THE SCEPTRE AND THE ROSE

Doris Leslie

THE SCEPTRE
AND THE ROSE

Published by Sapere Books.

24 Trafalgar Road, Ilkley, LS29 8HH

saperebooks.com

Copyright © Doris Leslie, 1967

Doris Leslie has asserted her right to be identified as the author of this work.
All rights reserved.

No part of this publication may be reproduced, stored in any retrieval system, or transmitted, in any form, or by any means, electronic, mechanical, photocopying, recording, or otherwise, without the prior written permission of the publishers.
This book is a work of fiction. Names, characters, businesses, organisations, places and events, other than those clearly in the public domain, are either the product of the author's imagination, or are used fictitiously.
Any resemblances to actual persons, living or dead, events or locales are purely coincidental.

ISBN: 978-0-85495-197-0

I dedicate this book to the memory of Naomi Jacob, who asked me to write it.

PART ONE

'Twas but a single rose
Till you on it did breathe
But since (methinks) it shows
Not so much rose as wreathe
   Robert Herrick

ONE

In the state cabin of the Admiral's ship she stood surrounded by those privileged to accompany her aboard. Very young, very small, and almost entirely extinguished by the circle of towering *hidalgos* and the sombre ladies of her mother's Court, she suffered a succession of lachrymal farewells with an equally, if artificial, lachrymose response.

Her brothers, Alphonzo, the King, and Pedro, the Infante, were the last to leave. Having indulged in the abundant celebrations preceding her departure, they plentifully wept; not so Catherine. She had shed no tears, not even at her mother's final blessing bestowed with oft-repeated gratitude to Almighty God for this most signal honour: an honour, however, that had been signally rewarded, for what other woman in Europe could bring to her marriage bed a dowry of half a million sterling?

At least, that was the settlement originally offered and thankfully accepted by the prospective impoverished bridegroom. But in consequence of Spanish aggression, so the Queen Mother with elaborate apologies conveyed to the British Ambassador, Admiral Lord Sandwich, she had been reluctantly compelled to spend half the monies intended for her daughter's marriage treaty to reinforce her troops in defence of the realm.

The residue, His Excellency was assured, would be paid within the year and surely such a valuable possession as Bombay, the entry to India — to say nothing of Tangier on the African shore commanding the Mediterranean — would have amply sufficed without additional endowment?

Apart from this munificence, the discomfited Lord Sandwich was graciously informed that a ship containing cargoes of sugar, spices, rum, which were more than worth their weight in gold, would escort the royal bride to England.

His Excellency, the Admiral, was now in sorry case. He could not recall the British troops already stationed in Tangier, having lost no time in taking full advantage of that part of the bargain; but how to account to his government for this last-minute alteration of the marriage treaty? And, besides the vast expense of bringing back to England a British garrison, how could he mortify the little bride by refusing her to board his ship unless she brought her portion with her?

As to the cargoes of merchandise in lieu of settlement, those, at first, he determinedly refused, but was overruled by the persuasions of Donna Luiza, the widowed Queen Mother of Portugal who, with indomitable suzerainty, reigned as Regent for her weakling son.

The cargoes, 'more than worth their weight in gold', that proved to be a thousand sacks of sugar, spices, and no rum, were duly loaded in the hold of the Vice-Admiral's ship, the *Gloucester*. The Queen Mother, all smiles at the success of her manoeuvres and further to evade her commitments, suggested that this 'rich merchandise' be traded in London by her Hebraic financial adviser, Senhor Duarte Silva, who would pay the King of Britain its price in ready cash. And, in addition, she handsomely offered to lend a proportion of her jewels as security for the remainder of the bond.

'God's truth!' exploded the vexed Sandwich to his second-in-command, 'does she take us for Jew pawnbrokers, by damn?'

But of these negotiations concerning the disposal of herself, Catherine was completely unaware. The long delay in the date of her departure had been caused, according to her mother's suave account of it, by the lavish preparations organised in Lisbon to speed England's future Queen upon her way. And now the day when she must leave her native land had come; and still no tears from her.

Alphonzo, slightly swaying, knelt to kiss her hand, but once down he found it difficult to rise. Giggling, she helped him up, flung her arms around his neck, and with a glance aside at the unprepossessing ladies of her entourage, judiciously appointed by her mother with regard to the bridegroom's amorous propensities, she whispered: 'Why must you endow me with these six horrid frights, about as handsome as a row of turnips?'

Said Alphonzo, between hiccups: 'They are of the Queen's choice, sweet, not mine, as you should know — and do by force of contrast — hic — enhance your — hic — your charms.'

'Let us hope the King, my husband, he will think so.' And to Pedro she turned, her lower lip caught under to stay the tremble of it. 'My dear, my very dear, write to me often as I will write to you.' For Pedro, of all her world, she loved the most, and it went hard with her to leave him, howsoever she rejoiced to leave the rest of them.

'Go now,' she said, 'or I shall cry, and I ... don't want to cry.'

He lifted her off her feet and swung her round, and made his voice firm to tell her, 'There's a time to weep, a time to laugh and a time to say ... goodbye.' Then he held her close for one last kiss and straightened and went from her blindly.

'Madam.' Lord Sandwich, Admiral of the *Royal Charles,* bowing head to knees in the doorway of the cabin, was admitted to the presence by Donna Maria de Penalva, first Lady-in-Waiting and duenna to the bride. 'I fear there will be some delay before we can put off.'

'Please?'

Despite her application to dictionaries and the tutorship of her chaplain — Dom Patricio, an Irish priest attached to the Court of Lisbon, better known to himself as Father Patrick — Catherine's command of English was elusive.

'Before we can come under weigh, Madam.' Lord Sandwich ineffectually attempted to explain. 'We are wind-bound.'

'What is vind— ? I no un'stan', milor'. Pleass'?'

More bows and an apologetic hem from the Admiral. 'Your Majesty —' for thus must she be addressed, by order of her betrothed, as if already she were his wedded wife — 'I am, by your leave, an ill-schooled sailor with my life lived in His Majesty's ships, and my knowledge of your lingo — of languages — is limited. Pray, ma'am,' to the dour-visaged Donna Maria, a moustached and grim virgin of sixty, 'have the goodness to interpret for Her Majesty.'

But Donna Maria's knowledge of English was even less than that of her young charge.

Lord Sandwich tried again. 'Countess, I regret to say that we must stay in port until the winds veer round.'

'*Grammerci, Senhor. Sa Machesta* is *molto fatigua* and *desire riposa*. Pleass',' was all he got from her, who held all men in abhorrence as monsters of vice — in particular the English, in view of the scandals attached to the name of their monarch. The entry of the Admiral to this chaste gynocracy indicated to the lady some ulterior, and lecherous, intent. Indignantly she gestured him to go.

He went, colliding at the door with Father Patrick. Having witnessed the Admiral's dismissal, he offered a jocular explanation for it.

'No! Good God!' exclaimed his horrified lordship. 'Does that dried-up old haddock think I want to tumble *her*?'

'Who dares say what she thinks?' chuckled the Father. But this I know: that these good ladies in attendance on Her Highness will not sleep in a bed where a man has slept, lest they be contaminated. How long d'ye reckon 'twill be before we are got under weigh?'

'Twenty-four hours, likely. I'll not run my fleet into gales. These winds are mightily ill-favoured.'

And ill-favoured they stayed all that day and night, until dawn brought a glorious sunrise. From her cabin porthole Catherine saw the coral-tinted clouds part unhurriedly, to stain the golden waters with crimson from the sky. The evening before, her brothers, and a selected few Court Gallants, had arranged to surprise her in their barges. Surrounding the galleries of the *Royal Charles* they serenaded her with viols and guitars, singing madrigals and choruses to wake the night and set the seagulls screaming. A gracious gesture, if a noisy one, that earned the disapproval of Donna Maria, who hastened Catherine to bed but not to sleep.

In the lamplight beside her couch, she read and re-read a treasured letter, although she knew each word of it by heart, transcribed into Portuguese by Dom Patricio.

My Lady and Wife,

Already at my request, the good Count da Ponte has set off for Lisbon. For me the signing of the marriage treaty has been great happiness ... I am going to make a short progress into some of my provinces ... Yet I do not complain whither I go, seeking, in vain, tranquillity in my restlessness, hoping to see the beloved person of Your Majesty in these Kingdoms, already your own; and that, with the same anxiety with which I desired to see myself within them...

The presence of Your Serenity is only waiting to unite us under the protection of God.

The very faithful husband of
Your Majesty, whose hand he kisses,
Charles Rex.
To the Queen of Great Britain, my Wife and my Lady

Her first love letter, to be cherished with his portrait in miniature. She drew it from its secret cache, suspended on a golden chain to lie between her breasts. Long she gazed at the pictured face of him, by whom her heart and her young ungiven body were possessed. Although he, as yet, was but a name to her, she knew herself his utterly, surrendered. And as she knelt before the image of the Holy Mother, enshrined in a corner of the cabin where lilies bloomed in chalices of silver, she prayed that she, his wife and lady, might be worthy of the love of him, her 'very faithful husband' and her lord.

At that moment, when dawn was in the sky, somewhat later over England than in the south, her very faithful husband lay sprawled upon a bed in a curtained chamber, sipping wine from a golden cup. The woman beside him, a lovely lady this, turned her mouth to nibble at his ear, and murmur into it, 'I will — I *vow* I will — you must promise that I will be her Mistress of the Robes.'

'Is it not enough,' came the lazy answer, 'that you are the mistress of me?'

'Enough!' She jerked away from him. 'You ask too much. Am I now to play the concubine for ever?'

His eyes, darkly shining between their hooded lids, twinkled up at her. 'Not for *ever*, may we hope? Repetition of a part played eternally grows stale.'

'Hah! So I grow stale, is it? I, who am bearing your son.'

He tweaked a curl of her hair. 'It may be a daughter.'

'I tell you, 'tis a son. I know from the way he lies and kicked so strong when he first stirred he almost threw me down. Ah! Why do you torment me?' She snatched the goblet from his hand and dashed it to the ground. The last of the wine trickled in a thin red streak along the polished floor. 'Do you believe I'll enjoy to see you wedded and — bedded with another? But I'll wager she'll not content you though you bring yourself to content her. She's dwarfish, swart and ugly, and dumb as a boot, they say.'

'Who say?'

'Bristol for one — he has seen her, and also the wife of the Portuguese attaché. She's of the Medina Sidonias, a Spaniard, and related to your Infanta's mother.'

'Yes.' A flash of white teeth in the lean brown face. 'Portugal tastes sour on the tongue of a Spaniard. Spain don't welcome the daughter of Braganza for England's wife. An alliance with Spain would have enriched their revenue by half a million. And since that wily old, er, witch, my future mother-in-law, has shaken off the Spanish yoke, Portugal regains possession of Brazil and, not the least of her territories, Tangier. You'll allow that even were my Catarina ugly, dwarfish, swart, which her portrait certainly denies —'

'Her teeth stick out,' sulked the lady.

'The better to bite me with, But you'll allow that the means she brings to me, whose fortunes are low though my hopes are high, justify their ends. What use am I restored to Britain, lacking the wherewithal to support my throne, my country and all this —' he touched her crudely — 'this pleasaunce where I stray for my delight? But,' his eyebrows quizzically lifted, 'the entrance fee is costly.'

'Do you grudge a paltry earldom to my husband, poor worm, for your right of way? And do you count the loss to *me* for the loss of you, who are my love, my very life?' The ready tears flooded her eyes. 'Were I in attendance upon her I could still be in attendance upon *you*, and so shut the mouth of gossip. I'll not endure —' she thumped the silken pillow where his long black tousled hair lay spread — 'I tell you,' she vociferated, 'I will not *endure* backstair intrigue, to have you sneaking in the night from her to me as if I were your whore!'

And then she fell to sobbing, and he, who could not bear to see a woman cry, as well she knew, must needs comfort her with kisses and promises. 'Yes, yes! The bedchamber, wardrobe woman, anything you like, only for mercy's sake stop blubbering! Yes, of course I love you, I adore you, but now, dear heart, I must away. The sun is up and I am not...'

Through St. James's Park he sauntered to his Palace of Whitehall, savouring the freshness of the blue and golden morning. Bird song was clamorous, the grass dew-spangled, and blossom burgeoning in every hedge. By the lake he stayed to watch the water-fowl he had caused to breed there: ducks, swans, moorhens, a stork — a rarity in England — and a melancholy crane, a gift from the Russian Ambassador. Having lost a leg in transit from St. Petersburg, it had been provided with a wooden one, jointed, to enable it to walk. At sight of his tall familiar figure, the birds came flocking for the titbits he always carried in his pouch.

Beyond the lake, deer grazed in the verdant spaces of the park; and roebuck, antelope, Arabian sheep, and mountain goats. As he approached, the deer raised startled heads; then, seeing no stranger, dropped again to their feeding. One, a dappled white doe, his especial favourite, came to nuzzle his hand and follow him almost to the entrance gates.

The sentries, saluting as he passed, waited till he was out of eye- and ear-shot before they exchanged indulgent winks and remarks aside concerning his nocturnal visits to 'the Lady', as she was known to them and to all of London Town. Who cared? Not they, nor those many loyal thousands of his subjects who had welcomed him, their 'Black Boy', on his exultant entry through the shouting streets of his capital to claim his throne after his long exile.

In the private chamber adjoining his bedroom, attended only by Chiffinch, his faithful closet keeper, the King, his appetite whetted after his walk, ate lustily, sliding pieces from his dish to his spaniels who sat waiting for their share of devilled kidneys and careful trimmings from loin chops.

'No! No bones for you, my lads, to perforate your guts. Nor for you, my pretty —' to a beloved bitch, due to whelp — 'but a double taste of this, for you've more to feed than one.' He pulled her on to his knees, running long expert hands over the small swollen body. 'A fine litter you'll be giving me tomorrow or today or — any minute. Have you seen to her bed, Chiffinch?'

'In Your Majesty's dressing room, as by your orders, Sire.'

Charles nodded, yawned, and said, 'Prepare me a bath and have the water cold to waken me. I'm half asleep.'

Chiffinch bowed, backed, and from the door returned to announce: 'His Royal Highness, the Duke of York, desires audience, Sire. Will Your Majesty receive him?'

'Of course. Bring him in.'

His brother James was brought in. Solemn-faced and point device in mulberry velvet, his light brown hair carefully curled and falling on his shoulders, he said worriedly, 'Charles. I — I — want — I must have a word with you. I trust you'll not take it amiss?'

The King lowered his chin and lifted his eyes. 'That depends, my brother. Chiff, you may go ... And I'll forestall you,

Jemmy. I know what your word, or words, will be before you speak them. Clarendon has primed you well. I must cease my visits to a, er, certain lady.'

Picking at his thumbnail, James said, 'Charles. For your sake, for my sake, for *all* our sakes, pending the arrival of your —'

Charles poured wine. 'You'll take a cup?'

'— pending the arrival of your bride,' continued James. ''Twere better so.'

Fondling the spaniel's ears, Charles slipped him a smile. 'You think?'

'We all think ... I, thank you, no. Wine doesn't agree with me so early in the morning.' The Duke took a chair to the table and, seating himself, leaned forward to say earnestly, 'Will you not be persuaded to break with her? There's too much talk afloat. It must be stopped. She and her partisans precipitate the scandal — to your discredit. I can't sleep o' nights for thinking on't.' He flexed his bony fingers, looking down at them. 'I know too well the poison that evil tongues can brew. Anne and I have had a taste of it. You remember how foully we were slandered?' He belched. 'Pardon me. I'll take a cup of milk. My stomach's queasy.'

The King called: 'Chiffinch!' who, removing his ear from the keyhole of the door, made his appearance with suspicious promptitude.

'Your Majesty?'

'Bring a jug of milk.'

Milk was brought; and James, searching in his pocket, produced a silver box containing tablets, swallowed two and drank a draught.

'A concoction of saxifrage and rhubarb,' he explained. 'A gentle purge. It expels the wind and settles the stomach.'

'May it settle your stomach as you and Hyde between you have settled me.' Charles grinned round at him. 'R.I.P. to all my peccadilloes. Henceforth I'm Benedick, the married man.'

'Now God be praised!' cried James. 'My prayers are answered.' He belched again. 'That's better. I'll sleep well tonight. You have lifted a load off my mind ... Bless me! What's the matter with the dog?'

She had clambered down from the King's knee, and rolled over on her side, panting, Convulsively her little body heaved.

The King started up. 'Chiff! Chiffinch!'

'Sire?'

'Minnie's whelping. Fetch her bed in here. Hurry.'

Chiffinch hurried, followed by the dogs who, at the first sign of the bitch's discomfort, had made a bolt for the door.

James, rising from his chair, said gloomily, 'My precious Phoebe died in whelp.'

'Because you overfed and coddled her. She was much too fat. Ah! Here's your bed, my pretty. Get in.'

The bitch got in and James got out, saying, 'I won't stay. I can't bear to see her suffer.'

'She won't suffer. She'll pass them as easy as a hen lays eggs.'

In the doorway the Duke blurted, 'One word more. Forgive me, Charles, but is it true that Lady Castlemaine is also due to —?'

'Whelp? As true as I am not.'

'Not?' James brightened. 'You mean it isn't yours?'

'Her husband vouches for it. Aha! We won't be long now. Chiff, let the council chamber know I am ... detained.'

The British fleet that had been sent to bring the Princess of Braganza to England consisted of fourteen men-o'-war. Although the heavy gales of the last few days had dropped overnight, the winds were still uncertain; but rather than risk more delay, Sandwich decided to put out to sea.

On the morning of 25 April, 1662, those fourteen splendid ships, all sails spread like the proud wings of swans, crossed the bar. From her cabin porthole, Catherine saw the seven lovely hills of Lisbon recede from the widening blue of the waters. The sun glistened on church spires, on palaces and white-walled villas, and on the small red-sailed boats rocking in the harbour. She watched until all she had known and loved of Lisbon lay far astern like the scattered petals of a flower, strewn on the rim of the horizon.

It was to be a long and stormy voyage. Strong north-westers followed the fleet to prostrate the courtly passengers of the *Royal Charles*, especially the ladies. Of them all, Catherine stayed unaffected save for a few days in the Bay of Biscay when the vessel plunged and tossed in the trough of angry seas, shuddering before the blast to right herself again and defy the winds, triumphant.

And while Donna Maria groaned on her bed, helpless, speechless, Catherine, disregardful of strict etiquette that forbade her to appear on deck unaccompanied, took advantage of her suffering duenna to venture from her cabin and brave the consequences should Donna Maria or any of her indisposed attendants recover sufficiently to recall or note her absence.

They did not; and Catherine, released from imprisonment, for although her state rooms lacked nothing of luxury if somewhat less of comfort, was stifled by stuffy curtains and longing for fresh air. Sickened of the sound through the cabin walls of her ladies' agonies, she took herself on deck.

Well wrapped, cloaked and hooded, she went unrecognised by the busy sailors who may have thought her, in her simple dress, one of her chambermaids. And if the officers sighted the gallant little figure go staggering along in the teeth of the wind with the spray in her face and the sun in her eyes, they kept careful watch and guard upon her from distance.

They were halfway through the Bay when, on a sunset evening, she was tempted out again. As a rule she allowed herself to play truant only in the early morning while her women believed her still asleep. By this time she had learned to yield herself to the swing of the ship, to know and love her antics; had learned, too, her every mood, tuned to all weathers; the shriek of the wind in her sails, the peevish mutter and growl in the rigging at the rise of a gale and, as the winds dropped, the laughing son of the breeze that, like a mischievous urchin, played with the bellying canvas as the ship swung between easy waves. And, on this evening, when the sea had ceased to gnash its teeth and lay pacified and shimmering, tipped with amber, saffron, gold, beneath the splendour of the sun's cremation, Catherine, leaning on the bulwark, saw one solitary star flicker in a space of cloudless light, and heard a voice behind her.

'Madam ... Your Majesty's pardon...'

She swung round. Her equerry and Master of the Horse, young Edward Montagu, kinsman of the Admiral, flushed, nervous, stammering, bowed low to offer her a handkerchief fallen from her sleeve. 'I ... I feared, Madam, that it would ... blow away.'

'I tank ... you verree kind, Senhor...' He had been presented to her when she came aboard, but even if she knew his name she could not have pronounced it.

From under her hood, her long dark chestnut hair escaped and was whipped about her shoulders, untrammelled by the hideous fashion of her mother's Court that demanded it be dragged up in a topknot and greasily plastered on the forehead. The functionary who attend to her coiffure was, as the rest of her retinue, laid low.

She stood swaying to the motion of the ship, a sprig of a girl; her deeply fringed eyes that seemed almost too large for the small face coloured shell-pink from the sting of the spray, were upraised to his as she sought about for words she could not speak. She wanted to share with this young Englishman, the only one of her age whom she had seen since she left Portugal, the beauty of the sunset and her enjoyment of the voyage soon to be ended. Too soon? Did she want it to end? Though she longed to meet her betrothed who wrote such charming letters and whose portrait fulfilled all her secret dreams of a handsome lover, yet, looming ever nearer in the arm of the sea — the sea that, for all its cruel capricious moods, she had grown to love — lay a new world, a new life, and she a stranger to it, a world unknown.

She shivered; the wind was rising, and the ship seemed to gather herself as a horse for the jump, when a sudden great wave crashed against the vessel's side; and Catherine, leaning over, saw the white circles of foam break in silvery fountains. The wind caught her hair again and lashed it across her face. She flung it back and laughed up at him who laughed down at her; a boy and girl in their fledgling youth, while the eternal cause called each to each to leave him breathless and her wondering. Nor neither knew themselves to be star-crossed…

'*Senhor! Sa Machesta* must not leave the *cabina*!'

This, and a volley of Portuguese, that might have been Hindustani for all the blushful Mr. Montagu understood of it, was followed by the person of Donna Maria. She, pale green and tottering, had staggered from her couch to find her Princess vanished, and, after frantic search, discovered in a situation that defied the rigid ethical behaviour demanded by the Queen Regent of her ladies, and her daughter above all. That the Infanta had escaped from the seclusion of her stateroom was bad enough; but to be found unattended in the company of one of 'those English' — to the lady a synonym for Beelzebub — was a lamentable breach of trust! Thus Donna Maria to her underlings, the elderly half dozen maids of honour, summoned from their sickbeds to be apprised of this disgraceful *contretemps,* for which the Condessa held the six of them entirely responsible. No matter they were ill. Was not *she* ill? And *how* ill, dear God! She had not ceased to vomit since this abominable ship had left dry land to bounce upon the sea! Yet did she lie bemoaning in her misery while the future Queen of England walked alone upon the deck to be accosted by a — man?

Had the future Queen of England been accosted by a man-eater, Donna Maria could not have been more shockingly disturbed.

There were no more sorties now for Catherine. Her dragonish duenna, and another noble lady of impeccable propriety, Donna Elvira de Vilpena, and the suffering six maids of honour, made shift, in turn, to keep watch on their Infanta in her luxurious velvet-curtained stateroom where no air, poisoned by the breath of man, could penetrate.

To Father Patrick, in the priest's cabin, the indignant Mr. Montagu disburdened. 'Do you mean to say that I, who am appointed by the King as equerry to Her Majesty, am not allowed to speak to her?'

'Sure, you're allowed to speak to her — to pass the time of day — but not alone,' was pacifically explained by Father Patrick. 'And by my reckoning, your passing of the time of day took more than half an hour. You were not unobserved.' The priest beamed kindly on the reddening Mr. Montagu. 'My cabin overlooks that quarter of the deck where Her Majesty is wont to walk.'

Spectacled, cherubic, stout of heart and body, was Father Patrick, who, prior to his chaplaincy at the Court of Lisbon, had served as parish priest at Pernambuco in Brazil.

'The Infanta,' he pursued, 'has scarce been out of the palace doors five times in as many years. From the age of eight until eighteen, upon the death of her father, the late King, God rest him, she was educated in a convent.' Removing his spectacles, the priest blew upon them, wiped them with his pocket handkerchief, replaced them on his button nose and, with a shake of his head, said, 'I confess to some slight — ah — some slight uncertainty as to how our little lady, with her conventual upbringing, will respond to the — um — gaieties, the free and easy manners, as I understand prevail at His Majesty's Court. A very natural reaction,' he smilingly offered to the scowl of Mr. Montagu, 'resultant on the Puritanical hypocrisies practised by the traitor Cromwell and his Roundheads. May God,' he signed himself, 'forgive them their iniquities.'

'My father and I,' retorted Mr. Montagu, drawing himself up, 'were followers of the *traitor Cromwell* as you call him, whose carcass, dug out of its honourable interment, now lies rotting in the earth beneath the gallows where they hanged his bones on Tyburn Hill.'

'Is that so? I did not hear of it, at all,' replied Father Patrick, with an aside to be forgiven that white lie, 'though, sure, you were too young to have fought in the wars that tore Britain in half from Land's End to John o' Groats? Yet certain 'tis that brother will fight against brother, and father against son in a house divided. And now, praise be, all's well — with the Stuart son of a murdered king come back to his rightful throne.' He got up from his chair and went over to a locker, taking from it a flagon of wine, his face so full of smiles that his eyes seemed quite to disappear in the roseate folds of his cheeks. 'Come, young sir,' he said, 'and drink a cup with me to the health of His Majesty and his Queen, my honoured pupil.'

The cup was drunk, and another and another, while Mr. Montagu waxed merry and the little priest waxed merrier; but his honoured pupil in her gilded prison, turned her face to the swaying wall and, for the first time, wept. For the life of her she could not have told why, with her 'very faithful' husband's portrait held between her breasts, and the words of his letter in her heart.

The fierce winds that had followed the fleet showed no sign of abatement, and did, in fact, increase in force, damaging some of the vessels, so that the Admiral had to run into Mount's Bay off the Lizard and wait until the gales moderated.

It was here that England gave the stranger queen her first welcome with a display of fireworks along the Cornish coast, and deep-throated salutes from cannon ashore. But with the calming of the winds, when sky and sea were wonderfully blue, and filled sails dipped to the gentle rhythm of the waves, the *Royal Charles* and her escort entered Portsmouth harbour.

The Duke of York, deputising for his brother, and accompanied by the Duke of Ormonde, Master of the King's Household, with other dignitaries of the Court, boarded the Admiral's ship to greet the bride.

Donna Maria, after much persuasion, had allowed Catherine to discard the national costume of a century before, with the monstrous *fardingales* worn by the retinue of *frights* or *Guarda Infantas,* as Evelyn describes them, whose *olivader complexions* and general appearance is noted by that meticulous diarist as *sufficiently unagreeable.* This opinion, supported by the Duke, may have caused him to wonder if his future sister-in-law would prove equally unagreeable. But the young woman who came eagerly to meet him in her stateroom, and whose warm brown hair framed a piquant little face endowed with a pair of velvety dark eyes — 'and lashes half an inch long, I give you my word' — so to his wife James afterwards reported, was, if not strictly beautiful, 'an engaging little piece, and sweetly mannered.'

'Well, to be sure,' placidly commented his Duchess, a fat sallow-skinned woman who had been Anne Hyde, daughter of the Lord Chancellor, Clarendon, married in haste and just in time to present the Duke with a son. 'There's a cat the Lady is to bruit abroad she's ugly. She won't be over-pleased to find she's not.'

'Charles will,' said James with a grin that youthified his elderly young face. 'Her portrait doesn't flatter.'

Anne took a stick of marchpane from a comfit dish and munched. 'Tell me what she wore.'

'How should I know? Something white and silver, I believe. But her women!' James turned up his eyes. 'Such a set of freaks were never seen outside of Bartholomew's Fair. Not one under fifty, and bearded.' He also helped himself to marchpane. 'They'd do well to shave.'

'I expect,' said Anne, 'the old Queen had her reasons for choosing Catherine's ladies less for their looks than their virtue, knowing Charles. Don't eat any more of that marchpane, love, it always makes you sickish.'

This conversation took place in the King's House at Portsmouth, where Charles — who had been detained on imperative business, so ran the message delivered by James — was to have met his bride. The 'imperative business' may have been conducted not only in Whitehall but in the house of Lady

Castlemaine, while Catherine awaited her bridegroom in maiden solitude at Portsmouth.

Yet the news of her landing had set all London in a stir. From every steeple joy-bells rang; bonfires flared at every door; but Mr. Pepys, trotting back and forth from his house to the Admiralty garnering gossip, observes that *there was no fire at the door of Lady Castlemaine with whom His Majesty supped nightly*, and that *the King and she did send for a pair of scales and weighed one another; and she, being with child, was said to be the heaviest* ... How or from whom Mr. Pepys is informed of these intimacies he does not divulge, but notes that *the Lady is now a most disconsolate creature*. So we may assume that Charles (Benedick) Rex had temporarily detached himself from his adhesion, and went jogging down to Portsmouth in his coach to meet his bride.

He had been writing to her daily. His letters lacked nothing of gallant devotion, to be treasured, kissed, and sneezed upon, where she lay in bed with a streaming cold, contracted — could anything be more vexing, and at such a time? — due to the change of climate, according to her doctor. But Donna Maria insisted it was due to her forbidden promenades upon the deck.

With what frenzied expectations, trepidations, palpitations did Catherine endure the suspense of those five days' delay, and now to have to greet him with a cold! The Portuguese physician attached to her Household, in consultation with the ship's doctor, had decided that Her Majesty was not ill enough for the King to be informed, but that she certainly must stay in bed. Which put Donna Maria in a taking: Her Majesty could not possibly receive the King in bed! And the nuptial Mass not yet performed...

The doctors were adamant. There was evidence of fever. In bed she must remain, and the meeting between the Royal bride and bridegroom be postponed.

'I'll not have that!' declared the King on his arrival. 'I demand to see her *now.*' Disregardful of the protesting, curtsying duenna, (*God's fish, and what a face!* parenthesised His Majesty) he commanded to be brought to his wife's room.

On the threshold, where her ladies clustered, he paused in a moment's apprehension. What was he about to see? Something dwarfish, ugly, swart? Which, to judge by the duenna and the vestal maids of honour, was not unlikely.

He braced himself to enter, and ... in a canopied four-poster hung with white and silver, propped on her pillows, her hair falling loose around her shoulders, he saw what he took to be a child. Her eyes, drawn to his, held that in them to twist his heart, so large and young and lost a look they had; a wisp of a girl lying there, her lips just parted by two little front teeth ... *Her teeth stick out,* he was reminded; but they didn't ... at least, not unattractively.

And, turning to the ladies, he said, 'Leave us.'

They left him, to stand outside the door, close enough to hear what might pass between the bride and groom at this auspicious meeting, and heard nothing save a silence. We may believe the King at a loss, for once, of words, since 'After the shock I sustained at the sight of her maids,' he later confided to James, 'I had thought they'd have brought me a bat instead of a woman. I was agreeably surprised.'

So agreeably surprised that he found himself breathless; and she, full of her cold and suppressing a sneeze, forgot the whole of the speech prepared by Dom Patricio, in English, with which to greet her husband, and which she had memorised verbatim.

The long-case clock in a corner by the window had ticked away a minute and a half before he approached the bed to kneel and take her hand that lay in his like a rose leaf — the thought struck him who was nothing if not a sentimentalist and inclined to be ashamed of it — and to which he added wryly, *in the paw of a baboon*. And then — the sneeze she had been holding she could no longer hold.

Releasing her hand she sought beneath the pillow for a handkerchief, could find none of the many supplied, and sneezed again. Miserably she strove, in halting English, to apologise. He laughed, the tension snapped. All now was easy. From his sleeve he produced a square of finest cambric, and with it wiped her nose, an adorably up-tilted nose, a trifle pinkened at the tip.

He also had prepared a speech and could say nothing of it. What he did say, still out of breath, was: 'But — you're lovely! And to think I've wasted days when I might have been with you. I'm yours entirely — for ever — my wife, my love, my Queen.'

All of which was charming, had she understood a word of it. Yet what were words when both could conjugate the verb 'to love' in any language?

Outside the door her women waited … and they waited. The indistinguishable murmur of voices, followed by intervals of silence, caused Donna Maria further shock. Dare she disobey the order of the King and interrupt this meeting between these two, as yet unmarried, and conducted, it would seem, with the utmost impropriety?

She dared not.

When at last the door was opened for the exit of the King he appeared to be in highest spirits, his flowing hair in some disorder, his face radiant. Distributing smiles among that agitated cluster of attendants, he buoyantly addressed them.

'*Mesdames* — er — *mesdemoiselles,* I have the pleasure and the honour to inform you that Her Majesty has given her consent that our marriage be performed, without delay, upon the morrow. *Comprenez-vous?*' Perceiving they did not understand, 'I have no Portuguese. I take it you speak Spanish?' And in Spanish he continued: 'I understand that arrangements for the ceremony are already made. I will notify Lord Sandwich, and the — where's the priest? Here, Montagu!'

The equerry, who had been hovering in the background, hurried forward. 'Sir?'

'The Queen desires that her chaplain — this, what's his name? Father Patricio — shall perform the nuptial Mass in private and before the public ceremony takes place. You will arrange it with the priest.'

She had begged, indeed insisted, she be married in the rites of the Catholic Faith. This determination came as a surprise to him, since it indicated a firmness of will contradictory to her childlike appearance, for despite that she was twenty-three she looked about thirteen. The letter he dashed off to the Lord Chancellor testifies to an almost schoolboyish elation.

I can now only give you an account of what I have seen abed, which in short is, her face is not so exact as to be called a beauty though her eyes are excellent good ... She has as much agreeableness in her looks as ever I saw, and, if I have any skill in physiognomy which I think I have, she must be as good a woman as ever was born, her conversation as much as I can perceive is very good, for she has wit enough and a most agreeable voice. You would wonder to see how well we are acquainted already! In a word I think myself very happy for I am confident our two humours will agree very well together. I have not time to say any more...

But he had said enough to convince Lord Clarendon that this young wife of Charles was found by him to be, in every way, agreeable.

And what of Catherine? Was she equally agreeable?

She lay where he had left her, bemused with the flood-tide of her first awakening. He was so unimaginably more than she had dared to hope. She believed herself reborn, or as if until this meeting she had never lived. And, lying there, she recaptured his every movement, every gesture, every line of his lean, dark, un-English face; those heavy-lidded eyes that dwelled on hers as it to draw the very heart out of her body; his mouth curving upward to his smile, the lips womanishly tender yet so strong, as though grafted upon steel. His voice that held a laugh as he looked down at her and wiped her nose. (How mortifying, cruel, to have a cold!) His hands that engulfed hers ... and his kiss folded into her palm.

He could not speak her language nor she his, but they could both speak fluent Spanish; and in Spanish she had said that unless she be married by a priest of her Church she would not be married at all. And she remembered the way his eyebrows lifted when teasingly he told her: 'You're a proper little Papist, as so is my mother — who, as you know, is French — so I'm half Papist too. But my father was not present at the nuptial Mass — he was represented by a near kinsman.' Then, hastily, he added: 'Have no fear, my love. I'll be there, in person, to marry you according to your Faith. It shall be held in private here, before the public ceremony.'

'Here ... in this room?'

'In this very room, my wife ... to be!' And then his face had clouded. 'You are so young,' he said, 'unspoiled, and untouched. I wish...' and he had hesitated as if to say more and said nothing, so she needs must ask him, 'What is it you wish?'

'That I were fit to ... touch you.' And he had slid his hand beneath the silver broidered counterpane to find her feet, uncovered them, and bent his head to lay his lips on each in turn and said, with a catch in his voice: 'Your hands are like feet and your feet are like flowers, and you are like a flower, too — a rose, one of those warm cream-tinted roses, the colour of old ivory, and I love ... I love you, Catarina, for all you are and, God be praised, for all that you are not.'

And he had touched her forehead with a kiss so light it was as if a moth's wing brushed it, and drew away from her, saying, 'I'll not trust myself longer alone with you until ... tomorrow!' With which he went, or rather bolted, from the room.

A shuddering sigh escaped her while cerebrally she fused and flamed to anticipatory delights of sense aroused, undreamed and unbelievable; unknown. She lay unstirring, spent, and very still 'until ... tomorrow.'

'Tomorrow' had been a fatiguing day for her, who, though recovered from her fever, was still in the throes of a cold.

The nuptial Mass, having been privately performed in her bedroom by Lord d'Aubigny, almoner to the Queen, and assisted by Father Patrick, was followed by the ceremony in the Established Church conducted by the Bishop of London. This took place in the Presence Chamber at the King's House in Portsmouth.

Lord Sandwich, who hurried up to London immediately after the wedding, reported to Mr. Pepys that *the Queen is a very pretty lady*, that she was greatly admired in her rose-coloured gown adorned with blue ribbons, but appeared to be pale and nervous. So nervous that her responses were inaudible, in fact, unuttered; she merely bowed her head as if in consent to take 'this man Charles to be her wedded husband'. It was evident she acknowledged no marriage but that, held in secret, according to the Church of Rome.

After the ceremony and so soon as the last guest had gone, Catherine, on her doctor's advice, was sent to bed; but when Charles took himself to his wife he was met at the door of her room by Donna Maria and — refused admittance.

'Be damned to that!' ejaculated, in English, the newly-wed husband, and, more politely, in Spanish: 'You will oblige me, Condessa, by conveying to Her Majesty that I will see her now.'

'But — Your Majesty —'

'Donna Maria,' came a soft little voice from the bed, 'you will admit His Majesty at once.'

The duenna, bridling, perforce must stand aside. The King bit his lip to hide a grin, and to the maids-in-waiting, on guard around the door, he bade them: 'Order supper to be brought here for the Queen and myself, alone…'

'That I should live to see our Beloved Infanta,' bemoaned the scandalised Condessa to her equally shocked six 'frights', 'take her first meal after marriage with the King — in her bed!' For exactly so it was; an impromptu supper with Charles seated there on the bed, a tray between them, picking turn and turn about from each savoury dish presented by Chiffinch, who had accompanied his master to robe him for his wedding and disrobe him for the night.

Alas for Charles! That night there was to be no consummation of the marriage. Apart from her cold, the excitement of these last few days had caused the bride an expedited condition resignedly accepted by the bridegroom, for *I think myself very happy,* he wrote to his sister, Henrietta Anne,

Duchess of Orléans. *I was married the day before yesterday, but the fortune that follows our family has fallen upon me, pour m'a fermé la porte au nez!* Which cryptic confidence was doubtless understood by his adored 'Minette'— his pet name for her — unsatisfactorily married to Philippe d'Orléans, brother of Louis, King of France, who loved himself and his own sex more than any woman. But to the bride's mother, Charles, with more decorum, writes that he is *greatly enjoying this springtime in the company of my dearest wife ... I cannot sufficiently look at or talk to her* which may have relieved the Queen Regent of uneasy qualms concerning her son-in-law's varied pre-marital interests.

The honeymoon was spent at Hampton Court: for Catherine a fairy palace. Charles had filled it with what Evelyn calls *incomparable furniture* and draped the bridal bed with silver cloth and crimson velvet. The park and gardens that, during the Protectorate, had been utterly neglected, were now planted with avenues of lime, chestnut trees, hornbeam hedges, and a flower-filled parterre named, not ineptly, Paradise Walk.

And in that country palace of her husband's forebears a continuous stream of courtiers came to pay homage to the little Queen Consort from over the sea. All day long the spacious halls were thronged, presenting a brilliant multicoloured spectacle of women's gowns, of men's extravagantly broidered suits and the glitter of jewels, while a babel of voices and laughter mingled with the strains of flute and viol.

Yet for Catherine the absence of formality, so different from the pomp and circumstance of her mother's Court, the endless presentations, the gabbling and jabbering in an incomprehensible foreign tongue, bewildered and dismayed her. But when the crowded days were ended, and she and her husband retired to their rooms, then, in his arms, did she know herself fulfilled, encompassed with the glory of her love.

As for him, who, since his early youth, had explored the depths of passion and all of passion's emptiness, her eager receptivity was an exciting new experience. This young creature, so strictly guarded, whose virginal small body — 'crocus-limbed,' he told her, 'and delicately modelled as a Tanagra figurine' — provided a delicious aphrodisiac to an appetite prematurely jaded. It was evident to all that the King seemed to be obsessed by this dark soft-eyed young woman, and were he not so much in love as entranced with a new toy, she, and Mr. Pepys was quick to note, had put *the Lady's nose quite out of joint*.

So, for the first few weeks of marriage, Catherine remained in blissful ignorance of the cloud, no larger than a woman's hand, slowly rising to drift across the golden light of honeymoon. Lady Castlemaine, who had just been delivered of a son, was not only well out of the way, but out of the King's sight and mind.

He, for the present, was completely absorbed with his little girl wife, his 'young rose' as he called her. She, in her naivety and innocence, contented him more than any of those others, schooled in all the artifices of the alcove. It amused him to watch her wonderment at the reckless frivolities of his giddy Court, to hear her lisped attempts to master English and make her repeat after him words whose meaning, meaningless to her, would convulse his lords and ladies. They scoffed at her childlike simplicity; found it prodigious droll that she should spend hours at prayer and her daily attendance at Mass in preference to the sylvan sports and picnics in the park by day, or the balls and masques and banquets prepared for her at night.

It was a boisterous rip-roaring company that Charles gathered round him, they who for thirteen years had been sickened of godly talk, Puritanical austerity, and the intolerable nuisance of casting eyes to heaven with no earthly hope of ever getting there. They had no use for religion in this pleasure-greedy renaissance of the Restoration. Charles, while respecting his wife's piety, may have deplored the hours she spent at her devotions that might have been spent more enjoyably with him.

This delightful state of things went on for some few weeks, when news was spread about, not for the ear of Catherine, that the Lady and her husband had quarrelled and — parted! The reason? That the son, presumably born to Lord Castlemaine and claimed as his own, had been baptised a Catholic in his father's Faith. But the Lady would have none of that. She insisted that the child was the King's and had him christened all over again in the Protestant Church, with Charles as one of the sponsors.

Thereupon the Castlemaine abruptly left her husband, carrying with her the infant and all the plate and furniture of her household, to take up residence at Richmond, easily accessible from Hampton Court. Lord Castlemaine, left behind in an empty house, departed in high dudgeon for Paris.

The gossips were enchanted; not so Mr. Montagu. Among all the courtiers who found the news side-splitting, he was unamused. He, who from a distance had dared to adore, suffered intensely of love that could never be requited or confessed.

A dreadfully earnest, sober young man was Mr. Edward Montagu, product of a line of country squires, bred of stern Puritan stock, and very much a Master of the Horse — and hounds.

With Father Patrick, always ready to receive latest news of the Lady lest any whisper of it be floated to the Queen, Mr. Montagu hurried to confer.

'I trust Lady Castlemaine will hold her place and distance, which is not here.'

'Amen to that.' agreed the Father, cocking a benevolent eye at Mr. Montagu. 'But we can only hope and pray that the King is well enough aware of the vows he has taken in Holy Matrimony to adhere to and respect them. A cup of wine, sir?'

'That woman must *not*,' emphatically stated Mr. Montagu, 'be allowed within the precincts of the Court.'

'Rhenish, Oporto, or Madeira?' winningly was offered, the priest's plump hand hovering above the flagons on the table.

'Rhenish, if you please. Then you think there is no cause for undue — apprehension?'

'According to Plautus, as he avers 'twas said by an old female slave: *Utinam lex esset eadem uxori, quae est viro.*' Father Patrick poured wine, passed the cup to Mr. Montagu and beamed upon him kindly. Your very good health, sir.

'And yours, sir ... Which means exactly what? Although tutored in Latin and a smattering of Greek, I am not well acquainted with Plautus.'

'Sure, he was poet of comical parts, something of a rogue, certain of a satirist, and all of a heathen.' The Father took a draught and savoured it, remarking: 'The finest cellars in the world are at Hampton Court, since the King is in possession to advise his cellarer.' He smacked his lips. 'Is it to your liking, sir?'

'Very much to my liking, I thank you. But what of Plautus?'

'Ah, yes, our friend Plautus, who says: "Would that the law were the same for a wife as a husband." I must remind you,' the priest twinkled, 'that the speaker was a slave.'

'As are all women,' gloomily commented Mr. Montagu.

'Slavery is not confined to the female sex, young sir. We, who are born of original sin, are all slaves to the powers of evil from which only the searching of our souls in the Confessional, and in constant prayer and faith in the mercy of Almighty God, can free us. So, my son, be comforted.' Father Patrick drained his glass and poured himself another.

Mr. Montagu curled his finely chiselled upper lip. *This Papist talk,* he inwardly observed, *gets us nowhere*; and rising from his seat, he said, 'I'll be about my duties. The King has bought a young Arab mare for the Queen, and I must try her mettle before I mount Her Majesty upon her ... No, I thank you, Father, 'tis an excellent good wine, but, no ... no more.' And he took himself off.

The priest's apparent indulgence for the weakness of the flesh and, as suggested for his comfort, the confession of his sins — to whom? To this wine-bibbing Irish priest? — caused all the Puritan in Mr. Montagu to recoil. Popery! And the Queen, so devout an adherent to the Church of Rome, an idolatress ... and idolised by him! He groaned aloud: '*Retro me, Sathanus!*' We must excuse him. He was very young.

Father Patrick, having emptied a flagon of wine, went over to a bell-rope, pulled it, and told the man who came in answer: 'The Queen desires that I wait upon her. Enquire if it be to the pleasure of Her Majesty that I attend her now.'

It was very much to the pleasure of Her Majesty, who received the priest in her private parlour. A sumptuous apartment was this, its walls decorated with tapestries and pictures from the King's collection, among them a Raphael, a Titian, and Mantegna's Caesarian Triumph. Above the marble mantelpiece hung a mirror framed in gold, a gift from Queen Henrietta Maria, the mother of Charles. There had been also sent from Portugal two magnificent Indian cabinets. Although accustomed to the splendour of the Lisbon Court, Father Patrick felt these lavish furnishings, and the heavily brocaded blue and silver curtains that draped the four tall windows, to be a trifle overwhelming. He, of simple tastes as he knew the Queen to be, wondered, again with some misgiving, how she would adapt herself to this extravagant new life into which she had so suddenly been jettisoned.

'My Father, be seated.' She gestured him to a high-backed chair, and stood before him, her eyes downcast.

She was wearing a dress of black velvet, possibly the same in which Dirk Stoop has painted her, the full slashed sleeves looped back over white ruffles; her hair, no longer tortured into a plastered stiff topknot, fell in loose ringlets about her neck and shoulders. She looked the merest child, as if her youth had been arrested between the bud and blossom. The thought crossed that corner of the Father's mind where he retained a secret store of quaint conceits in verse and prose, transcribed in a leather-bound volume.

'Well, my daughter?' Adjusting the spectacles on his snubby nose, he beamed upon her. 'You desire to consult me?'

'Yes, Father.' She drew forward a stool, sat herself upon it at his feet, gazed up at him solemnly and, speaking in her native tongue, said, 'As you know, dear Dom Patricio, it is my fondest wish that the King shall be led to the Faith, but I feel myself so inadequate and helpless to help him. This morning, I must tell you, he came upon me where I knelt before our Blessed Lady's shrine in my bedchamber. He saw my tears and asked me why. I told him it was because, unless he were converted to Our Mother Church, we would not be together in life everlasting. And he said that all roads lead to Heaven, but some take the short way and some take the long way. Father,' her eyes were dewy with tears unfallen, 'is that so?'

'Yes, my daughter, it is so, since all things work together for good to them who love God. But I have it strongly in my heart, and in my prayers, that before his earthly life is ended His Majesty will be brought the shorter way to the true Faith.'

Her face brightened. 'You feel that, too? I have so constantly prayed for it, I cannot but believe I will be granted this greatest joy of all the joys that God has blessed me with. It is the one and only shadow in my life that Charles and I are not...' Her voice faltered.

The Father laid a hand on her bowed head. 'I think the King is nearer to our Mother Church than you can know. Even as his brother James is secretly receiving instruction in the Faith, so in God's good time will the King, your husband, find the Way, the Truth, and the Life. Be of good cheer, my child. Watch and pray.' He smiled down at her, who smiled up at him, and wiped that dimness from her eyes.

Her one and only shadow, mused Father Patrick as he wandered back to his own quarters. *God grant there be no darker shade in all her life than this...*

TWO

Barbara Castlemaine, the 'Lady', was not in the best of good humours. Seated at her looking-glass on a summer's morning, her reflection should have given her cause for approval rather than the scowl that, for the moment, marred her beauty.

Beautiful undoubtedly she was. The voluptuous curves of her body, beneath a very transparent night-shift, defined an inclination to embonpoint that might well increase with age, but did not detract from, rather did enhance, her somewhat too obvious charms. Her complexion owed a trifle, but not much, to certain golden-lidded pots upon her dressing table containing rouge paste, lotions, and suchlike preparations devised by experts against 'all vices of the skin'. Her luxuriant auburn hair was arranged in the prevalent fashion of 'kiss curls'; her arms and bosom were no less white than the creamy asses' milk in which she took her daily bath, and which, in the kindness of her heart, when she emerged from her ablutions, she would charitably disperse among the poor.

The sun, high in heaven, poured its drenching light through her bedroom window where far below, from the heights of Richmond Hill, the Thames like some Titanic silver snake wound its translucent way between richly wooded banks: a view of surpassing loveliness had the 'Lady' an eye for it, which she had not. The loveliness of nature, as the loveliness of woman, other than her own, had no appeal for her.

Leaning closer to her mirror she carefully scrutinised her face, and discerning the droop of her blunt-cornered mouth, the knit of her brows that carved a gentle crease above her nose, she stretched her lips to their widest, then swiftly contracted them into an O. This ritual, repeated a dozen or more times a day to erase any effect that late nights and gallantries might impose upon her features, she practised with the same earnest devotion as the little Queen paid to her prayers.

Having finished with her face, she struck a small silver gong that stood among the toilet preparations on her table. Her confidential maid, Mrs. Wilson, appeared, between whom and her mistress was maintained a mutually profitable understanding.

'Send a messenger to Hampton Court with this.' The Lady took from a casket on the table a sealed letter. 'See it be conveyed at once and delivered to none but Chiffinch.'

The woman, with a comprehensive flicker of her eyelids, curtsied herself out. The Lady smiled, patted a curl on her forehead, and, from the same casket that had held the letter, she took a string of pearls the size of peas. These, a recent gift from the King, she clasped around her neck, and again she smiled, rose from her stool, pulled the shift over her head, and, mother-naked, admiringly posed before a full-length mirror on the wall. She then went back to bed, from which she had just risen, and lay there, her eyes to the ceiling where painted nudities of gods and goddesses were displayed in attitudes of amorous delights; but her thoughts were not of them nor of their activities.

With the business-like complacence of a tradesman she dwelled upon the value of her stock and the profit thereby appertaining: a duchy for herself and son; jewels to outvie those of the Crown entitled to be worn by 'that miserable little mouse-bitch' — thus did she agreeably designate the Queen — if any were left since Cromwell had his claws in them, and greater assets still than these. Another King of England had been rid of yet another Catherine to place upon his throne the woman of his choice, to sweep away all Papal legislation and make of Britain's Monarch Supreme Head of his Church and so ... divorce!

She writhed in ecstasy at the entrancing vista conjured: improbable, but not impossible.

'My lady.' The discreet handmaid was at the door. 'The message is delivered.'

'Good.' The Lady sighed her satisfaction. 'And now,' she snuggled lower, drawing the bedcovers up to her chin, 'we'll await the answer to it.' She often would adopt the Royal plural when in session with her confidential maid.

The answer to it came at sundown that same day. The Lady, who remained in bed on the plea of 'megrim', had ordered a meal to be brought to her which she heartily enjoyed. Her appetite, for food, appeased, she summoned her maid to prepare her for the visitor in nothing but the scanty gossamer shift, her hair arranged in careless curls, her face blanched with a concoction of white lead, that she looked to be in the final stages of decline. With the window curtains closed that the light should not too harshly penetrate, she lay in wait.

A long-case clock, another gift from the King, one of the first examples of marquetry brought from Holland, chimed the hour. As the last stroke died away the sound of hooves jerked the Lady from her pillows with a rush of colour to her cheeks beneath their plastering of white. Again the silver gong, that had been brought to the bedside, was struck to summon Wilson.

'Look from the window. Is it he?'

Cautiously the woman drew aside a curtain and peered out.

'Yes, my lady.' A pause. 'Cloaked, muffled, and — alone.'

'Alone? Not even Chiffinch?'

'Madam, I see no other with His Maj —'

'Quiet, you fool! Let none admit him but yourself. I told him in the message by which door he must enter. Alone, you say? Who holds his horse?'

'He has hitched it to the gate — the side gate, my lady.'

'Ah!' The Lady leaned back and closed her eyes; her head sank wearily, one pale hand pathetically inert upon the counterpane.

Within a few minutes, the visitor, announced as 'Mr. Rowley', was admitted. The maid withdrew. The Lady, weak, white, unstirring, lay as if the breath had left her body.

The door closed soundlessly behind him who stood aghast at the sight of that which appeared to be a cadaver, but second thoughts assured him it was not.

Leisurely he approached the bed.

'Why, what's this? And when did you sicken? At the christening you were well recovered from your lying-in. God's fish, my love, you do look poorly.'

Her eyelids fluttered open.

'Your ... love?' So low the words, so painfully uttered, they might have been her last. 'Since when was I your love? My messages ignored ... and I ... discarded. You kill me, Charles, have killed me ... see! I die from loss of ... you, a slow growing canker that eats away my heart to bring about my ... death.'

His eyebrows shot up. 'You look remarkably lively for a corpse, none the less.'

'O, cruel! To mock me who walk in the shadow of the valley ... I mean the valley of the ... my mind wanders.'

'It always was inclined to.' He bent over her, running a finger down her cheek. The deep furrows, carved from nose to mouth, eased into laughter. 'I' faith! You paint your face better than Lely ever could! Here's a pretty trickster's game you play.'

'God damn you, Charles!' She flung aside the bedcovers. 'That I should come to such a pass so I can only bring you to me by a trick is to your shame. What hell have I endured since you took that girl to wife!'

His heavy hair, in which some threads of silver gleamed amid the black, drooped down as he leaned closer to say, 'So! I'll share your hell with you on the same grid, pricked by the same devil's fork — and that's as near to Heaven as you and I together are ever like to be!'

And brushing her forehead lightly with his lips, he turned and left her.

The Lady's gentlewoman, Mrs. Wilson, had been her attendant since the days when a certain Mr. Butler had used to keep a shop on Ludgate Hill where he accommodated ladies for their assignations, among them one Barbara Villiers.

There, at the age of fifteen, before her marriage to Roger Palmer, later endowed by his Monarch with the Earldom of Castlemaine, Barbara was wont to meet Lord Chesterfield, the first in her long line of lovers.

Shortly after the Lady's unrewarding visit from 'Mr. Rowley', we find Mrs. Wilson in her private sanctum offering refreshment to and exchange of confidences with one Mrs. Sarah, housekeeper to Admiral Lord and Lady Sandwich, then at Hampton Court in attendance on Their Majesties.

Mrs. Sarah had all to give the rapacious Mrs. Wilson of — 'an almighty racket to raise the roof!' So did Mrs. Sarah describe the royal row between the King and Queen, of which the head and front of the offending was the name of Lady Castlemaine.

'May I perish, Mrs. Wilson, if I lie!' declared Mrs. Sarah with a rolling of her eyes, and a rolling of her tongue round this savoury titbit, 'but 'tis Gospel truth as I had it from one of the Queen's pages — at the keyhole. A nasty habit, Mrs. Wilson.'

'So 'tis, Mrs. Sarah,' was the virtuous agreement, 'and one to which no self-respecting female would stoop. But boys will be boys, Mrs. Sarah. You were saying?'

Mrs. Sarah was saying, between sips from the cup of wine offered by her hostess, 'scored off the list and heading it, believe me! Your lady's name, Mrs. Wilson, scratched out so violent as to tear the paper, so I am credibly informed.'

'Which is no news to us,' she was loftily assured. 'My lady is in consequence nigh mortified to death. Another cup of Rhenish, Mrs. Sarah?'

Another cup of Rhenish gratefully accepted, further divulgencies were then disclosed. How that Her Majesty — 'in whose mouth as we are told butter wouldn't melt, does scream at the King such words, Mrs. Wilson, that we — that they — did split their sides to hear. And how or where can this infantile Portuguese have learned them, who has no more of English than "yes", "no", "thank you", "please, good day, goodnight"? But "by cock", she says, and worse, Mrs. Wilson, which I'll not sully my mouth to repeat. And, "would you put the horns on me?" she shouts — yes, Mrs. Wilson, positively shouts! At which the King he laughs to kill himself and tells her, "You're an apt pupil, but let me remind you, no woman," says he, "can carry a horn!" Then followed the rest of it in Spanish, at which the King he laughed no more. So what's to be the outcome of this, Mrs. Wilson? Such an insult to your lady,' Mrs. Sarah said with relish, 'can surely not be tolerated?'

'No. It will not be tolerated, madam.' Mrs. Wilson, skinny, hen-faced, beak-nosed, drew herself up and set her cup down. 'We know what we know, Mrs. Sarah.'

Which was not all of 'that almighty racket' in the palace.

That his gentle Catherine, so acquiescent, so devoted, had known of his relationship with the Castlemaine, came as a shock to Charles; but a greater shock was the violence of her temper which his pliant little rose had displayed. Not only did she strike the Lady's name out of the list of those presented to attend her, but she positively refused to have 'that woman' about the Court, and, should he insist she receive her she declared she would return at once to Lisbon.

Then, after the first storm had passed over, and she, a little cooled, having let forth words in English he had mischievously taught her never dreaming she would understand them, which she evidently didn't, 'I was aware,' said she, 'of your previous association with this Lady Castlemaine, but that you propose I accept her to wait upon me, can only mean —' the proud young voice had for a moment faltered — 'that the intimacy you deny has been renewed, to the dishonour of your marriage vows and mine.'

In vain did Charles protest that there had been no familiarity between himself and the Lady since his marriage, nor would he ever be guilty of any such relationship again.

'Won't you believe me? Don't you know — can't you see that I love you — and none but you, entirely?'

Leaning against the oaken mantelshelf, his dark face clouded, his eyes beneath their hooded lids pleading for a relenting sign from her seated there enthroned in ice, he heard her say, 'If you will have me believe you love me entirely you will dispense with your mistress — entirely. If not,' she rose from her seat, 'I will dispense with you.'

And without another word or look she left him and went to her room. When Charles made after her he found the door guarded by Donna Maria, and entrance to his wife refused.

'A female Cerberus,' he complained to York, 'ugly as sin and as black-hearted. I'll have the whole lot of these Portuguese sent back where they belong.'

James, who felt that Catherine was justified in her refusal to have 'that trollop', as he named her to Anne, allowed about the person of the Queen, had little sympathy to offer.

'Catherine has every right to choose the women of her Household. I have already warned you that you tread dangerous ground should you still permit the Castlemaine those privileges which, as your mistress, she demanded, but not now, my dear, not now. I, too, have foregone and willingly,' said the pietistic James, 'certain — um — indulgences of my youthful past. We know such friendships as yours with the Castlemaine are not singular to monarchy, as in the case of our cousin Louis, but the French are more tolerant and intelligent than the English regarding extra-marital indiscretions. Also you must remember that England is only just recovering from a surfeit of Puritan cant and that many of your subjects still carry its taint, so it behoves you to preserve — at least to all outward appearance — the sanctity of marriage as a sop to the Puritan conscience.'

To which homily Charles, having had a dose of this from Clarendon, retorted, 'A pox upon your sermonizing! Do you think I give a curse for the Puritan conscience? A lot o' bloody hypocrites, and the sooner we round 'em up and string 'em up the better. As for women — damnation to them all! I've had a bellyful of women and their fantods. Here am I locked out of my wife's room, forsworn her bed and threatened with desertion, and all because I strive to keep the peace.'

'The only way to keep the peace between a wife and mistress,' James sententiously advised him, 'is to bring in legislative polygamy as in the days of Solomon. For all your experience, Charles,' he added with his slanting smile, 'you are uncommonly naive.'

But, 'Shut you your potato jaw!' was the hot reply to that, as Charles stalked out and James went in to pray for his brother's deliverance from 'that trollop' in the room he had fitted as a chapel. He much enjoyed the secrecy of his conversion, for a very secret man was James.

Although the 'racket' in the palace had blown over, it took the King a day and night to pacify his Catherine, assuring her he would have no more to do with Lady Castlemaine.

'If you don't wish to have her in attendance, then you needn't. I've done with her. That's a promise. Am I forgiven?'

Of course he was forgiven.

"Tis I should ask forgiveness for my wicked temper.'

'I love you in wicked or good temper.' He knelt beside her, covering her face with butterfly kisses. 'I love you as you are and every little bit of you.'

What more of Heaven could she ask than this after hours of anguish?

'Never, never —' with a fingertip she followed the curve of his upper lip under the black streak of moustache, so like an eyebrow — 'never must we come apart again.'

'We never will.' Lingeringly he kissed her mouth. 'Now let us visit the stables. You shall see the pretty mare I've bought for you.'

Joyously, her hand in his, she went with him through the gardens under the avenue of chestnuts, treading the thick fall of blossom that when she first arrived had been in full bloom of pink and white candles; and along the rows of lime trees, their frail yellow flowers perfuming the warm air. She had come to England in the late spring, yet the shores of Portsmouth had looked bleak and bare, the sea a pallid grey; but here at Hampton Court with the sun so radiant, the sky so blue, almost as deep a blue as the sky of Portugal, she felt to have come home. For this was her home, her England, now and for ever, and she her husband's love — and Queen. Such happiness was not to be believed!

Watched at a distance by strolling inquisitive courtiers, wagers were laid as to how long would last this infatuation of the newly wedded husband for the 'Portu*goose*', as the Lady facetiously dubbed her.

'A hundred guineas to one he'll not stay the course for a month.'

'Five hundred to one for a *week*! She's too simple for him.'

They stood to lose their bets. Her very simplicity was an added attraction. He had tired of experienced beauties. To initiate her in the joys of love-play was an unending delight.

Yes, and he'd teach her to dance. Her conventual training and the formalities of her mother's Court had not encouraged such trivial amusements; but she could ride, he knew that. He would dress her in a habit like a boy's. His mind designed it: red and white, long-coated, cocked-hatted, and but for the skirt who would know her for a girl? Delicious.

So to the stables; and Mr. Montagu, bowing to receive her, having been informed that she was on her way.

Here Catherine, who had learned to ride as soon as she could walk, was in her element. The chestnut mare, of Arabic strain, with a white streak to her forehead and a restless white to her eye, stretched her lovely arched neck to greet her who stood, tiptoe, to lay her lips against the satin cheek.

'Oh! You beautiful!' she cried. And to Mr. Montagu, 'Sir, I am much pleass' with my horse. I t'ank you. Is she good now me to ride?'

'The mare is high-mettled, Your Majesty, but docile enough.'

'Then,' said Charles, 'the Queen will mount her tomorrow.' And to Catherine, 'What say you, sweet? You have a riding habit?'

She had a riding habit, 'which,' Charles told her, 'will pass muster for a day or two until we fit you with another.'

So now, in her angry solitude at Richmond, the Lady heard how that the Queen — habited in white and scarlet 'like a boy' — must be up each morning with the sun and the King and young Mr. Montagu, too!

Very attentive, to be sure, was he, and much in favour with the Queen; also with the Castlemaine, who had an eye for pretty youths.

This latest information from her cronies of the Court, wherefrom she was excluded, heaped fuel on her smouldering fire. She summoned the King to her presence, not now by a trick as the last one didn't work, but on plea for right and justice.

Charles was received by the haughtily indignant Lady in her salon. She had dressed to part in funereal purple as for a royal death — 'Since death it is for me,' was her reply to his remark: 'Why these macabre trappings?' indicating the dark velvet, high to the throat with a train like a pall.

'Am I, who have given up my home, my husband and my life for you, to be discarded, thrown aside, abandoned? Your grandfather, *Henri le Grand,* did not dissemble his passion for the woman he loved but commanded she be paid the honour and respect that was her right, and —'

'*Their* right,' Charles interrupted with a grin. 'He had more than one.'

'Yes! And he gave them highest titles and obliged his wife to grant them grace and favour in her Household.'

Charles, reflectively appraising the outraged termagant who stood before him, her head thrown back, one hand upon her heaving bosom, mindful of Mrs. Knight's performance at the playhouse, said, 'You have missed your vocation. Had you taken to the boards, your talents would have met with more success than in the alcove.'

'You — you beast to mock me!' She raised a fist to strike the air as if it were his face. 'I, who am in all but name, your wife! Charles —' and now she changed her tactics and was on her knees to him in tears — 'how can you be so cruel, so hard, devoid of pity? How you are changed, bewitched by that sly foreigner who has no more of love in her for you than a cat that laps cream, as *she* laps the glory of her queenship. Do you think it is yourself, the man, she loves? I say it is your crown she loves. Already she casts about for one of her age. Watch out, Charles, and be warned. Young Montagu and she are more attuned together than you and she will ever be. Are you so blind?'

'What's that?' He who had listened to this tirade with half an ear was now brought to it with a jerk of his body as if pulled by a wire. Her hands were clutching at his legs; he stooped to disengage them and drag her to her feet. Her tear-wet eyes — 'like drowned violets', he once had called them when she wept — were raised to his. 'What's that you said?'

'Nothing. Forget it. Just the drift of idle talk that couples her with Montagu. I'll swear she's faithful — doting as one of your spaniels to lick the hand that feeds her. ('May it choke her,' was added *sotto voce*.) And lightly, on a laugh: 'My tactless tongue runs amok with me. I say forget it, but remember that youth will fly to youth so surely as a needle to a magnet.'

'Youth!' he snarled at her. 'A pox to that. Am I Methuselah at thirty?'

'— two,' unkindly she reminded him, 'and you've lived a hundred years in ten. She, for her age which is a woman's, is a child. What has she to give you who is witless as any dairymaid — a simple fool?'

'Neither so simple nor so foolish,' he said drily, 'as are some that set a higher price on their commodities, offered to fond customers who are greater fools to buy 'em.'

'So!' she flung at him, 'you heap insult upon injury to cast me forth unwanted, spurned. I, who only ask to attend her so I may still have sight and sound of you. Is that too much to ask? Is it? *Is* it?' And on that *fortissimo* again she smote the air. 'How can I be parted from you, never more to share those intimacies that belong to us alone? And what of our son? You have not laid eyes on him since you stood sponsor, and what then did you see of him, poor brat, who howled that the bishop's words of baptism were lost. But wait ... you shall see him how.' She ran to the door calling, 'Wilson! Tell the nurse to bring his lordship to me.'

Charles cocked an eyebrow. 'Lordship?'

'Yes!' she flashed. 'Have you forgot the name you gave him with the earldom to the heirs of the man who claims false parenthood to Charles Fitzroy, the Lord Viscount Limbricke, which in duty bound should be a dukedom?'

'As so it shall be.'

For not all her 'tear-drowned violets', not her histrionics could have won him had she not played this, her trump card, to place in his arms the babe, wide-eyed, dark-skinned, his head shaded with a down already almost black — 'and a nose,' his father chuckled, 'like to be as monumental as my own'.

'He is your own,' she whispered, as she took from him the 'Lord Viscount Limbricke' who was setting up a yell, to be comforted with tender coos and pats in this role of mother, played to perfection. 'Have you,' was asked of him who stood over her, melted, and moved to tears in his turn, 'the heart to deny your son — and me?'

He had not.

Catherine lay in her great canopied bed watching Donna Maria at her tambour frame. The duenna's sight was failing. So close did she bend to her needle, passing the silken thread through the rich embroidery, it was a wonder, thought Catherine, she didn't sew her nose to the canvas. And that whimsy brought a weak little laugh, caught back on a sob, quickly silenced, for Donna Maria, if myopic, was not deaf.

The crimson velvet counterpane, heavily embossed with silver, was too hot. Impatiently she flung it off. 'Condessa! Open a window. I suffocate.'

The duenna laid aside her work and came to the bed. 'No, Your Majesty, I cannot allow the damp air of this atrocious climate to penetrate. Each day it varies, blows warm, blows cold, and now it rains. It is time for your physic.'

The old lady carefully measured the dose into a phial and held it to Catherine's lips.

'I won't!' She pushed the glass away. 'I hate the stuff. It makes me sick.'

'Your English doctor's orders, Majesty,' said Donna Maria with a deprecatory sniff for the 'English doctor' and his orders, which must, however, be obeyed. 'I will give you a fondant to sweeten the taste of it.'

Resignedly Catherine gulped down the nauseating mixture, much favoured by Dr. Pierce, the Court physician, from a prescription of the famous herbalist, Dr. Culpeper, who declared it to be *exceedingly good for sad, melancholy, pensive, grieving, vexing, pining, fearful spirits, and helps such as are prone to fainting and swooning.*

'Ugh!' Catherine retched, crammed the proffered comfit in her mouth, and lay back on her pillows. Her bed faced the windows overlooking the gardens of the palace, their lawns sodden with the rain that had now lessened to a drizzle. The sky was clouded, dreary; no gleam of sun to brighten it; the trees dripped moisture shaken from their leaves in a slight rustle of wind; so sudden a change from the joyous blue and golden days of these last weeks. Even the birds were silent. Was it only yesterday that her whole world had crashed?

She closed her eyes and watched the scene unfold behind her shuttered lids; that scene imprinted there as on a living tapestry, crowded with figures realistically revived. How happy she had been when her women robed her to receive the ladies appointed by the King for her Household! She wore the white-and-silver gown, one of the many Charles had sent to Portugal for her wedding trousseau. Her maids had dressed her hair in the English fashion, with curls on her forehead and falling round her shoulders. And when she was ready, Charles had come to her room, and told her: 'You will outshine them all! You are less like a rose today than a dew-spangled lily.' And he had lifted her up and swung her off her feet as Pedro used to do … Darling Pedro. She owed him a letter in answer to his last, but she could not write to him now, not yet, with this darkness all about her…

And then Charles had tucked her hand under his arm and they went down to the Great Hall, along the serried ranks of bowing courtiers, and women in their gay coloured silks and satins, their billowing skirts spread out to the curtsy that they looked like vast flowers in a parterre. Charles had a word, a laugh, a jest for all on either side as he led her to the dais where stood the two great gilded chairs. But he did not seat himself; he left her there in solitary state, saying, 'I'll be back again,' and hastened away out of the hall and through the doors, unattended. She wondered if he had been taken with a need to relieve himself, for otherwise he surely would have stayed to support her through the preliminaries of this ordeal. For ordeal it was to meet so many unknown women and find words in their language with which to greet them.

The chattering and laughter were hushed as, one by one, the women of her Household, many of whom she had never seen before, were presented. Such a lovely day it was, of dazzling sun — how unpredictable the changes of this English weather! Light, as of a thousand fireflies, sparkled to draw flashes from jewelled necks, arms, and sword-hilts. Here and there, among the press of people, she saw a face she recognised. That squat, stout, red-cheeked man with two chins and the tuft of a beard on one of them under the straggling grey moustache, was the Lord Chancellor, Earl of Clarendon, father of her sister-in-law, Anne. Yes, she was there too, dear dumpy fat Anne — in yellow — just the wrong shade of yellow for her. An uncomely, ill-complexioned woman was Anne, but kindly natured. She had heard it said, from Donna Elvira who was a great tale-bearer, how that the Duke of York had married Anne not only because she was pregnant by him but because being plain she would more likely stay faithful, and how the Queen Mother had opposed the match. A lawyer's daughter for her son, heir presumptive to the throne! Even though the throne was in abeyance then, and Charles, James, and their mother, too, exiled paupers. And there was James beside his wife, so solemn. Catherine had never seen him laugh, always looking for trouble. Charles had told her how James had warned him not to walk alone in London's parks lest he be set upon by Cromwell's loyalists who thirsted for revenge in the cause of their dead Protector, and how Charles had quizzed him. 'They'll never kill me to put you on the throne,' and, 'No fear of that,' he had added, 'for you will give me half a dozen heirs.' And she: 'Pray God it may be so.'

She lay very still. It was as if by dwelling on trivialities she deliberately evaded the shocked recurrence of that outrage to her love, her dignity, her wifehood. Through her closed eyelids she forced herself to marshal that vivid pageant as a puppet master brings his marionettes to mimicry of life. But this she revisualised was no mimicry, no puppet play. In retrospect it was more alive to her than the sudden impact of it that had felled her as by a thunderbolt...

She saw her ladies file past, to kneel, to kiss her hand, and rise and drift away. Their names were called — these English names — so difficult to memorise. And then... she saw her husband with a lady on his arm. He brought her straight through the crowd about the dais, and the chatter of the courtiers, for a moment, ceased; a moment only before, with one accord, their voices rose again to drown the name her husband murmured as he presented the newcomer: a smiling woman, beautiful and gracious, magnificently gowned. Pearls circled her throat, diamonds shone in her hair as she bent to the bob, and kissed the hand offered by Catherine, who gave her, in her pretty broken English, warm welcome, for she was lovely to look at, and Catherine admired beauty in woman, man or beast.

And the Court held its breath.

'Your Majesty!' From her stance behind the high-backed chair, Donna Maria leaned forward to hiss in her ear, 'It is the Lady Castlemaine.'

Horrified incredulity struggled with a fierce upsurge of indignation. Not this! No. Surely not — after his fervent promise that never would this woman be brought into her presence, never be allowed within her sight — or his. He had done with her. He had promised to have done with her!

She started up. The walls of the room swayed and spun in a dizzy dance; she caught at the chair arm for support and felt a gush of blood to her nostrils. As a child in the convent she had suffered from nose bleeding if she had been naughty and reprimanded by Reverend Mother, but never since ... and how terrible and shaming that this should happen now!

There was a general confusion. Her women gathered round her; dimly she saw Charles take a step toward her, was aware of being raised, not by him, by Mr. Montagu ... Then a blackness came upon her and she knew no more.

Had it really happened? Or was it just a vivid awful dream? *If so,* she prayed, *then let me never wake from it so may I die!*

The Court was in a ferment, the Chancellor in a fuss. Writing to the Duke of Ormonde, guarding the King's affairs in Ireland, Clarendon expressed belief of a fight ahead which might necessitate the writing of his letters in cypher. The Lady had her spies and powerful supporters; not the least of them Lord Bristol and her cousin, the Duke of Buckingham, both sharing the Castlemaine's favours and both sworn enemies, as was she, of Lord Clarendon.

The Lady hath been at Court, he wrote, *and kissed the Queen's hand. I cannot tell you there was no discomposure...*

A 'discomposure' that was in everybody's mouth, the Lady triumphant, and the Court divided between the devil and the deep blue sea of Portugal. What to do, and which side to back? If the Queen should prove the winner in a three-cornered fight between man, wife and mistress, the wisest course would be to uphold the wife in anticipation of preferments. On the other hand, her youth and inexperience were no match for the worldly-wise sophistication of the Lady. General opinion gave it that the Queen stood no earthly chance against such odds, and with preferments in the offing it were best to back the Favourite.

They did.

Catherine, miserably rageful and though not yet recovered from the shock of the Lady's appearance at Court, was, at last, persuaded to receive Charles and his shamefaced apologies.

At this, their first meeting since that scene in the presentation room, 'high words' were reported by gleeful gossip-mongers.

Charles stood dumbfounded to see and hear her in a fury that entirely surpassed the previous exhibition of her 'wicked temper'! She stormed at him, in Spanish, her little body quivering, her cheeks aflame, her small fists clenched and rigid at her sides.

'You have deliberately insulted me by bringing that woman to my presence. Have you forgot your vows and promises? My country's ambassador shall be told of this. My mother, the Regent, will demand reparation. Portugal will challenge you!'

'No, no, my love, you exaggerate the incident. If you will give me leave to speak and to explain, I —'

He made attempt to take her in his arms. She dodged away and yelled at him in broken English — 'yes, positively yelled,' cackled the eavesdroppers — 'I finish wit' you. I no see you more. I will NOT,' — a volley of Spanish followed to the effect that she would return at once to Portugal, 'unless —' she flung an ultimatum — 'unless you break from that — that creature! You and she are in league together to humiliate me — your wife!'

'Listen! You *shall* listen. It is you I love — you only!' and at the time he meant it. 'You must believe me. I swear, before Almighty God, that I have had no association with that woman since our marriage.'

But this endeavour to make her see reason served only to make her see red. 'You to swear — to take God's name in vain! Out of my sight! Go — go!'

He went white-lipped and seething, bitterly hurt at what he deemed to be his wife's 'hysterical extravagancy', as he told Clarendon whom he sought to intercede on his behalf in this latest *crise*.

Facing the Chancellor's apartment, the lines from nose to mouth more deeply carved, his forehead under the heavy fall of hair more deeply furrowed, Charles said moodily, 'I cannot make her understand that I am in duty bound to shield Lady Castlemaine from the odium attached to her name because of our, er, former relationship, which is why I insist she be admitted to the bedchamber. It is the least I can do to vindicate her honour.'

The Chancellor rolled a gooseberry eye at him. 'Honour?'

'Yes!' Charles swung round. 'Her father lost his life in the service of the crown. Am I to discard his daughter who through my — my affection for her has provoked the insane jealousy of her husband, that he deserts her and — his son?'

'*His* son?' with marked emphasis repeated Clarendon, as he leaned his head against the chair back, his foot — he suffered sadly from gout — stretched for support on a stool. From him

Charles exacted no ceremony and had bidden him sit while he stood.

'Very well, then. *My* son, which gives me further motive why I should pay respect to her who bore him. But how can I make Catherine see this? How, I ask you — how?'

Clarendon who, as Edward Hyde, had faithfully served the martyred King and guarded his young son's interest during his long exile at his mother's needy little factious Court in France, sharing their poverty 'with scarce a sou to buy a faggot', as his contemporaries gave it, did not hesitate to remind him, 'Sir, do you forget that you have often criticised the conduct of your cousin, King Louis, in permitting his mistresses to live at the Court and —'

'I have never suggested,' Charles broke in hotly, 'that she should live at the Court, nor is she my mistress now.'

'— and, I was about to say,' doggedly pursued the Chancellor, 'that a woman who prostitutes herself to King or commoner is infamous to all women, be they wives, Queens, or whatever — Hey-hee — ah! God damn this bloody gout!' His pippin-red face turned puce with the pain of it — 'and I cannot advise a more sure way for you to lose the hearts of your people as well as the heart of your wife, than by your continuance of this association at the expense of your young Queen's happiness.'

'If you have done,' Charles told him, with ominous quiet, 'perhaps you'll allow *me* to speak.' And resuming his long-legged perambulation of the room: 'The friendship and respect I offer Lady Castlemaine, I owe as much to the memory of her father as to her, but I tell you —' he halted to glare at the Chancellor — 'and I swear to it, as I have sworn so to my wife, that there has never been a renewal of the intimacy between myself and Barbara since my marriage nor never will be again.

All I ask is that Catherine receives her with the same courtesy she would accord to others and that Lady Castlemaine, while in attendance, must show the Queen every possible duty and respect. Should she fail in the least degree I'll have her thrown out of Court, never to return. So take *this* to Her Majesty from me and let that be the end of it.'

But it was not to be the end of it.

Clarendon, bustling back and forth between two fires, in attempt to quench the flame of both by presenting the King's case to Catherine with the same forthrightness as he had presented hers to Charles, only caused a further conflagration.

He was impelled to suggest, said he, carefully, that 'Your Majesty should strive to comply with the King's — your husband's — will, according to your marriage vows in which you promised to love, honour and obey.'

Of this she understood enough English to retort in high passion, 'I have no marriage vows take but in my own Faith. You tell my husband he break *his* vows. I no listen to you, milord.' And she stamped her foot at him, pointing to the door. 'Pleass' to leave me.'

He left her, saying he would wait upon her the next day when he hoped to find her more composed. And the next day, finding her distinctly more composed, he offered her a sugared pill. His only desire, he said, was to serve her, and nothing could give him greater happiness than to promote complete sympathy and understanding between herself and the King, and to advise, for her sovereign good, how best to maintain that same sympathy in this — ah — most delicate situation.

To that, her lips trembling, tears springing: 'I know you are my friend,' she said, 'and I be glad for milord to tell me of my faults. I am not well yet in English ways — all is so new and strange to me. But I no' think to see my husban' engage wit' another lady — to break my heart.'

Which offered the Chancellor a loophole to continue with an eye to sentiment.

'Madam, I am come to you with a message from the King, who begs you to believe that whatever the — um — follies of his youth, when cast out of his kingdom, over-burdened with cares, broken with grief for his father's tragic end —' A tear rolled down her cheek. *I've got her now,* thought Clarendon — 'in whatever such youthful excesses he may have been tempted to indulge as diversions from his sorrows, to which I, too grievously, bear witness,' he achieved a break in his voice, 'I assure you that the King is heart and soul dedicated now to none but you.'

Phew! This heavy play upon her heartstrings had caused the Chancellor to break into a sweat. Did these black and bearded hags of hers never open a window? And had he won her or had he not?

He had; her face was radiant. Her tears dried in the warmth of her smiles. Her hands flew out to him; her words came in joyous little gasps.

'Milord! You make me happy — so happy! Pleass' to tell the King my pardon. I be sorry — so sorry I angry wit' him. I be always good now and obey him. Pleass'.'

All this was excellent, and Clarendon, taking her hand paternally to kiss, introduced the main purpose of his errand. If she would wish to prove her obedience and duty to the King, she must resign herself to His Majesty's command that she make reparation to Lady Castlemaine for having caused her such embarrassment when presented to Her Majesty, and accept her as her Woman of the Bedchamber.

For an instant she stared at him, incredulous. Then, as full comprehension of his words dawned on her, at once the fury of the day before was rekindled in another storm of indignation. It poured upon the harassed Chancellor in a torrent of Spanish from which he gathered that if the King insisted on enforcing such an infamous command — reparation, indeed! — it could only mean that he held her in contempt to shame her before the whole world, and lower her to the level of 'that woman'... Sooner than submit to such humiliation she would take the first ship back to Lisbon.

By this time Clarendon's patience was exhausted, his gout in ascendance — brought on, he savagely reflected, by her tantrums. A raging virago, forsooth! And who'd have thought it to see her so gentle, dove-soft? He broke in on her tirade, to sink her.

'I must remind Your Majesty that you have no disposal of yourself without the King's permission, and I should advise you not to repeat too often your intent of returning to Lisbon, for there's a plenty here who'd be glad to see you go.'

After that unkindest cut he finished by warning her not to give His Majesty any more of her temper, which might provoke him to similar retort in which case she would surely get the worst of it. So saying, he mopped his wet forehead, bowed, backed and hobbled away.

But that night, disregardful of Clarendon's warning not to give Charles any more of her temper, she gave it to him full measure. From behind closed doors their voices, hers in shrill *accelerando,* his booming *basso profundo,* were heard in concerted duet. That most of it was in Spanish made no matter. Buckingham and Bristol, both panders of the Lady and fluent in the language, rendered over the wine-cups their versions of the scene to delight their audience.

As relayed by Bristol, the Queen accused the King of having lied to her, shamed her, had neither love nor respect for her and so on — a repetition of previous wrangles, to which the King flung back: '*I* lie! God's fish! I like that! 'tis not I but your mother who has lied — tricked me into marriage by means of a false treaty!'

This, seemingly, they said, was the first the Queen had heard of it, and then did she squeal, according to Bristol, reproducing a fit of hysterics in squeaking falsetto to bring down the house: 'And if so be as you've made a bad bargain and not been paid your full price for me, I'll release you from your treaty and go back to my mother so you can trade yourself for another wife, the Lady if you will, and she not the first whore to share England's throne!'

Then Buckingham, profoundly bass, comes in with: 'So! You'll go back to your mother, and I'll not detain you, but let me suggest that you may not be welcome. Your mama had doubtless hoped to be rid of you when she handed you over to me at a price, as yet unpaid … How *now!* Oh, no, you don't! Why here's a pretty signature! Draw in your claws — a wild cat, i' faith! As I was saying, that I may be sure your Mama don't send you back to me I'll send back to her your Portu*geese*, ganders and gaffers and all, for we don't want 'em here, and in due course you may follow them!'

So that was the gist of it, with allowance for embellishment.

The company held its sides. They were easily amused; but Mr. Montagu, one of the party, got up and left the room. Lord William Brouncker, Catherine's secretary, went after him.

'I've an itch to call out that couple of whoresons,' muttered Montagu, red in the face. 'That they should make a mockery of her!' His knuckles were white, clenched on his sword-hilt.

'Best hold your hand and your tongue,' advised Lord William, his long blond hair precisely curled; the incline of his figure to avoirdupois was disguised by the cut of his suit and much of gold lace on his tunic. 'The Queen,' said he, 'may not have shown her claws to the King, but I'll warrant she shows him her mind. She can be waspish when roused, and with reason.'

'Do you think the King does honestly intend to dismiss her Household?'

'Honestly maybe, or honestly not, for honest is as honest does where the rights of Kings are concerned. But — yes, honestly, he does intend to send them packing and damn good riddance, for her women!' Lord William affected a shudder. 'May the devil disparage my parts if I'd bring myself to have at one o' them.'

'I consider,' said Edward between his teeth, 'that Buckingham and Bristol have been guilty of *lèse-majesté*.'

'Hearken to me, young man,' Lord William laid a hand on Edward's rigid shoulder. 'If you'd been at Court as long as I, you'd have learned to shut your ears to puffball chatter. But *should* you open ear to it, you'll find a particle of truth will settle there,' he flicked from his sleeve the gossamer shred of a dandelion clock, 'even as this,' and he blew it away, 'holds a seed — to sprout. In this tug o' war between the King and Queen they are both at fault. Were she less of a child, more schooled in the ways of the world, she'd know better than to deny him his pleasures that are no more to him than a hearty meal, and as soon forgotten. What's the difference between f—ing and eating? Too much of either will sicken us. And if our little Catherine would let him have his fill and not snatch the dish from him before he's finished with it, she'd soon find he'd turn to the more tasty and tenderer meal *she* can offer.'

'Sir!' said Edward, reddening. 'I find your comparisons disgustful.' His hand sprang again to his sword-hilt. 'I must ask you to retract them.'

'Pouf!' Brouncker grinned round at him. 'I see you're still tarred with the Puritan brush. Like mud it will stick. And here's a word of advice to you, lad. Don't wear your heart on your sleeve — but damme, I wish I'd a heart young enough to wear it where it's seen! Come on now, I'll play you at tennis. I need exercise to get rid of this.' He glanced down at a bulge above his waistline. 'I'll have my revenge for the beating you gave me yesterday.' Tucking his arm in Edward's, he walked him off, saying, 'There's time for three sets before we dine.'

Kneeling on the wide window seat of her bedchamber, Catherine looked out at the joyous green of landscape and gardens, where early roses offered their opening buds to the sun. This England, this land of capricious cloud, of tree-girt loveliness and the glory of meadows where pied cattle grazed in a carpet of gold — 'buttercups' they called them, those dazzling yellow flowers that grew in such wild profusion — this was now her land, and she a stranger in it, outcast, unwanted. Unloved.

Hot tears stung her eyes; she forced them back. Reverend Mother at the Convent used to tell her that self-pity is the greatest form of cowardice. Yet why should this complete collapse of all she had believed in have come to her? Swept away as by an avalanche: her joy of him, his love, professed with such passionate avowals. Was *that* love? No, never love as she could love, whose very soul was utterly possessed by him, who, at their marriage in his Church, had vowed to cherish, and …

'With my body I thee worship.' Was his love for her, as sworn before the altar and in their marriage bed, no more than satisfaction of the flesh, to be shared with another — to whom, he had said, he owed certain rights by reason of his previous association? Rights! Were these 'rights' he owed that he insist she receive his former mistress to attend her?

That he should dare impose upon his wife such humiliation!

She recalled the latest scene between them when she was lost to all control, as if the devil had entered into her. How terrible! She surely must be damned to everlasting now. If only she could remember the words she, or her devil, had screamed at him. And with what contempt, as it seemed, he had said, 'I cannot argue with a spoilt child.' That's what he thought her, 'a spoilt child', nothing of a wife ... And then, O, God! — she had flown at him, and Heaven knew what she might have done if he had not caught her hands and said, in English — what? If only she had learned to speak their hateful language!

Leaning on the sill she buried her face in her arms. 'Dear Jesus, Blessed Mary, forgive, forgive ... Merciful Lord, blot out my sins. Grant me grace to be truly penitent. I have loved God's creature better than Himself. O, *mea culpa, mea culpa, mea maxima culpa...*'

Men's voices floated up to her. She looked down to see Mr. Montagu and Lord William Brouncker returning from the tennis court. Two pages followed, carrying rackets and the netted bags of balls. Shadows were lengthening. Sunlight slanted through the full-leaved trees where birds chorused their evensong to the last of the sun; and then she saw advancing, a riding party; men, women and horses limned hazily against the misted green of distance. As they came nearer, the vivid colours of the women's habits, the plumed hats, the flash of jewels on gauntlets, formed a brightening pattern led by two figures: one tall in the saddle and hatless, his long dark hair sprinkled with blown petals of late hawthorn, the other ... Catherine's hands tightened on the windowsill. Could it be? ... Yes! It *was* she! In a crimson velvet habit with a fall of lace at the throat, her hat shading her face that laughed up at him, who leaned down to her; their laughter, as of some intimate shared jest, mingled with the voices of those that followed them.

Through a white-hot surge of fury, Catherine saw Mr. Montagu and Lord William, these two, her trusty servants, fall back for the riders to pass. Was it indeed this woman, *here*, or was her mind so distorted that it must conjure evil fantasies?

As she released her bitten underlip with an ooze of blood upon it, she heard: 'Your Majesty!' And turned to see Donna Elvira de Vilpena in the doorway. Forgetful of etiquette, so great her indignation, the Countess almost fell into the room as she advanced, to sink upon her knees.

Donna Elvira was 'plump as a pudding with a face like a pie', according to Charles, a description received by Catherine with delighted giggles. He would often tease her about her 'family', as he called her Portuguese attendants, how short a time ago, as time is measured! But an eternity of dark despairing days since this blight had fallen on her...

'Madame!' The high feathers in Donna Elvira's hair, worn as Portuguese fashion demanded, quivered as if in sympathetic frenzy. 'I cannot believe it is with Your Majesty's knowledge or consent that I, and all of us, are dismissed — ordered back to Lisbon. Madame!' She made a grab for the Queen's hand. 'I implore you to tell me if this infamous insult to Your Majesty's Household is true?'

'Good heavens!' gasped Catherine. 'Then he *does* mean to carry out his threat! Condessa, pray get up. What exactly have you heard? Explain yourself.'

Although encumbered by her monstrous farthingale, Donna Elvira did manage to get up and, her vast bosom swelling, eyes blazing, she explained herself in sentences excitedly escorted by exclamation marks.

'Your Majesty! We — all of us — to be driven away! Expelled! Returned in the next sailing vessel to Lisbon! Not even in one of His Majesty's ships! Not — indeed *not* — that I regret leaving this barbaric country where I have suffered agonies of rheumatism from this abominable climate! But to leave you! My beloved mistress! My adored Infanta!'

Rivulets of muddy tears, darkened from liberal application of kohl to her eyelids — the one assistance to nature permitted to the ladies of Lisbon's Court — rolled down her ample cheeks. 'This!' she dramatically shot out an arm, 'may likely bring about an international crisis! The King, your brother, and Her Majesty, the Regent, will not accept such indignity to Portugal!'

'Not only to Portugal,' flashed Catherine, 'but to me.'

'To you,' wept the Countess, 'most of all! My beloved child! How am I to bear this tearing apart from one I have nursed in her cradle!'

'You may not have to bear it.' Catherine patted the Condessa's heaving shoulder. 'There, then, there — oh, pray don't cry and upset yourself and me. Perhaps you won't be sent away. It may never come about.'

But it did come about. Not only was Catherine's Household dismissed in relays, with the exception of Donna Maria, Dom Patricio and his assistant priests, but the Queen Mother's Jewish factor, Senhor Diego Silva, was thrown into prison for not having paid the monies due to the Exchequer as part of the marriage treaty.

Meanwhile Clarendon, still hoping for peace between the two, again approached the King.

'I am bound to warn Your Majesty that, not only will you wreck your marriage if you continue to oppose the Queen's request concerning Lady Castlemaine's appointment — a very natural request,' he added, removing his sound foot from the interest of a puppy, 'but you may find yourself in bad odour with Portugal. The Portuguese Ambassador regards this dismissal of the Queen's Household as a personal affront, not to Her Majesty alone, but to the Queen Regent. He has lost no time in acquainting Donna Luiza of your decision, and the news of it will be in Lisbon before the Guarda Infantas and out-at-elbows lords and knights and what-not have come scrounging round for recompense. They demand remuneration overdue, which the Queen had not the wherewithal to give them. The Queen Regent is like to take it hardly.'

To which Charles, striding, as usual, up and down the room with a trail of spaniels at his heels, retorted, 'Do you think I care what that cheating cozening old hell-hag will take hardly — or softly — from me? And as for you,' Charles pointed a long finger at the goggle-eyed Chancellor, 'you can take this to my wife — as I've told her before — that I swear I will never again give her cause for complaint if she will accept Lady Castlemaine with the respect which is her due, but if she continues to oppose me then she has only herself to thank if I seek more agreeable company.'

So that was it; and Clarendon, heartily sick of the pair of them, gave up and betook himself to his son-in-law, James, who, as heir presumptive, should be primarily concerned in the upshot of this affair that looked to bring about an irreparable breach between the King and Queen. The wish may have fathered the thought of him whose daughter, should Charles predecease his brother without issue, might yet be Queen Consort of England.

'I would never have credited Her Majesty with so much determination,' said he, 'and should she carry out her oft-repeated threat to return to Lisbon —'

'In which event,' James interposed, elaborately casual, 'would the marriage be — possibly — annulled? There is talk of some doubt as to Catherine's fertility.'

'Pah! Talk.' Clarendon glanced uncomfortably aside. He too had heard talk of that. 'There is always talk where a union with so well endowed a consort is chosen for a monarch.'

'An endowment,' James reminded him, 'that has yet to materialise.'

'It will, it will,' Clarendon replied without conviction.

Said James, picking at his thumbnail, 'We hope so, and the sooner the better. There is much criticism from Portugal on account of the delay. There is also a strong faction here in favour of the Castlemaine's appointment. But I believe, were it not for continuous pressure from Catherine's Portuguese women and that sanctimonious old humbug, the Ambassador, who feathers his own nest, I'll be bound, with her overdue dowry, that the Queen would give way. She is deeply in love. The King is irresistible to women,' enviously added the King's brother, who was not.

Clarendon heaved himself out of his chair. 'Well, I've done my best with no appreciable effect, and now I wash my hands of it and them.'

The Court was on tenterhooks. What would be the next move in this battle royal? Which one would renew the offensive? Neither, it seemed, since they were not on speaking terms; and, disappointingly, there were no more rows. The Queen stayed in strict retirement, 'sunk in melancholy', as Clarendon reported; and if she did emerge from her seclusion to walk in the garden with Donna Maria and chanced to encounter the King, she would turn aside to avoid him, or, in passing, cut him dead.

And Charles, seeking 'more agreeable company', as he, via Clarendon, had warned her, sought it uproariously in every kind of frolic: banquets, water parties, rowdy moonlight revels to make hideous the night. Yet it was observed that he always returned to the Queen's apartments in the early hours of the morning.

Speculation ran high. Did they still cohabit? Unlikely, since, as was said, she locked her door against him so he must sleep in his dressing room along with his dogs.

But while Catherine never appeared at Court, the Lady exultantly did. The King rode, supped, dined with her and those of the company who flocked around the Favourite to gather the benefits she held in her hand to confer.

And now Catherine was faced with further trials. She must brace herself to part with her Portuguese 'family'.

Giggling courtiers watched the first batch of them depart. Loud were the lamentations of the maids of honour, wardrobe women, Guarda Infantas, and all; while a dejected train of knights and squires, pages, lackeys, cooks, were bundled into coaches bound for Portsmouth.

At a window overlooking the courtyard, Catherine stood to see them go; a dismal procession half obscured in the swirl of dust kicked up from the clatter of hooves and wooden wheels on paving stones ... Then a blindness came and hid them from her sight.

THREE

On a morning in July Father Patrick sat sunning himself on a bench in a secluded part of the palace gardens. Beside him, gloomily, sat Edward Montagu.

'Sure, 'tis by the intervention of our Blessed Lady,' the Father was saying, 'that the Queen Mother should return to England now, and for the first time since the death of her murdered husband, our late King, God rest his soul. This unhappy situation between the King and Queen cannot possibly persist when the Queen Mother arrives to meet and welcome her son's wife.'

Without turning his head, Edward turned his eyes to glance down at the beaming little priest. 'And her son's mistress? Will the Queen Mother welcome her?'

'My dear young sir!' The Father exhibited shock. 'Queen Henrietta is a Catholic.'

'What's that got to do with it?'

'It has everything to do with it,' was the equable reply. 'The mother of our King will never recognise the woman taken in — adultery.'

'Our Lord did,' said Edward. 'And as the King is endowed with Divine Right he may think himself justified in following example.'

The priest stiffened, and despite his stumpy figure he seemed clothed in simple dignity. 'With every respect and reverence for God's Anointed, there is only one man endowed with Divine Right: our Holy Father, the Bishop of Rome.'

'I see,' said Edward, who didn't.

'As all who have been led astray will see, in God's good time,' said the Father, mildly benign. Removing his biretta, he produced a handkerchief from the sleeve of his habit and mopped his tonsured head. ''Tis uncommonly hot today. Shall we find a shadier spot?'

Edward got up. 'Not for me, sir. I must be off to the stables. The Queen's favourite mare has gone lame.' His face darkened in an angry flush. 'Lady Castlemaine has been riding her without my knowledge — she's no horsewoman and has ridden her too hard, besides pulling her lovely mouth to pieces. By God! I could —' He stopped himself, adding in a surly voice, 'I've dismissed the groom responsible for taking orders from her.'

The Father blinked. 'Well, now. You did right to reprimand him, but 'tis hoped the fellow will not want for another situation. To be dismissed the Queen's service may go hardly against him.'

'You don't have to waste your sympathy on my rascally groom,' growled Edward. 'The Lady has taken him to Richmond as head groom for the four greys presented to her by the King to draw her gilded coach, which cost the Treasury another cool thousand or more.'

Noncommittally shaking his head, the priest replaced his biretta upon it, and peering through his spectacles said, 'There's a seat under that cedar. I will bid you good day, sir. I trust the mare will soon recover.'

He wandered away and, seating himself in the shade, took out his tablets and wrote the words of a poet he greatly admired:

Never was day so oversick with showres
But that it had some intermitting houres;

Never was night so tedious, but it knew
The last watch out and saw the dawning, too.

Preparations for the coming of the Queen Mother went apace. She, so long an exile from England, was due to arrive at Greenwich on 28 July, when Charles with his Court and his Queen set out to meet her.

To Catherine, having received from Father Patrick those lines from Herrick, contained in a little note with his translation of them into Portuguese, it was indeed as if her day, 'so oversick with showres', had seen its dawning, too.

On that day of brilliant sunshine, the small black-clad figure of Queen Henrietta stood alone at the head of the staircase in Greenwich Palace to greet her son and his young consort. As Catherine knelt to kiss the hand of the Queen Mother she was raised, enfolded in thin arms that held her close, and felt something warm and wet fall on her cheek.

'Do not kneel to me, *mon enfant*,' she heard. 'I would never have come back again to England but for the joy to see you whom I will love as my daughter and serve as my Queen.'

After the storms and despair the girl bride had suffered in these last weeks of her honeymoon, and the anguish of fear that the husband she adored had lost all love for her, his mother's tender greeting in her pretty French accent was balm to her wounded heart. She made attempt to answer, but could not just then speak.

The Queen Mother, still holding her hand, turned to her tall son, who knelt, and with her free hand she drew him to her to be kissed and wept upon.

'Charles! You look years younger than when I last saw you in Paris.' Her great black eyes set in the small dark face, once beautiful, now lined with markings of unforgotten tragedy, crinkled into laughter behind the tears that glittered on her lashes. 'Marriage, it agrees with you — and what a charming daughter you have given me. She is *délicieuse* with her air of a little nun! But where is James? Ah, James, my little — no, my big, big boy!'

He, the favourite of her three sons, loved even more than Henry, Duke of Gloucester, dead of the smallpox the year before, was in his turn ecstatically embraced. Then his wife, whose marriage she had so bitterly opposed, received her share, with tinctured warmth, of welcome. After which the reunited family retired to the Presence Chamber where the Dowager Queen insisted that Catherine should have place of honour on her right, with Charles on a stool at her feet, while Anne was graciously gestured to be seated beside him.

James, who stood behind his mother's chair, must have been no less relieved than was his wife at this cordial reception of Anne from the Queen, who had openly declared that no room should ever contain herself and the daughter of Hyde. 'If she enters Whitehall by one door, I will go out at the other!' So both the wives of Henrietta's sons had their 'intermitting houres', even if, for Catherine, short-lived.

It had been arranged that the Queen Mother should remain at Greenwich until Somerset House, which was to be her permanent residence and was now under repair, should be made ready to receive her. In the meantime she paid a return visit to the King and Queen at Hampton Court. It needed no prompting from her informers to confirm her suspicions that all was not well with the newlyweds. Quietly but firmly his mother took Charles to task.

'You cannot expect this girl of yours, brought up in *les convenances exigeantes* to comprehend the freedom that we women of France accept as a natural recreation of our husbands. Don't my darling —' her little hands, so thin they were like the claws of a bird, fluttered out to him — 'don't imperil your marriage and your throne by courting your mistress in public, for so may you be courting disaster. The English are hypocrites at heart, who make for themselves an eleventh commandment: "Thou shalt not be *found out in* adultery". Me, I know — I have seen this when, as a child of fifteen, I come here to marry that holy saint, your father. Yes, and they — those very Puritans who murdered him — were the first to say, "You shall not kill", and — killed!'

Charles, standing before her where she sat in the high chair, her feet scarcely touching the ground, took this lecture from 'Mam', as her children called her, much as when a boy he would wryly take the physic with which she dosed him.

'You have me wrong, Mam,' said he, with the forward thrust of the chin and underlip that she knew to be a danger signal. Charles could be led but never forced against his will. He had his full quota of Stuart obstinacy. 'Whatever former friendship has existed between myself and Lady Castlemaine is over and done with, I promise you.'

'So may you keep that promise,' said his mother, rising, 'and keep your former friend, *cette belle amie,* at your arm's length. Now we will walk in the gardens, yes? You have given back to them their loveliness, so full of heart-tearing memories for me.'

She slid her hand in his and together they went down the long corridor, her step still sprightly as a girl's.

The visit of the Queen Mother to Hampton Court gave Catherine a brief respite from the odious presence of the Lady. Charles, acting on his 'Mam's' advice, had the grace to keep his *belle amie* at arm's length, leaving her to kick her heels in various degrees of rage at Richmond. Yet if Charles, on secret sorties, did attempt to pacify her with promises that her absence from the Court during his mother's visit was but a temporary measure to guard against further objections from and rows with his wife, it is certain she was kept informed, not greatly to her joy, of the evident reunion between the King and Queen.

Mrs. Wilson had much to give the Castlemaine of news, gleaned from Mrs. Sarah, how that the Queen was in highest favour with the mother of the King.

'They are,' said Mrs. Wilson with some relish, 'so intimate and loving together and, both being Popish, 'tis natural, my lady, to be sure.'

'Very natural!' Her lady, at her toilet when these revelations were offered, slammed down upon the table the hand mirror she held, with force enough to break the glass and scatter a fountain of splinters.

'Mercy me!' cried Mrs. Wilson. 'That's seven years' ill luck for you, my lady.'

'Ill luck for you, more like — you lying toad!' Scarlet beneath the hare's foot upon her cheeks, the Lady swung round, demanding, 'What more have you heard from your chuff-cat of a familiar?'

'Little more, my lady.' Kneeling to gather the broken fragments from the floor, the mouth of Mrs. Wilson widened to a grin unseen by Lady Castlemaine. 'Only that the Queen, they say, is breeding. Hey, Lord! I've cut me finger!'

'Pity 'tweren't your throat. Ha! So that's it, is it? What a hope! He'd as well breed from a neutered bitch as from her. What more have you to tell?' Threateningly the Lady raised a hairbrush to brandish it above her handmaid's head. 'And tell me no lies or I'll brain you of what little wit you have.'

'Just this much more, my lady — no! I pray you do not beat me if I tell you that His Majesty sleeps no longer in his dressing chamber with his dogs, but, says Mrs. Sarah, having it from Chiffinch, he's as close as ever with the Queen — in her bed.'

'Pchah!' Or some such sound issued from the Lady's lips, snarled back against her teeth. 'He'd no doubt prefer the kennel with his four-footed bitch than with her, but for appearance's sake. And if you've naught better to tell than what all the world knows, then get out of my sight before I —' Another threat from the hairbrush to precipitate the exit of the handmaiden.

The Lady was left to dwell upon the divulgence of Wilson. 'Damnation take the pair of them!' said she to her dressing-glass. 'And may God blast him if he's using her to get him an heir.' With which amiable reflection, and lifting the corners of her drooping mouth, she carefully performed her facial exercises. Tension thus relieved, she struck the silver gong to recall Wilson. 'Habit me for riding. Their Majesties ride out this afternoon and — so do I.'

But though she took the route through leafy glades to Bushey, most favoured by the King and Catherine, and actually passed within sight and sound of the riding party, they did not see — or one of them at least may not have wished to see — the Lady Castlemaine.

And that good lady's nose was more than ever out of joint, her partisans uneasy. Had they backed, after all, the wrong horse? Since the widowed Queen's arrival it would seem they had. Hoped-for preferments looked to be sunk along with the odds on the Favourite. For, now that the Queen Mother was returned to London, her influence to bring about a reconciliation between the King and Queen might have weakened the Castlemaine's chances. Her supporters could only wait and see.

It was a day of radiant sun when Catherine made her first state entry into London from Hampton Court to Whitehall in the royal barge. All along Thameside the banks were lined with soldiers, and mobs of excited spectators, eager for a glimpse of their King's young wife where she sat in the gilded barge beneath a canopy of cloth of gold ornamented with enormous feather plumes.

The river was so crowded with boats and wherries, engarlanded, beflagged, come to watch and follow in the wake of the royalties, that hardly any water could be seen. Under the gilded canopy sat Catherine, delighted with it all, hands folded in her lap, her eyes dazzled by the sun and the pageant of colour, her ears deafened with the booms of guns from the Tower, resounding to mingle with the strains of music from the shore and watercraft, blaring welcome in a medley of discordance.

'You come in triumph,' said Charles. '*Vox populi* acclaims you!'

She slid her hand in his, felt the firm dry clasp of his fingers tighten on hers, and turned her head to meet his eyes with tears in her own; not now of sorrow, of joy and thankfulness, with God in His Heaven and all right with the world ... and Charles.

But all was not right with the Castlemaine. Clarendon, writing to Ormonde, tells him: *All things are bad here,* referring to the Lady, *but not quite so bad as you may hear.* Perhaps he was unduly optimistic, since *Everybody takes her to be of the bedchamber, but the Queen tells me that the King has promised her, on condition she will use her as she does the others, that she will never live in Court. Yet lodgings I think she has, although I hear of no backstairs.* If he did not, others did, for, in a burst of confidence, he adds a rider: *The worst is, the King is as discomposed as ever and looks little after business ... He seeks company who do not love him as you and I do.*

Among that company whom Charles sought, and who may not yet have loved him, was a fifteen-year-old *most pretty young spark,* as we hear it from Pepys, *who do hang much on my Lady Castlemaine and is always with her.*

'Always with her, I give you my word, Mrs. Wilson.' Thus did Mrs. Sarah give it, drinking this new-fangled 'tay' or tea, brought by the Queen from Portugal. 'As you, ma'am, should know,' Mrs. Sarah allowed, 'since talk has it that your lady, so I hear it from *my* lady, receives this young Master Crofts —' up went her eyes and down went her voice — 'in her chamber to be cosseted and more than would warrant a finely grown boy, no longer a child, shall we say?'

'You may say, Mrs. Sarah, but *I* say —' holding her cup and her temper, Mrs. Wilson darted a look of malice inconceivable at her smiling visitor — 'that my lady takes what might be called a maternal interest in young Master Crofts.'

'An interest maternally — misplaced?' queried Mrs. Sarah, her smile undiminished. 'For from what one hears he is the son born to His Majesty of an early indiscretion. Yes?'

'The son,' quoth Mrs. Wilson, 'of one Mistress Walters, as all the world knows to be the woman who caught in her toils the King when scarcely older than Master Crofts is now. A notorious bawd, Mrs Sarah.'

'Is that so?' innocently queried Mrs. Sarah. 'A bawd! You shock me, Mrs. Wilson.'

If anything short of murder could shock you, thought Mrs. Wilson, but this she did not say aloud. What she did say, with titters, and sipping scalding tea, was, 'Queen Henrietta dotes upon the boy as does Her Majesty — the Portugoose, hee-hee!'

'Madam,' Mrs. Sarah set down her cup. 'My mistress, Lady Sandwich, would abhor to hear you speak with such unbecoming levity of our Queen Consort. Pray reserve such remarks, which I gather you learn from your lady, for her ears and not mine. I thank you for the tay, ma'am, and will kindly take my leave.' And she flounced from the room with a hiss of petticoats as if she housed beneath their silken folds a colony of snakes.

That these two gentlewomen of their respective ladies voiced the Court's opinion concerning the parentage of young James Crofts did not unduly disturb Catherine. She had found a staunch ally in Queen Henrietta. Not only was their Faith a bond between them, but the Dowager Queen, who herself had come to England as a girl consort, could understand and sympathise with the difficulties and trials that beset this young wife of her son, whose subjects, while adoring him, looked askance at a foreigner and Papist. But of the agony she suffered as widow of a murdered king, a homeless exile in poverty unparalleled in the history of queenship, she did not speak; she told, instead, how she, too, as a bride, had been ordered to dismiss her French Household.

'It is *en règle,*' she said, with a sad little smile, 'that the foreign wife of an English King must be attended only by his people and not ours. We quarrelled bitterly. I was very young, hot tempered, obstinate, may God forgive me. I must have sorely tried him. I remember one night...' The small wrinkled face lightened to a grin which made her look like a little old child. 'I got up from our bed, shook that dear angel awake and put into his hand a letter I had written him and bade him read it. He told me *en bégayant* — how you call it? — stutt-stuttering — he had a terrible stutter, the poor dear —and told me to wait until the morning. He was so cross with me that I wake him. But I refuse to wait, so I read it for him, to say how I am miserable, and if he not let me have my servants and my ladies about me, I be finish with his kingdom and himself. I go back to my mother.'

'Yes,' Catherine nodded, 'as I told Charles. But you did not leave your husband, and I will not leave Charles, for I love him, Madame, I love him.' A sob rose in her throat, and she turned her head aside. 'I wish I do not love him, for to love … it hurts.'

'Love, my child, begets love. Charles,' said his mother, 'he, like all the Stuarts, is weak with women. My beloved too, he was weak, but with one woman only, myself. Yes, me, I am to blame. Much of these early quarrels with my husband were my fault. My mother was of the Medici, and from her I did inherit her fierce *jalousie*.' Then, seeing Catherine's hot flush she added quickly, 'My mother, the poor woman, she had cause enough for *jalousie*. My father, Henri *le Grand*, was a great King and a great lover. *But my mother,* she learn to go so —' Henrietta slid a hand over her eyes — 'that she see nothing and say nothing. I tell you now what my good friend, *le duc de* La Rochefoucauld, would say. We write to each other, for he has always the interest in me, my sons, and my dear daughter — he is with her now in Paris. She is married with my nephew, this little monkey of a "Monsieur". *Tiens!* How I run on so fast! What was I saying? Ah, yes, La Rochefoucauld, he tells me: *Il y a dans la jalousie plus d'amour-propre que d'amour.* Do you understand, *chérie?*'

'*Oui, Madame.*' Catherine's two little front teeth became visible in the smallest of smiles. 'Is it that *Monsieur le Duc* says there is more of self-love than love in — jealousy?'

'*Ça c'est excellent! Alors,* you soon learn to speak my language better than Charles. He was so slow to learn. James, he speak well French. You must speak with him.' Somewhere a clock chimed six silvery notes. 'Come!' The Queen Mother sprang up from her seat. All her movements were mercurial and young, as if her youth had been stayed in its flight. 'We go now to Benediction.'

Together, hand in hand, they went to the nearby Chapel of the Capuchins, where the cornerstone had been laid by Queen Henrietta when she came as a bride to England; a haven of refuge for Catherine. She would need it in the days to come.

That first summer of her marriage had drifted into autumn, and with it passed her hope of a child, which proved to be no more than a hope deferred.

From her lonely window at Whitehall Catherine would watch her husband stroll, pausing to set his watch by the sundial in the centre of the lawn, followed by his spaniels and his toadies, those gallants of the Court who had backed the winner, Lady Castlemaine.

She was in high fettle and highest favour now, with her lodgings in the palace and attendance on the Queen, as Clarendon in his letter to Ormonde had foretold. Although conditionally compelled to tolerate her presence, Catherine continued to ignore it. But Barbara, prepared for that, had gathered to herself a host of devotees in what was virtually a rival Court. Not only did her sworn adherents flock around her in loyal indignation at the Queen's refusal to 'use her as she does the others', as exacted by order of the King, but even the ladies of her Household, with exception of the few remaining Portuguese, went over to the enemy.

In the height of the conflict between himself and his wife during the honeymoon weeks, Charles might have given Catherine her way, since at that time he was in love with her enough to capitulate and heal her hurt, and his. For hurt he was at what he thought to be her unreasonable obstinacy; and, also, her outbursts of temper. He had borne with and been given his fill of his lady's splenetic convulsions, and now to find his dulcet 'little rose' could be equally contrary! 'A Megaera and all her sister Furies are personified in her,' he complained to his mother. 'Look you, Mam, can you not induce her to see how she is ruining our marriage by her attitude to Lady Castlemaine?'

'*She*, to ruin your marriage?' His mother dismissed that with a shrug. '*Cherchez la femme* — but not that *petite femme* of yours, not that poor innocent girl. It is not easy for a girl brought up in a convent to understand or to accept the lovers of a husband she adores. But I have tried for both your sakes to make her more amenable, and will try again, although you do not smooth the way for me by turning out her *ménage*.'

'I've allowed her to keep her priests and that scarecrow of hers, Donna Maria,' said Charles sulkily.

'Allowed?' snapped the Queen. 'You are *too* generous. I also had my *ménage* taken from me, and I raged at your father as does your Catherine at you.'

'As she did,' he retorted. 'She'll hardly speak to me now, and locks me out of her bedroom.'

'If you were all French instead of half English, you would break down the door.' His mother's eyes slipped past him, gazing through the open windows across the sun-lit lawns of Somerset House that spread green aprons to the Thames, shimmering like molten brass in the honey-gold light of the September afternoon. 'Yes, as I did break the casement of my room at Whitehall when your beloved father sent away my women. I made a frightful scene.' A hovering smile came upon her lips. 'They howled and so did I, screaming at the window that I would not let them go — they must come back or I go with them. I was an *enfant terrible,* and your father was an angel to put up with me. I yelled and beat my fist on the window to break the glass, and cut my hands.' Her little dark face broke into laughter. 'I bled like a pig, and your father, he did me comfort and take me to Nonsuch. So loving kind he was, so charming a lover, and that is where he got me with my first baby, your brother, who died on the day he was born.'

'Pity he did,' muttered Charles. 'He'd have had my crown — and welcome! 'Tis no joy to be a king. I'd liefer still be "one Charles Stuart" with a price on his head and on the run, chased by Cromwell's Parliament men, and I riding pillion as footman with the prettiest girl in the West Country, Jane Lane. I wonder what's become of her ... See what you can do, Mam, to bring this wife of mine to her senses.'

'I wish,' his mother said, lifting her dry withered cheek for his kiss, 'that I could bring you to yours.'

But if Queen Henrietta did not succeed in bringing her son to his senses, she may have persuaded his wife to accept the situation, in the hope that by so doing she would end that unhappy breach between herself and Charles.

A fatal resolution.

Not only did Catherine extend the olive branch to her hated rival, but offered it, as Clarendon disapprovingly records, with *familiarity in public, and in private used no one more friendly...*

The Court, sniggering scorn, was hugely diverted; the Lady triumphant, and Charles, far from viewing with relief this extraordinary reversal on Catherine's part was, contrariwise, irrationally angered at what he took to be a childish and mischievous caprice. Her determination to ignore the Lady's presence while allowing her access to the Court he had secretly applauded. Such strength of will in one, apparently, so pliable might have brought him not only to his senses, but in remorse and subjugation to his knees. Moreover, and this rankled further to dismay him, he believed himself the victim of deliberate deceit; her seeming slavish love for him an infatuation fostered, as the Castlemaine insisted, by the glory of his state and her elevation to it.

'I've been tricked!' Striding up and down his closet, he let forth to Clarendon. 'As that hell-hag of Portugal, her mother, has tricked me out of the marriage settlement, so did this wife of mine persist in her objection to receive the Lady Castlemaine that she may prove herself my master.'

'As the Lady seeks to prove herself your mistress,' countered Clarendon.

'But why?' — Charles rounded on the Chancellor, who goggled up at him in apprehension as to what was coming next — 'why,' came next, 'should I be forced to suffer the Queen's tantrums and her threats to leave me unless I dispose of her whom she is pleased to call my "whore", and now she falls upon her neck?'

Clarendon withheld on his tongue the retort that it was strange the King should be so put about at finding his wife had faithfully, if with *trop de zele*, followed his command to entertain the Lady. Instead, in an attempt to oil troubled waters, he temporised.

'Sir, did you not require Her Majesty to use Lady Castlemaine with the same courtesy she would accord to others? And now that she does so —'

'I did not,' Charles broke in loudly, 'require that the Queen prostrate herself before the woman she professes to loathe. More than according her mere courtesy, she hails her in friendship, calls her into corners, and there they sit, the pair of them, laughing together, merry as grigs. God alive! Such inconsistency can only be consistent with loss of reason. The girl must be out of her wits.'

'Which if it be so, Sir,' said Clarendon, bluntly, 'you have but yourself to blame — and to your cost!' For he foresaw that the King's behaviour to his wife and her enforced surrender to his mistress would give rise to scandalised astonishment far beyond the precincts of Whitehall.

Over ale mugs in taverns, grim and sober citizens muttered that the King danced to one tune only, played by the Lady; that he neglected, to his shame, his wife, and that she and the Queen Mother between them with their Popery would bring disaster to the Crown and Church. The country, prophesied these gloomy Jeremiahs, would find itself in parlous plight, up to its ears in debt and the government borrowing right and left from City goldsmiths. 'What little the King has managed to scrape from the pickings of Portugal — and not much of that, neither, since he'd been done out of the most of it — he hands over to be swallowed by his woman!'

'Aye, and look you, the government now sells Dunkirk to the French to supplement the needs of the Exchequer.'

'Bad management on the part of Ned Hyde, who is building a palace out of his pickings,' was growled by the followers of Cromwell, who would have wished to see Clarendon's head on a pike along with that of the traitor Monk.

'Yes! He who had gotten the King his throne, where old Noll should have sat to this day.'

There was evidently still some furtive hankering after a Protector who had protected them and their interests more than did the Stuart, with his giddy goings-on and his wenching in the Palace of Whitehall.

Clarendon was greatly bothered and his gout giving him hell, so he could not attend the council meeting at which the King had announced his intent to make an entire change of government. This would mean that the Chancellor's faithful time-servers, if not himself, would be thrown out and new blood brought in.

The Act of Uniformity, introduced on 24 August 1662, depriving two thousand Presbyterian ministers of office, had roused a storm of protest from the Nonconformists. Then Charles, wise after the event, brought in a policy to extend indulgence to all religious dissentients and terminate the penal laws exacted by the Established Church. The same toleration was, with equal liberality, offered to the Catholics. More trouble for the Chancellor, to start him from his couch and send him hobbling to the King in a sweat of pain and perturbation.

'Sir, I must warn you 'tis generally assumed that you have been coerced into this measure by Their Majesties, your mother and your wife.'

'Who,' demanded Charles, 'does so assume? And how can you know of such assumption with your foot in a bandage and yourself in your bed?'

'I still have my eyes and my ears,' grunted the Chancellor. 'Your people will excuse much in a monarch, but never his conversion to Rome.' Then, seeing the King's face darken with anger, his lower lip squared to retort, Clarendon — not disposed to argue — went hobbling out as he had come in.

But there were some who saw beyond the indolent and easy flexibilities of the people's 'Merry Monarch'. They knew that he who, it would appear, thought only of his pleasures, his lusts, and his laboratory where he dabbled in chemicals, physics, and — some said — necromancy, held his country's interests at heart before his own, and that his declaration of tolerance conveyed an earnest desire to bring about a more realistic approach to religious unity. This, however, did not popularise his marriage with a Papist. And Catherine, for her staunch adherence to her Faith and her unpredictable abasement to her rival, was regarded not only with suspicion but contempt.

Her sacrifice of pride had gained her nothing; and Charles, primed by Barbara, was convinced that her sudden change of attitude toward Lady Castlemaine indicated that she had never cared enough for him to oppose his dalliance with lighter loves. It was possible, as Barbara insisted, that her hostility to herself and his diversions was nothing but a blind to screen her own … with whom? Young Montagu? That mooncalf always at her elbow, bowing, scraping, riding with her daily and blushing to the ears whenever she addressed him? Very well, then, henceforth he need have no scruples concerning his inconstancy. He would go his own way and let his wife go hers.

And Catherine had staked and forfeited her all in one last misguided effort to regain his love. Although she would never more have cause to complain of his neglect; and while he bestowed on her every mark of respect combined with connubial duty, the deep-hearted enduring devotion that might have been hers, she had forever lost.

PART TWO

Dans les premières passions, les femmes aiment l'amant; dans les autres, elles aiment l'amour.
De La Rochefoucauld

FOUR

On the last night of December 1662, the ubiquitous Pepys got himself an entry to the palace at a ball given by the King, *in a room,* he tells us, *crammed with fine ladies ... Very noble it was and a pleasure to see.* Perhaps not so much pleasure for Catherine, who sat with her 'fine ladies' in the great Banqueting Hall, somewhat larger, one imagines, than a 'room', and saw her husband lead in the coranto with Frances Stuart, the prettiest and latest addition to the Court.

She, who had come over from Paris with Queen Henrietta, had been appointed chief maid of honour to Catherine by reason of her kinship to the Royal House. Upon this charming creature the Queen lavished much fondness, returned with a gratifying humble affection. That Frances was regarded by the Court as a stupid little fool, senseless to the verge of imbecility, did not trouble Catherine. What did trouble her was that the Castlemaine appeared to be equally fond of *la belle Stuart,* as she was known, and would frequently have her sup at her apartments, where the King supped every night, and not only to sup but to share the Lady's bed — so word would have it — with the King. 'A case,' the gossips giggled, 'of three's company, two's none.'

Such company and in such circumstances, if talk could be believed, caused Catherine some anxiety on behalf of her innocent young protégée. And it did a little irk her to see the lovely Stuart go prancing with the King, while she, who had not yet learned these frolicking English fandangoes so different from the stately dances of her mother's Court, must sit apart and watch the fun unable to join in it.

Above, in the minstrels' gallery, the harpists, the fiddlers and flautists twanged and squeaked and fluted, while the fun waxed faster and Catherine waxed furious to see the Castlemaine, whose jewels outshone her own, go romping round partnered by James Crofts, recently created Duke of Monmouth.

That Charles should give this bastard boy of his precedence over every duke in his kingdom with exception of his brother York, implemented, as Catherine guessed, by Lady Castlemaine, caused her more heart-burning. Charles had a conscience about his left-handed offspring and was more devoted to young Crofts than to any of them.

'Madam, is Your Majesty not dancing? Why so sad on this so joyful night?'

The boy James, disengaged from Lady Castlemaine, had darted through the whirling couples to drop on one knee before Catherine, his face coaxingly upraised with laughter in his eyes, and a warmth to bring a warmth to hers.

'I cannot dance these dances, James.'

'Then, Madam, I will show you how, if Your Majesty will honour me.'

He spoke with a slight French accent, having spent much of his short life in France, was bilingual, irresistible; nor could she resist him who had his father's charm. But there resemblance ended. Nothing of Charles was in that fair English face, framed in fawn-gold curls; a lovely boy. No wonder Charles adored him; yet rumour gave it he was not his son but the son of Robert Sidney, a former love of Lucy's. Catherine wished he might be proved as such; yet what proof would Charles accept to deprive him of a parentage of which he was so proud? *God send,* she prayed to her inner self, *that I may give my husband a son of whom he may be prouder.*

As James led her out, tall, long-limbed and graceful, if still a trifle coltish, tongues wagged again to see them.

'Oho! She follows Charles in the line of least resistance.'

'Which won't delight the other James, who looks — tee-hee! — as if about to vomit,' giggled little Henry Jermyn, one of Barbara's many adherents. 'Our York's queasy stomach don't take kindly to a nephew sprung out on wrong side o' the bed.'

Light from a myriad candles case a dust-dimmed glow on a bewildering pageant of colour, as couples revolved madly to the music, and boy choristers sang:

'The pleasures of youth are but flowers of May;
O, let me live well though I live but one day...'

And, as the fiddling and fluting rollicked to its end, the voice of the King rang through the Great Hall: 'Now for the dance of old England ... "Cuckolds all awry!"'

With which, amid the laughter and confusion, decorum was swept aside; and although a few of the dancers kept their places, most of them did not but went to seek seclusion in the shadows of the corridors, where bodies, strained together, stood or sprawled in the shrouding dark. Then as the bells of every steeple chimed the New Year in, shouts went up in welcome.

James, seated in the ballroom, long-faced, solemn, saw young Monmouth dart off in pursuit of Mistress Stuart, seizing her to swing her round and dance with him; he saw the Queen give the signal to her ladies that she wished to retire, and James, stroking his chin, muttered to his wife, ''Tis a dance well chosen, since my brother is the king of cuckold-makers.'

No cuckoldry for James who may have hoped — and hoped in vain.

'Yes, to be sure,' said Anne, stifling a yawn. 'And now the New Year's in, the Queen will go to bed — and so will I.'

The Whitehall Palace of Catherine's day, situated between Westminster and the village of Charing Cross, was a city in itself enclosed within walls that edged the Thames for half a mile. Inside those walls of many buildings were lodged the Court and high officials of the Household. Behind guarded doors in the long stone gallery lay the royal apartments and the council chamber where the King and his ministers conducted their affairs of state. But Charles, unlike his father, did not assert his privilege for privacy. Day and night the galleries, branching off from the main artery that ran through the palace, were open to the public, who would throng there to see the King pass and exchange words of greeting with all or any of them; and here too, among idlers, the gossip of the day would be exchanged while sightseers would come to gape at the pictures collected by the late King which had escaped the vandalism of the Roundheads.

Like his father before him Charles had a keen appreciation of the arts, and in his closet, where none save Chiffinch dared intrude, he kept his treasured Holbeins, Titians, Van Dycks, and the modern Dutch painters that were his pride: the seascapes and ships of Danckerts, the exquisite flower pieces of Verelst, and the Anglicised Lely, just come into fashion for his flattering portraits of Court beauties. Here, too, were his collection of clocks and watches, bric-à-brac and trinkets collected, he would say, 'upon his travels'; but where or how he obtained them when, a penniless outcast, he roamed through France and Holland, he did not divulge: possibly from the wealthy Duchesse de la Châtillon, whose name as a likely bride for him had been coupled with his, and who, it was said, rewarded his attentions in full measure. But more than all, his chief delight was his laboratory where, with his chemist Le Fèbre, he would distil physic for the sick and experiment with potions culled from his herb garden. In these, his more sober recreations, Catherine had as little part as in his merrier pursuits.

Determined to overcome the limitations imposed upon her by her convent training, she ardently attempted to adapt herself to the trivial frivolities of courtly life, where eroticism flourished in a labyrinthine *mise en scène* of disorderly example; a scene of alcoved intrigues where women engaged in outrageous adventures, romped like dairymaids with the lords of the bedchamber, sang lewd songs and looked upon chastity as something more shameful than sin.

Pathetically did Catherine strive to regain her husband's heart in her efforts to be as were these others whose company he sought as more amusing than her own. She took dancing lessons, diligently practising before her mirror the Court's outlandish capers. And, in order to be in the fashion, she discarded the Portuguese modesty in dress that covered all of her neck and shoulders and went to the other extreme, exposing her bosom as far as decency dared, bringing ridicule upon her from the Lady and her followers to see her romp and frolic with the worst of them, and with a gaiety assumed to hide the blight of resentment against the woman who was poisoning her life. For at all costs to her pride must she keep the peace between herself and Charles, even to acceptance of his woman to attend her in the bedchamber and with right of entry to it, of which the Castlemaine took full advantage. She would wait upon the Queen at her toilet to jibe, with veiled insolence, for the time she spent on titivating to attract her husband.

'Fie, Madam, I wonder at your patience to be so long a-dressing!' with a smile that suggested the result of it was scarcely worth the pains.

Stung to retort, Catherine replied, 'I have so much other cause for patience that this, compared to it, is nothing.'

But the Lady would not so easily release her 'little mouse-bitch' from her claws. Although the relationship between herself and Charles had been resumed, she realised her power over him was on the wane, notwithstanding the friction she promoted to disunite the husband and the wife. That her liaisons with other men were tolerated by Charles — among these the painted little fop Henry Jermyn, the sixteen-year-old John Churchill, future and first Duke of Marlborough, and one Jacob Hall, a tightrope acrobat of splendid physique whom she had picked up at Bartholomew's Fair — gave a certain indication of the King's declining favour. The unprecedented honours bestowed by Charles upon his natural son by Lucy Walters, were, as Catherine surmised, largely due to the connivance of Barbara to strike another blow at her, and at the same time to use this boy whom she had blatantly seduced as a formidable weapon for Catherine's undoing.

On a spring morning in 1663, at a summons from the Lady, came Henry Jermyn, recently returned from a visit to Paris, tripping on high red heels and dressed in the latest style favoured by 'Monsieur', Duc d'Orléans, husband of Minette. His golden peruke caressed his narrow shoulders; he was rouged and patched and powdered. So closely did his suit of amber satin, lavishly encrusted with sequins and seed pearls, embrace his puny figure, he looked as if poured into it as in a mould.

Barbara jerked her head from under Wilson's hands, engaged in threading ribbons through her curls. She turned upon Jermyn, volleying questions. 'Well? What have you gleaned from Paris? Have we started a false hare? Don't stand there grinning! Go on, man, say!'

Jermyn, grinning wider, said, 'I have just come from Somerset House with messages and gifts from Minette. Queen Mam confirms that her grandson — yes! grandson, mark you, as she calls him — is betrothed, and the marriage treaty ratified between Monmouth and the child, Lady Anne Scott — aged twelve!'

'Ah!' A gusty sigh escaped the Lady's lips. 'This is the best news I've heard since Cromwell's bones danced on the air. Charles shows his hand and I'll show my fist … Phew! For God's sake, Wilson, my perfume! Spray me. I can't stand the stink of Mr. Jermyn's civet. Is this the latest scent from Paris, Harry? Dog's turd would smell sweeter. Go on, then, tell what more you've learned from the Frenchwoman who hates my guts as much as I hate hers. How does she take this betrothal to the Scott child?'

'Not unkindly,' tittered Jermyn. 'She says it indicates there may be something in this talk of marriage between the King and the woman Walters since Anne Scott can bring a million to his son. A useful dower for a future heir.'

'Which being so —' Barbara, sorting patches from a gold box on the table, poised a tiny heart upon her finger, licked it and stuck in on her cheek — 'may I rot if I don't secure evidence of it to see our little rose plucked from its stalk.'

'Monsieur,' simpered Jermyn, 'wears a coach and horses on his chin to hide a pimple. He diets now to slim himself — he has a fear of growing fat. Yes, indeed, the Queen, as so often threatens, may find herself returned to Lisbon if Monmouth is *not*, tee-hee, born under the rose, but above it, and if — may I?' He paused to pick a comfit from a dish beside him. 'Sugared almonds are my delight. As I was saying, if he be proved the Walters' son — by *marriage,* we already have a Prince of Wales.'

The Lady's lips stretched to a smile. 'And that may be less difficult than to prove the Rose no wife.'

'Hey?' Jermyn, startled in the act of swallowing, choked, and spluttered, 'Wha — ouch! Ouch! How-ow-ow?'

'A glass of water, Wilson, for Mr. Jermyn.'

'Wha —? How-ow?'

'If you had kept open your ears instead of your eyes that see no further than your nose,' remarked the Lady, 'you would know there's been some doubt as to whether a Romish marriage between Charles and the Portugoose is valid.'

'But — huh — huh —' whooped Jermyn — 'a thousand pardons, madam, I hah-hah-have never been so mortified. This sweet has stuck in my gullet.' He grabbed the proffered glass of water, gulped, and recovering, said, 'They were married afterwards in the Church of England, so how —?'

'She refused to make the responses,' the Lady calmly supplemented.

'But how,' persisted Jermyn, wiping his streaming eyes, 'can her refusal to respond in a language she couldn't speak make the marriage invalid?'

'That,' smiled Barbara, 'remains to be seen.'

'Madam,' giggled Jermyn, 'you intrigue me.'

'Or heard,' she continued on a purring note, 'in the council chamber, where Clarendon won't be spared, neither. We know what we know. Now tell me of Minette. Is she breeding again from that puppy Philippe? It's a mystery to me how he's begotten two — is it? — who's as potent to beget as a worm or yourself with a prick so small as a thimble. Now you must go and I must go — about my business.'

Which brought her to call upon Lord Bristol. She found him in his library, a bottle at his elbow, himself upon a couch and in a coma, apparently induced by strong imbibition.

This imperishable busybody, Bristol, did, according to Clarendon, *value himself on the faculty of perplexing and obstructing everything in which he had a hand*, even to the extent of perplexing and obstructing Charles in the negotiations of his marriage with Portugal's Infanta. It was Bristol who, in order to keep on friendly terms with Spain and while in Paris after the Restoration, had informed the Spanish Ambassador of the English King's intent to marry the Portuguese heiress.

This news by no means delighted Spain's Ambassador, who had no desire to see England united with Portugal, only just released from Spanish shackles to regain her independence and her monarchy. From Bristol, also, came the inference that not only was the Infanta Catherine squint-eyed, humped and hideous — Bristol was unsparing of invention — but congenitally barren. How this condition in a convent-bred virgin could have been known to Bristol went unquestioned by the horrified bridegroom-to-be, until Louis of France stepped in with emphatic contradiction of these utterly fictitious and libellous reports. He had seen the Infanta of Portugal, he told his cousin, Charles. She was enchanting, adorable, petite, with eyes like saucers and a skin like a peach. If Charles refused her on account of these absurd lies he would do well to sign the marriage settlement without delay, or, if not, Louis would marry her himself She was far more attractive than that dowdy little frump, Maria Theresa of Spain, whom they were wishing on him. He finished by showing Charles a portrait of Catherine that sent him hurrying to finalise the treaty.

The disgruntled Bristol, having failed to bring off what he hoped would be a coup with Spain at some diplomatic advantage to himself (Earl of Bristol, British Ambassador to Madrid), in token of his Sovereign's gratitude for saving him from a disastrous marriage, cherished thereafter an unreasonable hate against Catherine, of which Barbara Castlemaine was happily aware.

So, certain of an ally in any scheme that she might entertain to thwart the wife of Charles and further the disruption of their marriage, she took her information — and herself — to Bristol.

Announced by a lackey to his somnolent lordship, who showed no indication of vitality, she approached him. 'Shake him,' she commanded the footman, 'and wake him.'

'My lord.' The fellow bent over the recumbent earl gingerly, as bidden, to shake him. 'The Lady Castlemaine, my lord.'

'P-p … wha'?' His lord opened an eye and blew bubbles. 'What th' hell? P-p … wha'?'

Bending lower: 'The Lady Castlemaine to see your lordship,' came louder repetition.

'Eh?' Both eyes were open now. 'Who?'

'You may go.' The Lady pointed to the door and, as it closed upon the lackey, she bade the startled Bristol: 'Come up, man, come up. A'hew! You stink like a tavern. I have that to say which can't wait, unless you're too raddled to hear it.'

'Not raddle', sweet. Dozin'.' He yawned widely. 'Been dicin' till mornin'. Buckin'am drain' me uva cool five 'undred.'

'Would you have me reimburse you to the double?' insinuated Barbara with a show of perfect teeth, not entirely her own.

Bristol sat up now, the wine fumes clearing. 'More'n ever gracious, but — why'm I so favoured?'

101

'To aid the cause we both uphold in the interest of the King to see him released from bondage, and to give him a rightful heir. There's a chance the Portuguese is breeding.'

'Eh?' Bristol sucked his dry palate. 'This is ugly news.'

'Not so ugly if 'twere proved she breeds a bastard.'

Bristol's jaw dropped. 'A what?'

'A bastard, darling.' Seating herself on the end of the couch, Barbara pushed aside the earl's stockinged feet, and said, 'which it *will* be if she bears it. I have somewhat here to lay before the council that should bring down Clarendon, who's been up too long, and will determine that Charles, at this present, has no wife.'

'Hey?'

Bristol was in a stare, and the Lady in a smile which looked to split her face in two, as, offering a parchment, she asked him, 'Can you read it? No, you can't. You're cock-eyed. I'll read it for you.' And she read:

'*...That the Lord Clarendon has brought the King and Queen together without any settled agreement about the marriage rites, whereby the Queen refusing to be married by a Protestant priest and in case of her being with child, either the Succession should be made uncertain for want of due rites of matrimony, or His Majesty be exposed to a suspicion of being married in his own dominions by a Romish priest.*'

'So what say you to this? It'll raise a hornet's nest I'm thinking, and —'

'— or a mare's nest,' Bristol doubtfully put in.

'Foh! You're white-livered. I tell you it will bring a swarm around the Chancellor, and in and out the queen's bedchamber, where she'll not lie, for long, aside o' Charles! Aha!' The Lady rubbed her hands. 'That'll teach her to despise me and then come wriggling up, all honey-mouthed, to make us both the King's fools!' She bestowed a kiss on Bristol's forehead. 'Go douse yourself, digest it and dish it up to Buckingham on the council table, and tell him his five hundred will be paid!'

The marriage of the sixteen-year-old Duke of Monmouth to his child bride, Lady Anne Scott, was the highlight of the season, the talk of the galleries, and in Thameside taverns far beyond the Palace of Whitehall. Over ale mugs the gossip, brought by journeymen, was all of the grand ball given by the King in Windsor Castle to celebrate the wedding of his son — and possible heir. This gleaned by Mr. Pepys from his confidant and crony, Court physician, Dr. Pierce, who had been present at the ball and had seen the Queen lead the young Duke for the opening Branle, or as more commonly known, the Brawl.

'Yes, honour after honour has been heaped upon this boy of Lucy Walters,' said the doctor, having invited Mr. Pepys to sup at his house hard by Whitehall and to give him all he knew of these events, 'and the Queen has made his little Duchess Anne one of the bedchamber women.'

'At twelve years old?' said the pop-eyed Pepys, imbibing this latest news with each draught of the doctor's metheglin; and how that when the Queen and the young bridegroom had only just begun to dance, the King took Monmouth, and for all the world to see, he kissed him and made him put on his hat which he had tucked under his arm.

'A sure sign of royal precedence, as well you know, Mr. Pepys. I tell you the whole company was turned to stone. The Queen stood there staring, white as death. She knew the significance of the King's gesture in making him cover his head before the Queen, that only royalty may do.'

'It must have been a bitter blow,' said Mr. Pepys, agog, 'for Her Majesty to see the King publicly acknowledge his bastard son as royal.'

The doctor nodded.

'The Queen did take it much to heart.' He raised his brimming goblet and screwed an eye at the ruby lights kindled in the crystal cup from candle gleams. 'Yet, as I was saying' — which Pepys had not heard him say — 'I think it possible that the King may have feasted a thought unwisely to look upon the wine when it was red and, in his natural elation at the marriage, to imply the Duke to be his heir presumptive in the event of the Queen's — ah — misconception. But for myself — I speak from medical observance — I believe Her Majesty to be fertile. We can only hope and pray it may be so.'

'Amen to that,' uttered Mr. Pepys; and walked somewhat unsteadily home, for he could not carry his drink so well as a camel or his good friend the doctor; and, after cooling his head, he made a note in his diary to the effect that:

It is made very doubtful whether the King do not intend the making of the Duke of Monmouth legitimate; but surely the Commons of England will never do it, nor the Duke of York suffer it…

The Duke of York would certainly not suffer it, and had already written to his father-in-law, Clarendon:

My brother hath spoken with the Queen concerning the owning of his son, and in much passion she told him that from the time he did any such thing she would never see his face more … I would be glad to see you that

I may advise with you what is to be done, for my brother tells me he will do whatever he pleases.

The fat was in the fire, but the fire did not burn; or it may have burned itself out in this last flare-up with which Catherine received her husband's alleged intention to legitimise young Monmouth. Yet, despite the seeds of doubt planted by the Castlemaine in the mind of Charles that his wife was incapable of child-bearing, the fact remains that Catherine's hopes deferred were realised; her prayers answered.

She was pregnant.

What now of the plans of Barbara, Buckingham and Bristol? 'Those three infernal Bs,' so the Chancellor named them to James. 'I tell you, Sir, they're out for blood — my blood and the Queen's blood, as if she'd not been bled enough — and your blood, too, if you should cross them.'

'Mine? Why, how's this?' James alarmedly enquired. 'If Catherine is breeding, then Monmouth is done for — praise be!'

He signed himself, at which Clarendon, with unease, warned him, 'Your Popery is like to bring you down as those three Bs and the queen B, God damn her — she is at the root of it — seek to bring down your sister, Catherine, with that same Romish weapon. I'll warrant there'll be fireworks in the council chamber when Bristol and Buckingham challenge the King's marriage with a Papist.'

James started up. 'They can't! The marriage was solemnised in the Established Church.'

'They can and they will.' Clarendon heaved himself out of his chair. 'There's no end to their machinations, nor to the fury of a woman scorned. Pity the Queen didn't open arms to receive the Lady in her bosom from the first, rather than despise and degrade her — not that she weren't already soaked in degradation. And now what's come of it? The Castlemaine has dug her talons deep in the little Queen to maul her — and me with her.' He limped to the door and turned to say over his shoulder, 'You may be called as witness to the Popish ceremony conducted privately at the King's House in Portsmouth. I thought I'd best prepare you.'

'Prepare —' The Duke's mouth sagged; he paled. 'Why should *I* be brought as witness? Surely the evidence of the officiating priests should be proof enough?'

'Much proof they'll swallow from a priest of Rome. Only the King's sense of justice can save the Queen and my Chancellorship, though I fear me I'm as good as gone since they accuse me of being a party to the Catholic marriage prior to the Anglican, and *that* they'll attempt to dishonour, and so — dethrone the Queen.'

'They will never do it!' James now was up in arms for Catherine. 'Charles hankers for an heir and if the Queen is ripe to give him one he'll not let her go. He loves her still. I'll swear to it.'

'You may have to swear to it before the council. Go now to your chapel, lad, and say a prayer for the Queen and — for me. I'm too old,' said the Chancellor, 'for this.' A wetness dimmed his gooseberry eyes. 'I served your father faithfully as I have served his son, and I didn't look to be thrown out in my sere and yellow.' His glance travelled to the window that framed the branches of a cherry tree in glorious full blossom. 'Nor in the spring of the year, neither, did I think to see myself fall. Autumn is the time for that with us of — winter's years.'

James went to him and laid a hand on the old man's sturdy shoulder. 'Sir, my brother will never have you leave him. He owes too much to you, as so do I.'

Clarendon grinned round at him. 'More to Monk, methinks, who turned his coat from Cromwell to cross the border with the Scots at his heels and bring back the Stuart to his throne.' Then he drew himself up. 'So! Let them do their devil's work. I'm ready for them, son.'

And out he went.

In the Queen's privy garden at Whitehall, where none but the King, her ladies and her priests had right of entry, the last of the tall tulips stood sentinel above a flame of wallflowers and low-growing pansies.

Father Patrick, at his window that overlooked the Queen's garden, wandered down to her who, with Frances Stuart in attendance, sat on the stone parapet that edged a lily pond.

'They call them heartsease in Ireland,' said Father Patrick, beaming cheer on the sad-faced little Queen as he stooped to pluck a full-blown purple pansy.

'Call who ... what, Father?'

He insisted she should speak English with him always now, and she had become quite fluent in her pretty soft accent.

'These gentle velvet blooms,' said he, and offered her the flower. 'That learned medico and herbalist, Dr. Culpeper — dead, alas, these nine years — declares them to be a gallant — ah — anti-venereal.'

'Anti...?' Her faintly surprised eyebrows lifted in slight puzzlement.

'Used,' the priest added in hasty confusion, 'with much beneficence for inflammatory conditions of the lungs, pleurisy, and scabs. It is also known as three faces in a hood.'

'Three faces in a hood! What a droll name!' giggled Frances. 'And so like my little cat's face.' She held in her arms a white kitten. 'Don't you think, Madam, that pansies' faces are like little cats' faces?'

'Yes, Frances.' Catherine gave her the smile, half quizzical, wholly affectionate, that she reserved for her alone. 'Just like your little cat's face.'

'Not *my* face, Your Majesty,' the large vapid blue eyes widened, 'Tiddy's little face. My face isn't like a cat's face, is it?'

'No, child, of course it isn't. We are speaking of the flowers that the Father calls heartsease.' She said it over, below breath. 'Heartsease. To ease the heart. A lovely name for a lovely flower.'

Frances jumped up. 'May I pick Your Majesty a nosegay? Just a pretty little nosegay of heartsease — heartseas*es* — if Your Majesty will hold Tiddy, for I can't pick flowers with Tiddy in my arms, and if I put her down she'll run away. She ran away yesterday when the King's dogs chased her … Oh, no, I can't! Here comes the King with his dogs. They will frighten her and she'll run away again.'

'So you had best take her indoors. Hurry, then.'

Frances, still hugging her kitten, curtsied, but as she obediently hurried, the King waylaid her, standing in her path and laughing down at her as she bent to the bob, while the spaniels set up a clamour of excited yelps, leaping to reach the kitten. Its shocked tail bristling, its eyes pinpointed in terrorised fury, it struggled from the arms of Mistress Stuart and like lightning streaked off with the dogs after it.

'Oh, no! Oh, Sir — Your Majesty! My poor little cat — I shall lose her!' She made as if to run, but the King barred her way.

'I'll back your cat to win a race against any of my dogs. See not — she's in the lilac tree, spittin' hate at 'em! Here, Minnie, Lulu! Dogs! To heel. Come here, come! You heard me!' They heard him and came, their pink tongues lolling, their feathered tails frantic. 'So you don't have to rescue your kitten,' said Charles. 'You can stay here with us.'

But the Queen had seen the hot look in his eyes as the heavy-lidded gaze fastened on the young woman who stood before him blushing, in a tremble; and to her lips Catherine laid the velvet-petalled pansy to hide the smile Father Patrick had come to see too often on her lips: a smile that like a breath on glass, as swiftly faded, held the flicker of an un-youthful cynicism ... *Yes,* mused the Father, *she is learning the hard way.*

'By Your Majesty's leave,' he said, with a bow to the King, 'I will take ... my leave.'

'Must you go, Padre? As it happens I was about to send you a message, for I have that to say which you may already have heard, since the galleries are a-buzz with it, and which I, as usual, am the last to know, although it concerns more closely me and my Queen,' he moved towards her, 'than any of those who bedevil us.'

The Father blinked, and bowed again. 'Your Majesty's servant, Sir.'

'Then pray be seated, Father,' Charles lowered his long frame to the edge of the pool where gold and silver fish flashed among the water lilies, and gestured the priest to sit beside him. 'You too, Frances,' he stretched out a hand to her, 'sit here between Her Majesty and me.' And he slid a casual arm around her as she sat.

Light, reflected from the shining water, wavered up and over the woman's fair young face that, for all its loveliness, was devoid of animation as a dummy's. The King's four dogs flopped at his feet; he touched the bitch with the tip of his shoe. 'Minnie's in whelp again. The spring is in her blood — and mine.' His hand stole upward to cup the breast of the

Stuart girl, firm as a little green apple, enclosed in the jade-coloured corsage of her gown, while his fingers explored to seek and find the tender stalk uprisen to the sweet surprise of touch. As if unaware of the young woman's hurried breathing, accompanied by a wriggle and a giggle, the King continued, 'I was saying, Padre, that you may or may not have heard this latest news from the council. Bristol has surpassed himself in chicanery by impeaching the Chancellor, whom he accuses of treason against us — the Queen and I.'

Catherine turned her head quickly.

'Have no fear, my love.' Without removing his hand from its stealthy caress of the fluttering Frances, he spoke across her to his wife. ''Tis but a clumsy attempt not only of Bristol, of — others, to denounce and bring down Clarendon, and find themselves the biters bit.'

Said Father Patrick mildly, 'I trust you may be right, Sir. But of what nature is this alleged impeachment against Lord Clarendon that can affect Your Majesties?'

'Ah! That's where you come into it, Padre. Bristol has the consummate audacity to call in question the validity of the Catholic marriage of the Queen and myself, and declares that the Chancellor promoted that marriage, which was secretly performed. Moreover, Bristol and — those others, maintain that the Queen's refusal to answer the responses during the Protestant ceremony, has exposed *me* to the suspicion of having already been married in my own Kingdom by a Romish priest! And that, according to the dictates of the Established Church of which I am the Supreme Head, is no marriage at all. So what say you, Father, to this calumny?'

'Sir, that it is — calumnious,' replied the priest, simply. 'There are no possible grounds for any such assumption on the part of Lord Bristol. Your Majesties were married according to the holy rites of our Mother Church, and no marriage ceremony in any other Church can add to or detract from the canonical legality of your union as man and wife.'

'Yes, that's what I told him. He'll not get away with it.' Charles released the fluttering Frances, and stooped to hoist one of the dogs on to his knee. 'I let him have it straight from the shoulder. I've forbidden him our presence and thrown him out of Court. He'll find himself in the Tower if not on the block, should he so much as show his face to us again. Here, child,' to Frances, 'See! Your kitten is down from the lilac. You'd best go and fetch and take it in before the dogs get wind of it.' He gave her a playful push to bring her to her feet.

'Oh, dear, oh, yes! I thank Your Majesty — I will — poor little —' dithered Frances. 'I wouldn't like Tiddy to be chased.'

The Queen, still with that smile on her lips, watched her run off.

Said Father Patrick, blinking behind his spectacles, 'It seems to me a trifle inconsistent, Sir, on the part of Lord Bristol, who has recently been received into the Church of Rome, that he should attempt to invalidate a marriage solemnised by the very Church of which he is a member.'

'My good Father,' Charles tendered him a specially fond look, 'it surprises me that you, who plumb the depths of man's self-deception to further his own ends, should find Bristol's attack on the Chancellor and his threat to my wife,' he drew her to him, 'inconsistent with his professed conversion. Yet, when I asked him why he had proselytised, he told me,' Charles gave a reminiscent chuckle, 'it was because he was writing a book on the Reformation. So I told him he had better write one on Popery.'

The Father, peering sideways down into the lily pool said, with a twinkle: 'Which reminds me of the reason given by a

Protestant friend of mine with whom I travelled to Florence some years ago. When I asked him why he had become a Catholic the answer was that it helped him to understand primitive Tuscan art ... is that a carp I see among the goldfish?'

Charles let forth a hoot of laughter. 'That's as good a reason for becoming a Catholic as any I've heard, and one which I'd endorse if ever I should come to the Faith,' his arm tightened round Catherine, 'in answer to your prayers, my darling. And, yes, Father, it *is* a carp. Tomorrow being Friday you shall have stewed carp for your dinner.'

The priest glanced apologetically up at the smiling king. 'May it please Your Majesty, I am not partial to carp, but I thank you for your gracious offer.'

'Then I'll send you a fine salmon from the upper reaches of the Thames. Come, Catherine, this talk of fish has given me an appetite, and 'tis near dinner time. You'll dine with us, Father, on good English roast beef?'

The priest rose to his feet with a jerky little bow. 'Your Majesty does me too much honour.'

'The honour is mine. As for that skunk Bristol, I swear before Almighty God, and you, Father, that should he or any man — or woman — wilfully seek to injure my wife and Queen, he shall be found guilty of high treason. Come, dogs, 'tis your dinner time, too.'

The attempted impeachment of treason against Clarendon caused, not the dismissal of the Chancellor but of Bristol from the council. Nor was that all. A further charge against Clarendon sought to implicate the Queen, in that she was accused of having petitioned the Pope to grant a cardinal's hat to her almoner, Lord d'Aubigny, which said charge was sarcastically refuted by Clarendon before his peers in the council chamber. It pleased him much, he said, that his lordship thought it so high a crime that Her Majesty should desire a cardinal's hat for a Catholic nobleman bred in the Faith from his cradle who had assisted at her Catholic marriage ceremony prior to its solemnisation in the Church of England.

The debate went on for hours, and by the time Clarendon had done with him, Bristol appeared to be, as reported, *in greatest confusion*, and complained that *by endeavouring to serve his country upon compulsion of his conscience, he was discountenanced and threatened with the anger and displeasure of his Prince.*

Whereupon his Prince, roused from his customary *laissez-faire,* indignantly retaliated with a warrant for the apprehension of Bristol who, more than ever 'discountenanced', went into hiding. None knew his whereabouts, not even the Lady, with whom it was said he had sought sanctuary only to find her door shut in his face and himself sent packing.

The wonder of these circumstances lasted no more than their nine days, before they were extinguished by a circumstance still more extraordinary to set the whole Court in a buzz: the Lady's suddenly avowed conversion to the Church of Rome!

One may believe Catherine could scarcely have been charmed by so unwelcome an acquisition to her Faith; nor were Barbara's intimates delighted with the news of it and approached the King with a plea to forbid her the Mass. To which Charles replied drily:

'I never interfere with women's souls.'

'Only with their bodies,' giggled little Jermyn.

He, and almost all of the Lady's satellites, had withdrawn from her orbit in view of her nearing eclipse. Buckingham, in company with Bristol, had already made himself scarce, while Barbara, infuriated at Bristol's failure, not only to invalidate the marriage of the Queen but to secure the downfall of Clarendon whom she detested, was now preparing for a reconciliation with her Catholic husband.

For some time she had known, but not cared to admit, that her royal lover, elated by medical confirmation of his wife's pregnancy, had returned his attention to Catherine, and, by way of variety, 'to that half-witted, sloppy, drooling, addle-pated' — the string of adjectives was inexhaustible — 'infinitely stupid Frances Stuart.'

Thus did she relieve herself to Henry Jermyn, the last of her adherents, who vengefully enjoyed his irascible charmer's discomfiture, having suffered much humiliation from her contempt of his prowess as *inamorato*.

So now the indefatigable Mr. Pepys had all to tell of how, when walking in the park, he saw the King and Queen ride by, and how the Queen *in a white-laced waistcoat and crimson skirt and petticoat*, presumably that boyish habit chosen by Charles, *her hair dressed à la négligence, was looking mighty pretty*. And mighty happy too, riding hand in hand with Charles as in their honeymoon days, and followed by her ladies, among them Barbara in a yellow plumed hat and *out of humour, very melancholy* ... *But, above all,* declares the fickle Mr. Pepys, *Mrs. Stuart in her cocked hat with a red feather was the greatest beauty he saw in his life, and if ever woman can do, does exceed,* he confesses, *my Lady Castlemaine*. Nor does he wonder the King changes, *which,* he hazards, *is the reason for his coldness to my Lady*.

Not the whole reason since, now that his expectations of an heir were assured, he had no eyes nor heart for any woman but his wife; not even *la belle Stuart*. It was evident to all that for the present, at any rate, the prodigal husband was devotedly repentant and entirely reformed.

In the early summer the Queen's condition decided her doctors to order her to take the waters at Tunbridge Wells, where, with the King and most of her ladies, with exception of the Castlemaine, went Catherine.

Yet the well waters of Tunbridge were not so beneficial as the doctors had expected, and a further cure at Bath was then prescribed; but this time the King did not stay with his wife. Having seen her and her cortège on their way, he returned to London. Important affairs, he said, engaged him in the council chamber; and also in the chamber of the Lady, as noised about Whitehall. Was this, then, a reunion?

Meanwhile Catherine, dutifully following medical advice, drank the waters and bobbed, dipped, and sweated in the Queen's Bath set aside for her. She and Frances, the only one of her ladies who dared venture in, were arrayed in formidable garments of stiff yellow canvas with enormous sleeves, similar to those of a parson's surplice, their hair tucked under huge mushroom-shaped bonnets. The water, rising beneath their bathing gowns, caused them to expand like balloons, to the terror of Frances, who shrieked that she was drowning.

'You can't drown in two feet of water,' Catherine told her. She was beginning to find the simplicity of Frances, and her artless delight in playing with dolls and at childish games and baby talk addressed to her kitten and often to the King, who would amusedly encourage her, just a little trying.

'B-but, Madam, the waters are too hot ... I'm being b-boiled!' sobbed Frances. 'Oh, pray, Madam, allow me to go ... oh!'

'No one is stopping you,' said Catherine, doubled with laughter and perhaps a little gratified to see the lovely Frances, her arms in their monstrous sleeves lashing at the water, her hair escaping from the bonnet, fallen damply out of curl in rats' tails on her shoulders, was anything but lovely at this moment. 'You insisted on coming in with me, so now you can get out.'

Thankfully Frances got, or rather, was hoisted out by a stout party in a mob cap and an identical calico canvas gown, watched by the Queen's ladies seated on stone benches raised around the bath, none of whom shared in Their Majesties' favour of Frances and her inanities. 'And of which,' remarked Lady Sandwich to Donna Maria, 'the Queen already tires. The girl has the brains of a louse.'

'Pardon, Madam?'

Donna Maria, gaunt, sallow and glum, did not at all approve of these English doctors who prescribed stewing and sweating in a kind of watery hell as assurance, they said, that the Queen would not miscarry.

'But that beauty of hers they all rave about won't last,' continued Lady Sandwich. 'Blondes don't wear so well as brunettes.' Lady Sandwich was a brunette and had worn well; but Donna Maria, who understood no word of this, could only sigh and offer up a prayer for the preservation of her Infanta from this purgatorial heat.

All the ladies were fanning themselves and perspiring freely in the vaporous steam, while Catherine, left alone in the bath, went on dipping and bobbing and splashing until Dr. Wakeman, her personal physician, who, watch in hand, had been timing her immersion, advised her to be done with it.

This drastic treatment persisted for three weeks, from which Catherine emerged the very ghost of herself. Always childishly formed as if in permanent adolescence, she seemed to have shrunk; but when Charles came to fetch her and escort her back to London, she, defying the advice of Dr. Wakeman, insisted on riding out to meet him.

'Very fond and touching, as I hear from Wakeman,' reported Dr. Pierce to the eager Mr. Pepys; and more than this was heard when the 'Royals' were again in residence at Whitehall: how that the Queen, exhausted by the journey, went to bed, and the King to sup with the Lady and Mistress Stuart on the very night of their arrival; and the next night ... and the next.

'So! She'll allow you thus far and no farther.' Barbara, reclining on her day bed, stretched her arms above her head and smiled at the ceiling. 'Poor Charles! But don't despair. The more guarded the door, the more pleasure when he who waits without is admitted. Have patience, Chanticleer. If you have not yet trod your little golden hen, you will in good time. We'll see what can be done to ease you and bring a just reward to me for giving you the key to the locked door of the hen-house. In France, as you should know, and as does your cousin Louis, the *demi-vierge* is greatly in demand as more exciting, when she learns to play the game to its finale. Witness la Vallière whom Louis found to be so maddeningly desirable in her pale primrose modesty... until he won her! By the way, they tell me your wife is ailing. Her bathing and her sweating and drinking of the waters has done more harm than good. But she rides in a coach with glass windows. I'd die for such a coach ... Pah! Charles, how you glower. If looks could kill I'd be a corpse. Come kiss me, then, and promise that you'll see your second son — our son — born to you come September, well done by and well placed. A duchy for me and mine, yes? That is surely the least you can give in return for all I have been made to suffer, cast aside and put down for her whom your sister so rightly calls the prettiest girl in the world — and the stupidest.'

Charles, who during this monologue had stood gnawing at his underlip, released it to say sourly, 'You shall have your glass-windowed coach when you've earned it — which is not yet.'

'No, Charles.' Rising from the couch, moving slowly and heavily, her body distorted with impending motherhood, she pulled aside the curtain of her window. 'I'll earn it now. Look.' She pointed. 'Beyond that clump of trees — you can't see it from here — lies the arbour that, as you know, the Queen ordered to be built while she was away ... Why, how's this? Did she not tell you? Yet I think there's much she doesn't tell you. For example, young Montagu, who is in constant attendance, accompanies the Queen to this rustic shelter that conveniently seats but two. Haven't you seen it? Ah, I was forgetting. You have scarcely seen the Queen since your return. Well, for your entertainment, and for what it may be worth to you, your charming Frances is to be found — alone — almost every evening in this secluded arbour, playing with her kitten and her toys. She has a doll and takes it to her bed for want of better company. She's down there now. I saw her go when I relieved her attendance on the Queen at six o'clock. Your lovely simple Stuart — and not so simple, neither, for she was quick to learn the game that you and I and she played together in *my* bed — you remember? Aha, I see you do, and should you care to repeat that little game, not with three but with two, I warrant she'll be a willing partner. See, 'tis sundown. Soon 'twill darken and she'll be hurrying back. Make haste if you don't want to miss your chance.'

He did make haste, and when he was gone the Lady took herself to Catherine. 'Madam, is it not a pity to stay so long indoors? Will you not walk in the garden?'

To this, and the Lady's respectful obeisance, Catherine briefly replied, 'I thank you, no.'

'Then, Madam,' was offered, undeterred by marked chill, 'allow me to open the window. The room is too hot for your health. Your women abhor ventilation.' Her hands urged the Queen to the casement, and flinging it wide, 'pray, Madam,' she begged, 'take the air. So necessary now for Your Majesty's condition. I am in like case, with my third, but not so Heaven-sent a case as yours, beloved Madam, who brings to the Kingdom, please God, an heir. I think Your Majesty is a thought too pale. I doubt if you have greatly benefited by your sojourn at Tunbridge and the Bath. How sweet the garden smells at evensong...' The Lady's nostrils expanded; she voluptuously sniffed. 'Can I not persuade Your Majesty to walk awhile yet before it darkens?'

'I appreciate your anxiety on my behalf,' said Catherine, icily inimical, 'but I have no wish to walk. If *you* would, however, I will not detain you.'

At this pointed dismissal, and with another deep obeisance, the Lady, well pleased with her manoeuvres, went. But Catherine at her window had seen, and stood transfixed at what she saw below, before the door of the arbour was shut.

To Donna Maria at her tambour frame, she said, white-lipped, 'I have changed my mind. I *will* walk in the garden.'

'Not alone, Your Majesty.' The old lady put aside her embroidery and rose stiffly from her chair. 'I will go with you.'

'No, Condessa, there is no need for you to come. Frances is there in the arbour.' Her tightened lips unfolded to say, 'She and her — her escort will attend me.'

The last pouring radiance of sundown probed fiery shafts of light through the late summer green of tree branches; all colours were intensified. The waters of the lily pool mirrored the glow of the burnt sky in a breathless pause that spread a bridge of dusk between night and the dying day.

Threading her way through a spinney of larch and beech, Catherine followed a path that led to the south wall of the arbour, and came upon a window that had been glazed to allow of light. There silently she stood, and, daring not to see, she saw, and, daring not to hear, she heard.

'I want never to possess you more than this ... this exquisite frustration, for to give and not to take is to prolong the quintessence of desire. Ah! Are you so greedy? There, then, there ... yes? ... yes! And this is but a taste of what I'll give you when you're ripe for it.'

How well she remembered those deep husky tones, and almost those same words as on their wedding night when, because of her condition, she must deny him his fulfilment, 'to give and not to take'.

And as, unseen and cowering, she watched against her will, against her instinct and her love for him who was her life, she experienced a secret vicarious echo of this mockery of love and passion played before her stricken eyes. And with a shudder she turned from it and, like a mad thing ran, and running caught her foot in a tussock of grass, and fell, where her women found her and carried her in.

FIVE

Charles turned in his restless stride to face Dr. Wakeman, who had brought him the latest bulletin of his wife's condition. 'Are you sure —' he had asked that same question half a dozen times in the last twenty-four hours — 'are you sure it was a boy?'

The doctor bowed his head. 'Yes, Sir.'

The King raised a clenched fist, and let it drop at his side. 'But it was not — was *not*,' he repeated loudly, 'the fall that killed my son, and looks, God forbid, to kill her. It was those damnable waters, those baths and those unnatural sweatings. Has the fever abated?'

'We regret to find no improvement for the better,' he was told.

'O, God!' Charles sank into a chair and covered his eyes. 'I must see her. I insist that I see her!'

The Court physicians attempted to dissuade him. Her Majesty was in high delirium. The King would be advised not to harass himself by visiting Her Majesty until —

'To Hell with you!' he stormed. 'I *will* see her!'

They fell back and let him pass.

Although after this premature birth Catherine had been seriously ill, the doctors did not then fear for her life; but the complications that followed, ambiguously diagnosed as 'spotted fever', gave rise to the gravest prognosis.

The King's grief and anxiety, shared by the whole Court, even by the Lady's late adherents, vented itself in accusative fury on her women for their negligence in allowing the Queen to walk unattended in the garden.

Donna Maria, poor soul, was distracted. She implored His Majesty to believe that the Queen had refused her attendance. Her Majesty had said she had seen Mistress Stuart in the arbour, and had gone to seek her there.

Charles, on his knees at his wife's bedside, suffered agonies of remorse. The ravings of her fever gave him proof enough to know what she had seen and overheard in the accursed arbour, the result of which had not only lost him his longed-for heir but might also lose him his wife.

Pitifully young she looked, lying there in the great canopied bed; and, with her hair cut short as advised by her doctors to alleviate the fever, she was like a pretty boy. In her bouts of delirium her mutterings, in a mixture of Portuguese and English, dwelled on 'Frances ... my husband ... I love him but he love me not. He bring her, Frances, to love him. He say I want ... to give ... I see what he do ... to give, he say, to give...' and so on and on to tear his heart.

'No, my darling, no!' Charles took her hands that were picking at the coverlet and held them fast. 'I love only you. I have given my love to none but you ... you must live for me. You must ... you *shall* live!' He was almost as much out of his mind as she, in the bitter gnawing of his conscience with the certainty that he alone had brought her to this pass; that her life was ebbing and he powerless to save her.

As the days slid by and still the fever fluctuated, and the doctors' reports gave little hope of recovery, it was noticed that the King had considerably aged. His luxuriant black hair was streaked with grey; his cheeks were hollowed and the lines from nose to mouth more pronounced. He could not be persuaded to leave the sickroom except for his evening meal, when, according to Pepys, whose pen had never been so busy, *he supped each night with Lady Castlemaine*; this a possibly incorrect assumption, as he had only been seen once on his way to the Lady's lodgings in Whitehall.

The whole Court was on tenterhooks for news of the Queen's illness, and from that fount of gossip Mr. Pepys, we are told, *The Queen grows worse, being so full of spots as a leopard ... and that the King do take it much to heart and wept...* Indeed, so much worse that Pepys, having ordered himself *a new good velvet cloak and other things modish*, suspended the making of them *till I see whether she lives or dies*. In which case he would have to go into mourning and forgo his *other things modish*, which included a periwig, the latest thing in men's fashions.

The wonder of it was that she did live, with those of her Portuguese attendants who had not been sent back to Lisbon in the general exodus, surrounding her bedside with prayers and lamentations that could be heard throughout the palace until Charles, half frantic with misery nothing lessened by their noise, ordered them to 'stop that God-damned howling and get *out*!'

Then, when the solemn-faced doctors pronounced her end was near, a priest was sent for to administer the Last Sacrament; after which, although still in high fever, she recovered consciousness enough to tell Charles, sobbing on his knees beside her, that he must not grieve, for, 'If it be God's will to take me from you I would be glad to leave this life.' And then, 'You must have no regrets. It is my fault,' she whispered — so faint the words, in Spanish, they seemed to fade upon a breath that his ear must lie against her lips to hear them — 'my fault if you have found other ... loves with more of ... charm than I.'

'Don't say it! You kill me!' He chafed her hot little hands in his, imploring her to live. 'You *must* live! I can't ... I can't bear it.'

Father Patrick, who had assisted at the last rites, and had left the room, tiptoed back again and stood in the doorway to hear Charles tell her, 'You must not leave me. I can't bear life without you ... Forgive, forgive...' But what she must forgive he did not say.

She asked one last request: that he would promise her body be taken back to Portugal to be buried with her own people. Agonizingly he promised, and Father Patrick, removing his spectacles to wipe a moisture from them, went silently away.

That the King's grief was genuine he did not doubt; and, when she again begged him not to mourn for her but to 'take a wife more worthy of you than I ... one who ... will bless you with the son that I have lost,' the King's sobs could be heard all along the corridor where her huddled women waited.

As the priest made his way to his lodgings he was halted by a white-faced Mr. Montagu.

'Will she die? Is she dying'?

'Not at all,' denied the Father stoutly, 'though 'twon't be the doctors who will save her with their potions and their pigeons.'

'Pigeons?' gasped Montagu.

'Yes, a pack of old wives who have slaughtered a dozen of her white fantails to lay at the soles of her feet, that their blood may soak and heal her. So much for their College of Physicians! I learned more of medicine from the Dominicans in Pernambuco than the whole College put together, who can't diagnose a simple case of chicken-pox.'

'Chicken —?' parrot-wise repeated Mr. Montagu. 'Not — what did they call it — "spotted fever"? *Not* smallpox?'

'No, though marvel 'tis she hasn't caught the great pox from her husband's straying fancies!'

And chicken-pox it most probably was, but not thus to be defined by the physicians, who still despaired of her life while the fever ran high to confuse her.

'The Queen is bewitched,' moaned Donna Maria, when Catherine joyfully told Charles that their lost son had been returned to them alive! 'But 'tis an ugly boy. Not fine and handsome as his father.'

'No, my love,' he humoured her. ''Tis as beautiful a boy as ever I saw.'

Then, waking from intermittent sleep, she said she had borne him a daughter. 'Your living image, Charles.'

'God help her if she is!' said he, who could even make a jest of it, having had it from Father Patrick whose opinion he inclined to believe rather than the doctors', that he had seen a similar case of hallucination after childbirth, and in this case augmented by the chicken-pox — 'A childish ailment that in an adult does cause an uncommon hurry of spirits but no danger of life more than high fever, so Your Majesty may rest assured. Only,' the Father warned him with a twinkle, 'don't tell this to your learned medicos, who would regard my interference as unethical.'

Yet unethical or not, the Father's favourable prognosis proved correct for, in November, Charles was joyfully writing to his 'dearest Minette': *My wife is now out of all danger, though very weak, and it was a very strange feaver* (sic), *for she talked idly four or five days after the feaver had left her but now that is likewise past.* And soon she was so much better that she was ordering herself a new gown, and going to Mass in her private chapel adjoining her apartments in the palace.

The New Year came in with jubilant festivities; masques, balls, banquets, and for Catherine some surcease in forgetfulness. By the time the first daffodils in her garden were trumpeting their welcome to the spring, she saw the slow but sure eclipse of the Lady. Those advancing summer days, if a trifle mixed with gall, were sweet. Charles, believing her snatched from the grave, was in constant devoted attendance; and that he made no secret of his infatuation for the Stuart she regarded as the lesser of two evils. The mistress must now endure the same humiliation she had forced upon the wife for, as the unflagging pen of Pepys recorded it, *although the King do not disown my Lady Castlemaine, he values not who sees him or stands by while he dallies with Mrs. Stuart openly; and then privately in her chamber where the very sentries observe him going in or going out…*

But thus far and no farther as the Lady had remarked, was all that the Stuart would allow. She drove him crazy.

'You make yourself a laughing stock,' his mother told him when she read a poem he had written to the elusive Frances from the fullness of his heart. 'You are behaving like an imbecile. Where's your sense? Be thankful for a wife who is as high above your woman as a star above a glow worm, or any vestal virgin in the Kingdom.'

These maudlin verses put into song were warbled by his minstrels to guitars:

Each shade and each conscious bower which I find
Where I have been happy and she has been kind,
When I see the print left by her shoes on the green
And imagine the pleasures may yet come again,
O, then 'tis I think no joys are above
The pleasures of love.

While alone, to myself I repeat all her charms,
She I love may be locked in another man's arms.
She may laugh at my cares, and false may she be,
To say all the kind things she before said to me:
O, then 'tis, O, then, that I think there's no Hell
Like loving too well.

But when I consider the truth of her heart,
Such an innocent passion, so kind without art,
I fear I have wronged her, and hope she may be
So full of true love to be jealous of me.
O, then 'tis I think no joys are above
The pleasures of love.

The Court was convulsed; and Catherine, who understood English enough to read into 'each conscious bower' a shattering reminder of the scene she had witnessed in the arbour, was at first in a fury and then in the giggles.

'My poor Charles!' She could laugh at and excuse what the Queen Mother called 'his silliness which you cannot take *au grand sérieux*, even if he does. Like all the Stuarts he will let his emotions run away with him. My Minette — *Dieu!* How I miss her! — I pray she soon will visit me here. She, too, believes herself in love with this one and that one, and my nephew Louis, also, whom she twists round her finger —' the Queen's dark little face, so like that of a marmoset, crumpled into laughter — 'in revenge for his having refused to dance with "that skinny little girl", as he called her when she was twelve and the King of France and no much older than she! But now, a few years later she plays him like a fish upon a line to make him jealous. *Et vois-tu* how Charles, in this nonsense rhyme, says he hopes *she* to whom he writes may be jealous of *him*?'

127

Catherine turned her head sharply.

'But you,' Henrietta added, forestalling her retort, 'have never given Charles cause for jealousy. It would be amusing to see how he would take it if you did.'

'No, Madame,' Catherine flushed deeply, 'I would not so demean myself to — fish, is it? — for my husband. And I think he does not care for me enough to be jealous, even if he had such cause.'

Said the Frenchwoman with a sidelong look, 'You have not tried him.'

Yet, if in those early years of his Restoration, the King's interests seemed solely to be centred in 'the pleasures of love', a more enduring passion than any ephemeral fancy was his pride in and love for his ships. Not only did his men-o'-war guard his island kingdom, they sternly threatened any would-be invaders. With their brass guns levelled in the south toward France, and in the east up the coastline from Margate to the Wash, all foreign ships that passed his own must dip their flags in homage to King Charles, unchallenged master of the sea, though not to stay unchallenged long.

In the previous decade, the naval war under Cromwell against the Dutch that vanquished the gallant Van Tromp and his fleet had conquered but not crushed the heart of Holland. England's one formidable maritime rival refused to acknowledge defeat. Wherever an English merchantman sailed, from Labrador to the Indian Ocean, there also would be seen a prowling Dutchman, not now to dip his pennant to England's flag but defiantly to follow him in competition with British world commerce.

Nearer home the sound of gun-shot in the North Sea could be heard by anxious fishwives of Yarmouth, whose husbands in their herring-boats met the insolent Hollander in daily fight.

Charles, however, was in no haste to renew hostilities. He would bide his time and opportunity, while in the interim he continued to enjoy his diverse amusements: racing at Newmarket or the chase of the stag in Windsor Forest, no less a favoured sport than the chase of the virginal hind, Mistress Stuart. Or, in the Botanical Gardens near St. James's Park, where mulberry and orange trees blossomed and fruited, the King could be seen any morning engrossed in the game of *pêle-mêle*. At the far end of the quarter-mile alley, now known as Pall Mall, an iron hoop was suspended from a bar of wood, and the game would be to strike the ball through the hoop and so score points, which needed some skill at such long-distance range. Then there were horse races in the Ring, or the Tour, as more commonly called, in Hyde Park; this the rendezvous of fashion where, as an anonymous contemporary ballad-monger gives it:

There hath not been seen such a sight since Adam's
For perriwig, ribbon and feather.
Hide Park may be termed the market of Madams,
Or Lady-Fair, chuse you whether.
Their gowns were a yard too long for their legs,
They shew'd like a rainbow cut into rags,
A garden of flowers, or a navy of flags
When they all did mingle together.

It was a motley crowd that thronged the leaf-embowered grassy spaces of the park in those early years of the Restoration: down-at-heel and out-at-elbows, out of service. Cavaliers, talking loudly of Edgehill and Naseby for all to hear and know them for King's men who had fought for him and his son to whom they doffed their bedraggled feathered hats and stood bare-headed as he drove by with a wave of that gauntleted long hand. There were sauntering gallants come to ogle the women as they minced along on their high French heels; there were pimps and prostitutes, courtiers, courtesans, and Lady Castlemaine, as seen by Pepys, *lying on her back in her coach asleep with her mouth open*; presumably snoring. He has perhaps become a little less enamoured of his lady since the King, he says, *is now stranger than in ordinary to her ... and doats on Mistress Stuart.*

Sometimes the King, driving with Catherine, would stop his coach and stroll among his people with a word here, a jest there for those crowding near enough to catch a glimpse of him while he bought nosegays from the flower women or fruit from the orange girls exchanging pleasantries, not always of the nicest, with young sparks to whom they offered something more than oranges.

On one of these occasions it may be that the King's attention was engaged by a saucy little redhead who flung an orange at him to be deftly caught, while his eye, for a second, may have lingered on the laughing freckled face of her as yet unknown to him, whose name was destined to be linked with his for all posterity.

Not always did Catherine accompany her husband's sorties in the park. She preferred to ride than to drive in a coach, and, with her ladies, was often to be seen in her white and scarlet habit mounted on her chestnut mare. That Mr. Montagu, her Master of the Horse, was ever beside her to lead the cavalcade gave ample food for talk, magnified by Castlemaine to reach the ear of Charles.

'I told you to have a care of your pious little wife,' the Lady warned him. 'Montagu's attachment to his duties in service to the Queen is *served,* she drooped an eyelid, 'with more warmth than discretion. One might believe her justified,' she lightly added, 'should she encourage service so ... devoted.' These gentle hints, and not the first of them, set thoughts churning in the mind of Charles, to make his temper fly as she smilingly repeated, 'Have a care lest she plays tit for tat with Montagu in retort to your tit-tatting with the Stuart.'

Fiercely red, he turned on her. 'Be damned to your foul insinuations! My wife is not and never will be tainted by your corrupt example!'

Yet, despite his hot dismissal of these 'foul insinuations', the poison seeds were sown to root and flourish. He took to watching Catherine and saw how 'that Roundhead fellow', whose father had fought against the Royalists, was held by Catherine in high esteem, and not entirely, so his jaundiced eye discerned it, for young Montagu's fine horsemanship.

Pacing his closet, Charles swore below breath: 'By God, the goose can drink deep as the gander!' And rounded on his servant. 'Eh, Chiff?'

Wise old Chiffinch, who knew his master's every mood, could hazard a guess at the cause of his fret, not altogether induced by the latest news of Dutchmen skulking off the Nore. A glance from the window, where the King halted his stride at the sound of distant voices and a girl's light laughter, gave Chiffinch an uneasy clue.

The windows of the closet looked out upon the gardens, their green lawns sloping to the Thames, where the sails of merchantmen swelled to the breeze outspread like the wings of white eagles. There, on the bosom of that splendid stream, flowed the life blood of the kingdom: the wealth of her realm along the world's trade routes from the Pool of London to lands beyond the seas.

Unlatching the casement, Charles flung it wide and leaned out. His hair, bereft of its periwig and ruffled in the wind swept up from the river, showed a crop of grey among the black, too grey for his age. Without turning his head, he said, 'The Queen is back from her ride. She has bought another horse — or Montagu has bought it for her.'

Chiffinch kept his silence.

'And who's to pay for it?' Charles squared his underlip. 'Not I. Not she, since Portugal still withholds her dower. Here, Chiff, my wig. I'll go down to meet Her Majesty!'

It was Father Patrick's custom to take a siesta in the afternoon, and on these late spring days he often would be seen comfortably dozing on a rustic bench in the Queen's garden to which he had been given access. So, having dined heartily on good roast pork, mutton pie and cheesecakes, he took himself and a book to his favourite seat.

A wealth of blossom glorified the flower beds; the sun, high in Heaven, brightened the leaves of an oak that cast a welcoming shade across him where he sat to enjoy the scent of hawthorn and opening roses. In the unshorn grass, hard by the Queen's arbour, where daffodils had spread a cloth of gold some weeks before, a haze of bluebells still lingered as if a patch of sky had fallen there. From St. James's Park a cuckoo called, and wood pigeons answered with their everlasting coo, abruptly halted and renewed again: 'Two ... ooo ... take two ... ooo, take...'

Tilting his biretta over his eyes, the Father murmured, ''Tis uncommonly warm, in spite of a sou'west breeze.' He stabbed with a finger at a cruising wasp. 'A queen, too, and so early in the year. There must be a nest nearby.'

He peered about; yawning, his head sank and, his mouth a little open, his jaw a little dropped, he slept.

And sleeping did he dream, or did roast pork incite hallucination? Or did the good old priest's cherubic astral presence escape its earthly bonds to see, screened from mortal sight in a grove of beech and silver birch, two who stood there in the dappled sunshine? And to hear, in a moment's breathless pause: 'Your Majesty ... my Queen ... I have been long constant but can no longer be ... contained.'

Did some such words drift upon the slumbrous ear of Father Patrick to steal from the silence a secret?

'That I dare love where I've no right to love more than as your servant ... that I dedicate my life, my whole heart's love and loyalty to you, Madam, then if this be too bold ... an inexcusable presumption, send me from you, Madam, if you will, for I have uttered the ... unutterable.'

As this outrageous declaration was falteringly stammered, the Father's inquisitive double may have seen a boy kneel bareheaded where last year's leaves still lay among the high grown grass and bluebells.

'Sir ... I would not send you from me ... no, I...'

The words died upon the lips of her whose hands leaped to her bosom as if to stay the pulse that beat unbidden there beneath the boyish riding coat of scarlet slashed with white; no whiter than her lips from which all colour faded.

Ouch! The Father belched, opened an eye and swallowed something in his mouth that tasted mighty sour of roast pig. His head nodded, sank, and, with a sigh he slept again, while his mind's ear listened to an Aeolian murmur of 'Madam, forgive me ... I am mad to speak of that which never should be spoken.'

'If you be mad,' came in whispers, 'then I love ... I like ... such madness.'

'Cheese cakes and roast pork,' said Father Patrick, waking with a start to belch again, 'lie sadly on the stomach. I must dose me a simple of cloves, liquorice, nutmegs and dill seeds. It notably helps the digestion, as Dr. Culpeper prescribes it.'

He got up, dazedly to look around and see the King go striding toward the copse that led from the stables to the Queen's apartments. Through the greenery and silver trunks of birches, he glimpsed a flash of white and red.

'Her Majesty,' said Father Patrick, beaming, 'is just now come home from her ride, and the King goes hurrying to meet her. All's well again with them, thank God.'

'Madame, but you have eaten nothing since early morning,' quacked Donna Maria. 'Will Your Majesty not oblige me by tasting this dish of chicken fried with rice; I myself have shown these deplorable English cooks how we make it in Portugal, flavoured with garlic that they never will use, although grown in the King's herb garden.'

Said Catherine at the window, and without turning her head, 'You know I abhor anything flavoured with garlic. And please to leave me, Condessa. I wish to be alone.'

'Madame.' Donna Maria curtsied, backed from the room and took herself to Father Patrick.

'Dom Patricio, the Queen is in great trouble. The King has been with her and I did overhear...' Tears brimmed and trickled down her hollowed cheeks that bore a network of frail lines, as of a skeleton leaf.

'If that, Senhora, which you have overheard was not intended you should hear,' the priest said gently, 'then I must not hear it.'

Donna Maria drew herself up; tears still trickled but her voice was firm. 'Your Reverence, the King spoke loud enough for anyone to hear and, as it seemed, in great passion to accuse Her Majesty of … no, I cannot speak of it.'

Dom Patricio, blinking at the carpet, jerked up his head to pull forward a chair. 'Pray, Condessa, be seated. Of what did the King accuse Her Majesty?'

'Padre, I hope,' that Countess deposited her person in the proffered seat, 'that I may be mistaken.' And she put her lips together as if she never meant to open them again.

'Yes, madame?' patiently interrogated Dom Patricio.

'I hope,' Donna Maria with marked emphasis repeated, 'that I am mistaken, but I am not deaf, Padre, and I distinctly heard the King comment upon the state of Senhor Montagu's knees.'

'Senhor Montagu's knees?' echoed the priest in mild wonder.

'Yes, Padre, and His Majesty remarked that they were green.'

'Green?' Again the Father blinked. 'Pardon me if I become repetitive, yet I fail to follow — did you say *green*?'

'As I,' rasped the Countess, 'understood the King to say — from kneeling on wet grass and, in this singular posture, did make the Queen a declaration of such a nature, Padre, as no gentleman attendant on Her Majesty should presume so to declare, and that our beloved Infanta should permit such declaration as repeated by His Majesty who, it seems, did interrupt Mr. Montagu's avowal and did remark upon the state of his knees — I cannot and *will* not believe!'

'Exactly so,' soothed Dom Patricio.

If this involved interpretation of that which the Countess overheard the King to say left the Father not unreasonably befogged, the Court was soon to find a more concise account of it, summed up by Mr. Jermyn as 'A case of the pot and the kettle, tee-hee! And a change for Charles to know *himself* cuckolded!'

The Court found it excessively droll, as did the Lady. She, for long, had nursed a grievance against Montagu, whose youth and handsome looks she much approved, and had hoped for a reciprocal response to her advances, from which she obtained persistent rebuffs; most mortifying to her self-esteem that demanded reparation. And now the fruits of her careful manoeuvres were gathered to lay before the King.

'Have I not warned you time and again of what your eyes and ears have witnessed, and that none would have believed of Caesar's wife, however critical they may have been of Caesar?' Since the birth of a second son, attributed to Charles, she had adopted toward him a tenderly assumed maternal attitude rather than that of the hitherto demanding mistress. 'If without complaint nor exposure of my own heartbreak I renounce you to another — this simpleton, the Stuart — it is surely proof enough that I want only your contentment and seek no reward for it more than your trust in me and my care for you and your welfare. The Queen is a slave to flattery, and who can condemn her if she favours him who grovels at her feet with an eye to preferment — so readily offered?'

Reclining on a day bed, her hair in loosened curls falling down and over her breasts, her face skilfully treated for pallor, she presented a fairly convincing picture of a woman suffering from 'heart-break' due to the renunciation of a lover who no longer loved.

'You are,' she said, 'so ingenuous, Charles.' She spoke as a mother to a recalcitrant child, with a small indulgent smile of her lips. 'You believe all you are made to believe, and not what your reason and sense *should* believe. But unless you would bring about a scandal to besmirch Caesar's irreproachable wife,' a little laugh escaped her; softly her glance rested upon him where he sat, leaning forward, his hands dropped between his knees, 'you would do well, my dear, to nip this romance in its bud before it is too late.'

Charles, gnawing at his underlip, released it to say, with ominous quiet, 'I mislike a lecture served to me half-baked on a used platter.'

Abruptly he got up, took a long stride to the door of the room where the evening light filtered through the windows, lingering to touch the elaborate furnishings with gilded fingers; and, turning on her who, still with that half-smile, watched him, he made as if to speak again, thought better of it and left her, slamming the heavy door behind him.

A moon path of silver was flung across the Thames and, on the far bank, the Surrey hills were spectral in the evening's grape-bloom mist. Under that pallid light all colours were submerged in a shimmering effulgence where the lanthorns of wherry boats and river craft bobbed and fluttered like will-o'-the-wisps in the slow falling dark.

Catherine knelt on the window seat of her bedchamber, her aching forehead pressed against the cool of the pane, her eyes unseeingly fixed on the tireless river in its eternal hurry to the sea. She had sent away her women and now waited for the answer to the message she had sent to Charles. She had *that to say which must be said*, so ran the note delivered by her page.

Would he come? Or did he fear a repetition of those scenes when, in their first weeks of marriage, she had agonised herself and him with her outbursts of uncontrollable temper? But never again ...

'When I was a child,' she whispered in her native tongue, remembering her convent school lessons of the Scriptures, 'I lived as a child, I thought as a child ... and now I have put away childish things.' *Yet Charles has not,* she thought, *put away childish things. He behaves more as a child than I.* Her lips moved in voiceless prayer. 'Lord, where there is hatred let me show love, where there is injury, pardon.'

A coldness seized her and she shivered, though the room glowed with the warmth of a sea-coal fire. And watching the fitful leap of flames she seemed to see, in their upward flight, a likeness to that strange haphazard thing called love, a fiery brilliance spun between brief burning ecstasy to sink into the dust of its ashes. These uncertain months that had followed the bitter loss of their son, had brought with them a return of his love, or the semblance of love, born of pity. And then ... was it only yesterday that Charles had come upon her and ... him, to shatter that still-born moment when she had heard him utter the 'unutterable' and seen his love, a fugitive, pierced as it fled with mockery? *How does your mistress, Mr. Montagu?* Those words, so lightly spoken, held a jibe, insolent and meaningful, or were they casually meaningless, a mere enquiry as to how his mistress had enjoyed her ride? O, God, let it have meant only that!

A step in the corridor caused her heart to beat too fast, knocking at her side to deaden all other sound, that he must hear it as he opened the door and stood there silhouetted against the candle-shine behind him. His face, framed in the heavy black of her periwig, was indistinct, the features blurred; his voice, borne to her across an empty void in the sudden pause of her racing heart, was a stranger's voice, politely formal.

'Your Majesty wishes to speak with me?'

She had turned at his entrance and had risen from the window seat; she felt herself tremble as she answered him, coldly, 'Am I to understand that Your Majesty dismisses my Master of the Horse without my knowledge or consent?'

'Yes.' A brief pause preceded the monosyllable, dropped in the stillness of the room as a stone in a stagnant pond.

'You have no right to do so.' She spoke in English. The words, carefully poised, held the slightest accent. Her eyes, set wide apart, looked up at him from under faint brows with a delicate uplift at the corners like the wings of a bird in flight. 'No right,' she repeated, 'and I will not agree to this dismissal. Mr. Montagu is my equerry and loyal servant, the only Englishman in my whole suite who — whom,' she corrected, as taught by Dom Patricio, 'I may call my friend.'

'There are degrees of friendship,' he threw back at her, 'that may be bestowed with favour on a servant, but the right to shield my wife from a servant's importunities is mine. Not yours.'

She held herself erect; she seemed to have grown taller. 'I,' she said, and now she spoke in Spanish, 'have not yet exerted *my* right to dismiss a servant of mine upon whom you bestow *your* favour that I am uncomplainingly forced to endure.'

There came a scuffling and scratching at the door. He opened it. His spaniel bitch had followed him; he stooped to lift her in his arms. She snuggled against his shoulder, licking his cheek.

'Such favours as this,' said he, fondling the satin head, 'permitted to a dog, must be denied a servant.'

For an instant the long lashes were lowered, and her mouth, childishly red, quivered in a fleeting smile.

'There is an old saying in my country, that dogs and women set men by the ears.'

A silent laugh bubbled up behind his closed lips; and meeting that level-eyed look of hers, he came to her where she stood.

'You can do with me what you will.' His eyes weighed on hers with that in them to cause her breath to quicken. 'You can *have* of me what you will, but — not from any other than myself.'

'No other man,' she told him clearly, 'has ever offered or taken from me that which is yours alone. Can the same be said of you — of other women?' She moved to the door. 'I see no point in continuing this discussion Sir, I will bid you goodnight.'

'No, you don't.' He took her hand from the door-latch and, letting the spaniel slide to the floor, he pulled her into his arms. 'I claim,' his mouth closed on hers to say, 'the rights that *are* mine — alone.'

SIX

The rights that were his alone claimed more than the body of his wife or his insatiable quest of the evasive Stuart. While onlookers enjoyed to watch the royal chase that never succeeded in capture, a sudden halt was called to turn the King about and engage him in another chase, not of any woman.

Those daily fights in the preceding months between the herring-boats of Yarmouth and marauders from the Netherlands could no longer be ignored. English rebels who, at the Restoration, fled to Holland and escaped the penalties suffered by their leaders, gloated at obscene cartoons and broadsides of the English King displayed in the print-shops of The Hague and Amsterdam. By the spring of '64 not only fisher-folk but every Englishman was up and ready to avenge Dutch insolence.

War was in the air. *With a great bragging and noise,* Charles wrote to Minette, *I never saw so great an appetite to a war as in both town and country ... But all this shall not govern me, for I will look merely to what is just and best for the honour and good of England, and if I be forced to a war I shall be ready with as good ships and men as ever was seen, and leave success to God.*

While spring blossomed into summer, his good ships stalked the Dutchmen warily but in no hot pursuit, for he still hoped to avoid hostilities, since France, as anxious for peace as himself, was bound by treaty to support Holland. Were Charles plunged into war with the Dutch, and Louis, however unwillingly, pledged to fight against him, he would be deprived of all communication with his adored Minette. The thought of that contingency caused him sleepless nights and *a vile headache*. This, however, was due, less to the anxieties of pending war, despite, as he told Minette, *I am the only man in my dominions who does not want it*, than to the fact that, when reviewing his ships in the Thames, which he did almost every day, he threw off his periwig during a heatwave, caught a chill, and lay sick of a fever for a week.

Meantime, his sea-hounds were hunting the Hollanders along the coast of Africa to harry them from Guinea, capture their forts, and sail off in triumph to America.

You will have heard, again he tells his sister, well aware that anything he writes to her will be read to Louis, *of our taking New Amsterdam which lies just by New England. It is a place of great importance to trade. It did belong to England heretofore, but the Dutch drove our people out of it and built a very good town. But we have got the better of them, and it is now called New York* — in compliment to James, Lord High Admiral of the Fleet.

All that summer, Catherine eagerly followed events. Born of a seafaring nation, she had a passion for the sea, possibly inherited from Henry the Navigator, her remote forbear; and thus, in September, Lord Sandwich at Chatham receives this message from the King:

My wife is so afraid she will not see the Fleet before it goes that she intends to set out from this place (Whitehall) on Monday next with the afternoon tide. Therefore let all yachts be ready at Gravesend by that time…

Summer was passing, autumn nearing, heralded by high winds and gales. Offshore the great ships lay tossing at anchor. Their brightly painted figureheads, carved into fantastic shapes of birds, beasts, and women with gilded breasts out-thrust, glittered in the light of fitful sun-gleams that they looked to be alive and straining against the wind as if at any moment they would break away and bear their walls of wood across the sparkling waters to where the Dutchmen waited.

But Catherine's first visit to the fleet was not enough for her; yet there may have been a warmer interest in her insistence to see these fine new battle ships. It is likely she had heard that Mr. Montagu who, under pressure, had handed in his resignation as Master of the Queen's Horse, was one of the recent volunteers to join the Navy; and in October Catherine was back again, this time at Woolwich where the latest vessel to be built and launched was officered, with other volunteers, by Lieutenant Edward Montagu.

She chose to go by water rather than to jolt over roads hock-deep in mud from recent heavy rainfall. She took with her a selected few of her ladies, but not Donna Maria to whom the voyage from Lisbon was an ever-present memory, so fraught with horror that she vowed she would never again set foot in a boat, royal barge - or nothing. Nor was Frances Stuart commanded to accompany the Queen. She, while still in nominal attendance, had now been allotted apartments in Whitehall, installed there as prime Favourite and with her own retinue in rivalry to the Castlemaine, who had been heard to declare, 'It is hard enough for any self-respecting mistress to play second fiddle to a wife, but to be put down for a common little slut and a simpleton at that is past bearing.'

Yet bear it she furiously must.

As for Catherine, she had become resigned to her husband's amatory excursions. With perception sharpened in a hedonistic atmosphere where human relationships were dedicated to erotic indulgence, she had come to realise that the pursuit of ephemeral desire bore no resemblance to love as she understood it. She had suffered, and in suffering had learned it is better to love than to be loved; that only in forgiving can we be forgiven, and in self-forgetfulness to find ourselves.

It was a day of brooding skies swept by a beggar's cloak of cloud, but the new man-o'-war about to be launched stood with her sails unfurled, splendidly defiant of threatening storm. Built by a brother of Commissioner Pett, another familiar of Pepys, she weighed twelve hundred tons and had, as Charles enthusiastically appraised her, 'the finest bow of any ship afloat'.

Conducted by Lord Sandwich, Catherine saw all there was to see on the upper and lower decks; the ordnance where the deadly guns were ranged; the galleys and the cockpit that, although brightly gleaming in its fresh coat of paint, was, of all berths aboard, the least inviting. Its two meagre portholes were insufficient to admit of adequate daylight, and the conditions of the midshipmen, whose sea-lives must be lived there, an unenviable contrast to the quarters of their superior officers. Then the Queen must be presented to the officers themselves, many of them old Cromwellians who had fought under Blake against the Spaniards in his triumphant last exploit at Teneriffe.

The King's unfailing charm which made slaves of his men and fools of his women was turned full battery on these, his former enemies, now prepared to die for him and the glory of his fleet. He chaffed them, bandied bawdy jokes with them and toasted them in rum, much to the disgust of the French Ambassador, invited by Charles, with possible intent to confound his cousin Louis, that he might gauge the invincibility of the powerful battle fleet he must oppose should he fulfil his obligations to the Dutch.

When the launching of the great sea-lioness was done, and she, magnificently poised, her sails filled, her flags and ensigns proudly flying, her oak timbers creaking as if she growled impatiently to free herself of anchorage that she might hunt and fall upon her prey, the royal party was regaled with dinner by Lord Sandwich in a frigate. It was then that Charles, who had well enjoyed the excellent food and wine supplied by the Admiral, decided to sail to the Nore, to the Queen's delight.

'Charles! I will go with you!'

'You will not. We are in for a squall. You'll be sick.'

'I won't. I am never sick at sea. I love a — how you say? — a *scole,* is it? That is the wind, yes? Please Charles, I must go with you. Please. I must.'

Laughing down at her, 'So be it. If you must — you must. But you'd best send your ladies back in the barge. They'll not stand up to a *scole.*' Teasingly he pulled a curl of her hair that had escaped from under the three-cornered hat she wore for her naval occasions, with a nautical costume of Navy blue fashioned after the style of her riding habit, its pockets embroidered with gold anchors, which Charles had said became her mightily. So mightily, indeed, that he could hardly let her out of his sight during her visits to the fleet, much, when they heard of it, to dishearten the two rival Favourites.

'Yes,' she agreed, 'I will send the ladies back up the river if they wish.'

They certainly did wish, and with exception of Lady Sandwich, who as a sailor's wife had no fear of the sea, were glad enough to go.

One of the officers attached to the frigate was Lieutenant Montagu, but not of those presented to Their Majesties at the launching. With a hurried glance in the direction of the King, Catherine found him engaged with the French Ambassador.

He, too, had sumptuously dined, disregardful of likely effects of the 'scole', and the King's twinkling advice that he should accompany the ladies in the barge.

'*Non! Non!*' Vehemently he refuted the idea. A dark ape-ish little man was de Courtin, whose elaborate politeness and reverence for monarchy did not at all detract from his astute and cunning statesmanship. 'I implore to tell *votre Majesté* that I have no greater pleasure than to ride upon the sea and suffer not, and never have, from *mal de mer*!' A gallant fiction in accordance with de Courtin's exaggerated code of etiquette, as evidenced in his *Traicte de la civilité*, which demanded he should pay all homage and respect, even at the expense of his stomach, to those waters surrounding the islands of the English King, and caused him infinite torture every time he crossed back and forth from France to Britain. Yet to confess to such weakness was not to be considered, so: '*J'adore* the sea! Your English Channel, Sire, and *la belle vue! Exquise!*' with a wave of his hand at the mudflats of Woolwich.

Charles gave him a grin. 'We don't pass through the Channel today. We sail westwards to the Nore, and the North Sea is blowing a devilish north-easter. Are you sure you will not change your mind?'

'*Jamais de la vie!* To be deprived of the honour of Your Majesty's company ... *non, Sire, vraiment!* If Your *Altesse* will allow me this privilege *ineffable...*'

While Charles was thus occupied with the polite de Courtin, Catherine smilingly gestured Mr. Montagu's approach. Detached from her circle of attendants she advanced to meet him, saying in her careful English, 'Mr. Montagu, I have not know that you did join the Navy. Under whose command?'

To which he found voice enough to answer: 'I am under no command, Madam, but yours.'

'Please? I did not command you to…' She lowered her eyes from his that searched her own to bring the colour to her face. 'I did not,' she repeated, almost in a whisper 'command you to leave me. It was not my wish. I hope you do believe?'

'As I believe in all that makes life bearable,' he told her below breath, 'which is my everlasting love for you while I live and … when I die.'

A moment of silence passed. She lifted her eyes to see his lips move and read their message, unconfessed.

Light flickered up from the smoke-grey water as a pale sungleam pierced the clouds, to battle with the wind that groaned in the wide-spread sails as the ship moved down the estuary between low-flying marshlands.

'Madam!' Clutching at the bulwarks, Lady Sandwich came stumbling along the deck. 'His Majesty desires you to go below. A storm is rising. The Captain will turn the ship and we will be put ashore.'

Poor Monsieur de Courtin! He, too, must be put ashore, bundled into a coach in a state of collapse. An unfortunate excursion and one that left the French Ambassador with a very jaundiced view of British naval manoeuvres to be reported to his King.

As Catherine stepped from the frigate into the royal barge, she saw Lieutenant Montagu, with his brother officers, stand at the salute.

Sight-blinded she saw him through a mist and as if he stood alone, his fair young face imprinted on her heart and memory, never to be seen again.

Tensely the nation awaited the New Year, and with it came a winter of unprecedented cold. There was skating on the lake in St. James's Park and on the Thames, so solidly frozen that stalls were erected offering roast chestnuts, hot pies, gingerbreads, flummery, and every kind of sweetmeat to tempt the taste of loiterers. Enterprising stall-holders did a roaring trade. The river had become a fairground where girls and boys frolicked, and slithered and toppled and fell, and were up again screaming with laughter and the fun of it all. But their elders in the taverns, and the King's councillors at Court, thumbed their chins and gloomed, beset with forebodings of war. Yet, while the Duke of York had hoisted his pennant in the *Royal Charles,* and with his fleet was scouring the North Sea for likely invaders, the King still hoped to come to terms with Holland: a lost hope.

Although war had not been openly declared, the Dutch and British merchantmen were at one another's throats again; and when spring danced in the gardens of Whitehall, Opdam, the Dutch Admiral, came out with his squadron to steal a march on York and bear down in all his might upon the English fleet.

In London the news spread with the thunder of the guns heard from Wapping to the Wash, that the Dutch, overconfident, were worsted: that Opdam's ship was sunk in flames and Opdam blown sky high! Whether by accidental fire in his gun room or by the fierce battery from the Duke's squadron was not known; but sunk she was, and every man and her gallant Admiral with her perished in the furnace as she sank.

Yet the mettle of the Dutch was not to be daunted by a first defeat at the onset of the battle. Spurred by disaster the Hollanders went to it with a more than ever fierce determination, though their losses greatly outnumbered those of the British, both in men and ships; ten thousand Dutch seamen were sent to the bottom or slain, while the English fleet, in hot pursuit, chased the Dutch out of sight to take shelter in their ports, lick their wounds and muster their forces for the next attack.

So unexpected and swift was this stupendous victory that Londoners roused from their sleep by the sound of joy-bells, could scarcely believe their ears nor yet their eyes to see great bonfires burning in the streets where citizens, delirious with triumph, joined hands and danced like madmen round them, and, as the fires burned down, they dragged furniture from their houses to heap upon the blaze. *A greater victory,* crows Pepys, *was never known in all the world! They are all fled ...*

But those about the King, and Catherine in their chamber, saw him troubled; and when she asked him, 'What ails you, love?' he told her, 'Nothing of my body, only of my heart that bleeds for my friends who are fallen.'

And taking her chin in his hands he bent his lips to hers; she felt his tears.

The jubilation of the people was short-lived. While wives and mothers mourned their men, lost to them, dead and dying, while the flags of captured Dutch ships flew from the Tower of London, a greater agony than war descended on the city.

It had been prophesied. Those who believed in omens — and who did not? — had foreseen it. In the spring of the year a comet had appeared in the sky, sure portent of evil, or Almighty God's warning that the world must be punished, was the verdict of long-lipped Puritans who never had and never would stomach an England under 'Charles Stuart'; an adulterer, a spendthrift of the nation's money, he who cried aloud his cuckoldry in the dance halls of his palace, who spread corruption, vice, and wickedness throughout his Court and country! 'And now see what he has brought upon us all, we innocents who suffer from his guilt!'

Red crosses on the doors of their houses; carts lumbering along the streets with the awful cry, 'Bring out your dead!'

The Plague.

Since the last days of May it had been creeping up from villages along the Thames, from Deptford and the poorest quarters of the city, writhing its loathsome way through narrow fetid alleys. At first the townsfolk punned it: 'Here's a plaguey news! The Plague has come to plague us.'

There had been intermittent outbreaks before, isolated cases, never epidemical as was this horror, spreading to strike with a virulence almost unexampled in any age or nation. As the summer advanced so did the pestilence advance, even to the gates of Whitehall.

Everyone who could escape into the country fled. Charles packed his seraglio and Catherine off to Salisbury. At first she refused to go without him. 'I stay with you and these poor people who have not the money to go away!'

'Go you will,' he told her firmly, 'and I'll follow you as soon as I can.'

'No!' She clung to him. 'You are in danger to stay. Let me be with you. I am not afraid, so I may be in danger too!' *For if he dies,* she prayed, *let me die with him...*

In the end she had to submit to his promise that he would join her when he had done all that was necessary for the relief of the stricken and their families.

This was his donation from his Privy Purse of a thousand pounds a week: six hundred was contributed by the Lord Mayor and Aldermen from the City funds and their own pockets; equally liberal gifts came from the Queen Dowager and others who could afford to give.

Catherine, who could not afford to give, consequent upon her much depleted dowry which had never yet been paid in full — so that the meagre allowance doled to her for her Household was scarce enough to supply them an adequate salary — gave her little all and went short of ready cash as result of it for years. That was why her calumniators, Castlemaine and Co., undeservedly reviled her for 'stinginess'. It stuck.

Having satisfied herself she had given all she could for the needy citizens of London, she set out for Salisbury filled with dread for Charles. As she jolted in her coach through the quiet leafy lanes she saw hordes of stragglers footing it along the highways, mothers with their babies at the breast; husbands, wives, children, and wagon-loads of those who had not the means to hire better transport; and slow patient oxen dragging behind them household goods piled on hastily contrived planks.

Catherine sat fingering her rosary: silently she prayed and silently she wept. Donna Maria was her sole attendant. The rest of them had gone before, but she had remained until the last minute in the hope that Charles would come with her.

A coachload of her Portuguese priests followed, but Father Patrick was not among them. He and Father Lord d'Aubigny, with many other clerics of all denominations, had stayed in the city to tend the sick, and administer the last rites to the dying.

The streets of London were deserted. Grass sprang up between the paving stones where unburied corpses, struck down as they walked, lay stiff and rotting, a feast for blowflies till the death carts came to throw them into the newly dug pits on the outskirts of the town. And, fearfully, to avoid the awful sights and sounds of those who, run mad in the fever's delirium, staggered to the Thames and plunged into the river strewn with corpses of other suicides, terrified men and women rushed to the taverns and brothels to souse themselves in drink or whoring. Maniacal laughter mingled with the shrieks of the afflicted; the wildest rumours were afloat of apparitions. The ghosts of the dead were said to haunt the pits where the heaped bodies mouldered. A flaming sword was seen stretched across the sky from Westminster to the Tower. It was the chance of their lives for fanatics who, defying infection, strode through the city yelling that 'In forty days London will be destroyed and all you sinners with it — cast into hell!'

One man, stark naked, bearing on his head a chafing dish of burning coals, proclaimed to all who had not fled at the sight of him, convinced he was a minion of the devil: 'The Almighty shall purge you with fire, even as this brazier that I will fling among you to scarify your flesh!'

More and more red crosses marked the shuttered houses with the words *Lord have mercy on our souls,* while higher and higher rose the Bill of Mortality. In less than a month it had leaped from two hundred and sixty-seven to one thousand and eighty-nine. By September the death roll had risen to near upon ten thousand.

It was from Deptford that the first cases of plague were reported; and to Deptford, on a September evening, went Father Patrick. He rode there alone, refusing the offer of his servant to go with him, 'for,' he said, 'I am so much with the sick I must be immune from infection, but you are not.'

'Pray God Your Reverence may run no risk.' Doubtfully the man watched him mount and ride away.

At a tumbledown cottage in an isolated spot near the river, the Father, having hitched his horse's bridle to the gatepost, knocked at the door and was admitted to a small dark room by a boy of some sixteen years.

'Sir! Thank God you are come!' His face bore signs of fatigue: his long fair hair fell straight and dank about his shoulders; he wore a blue smock and held in his hand what looked to be a scalpel.

'How is your friend?' enquired the priest with a glance at a truckle bed in a corner of the room. The floor was strewn with wood shavings; a table, under the window, scattered with the same. Among the litter stood a basket containing an exquisite nosegay of flowers, so light in their natural colour and disorder it was incredible to think them carved from wood.

'The fever is abating, sir,' the priest was told, 'but he is very weak.'

Father Patrick moved to the bed where lay a young lad. His dark curling hair was matted on his forehead; his lips caked with dried mucus, his face a leaden grey.

'Has a doctor seen him?'

'No, Your Reverence. There is no doctor hereabouts, and I daren't leave him while I seek one in the city. That is why I sent a message by a waterman for you, sir. He is a Catholic. Italian. And,' the boy's lips trembled, 'he asked for a priest, to give him the Last Sacrament. I had heard you was one of the Queen's chaplains and much about the city at the deathbeds of the Catholics, and so I ... I sent for you.'

'I am most thankful you did, but your messenger gave me no names. What is his name and yours?'

'Gibbons, sir, and he is Filippo. I know him by no other name. I found him there by the river,' he pointed vaguely, 'when he fell ill of the sickness a few nights since. He said he had recently come from Italy. He plays the violin and hoped to earn a better living here at the playhouses than in Milan, where he says there are so many more musicians. He has not been in England more than a month or two and speaks little English, but he made me understand enough to know that the landlord of the inn where he lodged turned him out when he sickened, so I brought him here. He is an orphan, as am I.'

'You did bravely to care for him, my son.' Father Patrick dived a hand beneath his habit to take from his pouch a phial containing a pink liquid, 'but you must also care for yourself. Here is a syrup of cloves, gilly-flowers and marigolds. Take it at intervals of every three hours. It will act as a preventive.'

'I thank Your Reverence, but I took the sickness at its onset here in Deptford. I believe it does not attack twice.'

'It is unusual but it can attack again, and is always more mild at the onset of the disease. It gathers virulence as the epidemic grows.' Father Patrick was now drawing phials from his pouch as a juggler draws rabbits from a hat, and these he placed on the table, saying — 'and the master-wort, a herb of Mars to dispel the green vomit, and the gentian brought from Portugal — an uncommon herb in England — it helps agues of all sorts and I doubt me not he's had the shivers — and the stinking gladwin, an ugly name for the flower-de-luce of the same family. It heals running sores, so you may bathe his mouth and eyes with it. Well now, there's enough for you to go on with, and — here's a charming thing. Did you carve and paint these flowers?'

'Yes, Father.'

'Sure, you have a remarkable gift.' Adjusting his spectacles, Father Patrick peered closer. 'I'll examine your work when I have examined the patient.' He returned to the bed and, sweeping the matted hair from the sick boy's forehead, laid a hand upon it. 'Ah, he sweats — a healthy sweat. Good, good! And the breathing is regular. If I'm not mistaken —' he pulled aside the bedclothes, felt beneath the sweat-soaked shift for the boy's groin, and turning to the other lad who anxiously watched him — "Tis as I thought. Glory be to God! The bubo has burst and suppurates to let out the poison. Bring me a bowl of water and I'll cleanse it. Your friend, Filippo, my son, is on the mend.'

At the mention of his name, the boy's eyelids fluttered open, and, at sight of the priest, his dry lips moved in a whisper: *'Deo gratias ... Dómine, non sum dignus ut intres sub tectum meum...'*

'Dóminus vobíscum.'

The priest made the sign of the Cross over the lad's forehead and, taking the bowl brought to him, he bathed the bubos, stripped off the damp shift and wrapped him in a blanket. 'If he should worsen — but I have no fear of that so long as he keeps up his strength — don't hesitate to send for me again. In the meantime,' he handed a purse to the boy beside him, 'here is money to buy our young friend nourishment: a capon to broil for broth. I take it you have the means for cooking? I see a cauldron on the hearth. Have you firing? ... Good. And eat well yourself.' His glance travelled round the room noting its poverty, the bare boards, a broken pane of the lattice stuffed with rags, a rickety chair or two. 'Do you live here alone? Your parents are dead, you say.'

'Yes, sir, they were Dutch. They came here from Rotterdam when I was a few months old, so although I am a native of Holland I am English in all but birth.'

'Your parents died — when?'

'Two years since, sir, of the smallpox. I did not take it for I was at school in London. My parents were fairly well conditioned and could afford to pay for my schooling, but when —' the boy steadied a shake in his lips — 'after they — left me, within two weeks of each other, I have managed to earn enough to keep myself with my wood carvings. I sell them in the streets of London and at fairs. Sometimes I am given so much as a guinea, but more often a shilling or two. It suffices.'

'Amazing!' Father Patrick, who had heard but half of this, so engrossed was he in and his imagination captured by the delicate loveliness expressed in the flowers arranged in a basket that at first sight looked to be woven from straw, but on closer inspection was also seen to be carved from wood. 'One would believe them to live ... this rose! It breathes. Only Della Robbia, whose exquisite garlands of fruit and flowers decorate the shrines of Our Lady, as I have seen in Florence, can compare with this. The King and Queen shall hear of your genius — for genius it is!'

The boy's face flushed. 'Your Reverence does me too much honour. I love my work, but cannot believe it worthy of comparison with the masters of sculpture. 'Tis so trivial. I am entirely self-taught. I copy the flowers I see in cottage gardens, and ... and the flowers of the fields.'

'Yet not even Solomon in all his glory,' tenderly the Father touched a frail petal, 'was arrayed as one of these.' Again his glance explored the room. 'We must find you a better environment than this for your work. I will endeavour to secure you a studio where there will be more light and more amenities ... No, no! Don't thank me. 'Tis I should thank you for the privilege of discovering so rare a gift. You will hear from me as soon as Their Majesties return to Court. The King is a great patron of the arts.'

But not until seven years later was that 'rare gift' brought to the notice of the King, and not by Father Patrick. It was John Evelyn who, in that same dilapidated cottage down at Deptford, found the young unknown wood-carver at his work, and gave to the world the name of Grinling Gibbons.

As Father Patrick rode back to Whitehall on that September evening the heat haze, rising from the river, came about him like a cloud that he must pass his hand across his eyes to wipe away a mist as of cobwebs. He had a fierce and sudden thirst. The reins slackened between his fingers and he was hard put to keep his seat in the saddle for the giddiness and nausea that overswept him. But his good horse, as if aware of his weakness, went gently and, unguided, brought him to the palace gates.

His groom who came to dismount him was waved aside. 'Do not touch me ... I am ... not ... well.' He spoke with difficulty; his tongue was swollen, his speech slurred. 'Send my servant to my room, but not to enter it. I ... will give my orders at the door. No, lad, keep away ... go bathe yourself in vinegar and ... leave me.'

The scared groom fled. The priest dragged himself, dizzily swaying, to his room, locked the door, undressed and examined his body to find on his stomach an eruption of pustules.

'So swift ... without warning,' he muttered. He burned and was cold, shivered and was hot, conscious of a painful inflammation in the groin and armpits.

'God's will be done,' he whispered. 'Not mine ... but ... Thine.'

His servant was hammering at the door: 'For mercy's sake, Your Reverence, let me in! You must not be left unattended.'

'I will sound the bell,' came the feeble voice in answer, 'if I need you to send ... for a ... priest.'

At his request they sent for Lord d'Aubigny to speed his gentle soul upon its way; and to Catherine came Father d'Aubigny to tell her, 'His was the greater love.'...

Yet, while the doomed city festered in putrescence; while rats swarmed over corpses in the empty streets; while the doctors, clergy, and the priests of Rome strove to stem the dreadful tide, and in their turn gave their lives in 'greater love', the Court, far removed from danger, frolicked carefree as ever through those months of death. Not so the King, nor Catherine.

Charles, sick at heart, gnawed with anxiety as each day brought him fresh news of London's devastation, fell ill himself. He could not sleep. Night after night, when in the halls below his minstrels sang and the flutes and fiddles set the measure for the 'Brawls', he paced his chamber fretting at his impotence to help his stricken subjects with more than financial aid. Willingly would he have worked among them with his doctors, and brought to the sufferers his knowledge of chemistry and physics, but that as Sovereign he would not be permitted to expose himself to any risk of contact. As for Catherine, her grief at the loss of him who, since her childhood, had been her spiritual guide, philosopher and much loved friend, was boundless. None knew of the lonely young woman's sorrow, and now she was called upon to bear another loss, unshared.

Within a month of the news brought to her by Lord d'Aubigny, she was told that in a sea battle off Bergen, Lieutenant Montagu had fallen.

To Catherine came Anne, full of it and of her second child born to the House of York.

'Well, now, my dear, this is doleful tidings. You were so attached to him and he —' the Duchess paused before she added — 'was so devoted.' Another pause. Anne's eyes were spherical, her lips rounded as if to say more, but said nothing.

'Yes, indeed.' Steadying her voice, Catherine, whose face had paled, returned Anne's stare with suitable dismay. 'Poor Mr. Montagu! I have ... I shall miss him greatly. He was very good with ... horses.'

But Anne had seen that sudden pallor, and, not remarkable for tact, hastened on with, 'We must find you another Master of the Horse.' She leaned forward from the high-backed chair, hardly wide enough to seat her bulk, to lay a hand on Catherine's knee. 'You must not grieve for him, my dear, but count it a blessing that he's gone, to stay a hundred tongues that wag too loud and shamefully of his ... devotion to Your Majesty.'

'Shamefully?' A wave of angry colour flooded those whitened cheeks. 'Who so dares?'

'You should have learned by now,' was Anne's reply, 'that in this Court what's on the lung leaps up on the tongue. His poor mother — she's broken-hearted. She had but the two sons and now she writes to beg me intercede with you to promote Ralph, the younger, as your Master of the Horse and so keep him safe at home. This dreadful war!' went on that placid monotone. 'I go in misery for James who is so brave and commands the fleet with no thought of his own danger or of me and my babes, for should you never carry — talk gives it that you can't, and if I don't have a boy — I lost my first — then some time, maybe, we'll have another Queen of England. And it took me four years to conceive again although James did his best — three times a week and often more. So think it over, Catherine, I mean about young Montagu, for his poor mother's sake who dreads lest he should volunteer, and then she might be lost of both.'

Catherine did think it over, yet against all persuasion from the Chancellor who seconded his daughter's proposal, she refused to have Ralph Montagu succeed his brother in her service 'unless of the King's choice and approval.' Never must those hundred tongues wag shamefully again!

But the King was not now concerned with the choice or approval of his wife's servants, or any pretty Master of her Horse. He and the Court were at Oxford when once more the Queen knew herself pregnant, to bring her hope and ease the ache of her loss in the death of Dom Patricio, and of that other who had dared to love where love must 'have no right'.

And Charles was quite schoolboyishly elated — 'As if he were fathering his first born,' tittered Harry Jermyn, 'instead of his fifth, or is it sixth?' This to Lady Castlemaine, recently delivered of a third son attributed to Charles. 'Although they do say —' he added, as he lolled beside her bed where she lay suckling her latest, whose indeterminate features, shell-like skin and the golden down upon his head, bore no likeness to that of any Stuart; more, indeed, to a certain yellow-haired Anglo-Saxon acrobat or the pink-and-white Mr. Jermyn himself — 'they do say,' he, with honeyed spite, repeated 'that I might likely claim the privilege.'

'As likely as a jellyfish,' rejoined the Lady.

She was no participant in the King's elation at his prospective parenthood. It sickened her to hear him joyously declare, 'Henceforth I'll prove myself worthy of God's blessing in giving me a son.' He was certain it would be a son. 'At last we'll have a Prince of Wales!'

The Court was one huge snigger in its sleeve at his renewed devotion to his neglected wife. He showered gifts upon her, was in constant attendance to put the Stuart in the sulks and the Castlemaine in fury, though not for long were the Favourites to be out-favoured by the wife.

Early in the New Year Charles returned to Hampton Court, but in view of Catherine's condition, he would not allow her to go with him who must be back and forth to London for consultation with his War Council; for despite the severe winter frosts that had somewhat decreased the spread of the plague, there were thousands already infected and the Mortality Bill had not yet lessened.

So, rejecting his wife's tearful inducements to take her with him, Charles rode off from Oxford with Chiffinch and a few other chosen attendants.

Catherine ran to the door of Merton College, where the Court was lodged, to watch him go; saw him turn in the saddle to wave his hand to her. She stood regardless of the biting cold on that raw February morning, unheedful of her ladies' protestations and the croakings of Donna Maria: 'Madame! You will catch your death!' For she stood bare-headed and uncloaked with the vicious wind whipping her loosened hair about her face and shoulders: stood till the cavalcade was lost in the icy river mist, that she could no longer see them nor hear the dying sound of hooves on the frozen road for the faintness that had seized her with a sharp tearing pain.

Her women ran forward; the more timid fell back, fearful that she sickened of the pestilence, as her hands groped into darkness and she sank.

'You are so credulous, Charles,' Lady Castlemaine, defying the plague, had come after him post-haste to Hampton Court. 'Did you really believe she was pregnant? Can't you see that she stages these false alarms in order to recapture your regard — she can never call it love, for you have never loved her. You should have listened when I warned you as did Bristol. He knew — before you signed the marriage treaty — that she was barren. This is no miscarriage, because she has never conceived. She would bribe her doctors to swear to it. I'd as soon trust a dicer's oath as the evidence of her Dr. Wakeman or your Pierce. My poor Charles!' She dropped on her knees beside him where he lay sunk in a chair, his long legs stretched to the logs on the hearth. 'I know what a grievous disappointment this must be to you, but you have other sons.' She took his hand in hers and laid her cheek upon it. 'You have three sons of mine — and a daughter.'

He snatched his hand away. 'I doubt if I'm responsible for any one of them!'

'Cruel! And each of them your image!' Mustering tears she let them slowly drip.

His mouth slid sideways. 'You have an ever ready aqueduct,' he said drily. 'I suggest you get up, for I must go about my business.'

'Which is —?'

'None of yours.' Rising, he pulled her to her feet, and pointed to the door. She went, with the backward look of a suffering spaniel, but outside in the long corridor, unwatched, she raised a fist and frenziedly beat the air.

'By God! I'll make you pay for this,' she said between her teeth, 'before I'm done with you — or you with me!'

All through the pestilential autumn months and into the New Year the war raged on. The battered Dutch, recovered from their first defeat, were out again encouraged by the weakening of the British Navy, for the destroyed had struck at the dockyards, where the battleships, halted in their building from the deaths of the workers, lay unmanned, unarmed, unready. And now, to reinforce the enemy, Louis of France had fulfilled his obligations that bound him by treaty to the Netherlands.

It was a bitter blow to Charles, not that he feared the strength of Louis as an ally of the Dutch, but that war with France must end his correspondence with Minette. In an earlier letter, having heard his sister was pregnant, he had written in his usual jocular vein:

I am glad to hear that your indisposition is turned into a great belly. I hope you will have better luck with it than the Duchess had here, who was brought to bed Monday last of a daughter. One part I shall wish you: that you may have as easy a labour for she despatched her business in little more than an hour. I am afraid your shape is not so advantageously made for that convenience as hers is; however, a boy will recompense you two grunts more and so ... goodnight.

And now it must be goodbye for the war's duration, since Minette was barred to him in all but thought.

The news of the King's daily visits from Hampton Court to London's shipyards where the fleet, re-manned, was ready to put out to sea, brought those who had fled flocking back to the city, ashamed of their fears when the Sovereign, against all advice, risked infection while the plague still ran its course. By the end of March Clarendon reported that: *The streets were so full, the Exchange as much crowded, the people in all places as numerous as they had ever been...* The worst was over, with the loss of more than a hundred and eighty thousand lives.

The Queen and the Court were back at Whitehall when the British faced the fiercest battle of the war. All through the summer in that life-and-death struggle, the thunder of the cannon could be heard in the Thames, in London's streets and in St. James's Park, where the King, his face haggard, his greying hair blown by the hot breeze — he had left off his periwig during the week's stifling heat — flung bread to his water fowl and waited and listened ... and waited again ... and prayed that the guns he could hear so near to his shores were his.

In her garden at Whitehall, Catherine could also hear the sound of the guns borne on the still close air. Was Britain to be invaded for the first time in six hundred years? Had this country of her adoption, this England she had grown to love, come under some dreadful curse wrought upon it by her 'Popery', as was whispered about and retailed by Donna Maria, whose hearing was acute if her sight was not?

'They'd have me burned for a witch or my head on the block if they could,' she said.

Donna Maria, at her everlasting embroidery, looked up to tell her, 'Speak not in jest to tempt the devil, who bestrides this land of misery. Even your goldfish are boiled.'

Catherine leaned over the lily pond to dip her hand in the water where the fish lay immobile among the leaves. 'My poor ones, yes — the water is too warm for them, but they are not dead, only sleepy. It is thunder, I think, and not the guns we hear, or both.'

She was in mourning, as were all the Court, for the recent death of her mother, the Queen Dowager of Portugal. This news had come to her soon after the loss of her child, of which the sex, a boy, had again been determined by the doctors. And Charles, against all the evidence of the physicians, was at last persuaded by the Lady to believe his wife incapable of bearing a child, and that he had been most monstrously deceived.

In her agony of grief and disappointment, Catherine had now none to whom she could turn for comfort, since the Queen Mother had gone back to France the year before. The London fogs, she declared, were killing her. She would take the waters of Bourbon and stay there for the winter months. She would 'return to England with the swallows', so she promised her son. But she did not return with the swallows, for the plague had intervened, and she stayed on at Colombes, her country house. Catherine remembered almost the last intimate talk she had with her mother-in-law, who had seen so much and said so little of her son's inconstancies; yet what she did say was always shrewdly to the point.

'The happiest marriage is between a blind wife and a deaf husband, but Charles is not deaf nor blind. He is *un gobe-mouches* — how the English call it? — too easily gulled, as are all the Stuarts. They are fated to be so. That is their weakness, and when weakness is allied to obstinacy, then weakness it becomes a mountain and not to be moved. It was just this weak obstinacy that gave his angel father to his murderers, and Charles to the Castlemaine, this bloodsucking *chienne,* whose place is in the kennel. *Mais, ma chérie,*' the Queen had taken Catherine's face in her hands, 'the good Lord gives us no greater burden than our spirit's strength can bear.'

But I, cried Catherine within her heart, *have surely borne enough?* She felt herself forsaken even by her God.

The Castlemaine, secure in the knowledge of her regained supremacy, assumed an attitude of overweening insolence when in waiting on the Queen. But her line of attack unexpectedly was parried. Catherine indeed had borne enough. While she met her adversary with deceptive calm, a well-timed thrust from her foil drew blood.

'I fear,' she hazarded, with careful nonchalance, 'that His Majesty has taken a chill.'

'A chill, Madam? How?'

'From staying so late in your ladyship's apartments. These August days are warm, the nights are not, and for the King to walk from a heated room into the cold of early morning is — inadvisable.'

Reddening beneath her paint, 'Should you believe,' was the Lady's sharp riposte, 'that the King is with me till all hours of the night, Your Majesty is much mistaken. If he does not pass his nights in your bedchamber, Madam, he must be in some one other's bedchamber. But not in mine.'

This statement, punctuated by emphatic pauses, did not decrease the Queen's preoccupation in the placing of a patch beneath her eye; but even as the Lady prepared to lunge again she heard, 'Be damned to you, woman, for your impertinence, you —'

Unobserved by the duellists, Charles had entered and stood at the door. Suppressing the more explicit epithet, his face dark with anger, 'I command you,' he hurled at her, 'to leave the Court at once, nor will you return until I send for you!' Saying so he turned about and, as silently as he had come, he went.

The Lady also went, but not in silence. Down the long corridor, past a group of scared pages, she tore back to her rooms, vowing vengeance for this insufferable insult, and dashed off a message delivered red-hot to the King: she would publish his letters for all the world to read!

Charles took alarm and the Lady took advice. Legal consultation affirmed that, since she was commanded to leave, or be driven out of Court, she was entitled to take with her the furniture of her apartments. She sent Charles virulent word to that effect. To which he inimically replied she could come and fetch her belongings herself.

She came with coaxings, implorings and tears that resulted in a half-hearted truce. Charles, sick of her paroxysms, succumbed. Her power over him was no longer that of mistress; he gave in to her from fear of her virago's tongue. Anything for peace and quiet.

But for him there was to be no peace or quiet, either at home or abroad.

While England was faced with defeat and disaster, while the plague still claimed its victims in towns and countryside, and while the Navy fought on against terrible odds, came the news that the French were out in the Channel to join forces with the Dutch under de Ruyter.

At once the men of England sprang to arms, standing at the ready to defend their shores from the threat of double invasion, when a fearful storm sprang up to drive de Ruyter and his allies, their ships severely damaged, to seek shelter in their ports.

Yet that storm, so providential to the English, hunting the enemies' battered fleets at sea, brought catastrophe on land. On 2 September 1666, in the early hours of the morning, Pepys was called from his bed by his maid to tell of a fire in the city. From his window he could see the flames but, thinking them at too great a distance to affect his house, he went back to bed and to sleep. Then, *By and by,* he records, *Jane comes to tell me that above three hundred houses have been burned tonight by the fire we saw and that it is now burning down all Fish Street by London Bridge.*

That same storm which had caused havoc among the enemy's ships was driving furiously inland, fanning the flames of a baker's house in Pudding Lane to a furnace that roared through the city in a molten blaze. The summer, one of the hottest and driest ever known, had rendered the ancient houses, built of timber with their pitch-plastered roofs, the more combustible; and the fire, driven by that relentless wind, devoured in its stride warehouses filled with tar and resin. Almost the whole city from the Tower to Temple Bar was soon one fiery torrent. For three days and nights the city burned, belching columns of smoke to cover the reddened sky in a murky pall through which the sun looked like a dried orange.

The King, aware that the flames, if not halted, would swallow the whole of London as a lion swallows meat, ordered the Lord Mayor — the most timid of men — to pull down all houses in the fire's path. But the terrified townsfolk, only concerned with saving their goods and chattels and making all haste for the river to take whatever watercraft were available to carry them away, offered no help to save their devastated city. The Mayor, who, according to Pepys, had brought him the King's message and was half fainting with fright, cried out: 'Lord! What can I do? The people won't obey me!' and took to his heels to save his own skin and what was left of his house and belongings.

On the second day the fire, gaining impetus as it scattered wind-blown sparks on the wooden houses in those narrow streets, was one flaming arch across the sky.

The Queen, with her cowering women, watched from her window the driven flames flash up to envelop the spire of St. Paul's. She could hear the mighty crash of its great roof falling.

'Sister!' Anne, with her eighteen-month-old daughter in her arms and the five-year-old Mary clutching at her petticoats, came from her room to say. 'Do you know that James and the King are out in the midst of it — blowing up the houses with gunpowder? James insisted on going. They will blow themselves up if not burned to death! To run into that danger — so foolhardy!'

'The King,' Catherine said, 'thinks nothing of danger to himself, only of danger to his people.'

'As so does James, but oh! — to escape death at sea only to be burned to death in London!'

At which Mary set up a howl, and Catherine knelt to soothe her. 'No, my sweet one, there's nothing to fear. God will protect your father and the King, and all his good people and us.

'They are saying,' Anne handed the other, now squalling princess to her nurse who had followed them — 'here, take her,' and, lowering her voice: 'they are saying, 'tis the Papists have caused it to destroy the city and dethrone the King ... Do stop crying, Mary! You heard the Queen tell you there's no danger.' And hustling her children out of the room, she drew Catherine aside to mouth in her ear. 'There's more danger, I'm thinking, from these wicked rumours that spread as wild as the fire.'

Rumours that were to bear poisonous fruit.

The King and his brother, regardless of risk from falling timbers, rode up and down in the thick of it, encouraging, commanding, calling for volunteers to fight the flames and, where the fire was fiercest, they dismounted and, leading their horses to safety, flung back into that hellish maelstrom to form a living chain, passing buckets of water to throw on the houses that burned like so many logs on a hearth.

After three days and four nights of it, the worst at last was over. The gaps where houses had been blown up by gunpowder baulked the fire of its prey: yet it had left almost all of the city in ashes, *The saddest sight of desolation,* as Pepys saw it.

But from that desolation, from its rubble and its ruins, rose the phoenix of a greater London; for even while the city still smouldered in its smoke, the King was closeted with his brother James and John Evelyn, who had brought him the plans for the new building of St. Paul's by a young architect, Christopher Wren.

Catherine, about to set out for her morning ride, was called to attend the conference. That Charles desired her approval of the architect's design gratified as much as it surprised her. He had never yet consulted her on affairs of state or on any other matter not of her immediate concern. Could this mean that he had come to realise she could no longer be treated as a child, or — a bitter smile came upon her lips — a wife?

'Your Majesty,' her dresser, hovering beside her, asked, 'Do you change from your habit?'

'No. I will go as I am. My horse can wait but the King cannot.'

And in her cavalier costume, with its feathered hat and short riding skirt, she went to her husband. Charles, bending over the table where the plans were spread out, turned at her entrance. His eyes — narrowing in swift appreciation, for she looked her best in riding kit — confirmed his brother's greeting: 'Madam, you are delicious — half girl, half Ganymede.'

Charles, wrinkling his nose, slipped James a grin. 'Has it taken you all of three years to know that? So, Catherine, let's have your epicene opinion on these designs for a new St. Paul's.'

The scaffoldings were up, and workmen swarming like ants on ladders, while the raucous commands of overseers accompanied the ceaseless hammering of steel on stone and brick, and creak of chains as the pulleys hoisted their heavy weights. But above all this stir and activity more sinister sounds were heard. The Dutch were in the Medway; panic was in the air, and along the Kentish coast guns barked defiance at the

Hollanders, triumphantly advancing to the Nore. The war had brought bankruptcy to the kingdom and the King, who was petitioned to forbid the Mass and to banish all Papists and priests.

Whispers flew from mouth to mouth. The Queen and the Catholics were in league with France to prolong this devastating war. It was they who had brought calamity upon the nation, they who had started the fire in that baker's shop in Pudding Lane. It was the Papists who had brought from their heathen countries those black rats that had spread the plague from their poisonous fleas! England would never prosper while a Catholic Queen shared the throne. Not only all Papists, but she, the King's wife — who was no wife — must go.

SEVEN

'Three sights here are seen,
Dunkirk, Tangier, and a barren Queen!

They bawled it in the taverns, they yelled it in the streets. They painted a gibbet on the gates of Lord Clarendon's house as reminder of the fate that should be his for selling Dunkirk to the French and for keeping, at the nation's cost, an army kicking its heels at Tangier. They accused him of having deliberately forced upon the King the one wife in Europe whom he knew to be sterile, that he might secure the throne for his son-in-law, York, and his grandchildren by his daughter, Anne.

The Peace of Breda that brought war to an end had brought no peace to Charles. He was torn between loyalty to a trustworthy friend and adviser, and the demands of his Parliament to drop overboard the faithful old pilot who had steered the ship of state too long.

So bitter was public opinion which threatened not only the downfall of Clarendon but of the throne, since there were still many who hankered after a Protectorate, that the King was faced with an alternative choice: to hand over his kingdom and likely his head to republican rule or — to dismiss his Chancellor. As he dared not risk another civil war, he chose the latter course.

Council meetings held in the Chancellor's house, where he lay gout-ridden, resulted in the old man's resignation. 'I give in and — give up,' he told James, who had unsuccessfully attempted to make Charles reconsider his decision.

'You can't be so ungrateful, so forgetful of all you owe to him.'

'Of all *you* owe to him, you mean!' Charles retorted, loping with his long-legged stride up and down the room. 'But don't imagine —' he swung round on James, who was picking at his thumbnail, a trick of his when worried, and so often of late was he worried that the skin round his thumb was picked raw — 'don't for one moment imagine that if I were deposed you'd sit where I am. Were you a Protestant they might set you up as their puppet King, but never a one that's a Papist.'

'Not yet publicly avowed,' muttered James.

Charles grinned. 'Nor am I — although I've a wife and mistress, for my sins, who are.'

James shook his head. 'I shall never understand how she got herself received.'

'Can't you? I can. In the same way as did the importunate widow, as told by the Word, who couldn't get the magistrate to try the case she was bringing in the hope of compensation, until she pestered him so much that in the end he allowed her a hearing to be rid of her.'

'You'll not get rid of your pest that way,' said James, glumly, 'but I see your point.'

The Lady, too, delightedly could see a point that offered further opportunity to break the King's marriage unhampered by warnings from the old watchdog. When Clarendon, at last defeated, got up from his couch to hand over the seals of office to the King, she ran out to her garden with very little on more than a gossamer shift, having been in bed all the morning holding conference with her disciples concerning this latest development. And there she stood, loud in laughter and jeering to see him, crushed and beaten, go limping back to his palatial home that would be his home no more.

With the fall of Clarendon, Catherine had lost her sole protector against the machinations of the Lady. Now that her hated old enemy was banished she had a clear field in which to pursue operations to rid herself of that other hated enemy, the Queen.

Never had the three Bs been so busy. Bristol, having sent scouts to Portugal to grub up any scrap of garbage that could be brought as evidence of Catherine's infertility, had sneaked back to the Lady and was again her tool. And Buckingham was back, having been detained in the Tower for some slight misdemeanour, from whence, after a stormy scene with Charles, the queen bee had obtained his release.

It was all around the galleries — the Lady could never modulate her voice — how that she had beleaguered the King for 'a fool! Only a fool would be governed by fools. You've had the sense, at *last*, to see your folly and throw out that old dizzard who has feathered his fine nest at your expense to drain you dry, and yet you place behind bars one whom of all your subjects would serve you and the country with honour!'

To which Charles was heard to retort: 'As much honour as is found among thieves?' And before she could take breath to hurl more abuse, he cut in: 'I'll thank you not to meddle with what doesn't concern you — you — bitch!' as those who gleefully listened would have it he called her, if not something worse.

But meddle she did and, by persistent barrage, gained her ends. Charles, sick of rows in his palace and rackets in his Parliament, let her have her way. He may have hoped that Buckingham, at large, would facilitate his own release from his limpet-like adhesion. He knew Buckingham had always received abundant fruits from the Lady's cornucopia. Also, he had become more than ever enamoured of *la belle Stuart,* who by her 'simple' methods, still held herself intact.

So besottedly infatuated was he that talk gave it he would sue for a divorce on the grounds of the Queen's sterility, and marry the Stuart. Why not? He needed an heir, and the country would never stomach his brother, a Papist, as his successor. The Stuart, although a commoner, was of Blood Royal by remote descent.

But none of this reached the ears of Catherine. She, just then, was immersed in disquieting news from Portugal. Alphonzo, the King, always weak-minded, had been pronounced insane, and also impotent. His wife, seeking an annulment of the marriage, eventually secured, was free to marry her lover, his brother, Dom Pedro, now Regent.

More ammunition for Castlemaine with which to bombard the Queen. If the House of Braganza bore the double taint of insanity *and* impotence, did it not prove the daughter of that House had inherited the taint to render her not only sterile but likely to run mad?

She called her drones in consultation. She had gathered to her hive a fourth whose name began with B. A pompous, oily divine was Dr. Burnet, destined for the bishopric of Salisbury.

Reclining on her couch, with Bristol at her feet, Buckingham at her head, and Dr. Burnet at somewhat less intimate distance, she cautioned them, 'We must go warily. In spite of incontrovertible evidence to the contrary, Charles still fathers the wish with the thought that his wife may yet get him an heir.'

'We might,' said Buckingham, 'procure him a divorce for desertion.'

'How desertion?' rapped the Lady. 'She'll never leave him.'

'There are means by which she may be made to — leave him.' And leaning his lips to her ear he whispered.

'What?' She jerked herself up from her cushions. 'Are you out of your mind? Kidnap her? Smuggle her off to America and dump her down in some cotton plantation?'

'It would offer,' said Bristol, 'a means to an end.'

She looked from one to the other. 'Oh? So! You've talked it over, have you? And how do you propose to get her out of the country — or, as you suggest, *kidnap* her?'

'By persuading her priest to induce her to retire to a convent,' she was told.

'Idiots!' snorted the Lady. 'For all her piety do you think she'd exchange a crown for the veil? Well,' she gave Dr. Burnet her dazzling smile, 'let me hear what the Church has to say.'

What the Church had to say was said at some length, and with frequent resort to a sheaf of notes. 'This is a resume of my thesis,' he pontifically announced, 'on the solution of two cases of conscience, one touching the Scriptures, the other divorce, and what the Scriptures allow in those cases.'

'According to *my* Church,' declared the Lady turning her eyes heavenward, 'the Scriptures allow no divorce.'

'Which,' Buckingham muttered, 'rather damps your chances.'

'Shut your mouth!' she ordered. 'Or if you must open it let it spew sense — if it can. Yes, Doctor?'

'I would refer your ladyship to —' the embryonic bishop hemmed behind his hand — 'to — ah — the Established Church in which I can find nothing against divorce and I, myself, see nothing so strong against it as the dangerous hazards that beset unfortunate individuals who are bound in — hem — what may be considered *un*-holy matrimony, as in the case of his unfortunate majesty who has contracted a marriage that can only be regarded as illegal.'

When, however, Buckingham approached the King with this incredible proposal to eliminate the Queen, Charles, in high indignation, rejected it as — 'an atrocity equalled only by its crass absurdity. It is no fault of my wife that she has no children. Do you suppose I would dissolve my marriage on that or any other unjustifiable count?'

Buckingham, who had hopes of taking the ministerial seat vacated by the Chancellor, at once realised his mistake, and assured His Majesty that he was in complete accord with his refusal to countenance so outrageous a scheme, which, he was bound to confess, had never met with his approval but had been suggested by the late Chancellor, who...

'That's a damned lie,' shouted Charles, 'considering Clarendon promoted the marriage!'

'Who, Sir, I was about to say,' Buckingham smoothly continued, 'having discovered the unhappy circumstances of Her Majesty's — ah — disability, had in mind the means of your release.'

Said Charles, his temper flying, 'I have no wish to be released, and unless you would have me regret *your* release — from the Tower — you will not falsely accuse one whose dismissal, against my better judgment, I shall all my life deplore, for there is none in my corrupt council whom I now can trust. *You* least of all.'

'Your Majesty!' Buckingham professed profoundest shock. 'Believe me there is not one of your subjects who would more readily lay down his life in your service than myself, whose counsel is prompted only by the love I bear my Sovereign, whom I —'

'Cut the puffery!' came stringent interruption, 'and — get out!'

Buckingham got out; but after further conference with his confederates he again approached the King to offer the suggestion that Her Majesty, who had always leaned, he understood, to the life of a religious, might be persuaded to retire to a convent.

This Charles was inclined to believe. 'Has she said so?'

'To her intimates, Sir, and, as I have been assured, with the approval of the late Father Patrick, her confessor, who,' fabricated Buckingham as he saw the King swallow the bait, 'was inclined thus to persuade the Queen in view of the irregularities with which, in all due respect, Sir, a priest of Rome would regard the — the lighter elements of Your Majesty's Court. I think it is apparent to all that the Queen has never been able to adapt herself to our English ways.'

He left Charles with the impression that Catherine had used Buckingham as her emissary to prepare the King of her intent. But when Dr. Burnet was commissioned to approach the Queen with this ulterior suggestion, she proved coldly unreceptive. She had no vocation, she assured him, nor desire to be a nun, or certainly not since she had been a wife. 'And who,' she demanded, 'dares so to presume?'

Dr. Burnet, whose face was the colour of underdone beef, and adorned with a bulbous nose that resembled nothing so much as a wine-stained cork, became a shade redder.

'None, Your Majesty, would dare so to presume, but that we — I — they —'

'They?'

'His Majesty's Council, Madam, who gave me to understand that Her Majesty herself did wish to retire from the — ah — the world.'

'You — they — whoever *they* may be, gave you to "understand"?' cried Catherine, as with a look of disgust she surveyed the unlovely sight of him upon whose forehead a faint dew had appeared. On the few occasions when she had been obliged to receive Dr. Burnet, she had found him distinctly unlikeable. She disliked his appearance, his fishy little eyes, and his oily voice — like a slug's voice, if a slug could speak, was how to herself she described it. 'You, sir,' she flung at him, 'you, and those who sent you to me must also understand that I will never leave my husband, whom I love, unless —' for a moment she faltered — 'unless he would wish it so.'

She had kept the would-be bishop standing while she sat; and, still seated, she gestured Donna Maria, in attendance, to show him the door.

So that was the end of that, and of the Lady's immediate efforts to obtain a divorce for the King, who it would seem was not now entirely opposed to the idea. Although grieved and conscience-stricken to think his neglect and infidelities might have driven his wife to seek shelter in a convent, it had occurred to him that if, of her own accord, she chose to disintegrate their marriage, he would be free to take him a wife who could give him an heir.

He had, by this time, become so obsessed by *la belle Stuart,* that he was ready to go to any desperate lengths to get her. He showered her with gifts. He offered to make her a Duchess. He had her portrait painted by Lely, who shows her in all her loveliness on the walls of Hampton Court. He commissioned John Rotier, the royal medallist, to use her for his model as Britannia in the new issue of coinage, and so to immortalise her on all copper coins to this day. It was the general opinion, both in and out of Court, that he would certainly marry her if he could not have her any other way.

But Buckingham had something else in view, even more far-fetched, by which the Queen would be out of everybody's way, including his own. He knew that Catherine would exert what little influence she had with Charles in the replacement of the ex-Chancellor; and, of all the council's candidates, were she allowed any voice in the matter, Buckingham would *not* be in the running. He was now prepared to produce evidence to the fact that before she married Charles, the Queen had been contracted to one of the many competitors for her hand and fortune, which would present a *prima facie* case for a dissolution of the marriage.

Then suddenly, in the midst of these preposterous intrigues, she who had sponsored them threw in her hand. It had occurred to the Lady that if the King were granted a divorce, and were to marry a wife who could bear him a child, and that wife, her loathly usurper, the Stuart, her last hold on him would be gone; and her own children, three of them, doubtfully, his, would never be raised to the semi-royal rank she coveted for them and for herself.

There had recently come to Court a cousin of Frances, another Charles Stuart, Duke of Richmond. Already twice married, twice widowed was he, though still in his twenties; not overburdened with wit, much overburdened with drink, whose attentions to Frances, the Lady discovered, were something more than cousinly. He was often seen to visit the virtuous Frances at all hours of the day and night.

To Charles she reported her findings. 'Are you so blind? She fools you to the top of her bent, to put you off and lead you on — to offer more than strawberry leaves. She can have those for the asking. When you bid her goodnight tucked up in her bed, Richmond runs in to — untuck her! If you don't believe me go and see.'

He went to see, and found his lovely Frances very much 'untucked' in bed, with her cousin there beside her on the pillows. They were playing cat's cradle.

'What,' the King demanded awfully, 'is the meaning of this?'

The meaning of that was clearer to him than to the pair of innocents, one of whom was rather drunk and whose unexpected visitor had reduced to a state of petrifaction.

Frances was the first to find her voice in a terrified bleat. 'Oh, Your Majesty, he ... my cousin, we ... we've done nothing wrong, Sir. He came to bid me ... goodnight. I asked him to ... stay and play a ... game with me because I couldn't ... sleep.'

'I know your game! You've played it once too often with me — because you couldn't sleep! As for you — you dirty little hound, I'll —' The King bore down on the Duke, who, foreseeing assault, made a dash for the window and was over the sill and into the garden below, where he sprawled, and was up to make what haste he could with a sprained ankle and a whizzing head.

Frances, left to deal with the infuriated monarch, reiterated, amid floods of tears, that 'nothing wrong' had taken place, that her cousin had asked her to marry him but that she would never — 'neh-ev-er,' she blubbered 'marry anyone without Your Majes-esty's consent.'

'Which you'll never have, to marry that tapeworm!' stormed Charles, and flung out of the room to hunt down Richmond and order his banishment from Court.

But Richmond was not to be found; he had fled.

And now the Court had food enough to fill it for a month. Every scrap of gossip to do with that sorry encounter was picked up, gobbled, to regurgitate *ad nauseam:* how that the

King had come upon the Stuart entertaining Richmond on, or in, her bed which, was hopefully surmised, would finish her and the Duke — were he to be found.

And Frances, thoroughly frightened, sought protection of the Queen, at whose feet she threw herself, hysterically imploring: 'Madam! If I have been thoughtless, forgive me. I was fl-flattered,' she sobbed, 'that His Majesty should fa-fa-favour me, but I ha-ha-have never permitted more than a — k-k-kiss. Madam!' She caught the Queen's hand and profusely wept upon it. 'B-b-b-believe me I am not dishon-hon-oured. I love and res-respect Your Majesty too much to do you wrong. Pray, Madam, b-b-believe me!'

Catherine did believe her. She knew Frances spoke no more than the truth that she had been flattered, as any young woman would be, by the impassioned advances of Charles; and that she remained *virgo intacta* against all temptation of wealth, jewels, rank. Refusing the proffered duchy proved her less wanton, Catherine ironically reflected, than fool. Had she succumbed to the King she might have been not only his mistress but his Queen. Yet here she was ready to wed with that much-married cousin of hers, brainless as herself, so to escape the King's pursuit...

'That's why I encouraged the Duke, who has been wanting to marry me this — ever so long — since his second wife died. Pray, Your Majesty —' another avalanche of tears — 'pray, I b-b-beg you ask the King to grant me permission to marry Richmond, or if not,' came the sob-impeded declaration, 'I'll take me to a c-c-convent.'

Catherine got rid of her at last by promising to obtain the King's consent to the marriage, or, for Frances was a Catholic, to place her as a novice in some religious order. In the meantime it would be advisable that she remain in her rooms and not be seen about the Court.

So implicitly did Frances obey the Queen's instructions that a week went by with neither sight nor sound of her ... until one night a figure, masked, cloaked, hooded, was seen by a porter to creep out of a side door from Mistress Stuart's apartments. When questioned she answered in a high squeaky voice: 'Don't tell on me. I'm off to Bartholomew's Fair.'

He guessed her a chambermaid out for a spree, and with a wink and a warning that she'd 'best not come back with a dose of the pox,' he let her go.

Up and down the palace, in and out the Lady's chamber, went the hue and cry: Frances had vanished!

Her women declared they had put her to bed the night before and left her, as usual, hugging her doll. She was afraid of the dark and always took the doll to bed with her. The maid who brought her breakfast found her room empty. They had searched high and low but never a sign of her. The night porter admitted that one of the maids had sneaked out, as they often did, to go off to the Fair. He had recognised the girl — to save his skin he swore to it — and that she had come back at midnight, and he had let her in by the side door.

Charles was frantic, Catherine no less. She blamed herself. If she had not offered to sponsor the marriage *this* would not have happened. And 'this' that had happened was elopement.

A pair of saddle horses had been seen outside the palace gates between Whitehall and Westminster; a man and a woman had mounted them. The woman was masked, as reported by yokels. They had taken the road southward over London Bridge into Surrey. And there in the Duke of Richmond's house and in his private chapel they were married by the Duke's own chaplain.

It was apocalyptic, catastrophic, unbelievable but, most shockingly, was true!

In the first heat of his fury Charles ordered the banishment of both recalcitrants. Never again, he declared, would he receive the guilty couple in his presence or his Court. So beside himself was he at the perfidy of Frances, there could be no doubt in any mind that he was, or had been, seriously in love with her. This runaway match he took as a deliberate insult, proof positive of her determination to escape him; and to have chosen 'that drunken sot', Richmond, in preference to the unlimited honours that could have been hers, heaped further insult upon injury.

As for the Castlemaine, her triumph — with the riddance of Frances — was complete, though not for long. Even while she and her allies were resuming operations to annihilate the Queen, they were again frustrated. For the third time Catherine had hopes of a child, and Charles was all devotion and *mightily reformed*, says Pepys.

But three months later, *My wife miscarried this morning,* Charles wrote to Minette, with whom, now war was over, he could resume his correspondence, *yet I am glad 'tis evident she was with child, of which I will not deny to you I feared she was incapable.* It had been dinned into him enough to make him think so. Their mutual disappointment drew them closer together.

Not since the honeymoon had Charles been so attentive to his unhappy little wife, for her comfort and her joy; and she had reason enough for rejoicing. The Castlemaine's reign of tyranny was nearing its end. Although she still extracted enormous sums from the King's Exchequer, she had lost her power over him. Deprived of Frances, he turned for consolation not to her but to the Playhouse, where Moll Davis, an enchanting little warbler, charmed his eye and fancy with sentimental song.

My lodging is on the cold hard ground,
And very hard my fare,
But that which troubles me the most
Is the unkindness of my dear.

The unkindness of her 'dear' may have been attributed to Charles Hart, leading actor in the play when the King first saw her, soon to be supplanted by one dearer who could offer a more comfortable lodging than the cold hard ground.

This addition to the King's seraglio, while it infuriated Castlemaine, caused Catherine no heartache. She loved her husband too deeply to interfere with his enjoyment of footlight attractions. Even when one morning she came to his bedroom unannounced, and saw a woman's night-shift and slippers on the floor beside his bed, she could laugh and tell him it was time she went lest what was hid behind the curtain, 'underdressed', might take a chill. Yet the interlude with Moll was of very short duration. Within a year she lost him to another whose gamine wit and Cockney humour delighted her audience not only at the Duke's Theatre, but at the royal supper table in Whitehall.

When aware of her husband's latest diversion Catherine, far from resenting it, encouraged it. These actresses were of a different world from those others of his harem; and this one who danced her way into his heart as she danced into the hearts of his people, had no ambition, no avarice for honours in return for what she gave him. She was full of quips and laughter; and if her jests were bawdy, her language coarse, who cared? Not the King nor anyone else. She was his and everybody's darling, this 'pretty, witty Nell' of Drury Lane.

Not without a struggle did Castlemaine renounce what she chose to call her 'rights'. The marked indifference of the King to her enticements brought about a series of brainstorms concerning this new acquisition.

'How can you so demean yourself with these strolling play-actresses? And this one from the gutter who began life as a fish-fag, an orange girl — a whore!'

To which Charles returned a nonchalant reminder of her own misdemeanours with the acrobatic Jacob Hall and his many predecessors, not excluding the most recent beneficiary of her favour, young John Churchill, the Duke of York's sixteen-year-old page.

'That boy! A child!' Her paroxysmal rage was augmented by the fact that for all her blandishments she had not so far succeeded in seducing the future Duke of Marlborough. 'Have you sunk so low, that you can heed the lying tongues of demireps? To dare accuse me of tampering with the son of my own cousin on whom I have bestowed a mother's love!'

'As might the mother of an Oedipus?' suggested Charles in quiet laughter, to induce a volley of vituperative threats. If he persisted in shaming her and his royal dignity by his association with a pack of harlots, she would dash out her children's brains at his feet sooner than see them half kin to the bastards of a strumpet! She would expose him to his people for a ruttish lecher soaked in fornication — she'd set fire to his palace with him in it 'so you may roast there and burn before your time!'

He let her go on till she and her hysterics were exhausted. He was sick to death of her, disgusted by her frenzies; but because it was not in him to abandon that between them which once had passed for love, he placated her with offers of the duchy, long delayed ... 'Yes, yes! And the manors of Nonsuch and the parishes of Cheam, O, God, yes!' Anything and all of it if only to be rid of her.

Her day, at last, was done.

The excitement occasioned by this penultimate row before the final departure of Castlemaine was less than a nine days' wonder. Everyone had seen it coming and the only wonder was that it had come so late. The reason given by the Lady for what she called her 'voluntary retirement' was the return of Frances, Duchess of Richmond, to be appointed, in her stead, as Lady of the Bedchamber. This by Catherine's request, and perhaps as a tacit acknowledgement and reward to Charles for relieving her, no matter how belatedly, of Castlemaine's hateful attendance. Frances and her husband were given apartments in Somerset House, again by desire of the Queen and until such time as the Queen Mother should return to take up residence. But she was never to return. On the last day of August, 1669, she died at her château of Colombes.

The Court was again plunged into mourning, but James, who had always been his mother's favourite, grieved more for her than did Charles, although he took it hardly. Three deaths in eight years! Since his Restoration he had lost his sister Mary, wife of the Prince of Orange, and his young brother, Harry of Gloucester. Both died of the smallpox during a visit to Somerset House.

'There's a curse on the place,' Charles declared, when Frances, Duchess of Richmond, went down with it and lay at death's door for a month. Yet the curse, if any, in the days when disinfectants were unknown, might well have been attributed to the virus that still hung about the bed on which Frances slept, and where those two had died.

Charles, who had not seen her since her reinstatement, called to enquire daily, and once or twice visited the sickroom during the height of the infection. She recovered slowly, but her beauty was impaired and she had lost the sight of one eye, much to the satisfaction of the Lady. She, although no longer of the bedchamber, had not yet been formally dismissed and refused to leave her apartments in the palace until the promised duchy should be confirmed by letters patent.

The King's concern for and attention to Frances in her illness gave everyone but Catherine reason to believe him as enslaved as ever by the Stuart. Catherine knew better. When Charles heard of her intent to visit Frances, he forbade it. He would not have her run the risk of contagion, he said, and went himself, as in duty bound to one of royal blood and his own kinswoman. And to Minette, always inquisitive and ready to tease him in her letters whenever she heard of his various entanglements, and particularly to do with the Stuart, whom she had known at the Court of France, Charles sent a chaffing contradiction to rumour.

You were misinformed in your intelligence concerning the Duchess of Richmond. If you were as well acquainted with a little fantastical gentleman called Cupid as I am, you would neither wonder at nor take ill any sudden change in the affairs of his conducting, but in this matter there is nothing done in it...

As for Catherine, she had no fear of Frances nor of any other rival now that the woman who had sought to wreck her life was no longer a menace. She had come to accept her husband's infidelities as one accepts a climate. 'He is — how you say? — a weathercock to turn as the winds of fancy take him,' she confided to the Benedictine priest who had replaced Father Patrick as her English tutor and confessor.

Father John Huddleston had been out of England for some years, but because he had assisted the King's escape from Boscobel after the Battle of Worcester, he was one of the few practising priests to be received by Charles since the Proclamation of Parliament in 1663 had ordered the banishment of officiating Papists.

From Father Huddleston, who was in charge of the Whitehall Oratory, Catherine heard all he had to tell of his first meeting with 'a long dark man above two yards high'. 'A scruffy crop-haired fellow,' as described by the Father, 'and wearing a sweaty leathern jerkin, a five-days' growth of beard on his chin and a grease-sodden steeple-crowned hat on his head that was worth a thousand pounds to whomsoever should find and betray him.'

Catherine shuddered.

'But they didn't find.' The priest's deep-set eyes under gabled brows pierced the walls of memory. 'No, although the hunt was after him for forty days and nights they didn't find — to kill. He broke cover with the hounds at his heels and bore straight for Moseley Hall, the house of Mr. Whitgreave — that's where I first saw him, nor never knew him for the King.' A whimsical smile came upon his lips. 'Believe me, he looked as scurvy a rogue as you'd meet in a day's march. Nor did His Majesty know me for what I am, since I wore a layman's habit — for discretion's sake. We priests were all potential victims of Cromwell's butchery.'

'And then?' persisted Catherine, who had heard all this before but could never have enough of it.

'Why then, Lord Wilmot — he had come there to meet the King and Richard Penderel, one of those five Penderel brothers, wood-cutters of Boscobel, who hid him in the oak while the hunt crashed through that little copse, under the very tree where the King sat straddling a bough, and how they didn't see him is just another of those miracles in his God-sent escape. It wasn't his time,' mused the Father. 'We none of us goes till we're invited ... Where was I?'

'Lord Wilmot,' prompted Catherine. 'Was it not he who told you that...?'

'Yes, but there was little light to distinguish one from t'other for all the five Penderels were with him and all in peasant dress, dishevelled and dirty, until in the hall, where one oil lamp burned, Wilmot fell on his knees before a tall lad, brown as a gipsy — they'd cut his hair. It hung in elf-locks round his face that they'd stained with walnut juice, and — "this is your master," said Wilmot, in tears, "and the master of us all."'

Catherine, too, was in tears.

'So then,' Father Huddleston roused himself from that scene re-enacted in his mind's eye, 'we bathed his feet that were raw and blistered — he'd been footing it for hours — and we changed his filthy shirt for one of mine and then his nose began to bleed. I kept that shirt and the blood-stained handkerchief with which we staunched the flow. I gave it to the King — the handkerchief, I mean. His Majesty used it to touch for the King's Evil. 'Tis said to have healing properties.'

The story of his flight, or so much as Father Huddleston had to do with it, was given to Catherine in relays, nor did frequent repetition stale curiosity. But the supreme moment of that meeting with the King, the Father hoarded to divulge after these episodes from hearsay and his own account of them had been exhausted.

It was while they sat at supper that Charles told Father Huddleston he knew him for a priest — 'And that if it should please God to restore him to his own, we of the only living Church would never more be forced to keep our Faith a secret.'

Then he asked to see his host's private chapel. 'A plain white-washed room it was, with the Crucifix and candles and a few images of saints and Our Blessed Lady's shrine, the only indication of our trust ... "So," said the King, "you face capture and death and torture on the rack and at the rope, that you may fulfil that trust and serve the Mass to them who would also die for it?" ... Yes, he said that to me.' The Father's eyes were suspiciously bright. 'And when I saw him kneel before the altar in God's Presence I knew that the King had come into his own...'

That incident recalled by Father Huddleston, she had reason to remember during her recovery from her fourth and last miscarriage.

The King's predilection for curious pets, not only in his Park but in his palace, had caused him to adopt a fox cub rescued from his hounds in Windsor Forest. He brought it back with him to Hampton Court, tamed it to feed from his hand and to follow him from room to room like any of his dogs. One night it sneaked into Catherine's bedchamber when she was three months pregnant. It leaped on the bed and on to her pillow while she slept, and woke — to find its mask in her face and its tongue on her cheek. Her terrified shrieks brought her maids running, and Charles on his knees to soothe her, but the damage was done.

During the aftermath of abortive travail, a sense of tranquillity had replaced the first anguish of her loss. In these mutilated years of her marriage, when helpless to defend herself against the forces of enmity and evil, it was as if she had been tossed adrift in a devouring sea, to find herself cast upon some quiet shore, remote from the inexorable buffetings of conflict and this torture of loving too much.

But that final loss of a prospective heir had again brought up the question of divorce. This time it was Buckingham who, lacking the Castlemaine's co-operation, had taken on himself to spread the report that the Queen was incapable of childbirth.

Yet Catherine, secure in the knowledge that her husband's sympathies, if not openly declared, were with the older Faith, could suffer unprotestingly these recurrent iniquitous intrigues against her; though not until this last bitter disappointment did Charles disclose to her his secret allegiance to Rome.

Memory went searching.

That day at Hampton Court — the very first day of her recovery when they brought her couch into the garden, he had sent away her woman and sat with her to tell of a 'grand design', as he called his proposed treaty with France. He said that Louis had 'fallen out' with him over the Triple Alliance — 'You remember the Triple Alliance between Holland, Sweden and us?'

And she had nodded her head very wisely. Of course she remembered. But she mustn't let him know that not till then had she clearly understood with whom that Triple Alliance had been made; nor did she understand why Charles should now, for the first time, discuss affairs of state with her.

Briefly, if a thought shamefacedly, he explained that Louis had approached him with an ultimatum to break the Alliance and unite himself with France in a treaty that would be of incalculable benefit to Britain. Louis' invasion of the Low Countries had made war between France and Holland inevitable — 'in which case, under the Triple Alliance, we would be involved.'

'Not war again!' cried Catherine.

'I have the ships, I have the men, but,' Charles said, avoiding her eyes, 'I have no money for a war with France, even with Holland to back me. Yet if Louis will finance me — he is out to seize Holland and her Spanish possessions — then together we could change the face of Europe, to make me master of the sea as Louis is master of the land.'

'To break your trust with Holland!'

'The Dutch burned my ships in the Medway and the Thames,' Charles had said, tight-lipped.

'Would all the money in the world compensate for the loss of thousands of brave lives?' And saying that she had forced him to look at her, and saw the deeply furrowed lines from his nose to mouth relax.

'Yes, if those thousand lives can gain one soul's salvation. Louis stipulates to pay me sufficient to conduct a second war with Holland — on condition that I declare myself a Catholic.'

And while on a June morning she drowsed in her garden at Hampton Court, and relived that marvellous moment of his revelation, she realised how the whole fabric of her being, from its cloistered adolescence to her frustrated womanhood, had been shaped to this fulfilment of her heart's unending prayer. Nothing now could tarnish the lustre of her love that lay beyond desire, beyond regret, beyond the laceration of life's crises and suspenses and the agonies of jealousy she had suffered and endured: her crown of thorns. Nothing now could come between her husband and herself. His transient indulgences, in the name of love — what mockery! — were no more than a schoolboy's robbing of an orchard. The knowledge that he had never loved nor ever could love her as she loved him, was no longer a wound unhealed, for as Dom Patricio had often said, 'Man loves nobody and nothing if he loves not God...'

A deep sigh of thankfulness escaped her. She stretched out her arms as if in an embrace, let them fall to her side and felt the thrust of a cold nose nuzzling her palm. One of his dogs had come to her, so Charles could not be far away.

Shading her eyes with her hand against the sun's hot glare, she saw the distant groups of figures imposed against the trees as upon a tapestry. The flickering light shone on the satin of women's gowns, on the bright harsh colours of men's suits and their wide slashed breeches that were like petticoats. She felt to be watching a masque played by voiceless mummers, and, as they strutted, bowing one to the other, she was reminded of the movements of her white fantail pigeons ... Some of them had flown down from their dovecote over the stables. One alighted on the shoulder of the tallest man, who towered over those who postured round him, and as he left that chattering circle of courtiers the bird spread its wings and fluttered after him. Her eyes followed its flight with half a dozen others as Charles came toward her, calling, 'Why are you alone? Where are your women?'

'I like to be alone. They are over there,' she pointed, 'if I want them.' And, as she held out her hand to him, one of the fantails swooped down to perch on her finger. 'They won't come to me,' she said, 'unless I am alone, but they will always go where you are.'

There were stools about her couch and a table with a flagon of wine and a dish of cakes and fondants. She took and nibbled a stick of marchpane and placed a piece of it between her teeth. 'Now look, this one she will feed from my lips. She is the tamest of them all and the most old.'

'Eldest,' he corrected, smiling down at her.

'Thank you. Eldest.' Her dark little childish face answered his smile. 'She is a great-great-great — so many greats — grandmother.'

'How do you know?' he asked, amused.

'Because,' as the bird flew off with the titbit, 'she is here always. When others go and others come, she stays. 'Tis years now since she was a — how you say? — a fledgling. And I know also because she is the only one who is not pure white. If you look at her wing you will see a small little patch of grey. Please, Charles, sit. You are so high it breaks my neck to look at you.'

'My legs are too long for these stools,' said he, 'which could only accommodate a dwarf.' He lowered himself to the grass, and the spaniel that had clambered on to the couch jumped down and into his arms.

'I have heard from Minette today,' he went on. 'She will be coming to visit us some time this year.'

'Minette!' she echoed delightedly. 'At last! I have longed so much to see her.'

'So,' said Charles, 'have I.' And at the glowing light that transformed his sombre face she thought, *Yes, Minette. She is and always has been the one love of his life...*

This year, next year, sometime ... never?

How often in the coming months did Charles fret against the repeated delays that had held up Minette's arrival? All through that year, since the negotiations for the 'grand design' had been first discussed with France through their respective secret agents, he had insisted that none but Minette should be entrusted with the final and innermost condition of the treaty, by which he would be empowered, under subsidy of Louis, to declare himself a Catholic. Only to his wife and James, already a convert, had he told of that clause which none other in his kingdom must know. But what Catherine must never know were the perils that would involve his conversion, to endanger his Crown, his very life — and hers.

In the quiet of his closet he would ask himself: Was this tremendous step he was about to take prompted by a true vocation or by his urgent need for money, that hundred and fifty thousand pounds promised by Louis as the price of his apostasy when it should be expedient for him to reveal it?

Charles had no illusions as to his cousin's motive in forcing his hand. Not from religious conviction was Louis using Minette as his pawn on the chequerboard of France's foreign policy. She, whose nurtured dream and dearest wish had been to see her beloved Charles and the heretic peoples of her native land brought back to the Church in which she, of all her mother's children, had been reared, had fallen, a ripe plum at the feet of Louis, who by a union with France and England thought to gain mastery of these coveted islands.

Yet should his Protestant kingdom get wind of this intent, Charles believed revolution to be certain. Already there were rumours that he was prepared to abandon his part in the Triple Alliance, and if his secret conspiracy to join Louis in a war against Holland and become a paid vassal of France were known, he would earn the contempt of his subjects and possibly the loss of his throne.

Such were the nagging anxieties with which he had battled all through this past year while outwardly, seeming, he played the 'Merry Monarch' without a care in the world. But now all indecisions were dispersed, as a vapour melts before the sun, in the joyful anticipation that Minette was on her way to Dover ostensibly to visit the brother whom for nine years she had not seen, but in actual fact to conclude the secret signing of the treaty.

The fatal die was cast.

In a dawn of pink and pearl on the morning of 24 May, 1670, Minette, on the deck of the ship that Charles had sent to fetch her with an escorting fleet, saw the nearing cliffs of Dover rise from a mantle of white mist.

'Louise!' She turned to the young woman beside her. 'Look! Do you see? That is my England. I have waited for this moment all my life since I left here as a baby of two-three years old. I was in the care of my nurse, Lady Dalkeith, when my father was in prison and my mother fled to France.'

She leaned over the ship's side, her eyes straining for that ghostly glimpse risen from the sea. As the sun rose higher, its rays enmeshed the cliff tops in a metallic brightness deepening to crimson. She caught her breath. Her thin, too-slender body quivered with excitement. Her dark hair, blown by the breeze, escaped her hood and fell in wisps across her face. Impatiently she swept them back. All her movements were arrow-swift, as if she raced with time. 'My dear Dalkeith — she disguised herself as a beggar woman with a hump on her back.' Tears and laughter struggled with the words, 'I was the hump, and dressed as a boy! But when she found me too heavy to carry, although I was only a bag of bones — I still am! — and so was she, for we never had enough to eat until my cousin, King Louis — he was only a little boy himself then, and almost as poor as we were — had us to live with him. Then when she set me down to walk along the road — such a long, long road to Dover — and people stopped to talk to me and asked my name, Lady Dalkeith told them I was Peter, but I told them, "I am not Peter, I'm a princess!"'

All this was spoken in voluble French to Louise de Kerouaille, the young Breton whom Minette, known to France as 'Madame', had brought with her as one of her five maids of honour on this momentous mission.

Minette suddenly stiffened. 'That barge!' she cried. 'There's a barge coming to meet us. My brother, the King and — James, and another — who is it? Ah, yes! my cousin, Prince Rupert.'

'Madame has a very long sight,' said Louise. She had a gentle voice, a baby-faced prettiness, and large brown eyes, their beauty somewhat marred by a slight cast in one of them. 'Which is His Majesty, Madame?'

'The tall man in the bowl. Charles!' She made a trumpet of her hands and called to him in English in shrill lilting French accents. 'Charles, tell the men to row more quickly or I shall jump into the sea and swim to you!'

Within a few minutes the boat came alongside. The gangway was lowered and she was in her brother's arms. And then she pulled away from him, gazing up into his face. 'You look so much older than you used to look. Is it love or marriage that has aged you? And your wife — I long to see her, poor little thing.'

'Why "poor"?' His deep voice held a note of aggression. 'She is not to be pitied.'

'Any woman who loves you, Charles, is to be pitied, and the more if she is your wife … Ah, James, my James! Yes — and you, too, have aged. But naturally. I've not seen you since — how long? I've seen Charles since I last saw you — ten, twelve — how many years ago!' She tiptoed to meet his kiss and, turning to Prince Rupert, she gave him her hand. 'Dear cousin.'

He bowed over it formally. 'Madame, welcome to England.'

She could hardly remember him, this warrior prince, whose dark saturnine beauty and ruthless courage had earned him the nickname of 'Rupert the Devil'. Minette had been told how Charles, as a boy, had hero-worshipped him who fought so valiantly in their father's cause, but was there not some sort of quarrel between them to do with Rupert's surrender to the rebels at Bristol? She had heard her mother speak of it and how the King, her father, had deprived him of his command and ordered him out of the country. Her mother had always nursed a grievance against Rupert for that, and believed the disaster of Naseby had been the result of it…

While these random flashes of thought darted through her mind she was gaily chattering to her brothers and this solemn-faced Rupert, who was little more than a name to her.

As the ship sailed into harbour she was telling them of 'our most horrible journey here. I thought we would never arrive. It poured with rain. The coach was stuck in the mud where the river had flooded the roads, and the bridges were broken down. We had to sleep in a barn on straw mattresses until they mended a bridge for us so that we could go on our way. We sat on the floor and ate chicken with our fingers because we had no knives and forks. It was quite an adventure, wasn't it, Louise? Ah, but I forget, you don't speak English, so you don't know what I'm talking about … Charles, this is a new addition to my suite. Mademoiselle de Kerouaille.'

The young woman curtsied low, and her eyes, as she rose, met those of the King, which held hers in a long close look from which both seemed to find it difficult to disengage. A moment only, then all was hurry and bustle on deck as the seamen again lowered the gangway and the ship came alongside the quay.

Never had the little fishing village seen such festivities nor so brilliant a retinue as that which accompanied the King's sister from France. 'These French,' muttered suspicious islanders gathered at their cottage doors to watch them drive in their coaches along the cobbled streets. This sister of the King, an English-born princess, married to the French king's brother, received but tepid welcome from the natives of Dover, for all the flying of flags from the castle and bonfires lighted on the Downs. Bad enough to have 'that Portuguese' and her Popery as their Queen, without filling the town with a horde of foreigners lodged on them, since the castle couldn't hold them all. Two hundred and forty, or thereabouts, this 'Madame' had brought with her. And she and every one of them Papists!

But Minette, indifferent to or unaware of insular hostility, lived to its fullest every hour of the ten days grudgingly allotted by her husband for this visit.

'If only I need never go back. I dread to go back,' she confided to Catherine, who had given her heart to this adored sister of Charles, so frail and exquisite in her flower-like grace; not beautiful, yet she had about her a quality of beauty that owed nothing to feature or form. Too thin for health, with one shoulder higher than the other, her endearing charm was less outwardly manifest than in her quickened sense of life and living; her every word and action seemed to spring from some passionate desire to grasp at and share with others each vital new impression. It was as if she knew her time was short.

Those were halcyon days for Catherine; life narrowed to the hours spent with Minette. She loved to listen to her tell, in her pretty French accent, of that world beyond the strip of water in which this new-found sister moved and had her being, Queen of France in all but name, beloved of every man — and 'loving none, save Charles', as she laughingly confessed on one of these occasions when they walked together in the castle grounds.

'Your husband? You do not love him?'

Catherine stole a glance and saw Minette flush: the faintest suffusion, to leave her transparent skin uncoloured as a white rose petal.

'Him? No,' she answered lightly. 'Him least of all, for he is not a man, nor is he a woman, although he tries so hard to be! He has all our faults and none of our virtues. He is one of nature's mistakes — as is my marriage.' She half whispered it, gazing out over the wall of the castle to where the fleet lay gently rocking at anchor. It was a capricious day of sun and cloud driven by a flighty breeze across a blue-grey sky, that the sea looked like some vast translucent opal in the dappled gleam of light and shade cast by the ships' spread sails.

'He, Philippe —' without turning her head, her eyes slid round to Catherine — 'he told me had ceased to love me two weeks after our wedding night. *Mon dieu!*' She laughed again, on a high shrill note. 'That night! I think we hated each other. If he ever loved me it was certainly not then. I think he cannot love a woman — his tastes lie in other directions. He cried. He was hysterical, and so was I, to see him decked out like a girl in a frilled nightgown and ear-rings with paint on his face. He was twenty but he looked about twelve, very small and pretty. Nothing happened. We spent most of the night eating sweets and asking each other what to do, and if it would hurt! He wouldn't know, never having had a woman. And then it did happen, two or three nights later, it was a miserable failure. How my "Monsieur" ever got me with child will always be a mystery to me. I had three, two girls and a boy — my darling who died two years ago.' She stretched out her hand to

Catherine. 'And you, my poor dear, have lost all yours before they were born.'

Catherine's fingers were laced in hers; out of some far-off vacancy she heard herself say, 'If only one of them had lived, Charles might have loved me.'

'He does love you, he does!' cried Minette. 'All these others, they —' And at the slight negative shake of Catherine's head and the tremble of her lips that tried to smile, her words dwindled into silence.

'It was my fault,' that far-away voice went on. 'Love is giving, not taking, as I have learned — too late.'

'Pah! This love!' Minette jerked up a shoulder. 'It is too serious to be taken seriously. Charles knows that.'

'I wonder.' Catherine's eyes strayed to him who now strolled down the sloping lawn with young Monmouth, followed by a flock of Minette's girls, foremost among them Louise de Kerouaille. She walked alone, speaking to none of those others chattering like starlings in their gesticulatory French. Charles turned to throw a laughing word to her and beckoned her alongside to be presented to his reputed son. Monmouth had driven post haste from London a few days earlier to join the royal party, and had made himself the life and soul of it before he had been twenty-four hours at the castle.

'I'd stake my life,' said Minette, 'that Charles is not his father. There's nothing of the Stuart in him. I have seen a portrait of Robert Sidney, one of Lucy Walters' *amoureux*. Old Hyde, who was with us at St. Germain, showed it to my mother. He always believed — the wily old fox — that James Crofts, Lucy's byblow, was not by Charles. But Mam would have it that he was. She adored him. Yet this portrait of Sidney, unless it lies, might be Monmouth's twin. He is beautiful and bad, and if not Sidney's spawn then he's the devil's — sh!' She clapped a hand to her mouth. 'Here he comes. Never tell Charles what I've said — he'll not hear a word against him, but I know and my brother James, *he* knows, and Charles will know some day — you'll see!'

'Dear Aunt!' Monmouth ran forward to greet her, 'How lovely you look!' And to Catherine he dropped on one knee. Lifting the hem of her gown, he raised it to his lips. 'You too, Your Majesty ... my lovely mother.'

Minette gave a little gasp, but Catherine merely smiled. He would so often address her in the presence of the King; it didn't hurt her and she knew it pleased Charles.

Raising himself, he rattled on: 'I have arranged a cruise for you this afternoon, sweet Aunt, in the *Royal Charles*. We'll have a picnic aboard and you will see the coastline from here to Portsmouth. The winds will stay fair today. You will like that, won't you? I'll go tell them to have all ready for us to embark by two o'clock.' Without waiting for an answer he dashed off.

Charles watched him go, saying indulgently, 'James is master of the revels here, so 'tis not for us to tell him yea or nay.' And to Louise de Kerouaille, standing with eyes downcast beside her mistress: 'I trust, Mademoiselle, you are a good sailor, for I think my son may be mistaken in the fairness of the winds. They can be as fickle as a woman's heart. *Comprends-tu?*'

Her eyelids lifted; her lashes curled upward to her eyebrows. '*Oui, Sire, je comprends, mais* ... I love the sea.'

'Then you should come and live with us upon this island where you can always be surrounded by the sea.'

'*Alors, mes enfants!*' Minette shattered the pause that followed the King's remark as his narrowed glance lingered on this demure little mademoiselle. 'We must go and dress ourselves for our voyage. Louise, *dépêche-toi.*'

'Madame.' The young woman curtsied, but she did not hurry. She, who had come in advance of the others, now walked behind them, a small secret smile on her lips.

Minette, with an arm in Catherine's, moved away, saying, low-voiced, 'I was a fool to bring her here.'

And Catherine, her eyes on Charles, asked delicately, 'Why?'

On the last night of Minette's visit, Charles said to his wife, 'Did you and my sister ever discuss the treaty and my — intended conversion?'

He had come to her room, for she had gone to bed early to be up betimes to see Minette aboard the ship that was to take her away next morning. He stood at the open window, from which he had drawn aside the curtains. A moon-shaft sliced the shadows cast by the wavering candlelight. From below, in the Great Hall, could be heard music and girls' laughter, mingled with the shouts of men, Monmouth's high among them; they were playing Blind Man's Buff.

'You told me it was a secret,' she said quietly. 'Nor did Minette speak of it, for it is her secret, too.'

'Yes.' Leaving the window he approached the bed. His face was sphinx-like, his low-lidded eyes stayed on hers where she lay propped on her pillows, her hair loose about her shoulders, her hands crossed under her chin. His heart twisted to see her lying there, so small and childish. 'Yes,' he said again, 'it is our secret. The deed is signed — the darkest deed of my life.'

And at that young lost look of hers and the startled unvoiced question on her parted lips, he folded his. The window curtain bellied in a sudden gust of wind; somewhere out there in the night an owl hooted.

'How,' her words came to him softly, 'can a deed be dark that gives you ... light?'

'To light a conflagration,' he answered her from a dry mouth, 'that will set Churches and nations one against the other to slay and be slain. I have betrayed my trust with Holland.'

'No, Charles.' She held out her hand to him. 'You have fulfilled your trust ... with God in seeking Him, but I think you would not have sought Him if you had not already found Him.'

'Minha pequena rosa.' He laid his head on her frail shoulder. 'Why are you so loving-kind to me? I have given you nothing but sorrow.'

'You gave me all the happiness I have ever known when you gave yourself to Mother Church with the signing of that treaty,' she whispered; and felt something like a sob shake through his body.

The candles guttered and burned down. The room was panoplied in the cold light of the moon. She could hear the sound of the sea like a rustle of leaves as it swept the beach, and the sigh of the wind in the sand-hills. Below, in the hall, boy choristers sang:

'All our pride is but a jest;
None is worst and none is best.
Grief and joy and hope and fear
Play their pageants everywhere.
Vain opinion all doth sway,
And the world is but a play.'

'Aha! I've caught you, Mademoiselle Louise!' Monmouth's voice rang out above the chorus and the laughter. 'I know you by the feel of your nose that points to heaven. I demand your forfeit ... *Merci, mademoiselle!* But an elf's kiss would be warmer.

And now I'll bind your eyes that you chase me. I'll not be caught!'

'Those girls,' said Charles, 'should be in bed. They must be up at dawn. The ship sails with the tide at six in the morning.' He brushed her forehead with his lips. 'Sleep very well, my love. Goodnight.'

The door closed behind him.

The long-case clock ticked away the minutes, or it may have been an hour. The room darkened, and a cloud bronze tinted, crossed the moon seen through the window in vaporous mist. She dozed, and was suddenly alert to the murmur of voices under the window.

'So, *mademoiselle*, you are sorry to be leaving my England?'

'Si, *Sire, J'adore* ... I love ... your England.'

'You must come back, and God willing, you *shall* come back.'

And down in the hall the choristers sang:

'Seas have their source,
And so have shallow springs.
But love is love in beggars,
And — in Kings!'

The sun rose clear and splendid out of a cloudless dawn, and so crystalline the air that the coast of France was a silver shade limned in the circle of the near horizon. Minette, with Catherine and her brothers, stood on the deck of the *Royal Charles* for her one last look at England.

'My little dear sister!' She flung her arms round Catherine. 'I'll not say goodbye. I hate goodbyes. If I only could have stayed with you for ever!'

'Minette...' was all that Catherine could say for the rock in her throat, but she took Minette's hand and held it to her lips, and 'Louise!' Minette beckoned the Breton girl standing with a group of her maids. 'Bring me the casket.'

The casket was brought and offered with a curtsy. Minette opened the ivory lid to disclose its sparkling contents on a bed of ruby velvet. 'This for you, sister — a parting gift.' She lifted a diamond cross suspended from a slender chain of gold. 'Wear it for me.' She clasped it round Catherine's neck — 'such a lovely little neck, and how prettily your hair grows here.' She kissed her nape. 'And for you, James — this.' She handed him an image of the Blessed Virgin. 'Her robe is of sapphires and the diamonds in her crown are seven.' He murmured something inaudible; tears, always a ready fount with James, gushed from his eyes. More kisses ... 'And now,' she turned to Charles, 'choose what you will from any of these.'

'The only jewel I want from you,' said he, 'is this.' Taking Louise by the hand he drew her forward. 'Give her to me for my —' between a second and a second he added to his pause — 'my wife, as maid-in-waiting.'

'No.' Minette stood very still, but she answered him banteringly: 'She is not mine to give. I promised her parents I would bring her back to them safely, unharmed by contact with your wicked Court. The Bretons are very particular. And so is my little Louise.'

There was a ripple of laughter from among the girls, some of whom understood English. Charles wrinkled an eyebrow, dropped the hand he was holding and, with a shrug of his shoulders, chose at random a ring of lapis lazuli.

'But that,' cried Minette, 'is of no value!'

'The one thing of value I would want,' he said, 'I mustn't have.'

On Catherine's face a smile wandered up; her hand touched to linger on the diamond cross at her breast, and her eyes strayed to Louise whose long lashes veiled her eyes. The only colour in her round babyish face was the pale rose of her lips, like the staining on a mask.

'Your Majesty,' the Captain stood at the salute before the Queen, 'the tide is on the turn...' And time for Catherine to go ashore.

From the quayside she watched the ship that was carrying Minette back to France cut through the blue sun-dazzled water. Charles and James were to go with her part of the way and return in the royal barge.

The sound of music aboard drifted to her above the screech of gulls and the soft suction of the sea on the pebbled beach below. She watched the spreading canvas and the silvery wash of the waves trailing the stern of the great ship as she leaned to the wind. Her eyes strained for a last glimpse of her until she and the white winged fleet were no more than a memory between the sea and sky.

PART THREE

The ruling Passion, be it what it will,
The ruling Passion conquers Reason still.
Alexander Pope

EIGHT

Mrs. Wilson, in a state of suppressed excitement, hovered about the tea-table with one eye on the clock, the other on a dish of cakes ordered from Her Grace's chef for this occasion; the first entertainment offered by Mrs. Wilson to her dear friend, Mrs. Sarah, since the bestowal of her lady's duchy.

Duchess of Cleveland! And with the endowment of a ducal coronet upon the Castlemaine, Mrs. Wilson basked in a glitter of reflected glory. For, in token of long and confidential service, Mrs. Wilson had also been elevated. Not now was she in menial attendance at her lady's beck, but had been appointed Woman of the Bedchamber to Her Grace, the Duchess, nor did His Majesty's beneficence stop at what was tantamount to semi-royal rank. Her Grace's natural sons had also been endowed, and only Mrs. Wilson, well paid to keep her mouth shut, could prove who, if not the King, were the respective fathers of these latest additions to the peerage: the Earls of Southampton and Euston, with the promise of dukedoms for each, should their mother, Her Grace, retire *grace*fully. Mrs. Wilson chuckled at the woeful pun. And why should she not retire gracefully on her hard-won earnings? The palace of Nonsuch, and the parishes of Malden and Cheam in Surrey, with a more-than-ample income to sustain them? *But everything,* decided Mrs. Wilson, *comes to them that wait and she and I have been long enough a-waiting, surely.*

She gave a final touch to the silver dishes and the tea urn cast from Her Grace, who now must only eat off solid gold; a rearrangement of the roses in their bowls; a satisfied survey of her person in the circular wall mirror brought from Holland by the Princess of Orange, the King's late sister Mary, as a gift to him, appropriated by the Lady and handed to Mrs. Wilson along with other perquisites: the price of her silence to do with certain of her visitors.

Revealed in the Dutch mirror, full length but diminished to a midget's size, Mrs. Wilson saw herself elegant in a gown of mourning purple, another presentation from her mistress, since the Court was once again in mourning for His Majesty's bereavement.

A tap at the door heralded the entrance of Mrs. Sarah.

'Mrs. Wilson!'

The ladies effusively embraced. Mrs. Sarah was not in mourning. Still in comparatively humble employment as housekeeper to Lord and Lady Sandwich, who were *not* semi-royal, she was not required outwardly to mourn.

'Well, now, Mrs. Sarah,' the least suspicion of patronage accompanied the request, 'pray be seated.'

Mrs. Sarah sat. She had stoutened, Mrs. Wilson was gratified to note. 'Milk and sugar?' graciously was offered.

'No milk, but sugar, I thank you. I have,' said Mrs. Sarah, 'what is called a sweet tooth.'

'Which is very evident,' smiled Mrs. Wilson.

'Evident, madam?' innocently echoed Mrs. Sarah.

Heaping sugar in the cup, Mrs. Wilson passed it, saying, 'Your figure, madam, indicates that you have put on weight.'

'And thankful for it, madam. Better be well covered at our ages, Mrs. Wilson, than a broomstick, as some I could name. Is that marchpane? May I help myself?'

Mrs. Sarah helped herself, and while Mrs. Wilson sought for a suitably crushing retort to that oblique allusion to her angularity, Mrs. Sarah removed from a tooth an adhesive morsel, and with a sigh that creaked her corsets, said, 'My Lord and Lady Sandwich are broken-hearted. 'Twas he who conducted the fleet that brought the Duchesse d'Orléans to Dover. Oh, the tragedy of it! The sorrow! So sudden. They say —' Mrs. Sarah allowed a moment's interval for this to sink in — 'they say 'twas not a natural death.'

It sank. Forgetful of her grandeur, Mrs. Wilson swallowed tea too hastily and fell into a choke.

'Count ten and hold your breath,' Mrs. Sarah advised with satisfaction. Here was something this high-and-mighty Wilson and her Duchess *didn't* know! 'Then you haven't heard all the talk about the Court? But of course, your lady, no longer of the bedchamber and paid off —'

'Paid off!' croaked Mrs. Wilson, between splutters — 'paid off! How — ouch — dare you — paid — ouch!'

'I beg you, ma'am,' complacently continued Mrs. Sarah, 'to keep this confidential, although 'tis common knowledge to the Court, but as your lady, living so retired, hasn't heard of it, 'twere best it doesn't come from me that Madame, the King's beloved sister, died of — poison!'

'Who,' wiping her streaming eyes, Mrs. Wilson recovered breath enough to ask, 'who would poison the K-K-King's sister? I wonder you repeat such infamous talk — gleaned from your familiar, Mr. Pepys, no doubt.'

'Mr. Pepys, ma'am,' said Mrs. Sarah mildly, 'is not my informant.'

'But who,' repeated Mrs. Wilson, enormously intrigued, 'would wish to poison that excellent princess?'

'Her husband, so they say,' came alarmingly the answer. 'Monsieur, as they call him — over there.' Mrs. Sarah gave a sniff for 'over there'. 'Him being jealous of his favourite gentleman, who had been paying court to Madame, as I've heard from Lady Sandwich. Not being partial to the ladies, so they say, he seeks vengeance by poisoning his wife for his fancy gentleman's infidelity.'

'Gracious goodness!' ejaculated Mrs. Wilson. 'What do you — insinuate?'

'That the Court of France,' Mrs. Sarah turned up her eyes till the irises almost disappeared beneath their lids, 'is a Sodom and Gomorrah, with the emphasis on Sodom, as they say.'

'You are too easy with your "say",' gave out Mrs. Wilson, still a trifle short of breath. 'This is slander, Mrs. Sarah.'

'If so then the King himself is guilty of it, for 'tis His Majesty who first spread the tale, so they s— um. May I beg,' asked Mrs. Sarah, winningly, 'another cup of your delicious tay?'

The news of Minette's sudden death, so soon after her visit to England, had been brought to Charles by Sir Thomas Armstrong, a young attaché at the British Embassy in Paris.

In the first flood of his grief, Charles, stunned with the shock of it, could hardly bring himself to listen to the tale of the tragedy jerked out by Armstrong. But later, when more controlled, he heard that Minette had been ailing for some days before the end. She had complained of a pain in her side, although not until 28 June — 'which would be about two weeks after she came to St. Cloud, Sir, was Madame seized with the — fatal attack.'

'Well?' uttered Charles, as Armstrong paused.

'She dined with Monsieur that night, Sir, and then asked for a glass of iced chicory water. She said she was thirsty. She drank some of it and was at once taken with violent pains. She cried out that she was poisoned. Her ladies got her to bed and —'

So motionless the figure stood, one might have thought it had ceased to breathe.

Shifting his eyes from that rigid figure, Sir Thomas, in a sweat, uncomfortably pursued: 'When Madame insisted she was poisoned — although the doctors said it was colic — Monsieur ordered what was left of the chicory water in the glass from which Madame had drunk should be given to his dog — his favourite dog.'

'So?'

'The dog lapped it, Your Majesty, and suffered no ill effects, which —' *And why,* young Armstrong asked his inner man, *should I be sent to tell him this?* — 'which should go to prove that Monsieur is not — I mean — is unlikely to have given his dog poison if he had — if he knew the water her Royal Highness drank had been —'

'Why not?' came the snarled interruption from those grey lips. 'Monsieur is no man, he's an ape with all an ape's mischievous cunning. Go on.'

Armstrong went on: he made it brief in order to spare the King the agonies of those hours while she lay on her bed of death, racked with torment yet conscious to the end.

'Madame knew she was dying,' Charles heard, 'and she asked for a priest. She received Extreme Unction and —' young Armstrong's voice faltered — 'her last words and thoughts were for Your Majesty. You will find her message in this letter from the Ambassador, who was with her at the — last. His Excellency also bade me give you this ring, a gift from Madame.'

A hand, dark veined and hairy, took the letter and the ring. He did not look at it nor at Armstrong, nervously bowing and backing. His eyes stared straight before him to see a small, white shrouded form … and cold; she who had been his life's warmth.

In the quiet of his closet Charles read:

When Madame fell ill she called for me ... As soon as I came in she told me 'I am going to die. How I pity the King my Brother. For I am sure he loses the Person he loves best in the world that loves him best.' ... She then asked if I remembered what she had said to me of Your Majesty's intention to join with France against Holland. I told her Yes. 'Pray, then,' said she, 'tell my Brother I never persuaded him out of my own interest but because I thought it for his honour and advantage. For I have always loved him above all things in the world, and have no regret to leave it, but because I leave him.'... I asked her then if she believed herself poisoned. Her Confessor that was by told her, 'Madam, you must accuse nobody, but offer up your death to God as a sacrifice.' So she would never answer that question though I asked her several times but would only shrink up her shoulders ... She recommended you to help as much as you could all her poor servants...

Of all her poor servants only one was remembered, and she, for consolation in his sorrow and who had been the favourite of his beloved Minette, was brought to him as her memento: the little maid from Brittany, Louise.

Although Catherine had known Minette so short a time she had come to love her and deeply felt her loss. She was thankful that King Louis had allowed Louise to leave his Court for hers, to be appointed maid of honour. This shy demure young person soon became her favourite, as had the Stuart before her; perhaps because, like Frances, she resisted the pursuit of Charles, who from the first had been attracted to the pretty little Breton.

When, on her arrival, she was presented to him by Catherine, and Charles saw again the girl who had been so closely connected with Minette, he wept. Catherine wept; Louise wept; and the sycophantic ladies round them wept.

'Very touching,' sneered the Duke of Buckingham, who had been sent to bring her over in the royal yacht and kept her waiting ten days at Dieppe. Ousted from the chamber of the Lady, now the Duchess, in favour of sundry other recipients of her bounty — including two latest acquisitions, the young dramatist, Wycherley, and 'that scrubby schoolboy, Churchill,' as Buckingham named the future hero of Blenheim, whom he had surprised in the Lady's bed and flung him, naked, out of it — Buckingham was delighted to see the King's attention turned upon the fair Louise.

Yet his interest in her was not entirely due to her baby-faced charm. Since Charles now had no intimate link between himself and France, Louise, his sister's protégée, might well supply the deficit.

At Versailles, Louis, cold-eyed, calculating, was of the same opinion, but from no sentimental motive. He thought to use Louise to ensnare and bind Charles by those silken fetters, loosened since the death of Minette, and so make of England's king his dupe.

But reports from his Ambassador Colbert de Croissy, successor to de Courtin, proved disappointing. De Kerouaille was coyly unresponsive to the favour of Charles. Unlike Frances, she permitted no familiarities, no fumbling in corners, not a kiss. She shrank from his advances beneath the Queen's protective wing. Catherine believed her the epitome of virtue, untouched, untouchable, and exceedingly devout. She was often to be seen — where Catherine might see her — telling her rosary or reading holy books. Frances, also born a Catholic, had never been so earnestly devout as was Louise.

But Catherine, poor innocent, for all her years of contact with a Court of uninhibited vice, had never learned the creed that these others had suckled at their mothers' breasts: 'I believe in one God, the Father Almighty, my Ego'. And the knowledge that her chaste and virtuous Louise had likewise imbibed from her birth this *credo,* leading her to scale ambition's highest peak with a craft surpassing all the cunning of a Castlemaine, had yet to be revealed.

The year of mourning ended, and once again Whitehall was festive with banquets, balls, and a ballet in which the Queen, the Duchesses of Richmond, Monmouth, Buckingham and all the ladies of highest rank took part: among them, specially selected by Catherine for her graceful dancing, was her maid of honour, Mademoiselle Louise.

The public, admitted for this gala occasion, were allowed to watch from the gallery above the Great Hall, where Mesdames Wilson and Sarah, with other ladies' ladies, and the gentlemen's gentlemen, had been given reserved front seats.

The Duchess of Cleveland, who, for this occasion, had emerged from her retirement, attracted much attention, being dressed *very fine* as reported by a Court diurnalist, in *a rich petticoat, half shirt, and short man's coat, a periwig and hat.*

'I wonder her ladyship should choose so uncommon and unladylikely a habit,' remarked Mrs. Sarah to a long-faced Mrs. Wilson.

'Her Grace,' corrected Mrs. Wilson, 'has but just returned from Newmarket and had no time to change. She did not wish to miss the ballet.'

An apocrypha: for, in truth Her Grace had not been to Newmarket, but to St. Bartholomew's Fair to see her stalwart Jacob perform upon his tightrope, and had come back in a state of near inebriation after entertainment in the dressing room of Mr. Hall. Nor could Mrs. Wilson persuade Her Grace to discard her 'unladylikely' habit for one more suitable.

'Indeed,' Mrs. Wilson devised, 'I was confronted with some difficulty to induce Her Grace to attend tonight, even at the pressing invitation of His Majesty, since she is at present much occupied with her removal to Cleveland House.'

The difficulty with which Mrs. Wilson had been confronted was due less to the fact of her preoccupation with the removal of Her Grace to her grand new establishment, than with her lady's further imbibation when escorted back to her apartments by Mr. Jacob Hall.

'Cleveland House,' reflected Mrs. Sarah, 'is yet another handsome recompense for discarded service to His Majesty.' And, frustrating Mrs. Wilson's hot retort — 'Discarded service, madam, of a lifelong devotion —'

'*Life*long, Mrs. Wilson? Surely her ladyship, beg pardon, Her Grace, is more than twelve years old? And I declare,' cried Mrs. Sarah, 'if the young French lady is not dancing a finale with a little blackamoor. That would be the boy to whom Mademoiselle took a fancy when, in attendance on the Queen at the Playhouse, she saw him serving oranges to the Royals in their box, and the King bought him for her as her page. His Majesty is always so generous to the Queen's ladies. They say she dotes on Mrs. Carwell, as they call her — for her tongue-twisting name. Pretty creature.'

'Pretty!' snorted Mrs. Wilson. 'I've seen prettier sheep's heads in a butcher's shop.'

While these pleasantries were exchanged above, the curtain having fallen on the ballet below, the King called for a coranto.

The dusty light of candles presented to the watchers in the gallery an empyrean vision of figures woven in a brilliant pageantry of colour, flashed with the sparkle of jewels to merge in a bewildering confusion of crimson, amber, rose and gold, the pale lavender of the French girl's gown and the white and silver of the Queen's as the King led her out; but his eyes were not for her. They strayed above her head to where de Croissy bowed before his young compatriot, inviting her to dance.

The music sighed and sang, the fiddles squeaked, and Her Grace of Cleveland, carefully rising from her seat among the serried ranks of privileged spectators, was seen, swaying dizzily, to join the throng and make a grab for young Mr. Churchill as he passed.

'John,' her voice, always resonant if just then a trifle slurred, commanded, 'dance 'ith me!'

They danced, the Duchess with so much zest that John had all to do to guide Her Grace's steps. She had lost her hat and she had lost a shoe, kicked off in her exuberance.

'Your lady,' remarked Mrs. Sarah, 'appears in highest fettle — Dear me! She tumbles down!'

And was hoisted up by Mr. Churchill, and, her shoe recovered, steered away amid loud laughter in which Her Grace was heard to laugh the loudest — 'who laughs last', muttered Buckingham to Bristol from the corner of his mouth. The love of both for their fair lady, who since her decline could no longer profit them, had turned to hate.

'Madam, may I have the honour?'

James, in full fig of crimson velvet, elaborately laced, was ceremoniously bowing before Catherine; but she, with a shake of her head, told him, 'No, James, if you will excuse me. I dance no more tonight. I am tired for I have danced so much in the ballet. Please, I would like to visit Anne. She must be lonely lying ill in bed and unable to be with us here. How is she?'

His solemn face lengthened. 'The doctors say there is little improvement. I will take you to her. I know she will be happy to see you.'

'No, please, you have your duties — to dance with my ladies.' Her eyes wandered to Charles, who had now called for the Brawl and had claimed Louise for his partner.

'But Your Majesty,' said James, politely punctilious 'must allow me to escort you.'

They left together, followed by two of their pages. Anne's apartments were some distance from the Great Hall, and their footsteps echoed eerily on the wide tessellated pavement of the corridor, empty save for the sentries on guard. The walls were hung with some of the King's pictures, precedence given to the portrait of Charles I and his Queen with their two eldest sons: Charles in petticoats at his father's knee, and James in his mother's arms.

Catherine paused to look up at it. 'You were such a pretty baby, James, but Charles — he was never pretty. His nose was always too big.'

'A sign of intelligence,' said James.

'Then I must be very stupid for I have a so little nose.'

'A lovely nose,' James turned his eyes upon her with a sudden heat in them as the thought crossed his mind that, had she been his wife, he would not have sought satisfaction elsewhere — at least not in such variety as did his brother Charles. And with a twist of his conscience for his own infidelities, James could not help contrasting Catherine's beautiful long-lashed eyes and her still-childish figure with those of his colourless, short-sighted Anne — she had lately taken to spectacles, poor soul — bereft now of any pretensions to charm, and no chance, the doctors had told him, should she live, of giving him another child, the son for whom he had always longed.

'Brother,' with a look behind at the following pages, Catherine lowered her voice, 'I know you are in the secret, are you not — about the treaty?' And at his assenting nod, 'but Charles,' she said, 'has not yet declared —' and to the pages she called, 'You may go back to the ballroom and — enjoy yourselves.'

Thankfully they went, and so soon as they were out of earshot she continued, 'Charles has not yet declared his conversion. I wonder why.'

James began picking at his thumb. 'I think the time is not yet ripe for a public announcement. The anti-Catholic feeling is very strong at present, and Charles thinks it would be too great a risk to proclaim his Faith until the country is prepared to recognise a union with France and — a Catholic King.'

'Which England will *never* recognise,' murmured Catherine.

Passing his thumb across his lip, James said with a sort of glum fierceness, 'Some time or other England will be forced to recognise a sovereign who has restored to them the one and only Church.'

They had come to the entrance of Anne's suite, where a couple of pages engaged in a game of marbles sprang to attention; bowing either side the door that their heads all but collided, they flung it open.

A lady-in-waiting received them, who, at the bidding of the Duke, conducted them to his wife's bedchamber.

They found Anne lying on a couch and reading from a missal while her two young daughters romped with a spaniel puppy. As the Queen and their father came into the room they dutifully curtsied to Catherine and both rushed to the Duke to be kissed and told:

'Run away, children, you must not disturb your mother.'

'They don't disturb me.' Removing her spectacles, Anne stretched a hand to Catherine. 'How good of you to come, dear sister. I can hear the music and I wish I could have seen the ballet.'

'You have not missed very much by not seeing it.' Catherine seated herself beside the couch and, as she took Anne's hand in hers, saw with a pang how wasted it was. 'The dancing,' she continued cheerfully, 'was not very good, with exception of my Mademoiselle Louise.'

'Did *she* take part in it?'

'Yes, she is a beautiful dancer.'

'Why couldn't *we* have taken part in it?' Mary, now a self-assertive ten-year-old, demanded of her father.

'Because you are too young.' James stooped to the puppy that had come lolloping to greet him. 'This is something new. I've not seen him before.'

'You would have seen him, Papa,' said Mary, sulkily, 'if you came to see us —' with an emphasis on *us* — 'more often.'

'That is not polite,' her mother told her weakly. 'You must apologise to your dear papa for your rudeness.'

Mary's lower lip bulged. 'I didn't mean to be rude. I 'pologise, Papa.'

He patted her head. 'I accept your apology. Where did you get him?' He ran a practised eye over the puppy's points. 'I don't think much of him. Too long in the nose.'

Mary giggled. 'That's what Uncle Charles said when he gave him to us. A proper nosy Stuart, he called him.'

'He'th my puppy, not yourth.' Anne flopped down beside him to lift the sprawling bundle in her arms. 'Uncle Charleth gave him to me becauthe he gave you one from the lath' litter.' She was a squarely built, stolid child with full round cheeks that dimpled when she smiled. She was smiling up at her father now, showing gaps in her upper gums where two of her milk teeth were missing.

'Then if he's your puppy you should teach him better manners,' Mary told her with an elder sister's superiority. 'Look! He's wetted all over your dress. That's the second time today it will have to be changed.'

'He'th only a baby — he can't help it. We all do that when we're babieth,' said Anne comfortably. 'My poor little bubby boo ... pim, pim, pim...' She crooned over him with kisses.

'Darlings,' their mother called from her couch, 'you must take him outside. I can't have my room turned into a kennel. These Stuarts,' she said fondly. 'I think they all love dogs more than they love people.'

'Go along, children.' James hoisted the squatting Anne to her feet. 'Time you were both in bed.' And when these two future Queens of England had curtsied themselves out, he went over to his wife to tell her, 'And you must go to bed too, my love. I won't be late back.'

'You mustn't leave the ball before the King so don't hurry, and don't,' with an upward glance at his anxious face, 'worry about me. I am much better, truly.' Anne took his hand and examined his thumb. 'I see you *have* been worrying. I'll put a sticking plaster on these thumbs tomorrow or you'll have no skin left on them.'

In this last year Anne had been converted to the Church of Rome, 'for which I thank God,' she said, when her husband had gone. 'It is as if James, who urged me to it, must have known that I am going to die.'

'No, my dear, no,' Catherine soothed her. 'You will soon be well again.'

'Soon, yes ... well again, where there is no pain, no cuppings, no bleedings, no purges — these doctors! What do you think?' Anne raised herself on an elbow; her voice, for all its weakness, held a chuckle. 'They gave me a disgusting mixture said to cure the falling sickness, which is what they tell me is my malady. Dr. Pierce wrote out the prescription — it was in English, not Latin — and left it lying on the table here. So I read it and, believe me or believe me not, it contained, among other things, the blood of a he-goat, the urine of a stag and the liver of a hedgehog, all beaten into a pulp and administered in wine, as prescribed by the College of Apothecaries! When the King came to visit me he saw it and called it an old witch's brew and laughed like anything, and said "I'll tell you what to do with it — which is not to swallow it!" And he brought me a phial of physic distilled by himself in his laboratory. Charles knows more of medicine that any of these doctors. But — the urine of a stag! How do they think they'll get it — by holding a pail under him to catch the piss?' She achieved a little crow of laughter, and Catherine laughed with her with a brightness, not of laughter, in her eyes.

'James said,' the feeble voice went on, 'that you make a round of visits in the next few weeks. Do you take the French girl with you?'

'Yes, all my maids of honour,' Catherine told her, 'will come with me.'

Anne leaned back against her cushions and gazed up at the painted ceiling where satyrs chased and tumbled naked nymphs. 'Is it true that the King has given her a suite of apartments in the palace?'

'Quite true. Charles and I,' Catherine flexed her fingers, looking down at them, 'we both agreed that Louise should be given precedence above my other maids, out of respect to

Minette.' And on a faint note of defiance she added, 'I am devoted to Louise and she to me.'

Still with her eyes on the ceiling, Anne murmured, 'My father always says that none is deceived save those who trust.'

'Your father,' replied Catherine with a smile, 'is a lawyer, and *my* father used to say that lawyers trust none but themselves. And now, my dear, we have talked long enough. I must not tire you. Your women wait to put you to bed.'

'Come soon again,' Anne whispered. 'And remember what I've said … when I'm not here.'

She died in the spring of the year, and Catherine, who, with James, was beside her to the end, had reason in the coming months to remember what she had said.

NINE

The visit of the King and Queen to country houses had been postponed until the autumn when, for the third time in as many years, the Court was again in mourning, for the Duchess of York. But although there were no outward festivities there were plenty of mild amusements: hunting, hawking, coursing, and various other diversions, which, however, did not interfere with the political activities of Charles. He knew that the Treaty of Dover, and in particular, the clause relating to his apostasy, would, if the secret leaked out, be disastrous to him and to the realm. It was therefore imperative that it be kept dark.

In the preceding year he had formed a Committee of Foreign Affairs consisting of Sir Thomas Clifford, Ashley Cooper, Buckingham — for whom Charles had always retained a sneaking fondness for the sake of their early friendship in the days of his exile — Arlington, and, the last but not the least of them, Lauderdale, a Presbyterian Scot.

This, the famous 'Cabal', so-called for the first letters of their names, was entrusted with and witnessed his signature to a second treaty, in all respects a facsimile of the first, but that the hundred and fifty thousand pounds promised by Louis as the price of the conversion of England's King was now described as part of the war subsidy.

Only to Clifford and Arlington, both Catholics, did Charles divulge the truth. He had staked his all on a gambler's throw, committed in an alliance with Louis by which he was pledged to destroy the Dutch States and share with France the spoils.

Meanwhile Louis craftily wove the web into which he would entangle Charles by means of his infatuation for the young Breton woman. As mistress of and in closest intimacy with his cousin of England, she would prove to be a useful, and well rewarded, *agent provocateur*.

Yet still reports from de Croissy gave no indication that the chaste Louise was prepared to surrender her guarded citadel. She accepted the King's gifts, the luxurious lodgings he had furnished for her in Whitehall, and the payment of her card debts — she was an avid and very bad card player, and invariably lost — and he gave her costly jewels, for she had come from France with scarcely an adornment and only three presentable gowns. So a dozen new gowns were also humbly accepted ... and nothing more.

But by this time the patience of France was exhausted. She had repulsed the English King's advances longer than Louis had bargained for.

The Court was visiting at Audley End, the seat of Lord and Lady Suffolk, when de Croissy, acting on instructions from Versailles, approached the bashful Louise with an ultimatum. Unless she fulfilled the mission for which, as a loyal subject of His Most Catholic Majesty, she had been brought to England, she would be sent back to France and to a convent, where she would remain for the rest of her life. The choice was hers: acceptance of the English King's good graces, or the veil. She must choose.

She chose, but begged his Excellency to believe it was against her principles and her Faith to enter into an adulterous relationship with any man, be he King or commoner. She could not and she would not, she tearfully told him, be committed to a mortal sin.

Within himself de Croissy grinned. As ever, the Sun King's unerring perception had not been at fault in selecting this chaste Lucrezia as his decoy.

So this was *her* ultimatum. Marriage! He might have known that her chastity belt was waiting only to be unlocked, or if when divorce, by Papal dispensation, could be obtained ... Why not? Better a French wife for England than a French mistress, but failing that, and to satisfy the scruples of these innocents *(mon Dieu, innocents! Comme le diable!)* why not a morganatic marriage?

De Croissy thumbed his chin, Louise lifted hers. Their eyes met: at least one of her eyes met his, the other ever so slightly wandered, for which Nell Gwynne, when she first saw her on the racecourse at Newmarket, mischievously dubbed her 'Squintabella'. Then the pale lids were lowered, and, her lips scarcely moving. 'Your Excellency,' she murmured, 'I am honourably engaged to render great honour to France and my King, but I must also guard my own honour.'

'Précisément, mademoiselle.' De Croissy, bowing to her bob, raised her hand to his lips. 'That goes without saying.' And with exaggerated homage he backed from her and, nose to knees, he bowed again. *'Madame.'*

From Audley End the royal party moved on to Euston Hall, Lord Arlington's place near Newmarket, where Charles had built himself a house in an unpretentious little street overlooking the Heath. He was there for the October meeting and spent almost every day on the racecourse, returning to Euston at night.

The staid John Evelyn, one of the house party, reported it *filled from end to end with lords, ladies and gallants, there being such a furnished table as I have seldom seen, nor anything more splendid and free.*

So free that, under the watchful eye of Colbert de Croissy, the reticent backward Louise was persuaded, at last, to come forward with the high light of the 'lords, ladies, and gallants' focused full upon her. Yet Evelyn, that meticulous scribe, writes he was *out of all this*, the crowning episode of an eventful week.

It was on a wild October night when the younger members of the company, at their most hilarious, toasted the King, who, the day before, rode in the amateurs' race at Newmarket as the winner of the Plate. After the banquet, so *splendid and free*, there were cards and dicing, but no dancing, out of respect for the bereaved Duke of York.

Evelyn, no gamester, went early to bed; and Catherine, who could enjoy a game of cards with the best of them — she was, incidentally, a very good player — had also gone to bed, having developed a headache: so she too, was 'out of all this', which, however, could scarcely have taken place in her presence.

And what, may we ask, was 'all this', excitedly buzzed about the Court next day? No less than a mock marriage, with the King and Mademoiselle as bride and groom, the ceremony performed by one of the gentlemen correctly attired in a cassock.

But, declares the shocked Mr. Evelyn, *I neither saw nor heard any such thing.* Though he admits, *'Twas universally reported that the fair Lady* Whore *was bedded one of these nights and the stocking flung,* as was the custom in the case of a just-married bride. *I acknowledge,* he shudders, *she was for the most part in her undress all day, and there was a fondness and a toying with the young wanton.* Presumably on the day following this interesting event, which same familiarity, Evelyn records: *I was myself observing with curiosity enough,* loitering in corridors, his eyes on stalks, and his pen at the ready to note, *'Twas with confidence believed she was first made a* Miss, *as they call these unhappy creatures, at this time.*

That these 'unhappy creatures' should be called 'Miss' at any time would seem to be a slight misnomer; nor was 'Miss' Louise in the least unhappy. She had salved her conscience, though not in Church, and was married! To the delight of de Croissy and the approval of His Most Catholic Majesty. Through his Ambassador he presented congratulations on her conquest. He had secured for Charles a *maîtresse-en-titre,* binding England to France with the silken girdle of Mademoiselle, now 'Madame', de Kerouaille.

Louis expressed himself well satisfied, as so indeed did Charles.

'The chrysalis emerges!' cackled Buckingham, when he hurried from Euston to London to retail the triumph of the new *maîtresse-en-titre* to the Duchess of Cleveland. She took it with unwonted calm. She had reaped a rich harvest to fill her coffers and to gain for her sons, irrespective of their claim to royal parentage, a dukedom for Charles Fitzroy, Earl of Southampton; for Henry Fitzroy, Earl of Euston, the dukedom of Grafton; and for George Fitzroy, her youngest son, the earldom of Northumberland. Her two daughters, the Ladies Anne and Charlotte Fitzroy, although of equally doubtful fathers acknowledged, by Charles as his, were married, the one at the age of ten, the other at thirteen, to the Earls of Sussex and Lichfield. She could well afford to abdicate with an income of something in the region of fifty thousand a year, to say nothing of the bonuses supplied for past services and present honours.

As for her usurper, the inconsiderable Louise, disregarded, overlooked, so modest, so shy, she had in truth emerged from a chrysalis to flash in one night and a day upon a dazzled world, greedily to taste and gather in the fruits of her surrender. Men adored her, women loathed her, and the King was at her feet. Her power over him far exceeded that of any other he had taken to himself.

When the Court returned to Whitehall it was evident to Louis, watchfully alert for the result of his threats, that his choice of this young person to serve his purpose was indeed a *coup de grâce*.

Her provocative charm and gentle submission to her inflammable lover's demands masked a subtle artifice and a keen diplomatic intelligence that induced Louis, ensconced in his glittering web at Versailles, to seize this golden opportunity to strike. But first he must force his vacillating English cousin to fulfil his obligations, which he was now prepared to do, with one exception.

Although held in thrall by the spell of Louise, not even when within three months of her 'marriage' she announced to Charles the joyful news that she was pregnant, could he bring himself to make a public declaration of his Faith. With France on the brink of war against Holland, and he committed to Louis in alliance by Minette's fatal 'treaty'; with a wave of anti-Catholicism flooding the country, and every man spoiling to fight for and die for him, he dared not disunite the nation by an eruptive convulsion between Rome and the Established Church of which he was the Head.

Yet none of his subjects, his citizens, the rich, the poor, tradesmen, merchants, the girls and the boys, who adoringly dogged him as he strolled through his parks, or chatted with Nell where she sat perched on the garden wall of her house in Pall Mall, impudently quizzing him concerning 'Squintabella', could guess he walked a rope as tight and dangerous as that of any acrobatic Jacob Hall.

The first of May, and the milkmaids were making merry round the maypole in the Strand. This was their own festival when bedizened with ribbons and garlands of hawthorn, their pails slung across their shoulders, filled, not with milk, but with fruit and flowers, they danced, sang, and frolicked, accompanied by pipers, fiddlers and Jacks-in-the-Green. From the village of Charing Cross to Cheapside and back again they danced till sundown, holding up the traffic, and followed by a mob of townsfolk come to watch and join in the fun of May Day.

Catherine, who, with Frances in attendance, had gone to the Exchange that morning to buy a gift for the birthday of Donna Maria, was caught up in the midst of it and her coach halted while from behind her curtained window she, too, could watch the fun. There were others whose carriages and coaches were held up. The first of these, far more splendid than that of the Queen, was a gilded chariot drawn by six white horses, with postilions and footmen in liveries of canary plush, braided with gold. At sight of this magnificence, those foremost in the crowd fell back, and their laughter faded into menacing undertones like the mutter of thunder, capped, after a moment's pause, by jeers and catcalls from the lads of the town.

Battle-scarred old Cavaliers and Roundheads, many of them crippled, armless, wooden-legged, all differences forgotten now, joined their husky voices to the yells of: 'See! Here comes the King's Papist whore!' when the coach of 'Madam Carwell', as they called her for her unpronounceable name, forced its way through the mob, the postilions striking right and left with their whips at those who pressed too near.

Screened by her window curtain, Catherine went unrecognised, for she wore a velvet mask as did all women of rank when they shopped in the Exchange, and the crowds were too great to have noticed the royal coat of arms on the panels of her coach, so she heard none of this; nor did she hear the lady's reply to it when, in blazing indignation, she showed her face at the window of her coach to shout, 'Me no bad woman! If me bad woman — me! I cut my throat!'

'*Me!*' they mimicked, '*mee*-hee-hee! Yah! We'll cut it for you!' yelled the crowd. 'We'll have no French trollops here, King's whore or none!'

'No, nor a Papist Queen, neither!'

But what Catherine did see and hear was one of those new sedan chairs carried by four footmen that had halted alongside her coach. The occupant of this conveyance also came in for her share of attention, at first not friendly, from those who baited 'Madam Carwell', recently created Duchess of Portsmouth. They were only too eager to mock at and heckle any one of the King's 'chargeable ladies', as known to the sorely tried men of the Royal Exchequer. But when greeted with cries of 'Here's another of 'em!' and 'Down with all Papist whores whelped in a kennel!' she, who was their target, dodging a slab of stinking fish and a volley of rotten apples, stuck her head out to yell back at those who pressed around her: 'You've gotten me wrong, folk! I'm the *Protestant* whore — and was whelped in old Drury!'

Then at sight of that impudent laughing face framed in its crop of red curls, a mighty shout went up to hit the sky: 'Nell! 'Tis our Nell! Nelly Gwynne, God bless her!'

'Ay,' came her answer in shrill Cockney. 'And may God damn you for falsifying me. I ain't no Squintabella! And here's somethin' to prove it!'

With which she flung a handful of gold and silver coins among the rabble, who, amid more riotous yells and God-blessings, were down on all fours in the dirt to fight for and grab what they could get, which, for most of them in their scrambling greed, was nothing at all.

'Your Majesty,' Frances plucked at Catherine's sleeve, 'shall I tell them to drive on? Or we may be here for hours.'

'Yes, if he can.' Catherine was shaking with silent laughter at the scene. Seldom did she laugh these days, and since the ascendance of Louise she had quietly removed herself from Whitehall to Somerset House, which, by the death of the Queen Mother, had reverted to her. And from there it was announced that the Queen, when in London, would hold her Court; this her sole unvoiced protest against the juxtaposition in those State apartments at Whitehall of the girl whom she had loved and trusted, and by those whose treachery she had been betrayed.

But when Frances tapped on the window glass to give the order to a footman, the royal coach was recognised and, as if by lightning struck, the noise and jollity were silenced with no sign of greeting on any face. It was as if a dark threatening cloud had enwrapped them — for a moment only, until she in the sedan called out, 'Hey, folks! Where's your manners? Can't you see who comes to honour you, this May Day? Come on, then! 'Ip, 'ip, 'ip, 'uzza f'r Majesty, the Queen!'

At once they took it up in a concerted shout of 'The Queen! God bless her!'

'Show yourself, Madam,' whispered Frances. 'They want to see you.'

She pulled aside the curtain, and at sight of that small pale face which many had never seen before and none at such close quarters, another great shout went up, led by Nell: 'God save the Queen!'

Tears smarted in Catherine's eyes. She had long been aware of her unpopularity with the citizens of London, which had increased in this past year since Charles had introduced his Declaration of Indulgence, by which the penal laws against the Catholics and Nonconformists were suspended. As soon as the news of it filtered through to the man in the street, general opinion gave it that this latest toleration of Popery on the part of the King had been prompted by his Papist wife, and indicated a revival of those burnings at Smithfield. Hot arguments between Catholics and Anglicans were hurled over the ale mugs, and not only in taverns. In Parliament the anti-Catholic contingent was also forcibly opposed to a Catholic and barren Queen Consort.

Ashley Cooper, now raised to the Chancellorship with the Earldom of Shaftesbury, saw a menace to the realm and constitution in the King's partiality to the Old Faith, even though he was not in the secret of that final clause enforced by Louis and urged by Minette. If Catherine but knew it, Shaftesbury was her bitterest enemy, as she later would learn — to her undoing. So this unexpected and sudden acclamation was a grateful heart-warming surprise.

She leaned forward to wave smiling acknowledgement to it; and to Nell, blowing boisterous kisses at her, the Queen's hand in its gauntleted glove was raised again, in a gesture that seemed to linger. Then the coachman cracked his whip, the horses plunged forward and the incident was closed, but by Catherine not forgotten. She would for ever hold and cherish in her memory that glimpse of this girl of the people whom she knew to be their idol; and, of all her husband's women, the least acquisitive, the only one who asked of him no more than love.

To avoid another hold-up, the coachman drove back to Somerset House by devious ways. Passing Belle Sauvage Yard, Frances drew Catherine's attention to 'that young man there with the tray of flowers and things. Don't you remember, Madam? It was Mr. Evelyn who presented him to Your Majesty, just before we went to Audley End last year?'

Yes, Catherine did remember; a little rueful smile curled her lip. 'And Mr. Evelyn, he has never forgiven me because I didn't buy his work — I mean this boy's work — so beautiful, only I couldn't afford it, but — wait! Stop the coach and call a footman.'

The horses pulled up and a footman came down to take an order.

'Tell the young man selling flowers — are they real? Ask him, and have him bring them to me at Somerset House today.'

In that same miserable hovel at Deptford, where Father Patrick had been called to a boy, sick of the plague, Evelyn had discovered this young artist at work on a copy in wood of Tintoretto's *Stoning of St. Stephen*. So impressed was he by the lad's remarkable gift that he brought him and his carvings to the King, *who*, says Evelyn, *was astonished at the curiositie of it, and having considered it a long time he commanded it be immediately carried to the Queen*. Obviously Charles had not the ready cash to pay the price demanded by Evelyn for this colossal work, having been drained dry by his *Ladies of Pleasure, the curse of our nation*, groans Evelyn. And so young Gibbons was passed on to Catherine. She, poor girl, had even less than Charles to spend on any personal indulgence — her dowry, after all these years, was still in arrears — and although delighted with the boy's wonderful carving, she didn't buy it, which much offended Mr. Evelyn, who, he tells us, 'finding this incomparable artist had his labour only for his pains', and 'in a kind of indignation' took Grinling Gibbons and his carvings back to Deptford.

But this chance encounter with a young man selling flowers — 'are they real?' — outside Bell Sauvage Yard on that May Day, three hundred years ago, is, though unrecorded, how Nell Gwynne received the anonymous gift of a single rose, carved in cream-tinted satinwood, so delicate and frail in its airy lightness that the petals seemed to breathe. The message inscribed on the note that came with it in an unknown hand, bore no address and only the words: *From a friend.*

'For the young, Time is a tortoise,' said Donna Maria, 'and for the old, Time is a hare.'

Suffering from no ailment worse than old age and inclined to be light-headed, she believed herself to be at death's door although the Queen's physician, Dr. Wakeman, declared her to be in excellent health for her years. They had brought her couch out to the terrace overlooking the gardens of Somerset House, for the autumn day was unusually warm. 'You cannot,' she said, 'hold Time on a leash like a dog. He will run away with us, for all your doctor's physics that they think will pull him back.'

Her dimmed old eyes gazed out across the lawns that sloped to the river bank where the young daughters of the Duke of York played at battledore and shuttlecock. They were staying at Somerset House pending the arrival from Italy of the late Duke of Modena's daughter as bride to the widowed James.

'The Infantas,' Donna Maria complained, 'are very noisy. The English and their children have no manners.'

'If they disturb you,' Catherine told her, 'I will have them play elsewhere.'

'No, let them play while they can. They will be halt, lame, half blind and dead soon enough — as I am. There's a summer's day it is for October. The grapes are ripe in the vineyards now and so quiet except for the Infantas and the cannon. Always one hears the cannon and always in England it is war and war again; as it is written, nation will rise against nation and the horned beast shall bestride the world.' The Countess sucked her tongue and said, 'I'm thirsty.'

Catherine took a flagon of citron water from a table by the couch, filled a cup and held it to the old lady's lips.

'Not,' she squawked, 'this poison of the doctor's. Mine — I will have my own mouse physic obtained from a flayed mouse dried and beaten to a powder taken three times a day brewed with a simple of valerian, parsley and carrots. Thank you.'

'This,' Catherine told her patiently, 'is not physic. It is lemon water. Drink it up, and try not to talk so much. You tire yourself.'

'Pardon, Madame.' The Countess inclined an ear. She was now not only half blind but deaf, to which she would never admit. 'You said?'

'That you must drink this delicious citron water and — not — to *talk*. You *tire* yourself.'

'Please not to shout. Everybody shouts,' complained Donna Maria, whose attitude toward Catherine had, in these her later years, reverted to the days when her Infanta was in the nursery, and she her governess. 'Your Highness must modulate your voice.' She sipped the proffered cup, made a face and spat what she had taken. 'It is sour. Give me wine.'

Wine was brought by a page, which she drank at a draught. The Countess smacked her lips. Her teeth had fallen out and her mouth had fallen in, and although the sun was hot she had her face swathed in a shawl and her shoulders in a tippet. Her hands, their knuckles rheumatically knotted, went groping. Catherine took and held them.

'What is it, dear?'

'Those guns. They are in the river — the Dutch ships. If they land we shall be invaded. The women have orders to pack our baggage and we will board the next vessel for Lisbon. I must take my Infanta away from this abominable island in the middle of the sea inhabited by barbarians and Jezebels.' She made as if to get up from the couch. 'Come, child, we must go. I will not stay here to see you and myself violated by Hollanders and drunken English soldiers. So! We go!'

'Madame, no!' Catherine composed her face. 'You cannot hear any guns. The fighting is almost over in this second war — I said *second* war — with Holland. They are already arranging a peace settlement.'

'Yes. Jezebels,' stonily agreed the Countess. 'The King, your Highness's brother, shall be told of this city of Babylon where you have been imprisoned this many a long year.' She began to scratch, lifting her petticoats to fumble at her parts. 'I have the itch.'

'Madam!' The two princesses came running to halt beneath the terrace. Anne held something wrapped in a handkerchief. 'Look, we've found a hedgehog. May we show it to you, Madam?'

'Yes, but —' Catherine glanced aside at Donna Maria whose head was nodding and whose bleared old eyes had closed — 'come quietly.'

They tiptoed up the steps to the terrace, where the hedgehog, having rolled itself into a ball, was deposited by Anne, who at once let out a squeal. 'Ooh! My finger — it's pricked me!'

'I told you it would if you picked it up,' said Mary.

'I didn't feel its prickles through the handkerchief — and now I'll be poisoned — ooh — ooh!' Anne was jumping about, wringing a finger.

'Such a fuss!' scoffed Mary, a handsome dark-haired child. 'I told you not to touch it.'

'Don't keep on at me!' blubbered Anne. 'You're always such a know-all — telling me this, telling me that. It was you saw it first, anyway. I'd never have seen it if you hadn't said —'

'Let me examine this fuss.' Catherine stretched out her hand. 'Yes, there is a *tiny* little speck of blood.' And to the hovering page, 'Bring a bowl of warm water, and a saucer of milk for the hedgehog.'

'Milk!' squealed Anne. 'Will it drink milk?'

Catherine smiled. 'When I was at convent school we had a family of hedgehogs in the garden and the nuns used to leave dishes of bread and milk for them. They would come every day to eat and drink it. They are friendly little creatures and very good in a garden. They eat the slugs.'

''Tis not very friendly of it to prick me,' said Anne, 'and draw blood.'

And Donna Maria, sitting up with a jerk, croaked in guttural English, 'Blood! Who say blood? It is the Dutch who come to kill us! I knew it — me! Now we go, and we tak' the two Infantas wit' us. We leave them not here to be rapit!'

'Whatever,' tittered Mary, 'does she think we said?' And coming closer she shouted in the old lady's ear, 'There's no Dutch here, Donna Maria. 'Tis only a hedgehog.'

'A — what is it she say?' appealed the Countess. And when Catherine translated into Portuguese: 'Ah, so! Then tek' it away. That t'ing, it bring bad luck.'

'Bad luck!' Mary touched the prickly ball with her toe. 'As if we hadn't enough bad luck already with a stepmother coming to marry Papa. I know we shall hate her and she's sure to hate us.'

'You mustn't say that before you have even seen her. That is naughty of you, Mary. If you love her she will love you.' Catherine took the bowl of water from the page, and busied herself with Anne. 'No, child, it cannot possibly poison you — it is no more than a pinprick. Now! I bind it with my handkerchief so you keep it clean.'

'But Madam,' persisted Mary, 'suppose your Mama had died and your Papa had married again, would you have liked a stepmother of almost your own age to order you about? She's only four years older than me.' And not waiting for a reply to that, 'I think,' grumbled Mary, 'that it is rather dreadful of Papa to choose so young a wife for himself as stepmother to us.'

'You have no right to criticise your father, Mary.' Although secretly Catherine could not but agree with her. 'Now go indoors, both of you. It is time for your dinners, and Donna Maria's woman waits to take her to her room.'

When the children had gone and Donna Maria had been hoisted from her couch and led away, Catherine was left to enjoy the quiet of that golden afternoon. It had been a wet summer and the trees had scarcely lost the spinach green of August. Bees hummed in the herbaceous borders; the scent of a late bloom of roses was borne to her on the breathless air. Beyond the sweep of lawn, hedged about with box and privet, the river shone like a giant's brazen shield in the honey-thick light of the October sun. Slow-moving barges, wherries, and wide-sailed merchantmen had a phantasmal unreality seen through that gilded haze.

How still it was, how silent. Even the voices of her women strolling among the trees came to her thinly: elfin voices. The pastel colours of their gowns, submerged in the green distance, lent a pellucid impermanence to a scene that might have delighted a Watteau, yet to be born.

Her thoughts went straying in a labyrinth of disconnected fragments, gradually solidified into one consecutive design in which she saw herself a remote, impersonal spectator. Impersonal? Yes, strangely that. For in these solitary years when she had plumbed the depths of loneliness, she had learned to renounce her dependence on him to whom her whole life's love was rendered. Here in this tranquil Dower House, removed from the agonies of her humiliation, she had been soothed into a state, if not of hopefulness, of contentment. She had suffered, as God alone could know, to see honour after honour heaped upon the young woman she had befriended and loved.

She recalled Anne's warning ... dear Anne, who had faced a lingering death with such patient fortitude: 'None is deceived save those who trust.' But how could one live without trust for one's fellow creatures? Nothing had prepared her for Louise's treachery, the more bitter in that she blamed herself for it, as for the failure of her marriage. In those early days Charles had been hers, as he told her, 'entirely'. Then how did she come to lose him? Was it because of those childish scenes when she, so shamingly, had raged at him with threats and accusations? Had she been more restrained, the 'complaisant' wife — a little laugh, unmirthful, escaped her — as so many men are 'complaisant' husbands, would she have held him? Never. No woman could hold Charles in marriage, which, he had often said in jest, though she knew he half believed it, was but 'legalised concubinage'. His passions and desires were as uncontrollably instinctive as the coupling of birds. If she had borne him a child…

She moved her head impatiently. *If, if, if! Why torment yourself? You would have lost him just the same. He has a dozen children, supposed to be his, and how many more unknown?* And now Louise had given him a son.

It was after the birth of this son born to Charles nine months to the day from that 'wedding' at Euston when Catherine fell ill. The doctor attending her, Sir Alexander Fraser, one of the Court physicians, found her to be in a consumption and said she had but a year to live. This prognosis, indiscreetly circulated by Sir Alexander, gave Louise to hope for still higher elevation. Colbert de Croissy, writing to the ever-watchful Louis, who had no reason to regret his confidence in Madame la Duchesse de Portsmouth, tells him, *She has got the notion that it is possible she may yet be Queen of England. She talks from morning till night of the Queen's ailments as if they were mortal…*

Much to the disappointment of Louise they were not; but Charles, who believed his wife to be dying, was distraught and, as ever, conscience-stricken. She could not help teasing him.

'Why should you grieve? You should rejoice to be free that you may remarry and get you a lawful heir. I have had all I ask of life and am happy to be leaving it, though I regret to leave you.'

'No! You must never leave me, never!' It was a repetition of that scene when she was really dying after her second miscarriage. 'I can't,' he sobbed, 'live without you!'

'You have managed very well to live without me this past year,' said she, with a private little smile. Then she saw his eyes that clung to hers with a kind of dumb pleading, and her heart turned over. There was so much, endearingly, in him of the schoolboy expectant of the thrashing he deserved. Impossible to reconcile this complex personality, the man of affairs, dedicated ruler of a turbulent people, with the amorous dilettante who put pleasure before purpose, the vacillating slave of his ministers, first to declare independence for the

Catholics, then to withdraw his Declaration and their promised rights in it; he, in whom his subjects saw only their indolent, good-natured King exercising his dogs or off to the hunt in Windsor or Epping Forests; or chaffing Nell over her garden wall, and squandering the nation's money on his French Madam who looked to see the Crown on her head, and likely would if his Papist wife lost hers! So ran the talk of him, that Catherine, although isolated in her Dower House, had gleaned from certain sources, not the least of them the ever adoring faithful Frances, Duchess of Richmond.

From a group of women clustered beneath the trees, she saw Frances detach herself and come running. She was in black for the death of her husband; he, the year before, had been appointed Ambassador in Denmark, for Charles had long since forgiven him his abduction of *la belle Stuart*. And at Copenhagen, where he contracted a fever, he died, not greatly to the sorrow of his wife, who found leisure to repent her hasty marriage.

'It grows chilly, Madam.' Panting with her hurry, Frances, now chief Lady-in-Waiting, had been given her own apartments at Somerset House and was, of all Catherine's women, the only one upon whose loyalty she could rely even though her unceasing solicitous attention was sometimes a little too much. 'You mustn't take cold, Madam. You know what the doctor said.'

'That I'd be dead within a year and except for occasional headaches have never been better in my life. Very well, we will go in.'

Later, when she and her ladies had dined, and the Queen played at basset, Frances regaled those who were not in the card room with a rigmarole concerning Louise and a highwayman.

'My dears, if I tell you what one of her dressers told one of *my* dressers — you'd never believe!'

This knight of the road, known and feared as 'old Mobb' had, according to Frances, held up 'Madame Carwell', 'or Cardwell', giggled Frances, 'as the common people call her, and she *does* care well for herself and her son to badger the King for my poor Charles's dukedom.'

But what of the highwayman, they wished to know.

'Oh, well, he — now let me get it right — he told her that as a gentleman collector of the road he considered it his duty to seize any foreign commodities that came his way.'

The girls — they were all young — doubled with laughter; they hated that 'highty-tighty-nose-in-the-air, imperial whore, Louise', as they dubbed her for her over-weening arrogance and greed. 'And then,' Frances recounted with relish, 'he told her that all the jewels and money she had about her were confiscate to him as bestowed on a worthless bitch! Yes, he did — in front of her women he called her a bitch, and he said — oh, dear, I hardly like to say it — but he said he had a bawd of his own to keep on public contribution as well as the King.'

'For gracious sake!' screamed a newcomer to the Court — another Frances, Miss Jennings who, with a younger sister, Sarah, was temporarily in waiting on the Queen until the arrival at St. James's Palace of the future Duchess of York. 'You'll kill me! And pity 'tis he didn't kill *her*!'

As he might have done, according to Frances, ever a stickler for truth or at any rate that which she thought to be the truth, for he pointed his blunderbuss at the terrified Louise ready to fire it had she not allowed him to strip her of her jewels and her money in lieu of her life. This, just one instance of the general disfavour in which the Favourite was held, not only by the gentlemen of the King's highway but by the citizens of London.

It had come to the taverns from the Whitehall galleries that the 'French bawd' had got her deserts, with a dose of the pox. Her rageful accusations and threats to expose the King as the cause of it were heard all over the palace. Never could a royal row pass unheeded with an ear at every door and an eye at every window. And then there was the time when 'the Carwell' had ordered for herself, at the King's expense, a magnificent tea service of gold complete with urn and salver. The shop of the goldsmith commissioned to supply it was almost opposite the house of Nell Gwynne in Pall Mall. When displayed in the shop's window a crowd collected to gape at and unanimously to declare it were better given to 'Our Nell' than that the French whore should have it — she who gave nothing to the King except the clap!

And then a voice, loud above the rest of them, shouted, 'Better still to melt it and pour it down her throat!'

Much of this hate against the Duchess of Portsmouth was due less to personal dislike of her as the King's mistress than of her religion. The wave of anti-Catholicism that had overswept the country during the past three years had increased with the coming of yet another Papist as possible future Queen Consort: Maria Beatrice d'Este of Modena, the Duke of York's fifteen-year-old bride.

On a raw November morning his child wife arrived in London and at a time when the anti-Papist demonstrations were at their height. Effigies of the Pope were paraded through the streets, flung on to bonfires and burned, to the delight of a hooligan mob. The sickening sight of tortured cats, crucified by ardent Protestant apprentices, provided a comical fillip to an evening's amusement and all in the good of the cause as protest against evil Romish influence in highest quarters. Rumour gave it that the King had leanings toward Popery, and it was generally known that the Duke of York, an avowed Catholic, had latterly refused to attend service in the Royal Chapel and now had got himself a Papist wife!

Chancellor Lord Shaftesbury, known as 'Shiftesbury' by derisive detractors for his continuous change of sides, had early in the year brought in a Bill, to which the King had been forced to consent, for the removal from official status of all persons who refused to take an oath against the Sacrament of Transubstantiation. James, the first to suffer under this 'Test Act', as they called it, had been deprived of his office as Lord High Admiral, notwithstanding his distinguished and courageous service in command of the fleet during the two Dutch wars. The King's Catholic servants had to go, with exception of his barber, from whom he refused to part; and the Queen's ladies must go, whether Catholic or not, but she was allowed to keep nine of them including Donna Maria, a permanency, Frances, as kinswoman of the King, and Louise, in her entirely nominal post as Woman of the Bedchamber.

In view of these upheavals both in and out of Court it is not surprising that the Duke should have wished to spare his young Catholic wife a hostile reception from the citizens of London. 'To avoid this great concourse of people come to welcome her,' the harassed James explained to his mother-in-law, who had accompanied her daughter from Modena, 'it were best we enter London by barge.'

So Maria was stealthily smuggled up river under cover of the fog, and brought to Whitehall stairs, not without much heated objection from the old Duchess and floods of tears from the young one. She had never ceased to cry since she left Dover after her private marriage in the rites of their Church to her forty-year-old bridegroom.

'Me not know he *old* man!' she sobbed to Catherine, who had taken the child to her heart at first sight of her. She was a lovely little creature, dark-haired and olive-skinned, with large beautiful eyes, despite they were red-rimmed and swollen from weeping. Catherine remembered her own loneliness and desolation when she had waited five days at Portsmouth for her errant Charles; but he had been a Prince Charming and a perfect lover. She could well understand the shock it must have been to Maria when confronted by 'Dismal Jemmy', so named by the irrepressible Nell. He had decked himself out in mulberry satin and a blond periwig, new for the occasion, that was by no means complimentary to his leathery lined face, aged beyond his years from his arduous service at sea, and pockmarked. Poor James! Nothing of charm about him, although Catherine had heard that in his youth he had been far the best-looking of the three Stuart boys.

When, as was the custom, the King, the Queen, her mother and her personal attendants prepared the bride for the nuptial bed, she was in hysterics. There they left her with her 'Dismal Jemmy' and the jocular injunction from Charles: 'Now, James, get to work and do your damnedest to give us a boy to the succession — instead of a couple o' girls!'

It is doubtful if James did get to work or do his damnedest that night for, so went word of it gleaned from pages giggling at keyholes, his bride would have none of him, and, expressing her rejection in terrified shrieks, finally took refuge in a cupboard: a report that for want of eye-witness verification is likely controvertible. But we may believe the bridegroom had all his work to do in placating her, if in a cupboard or out of it.

Catherine, who had returned to Whitehall that she might entertain the honeymoon couple in her State apartments, was thankful when the celebrations were over and she could go back to the quiet of Somerset House.

But not for long would she enjoy uninterrupted tenancy of her haven by the Thames. She could not know that when the first crocuses should herald four more springs, the wheel of destiny would whirl her and many others with it into abysmal danger. No pricking of her thumbs, no premonition warned her that within a crow's flight of a mile from her pleasant tree-girt palace, the block on Tower Hill would cast its shadow ... upon her.

TEN

Would you send Kate to Portugal
And James to be a Cardinal
Banish rebels and French whores
The worser sort of Shores
This is the time!

Would you make our Sovereign disabuse
And make his Parliament of use
And not be changed like dirty shoes
This is the time!

It was the wolf cry of an infuriated pack led by Shaftesbury, fallen from office with his tottering Cabal. Charles, as always in a crisis, spurred by his uncanny intuition for finding the right man at *his* right time, picked the one on whom he could rely to hold at bay the shiftless 'Shiftesbury', hot to revenge his dismissal.

Sir Thomas Osborne, late of the Cabal, created Earl of Danby as Shaftesbury's successor, was a hard-headed, rock-solid Yorkshireman in whom Charles saw a powerful resistance against the Opposition, now self-styled 'Whigs'.

In his laboratory labelling his phials, pounding with his pestle, mixing his potions and dissecting frogs, Charles would let his mind side-track to see the tenderly reproachful shade of Minette, and their shared secret vanished: a dream within a dream, forsaken, a hope lost; his alliance with Louis abandoned for an Anglo-Dutch peace...

It had to be. Not only was he faced with the likelihood of setting out again upon his travels, a homeless wanderer, as alternative to the continuance of war and inward strife at home, while his people fought it out among themselves to have him back or thrown to the dogs, but also he was desperately hard up.

The war, that in one year alone had cost a million and a half, swallowed at a gulp the subsidy granted by Louis; and the peace that Shaftesbury had formerly demanded, when at last accomplished, was, for the ex-Chancellor, an added grievance. Anything brought about by that 'Yorkshire Ham', as he designated Danby, was damnified by him. The rise of prosperity as result of the cessation of hostilities empowered Charles, ever generous to folly if he had anything to spend, to share his good fortune with his 'Chargeable Ladies' and their various offspring. Louise got the rope of pearls for which she had been pestering him, and for her son the Duchy of Richmond that had reverted to Charles as the deceased duke's next of male kin.

Nelly, the least demanding of them all, also got a dukedom for her son. She hadn't asked for it: the gift was a surprise, and entirely spontaneous. As usual the gossips had the story before it was out of Nell's mouth, how that the King, on one of his visits, had seen the child playing in her garden; he had dirtied his hands, and his mother from the window shouted: 'Come in at once and clean yourself, you little bastard!'

Whereupon Charles turned on her indignantly to say: 'Don't you dare call him that!'

'Well, what else should I call him, who hasn't a name?'

'Yes, he has,' was the prompt reply, 'he is the Earl of Burford.'

And more cost to the Exchequer to go with it; dukes right and left, their estates to be endowed, and their mothers to receive the wherewithal for the upkeep of them and for the marriage of Barbara Cleveland's son, Henry Fitzroy, now Duke of Grafton, to the five-year-old daughter of Lord Arlington.

Then, to crown all, comes another to exhaust the Privy purse and add more burden to the Treasury.

'Off with the new love and on with the old!' cackled the wags of Whitehall. She was not old, nor was she very young, the notorious Hortense Mancini, Duchesse de Mazarin, ravager of men and, as was said of her, of women, whom Charles in his youthful exile had wooed but not won. Her uncle, Cardinal Mazarin, had higher ambitions for his niece than a throneless king.

The loveliest of *'les Mazarinettes'*, as she and her sisters, wards of the cardinal, were called, came to conquer and recapture the heart of the susceptible Charles. He, as all men who had known her in her heyday, had been captivated by her beauty, but not until later did she develop that singularity of conduct which set all tongues in Europe licking at the scandals that followed her trail wherever she went.

The cardinal did not live to regret his refusal to marry her to England's King when, on his death, she was sacrificed to a man twice her age. Armand de la Porte, Marquis de Maillery, who, immediately after the wedding, assumed the name of Mazarin.

To Hortense, his favourite niece, the cardinal bequeathed the bulk of his enormous fortune, the Palais Mazarin, and all its rare treasures of art, paintings, sculpture, jewels. Armand, husband of Hortense, saw visions and, obsessed by religious mania, declared the work of the great *cinquecento* masters, decorating the walls of the Palais Mazarin, to be thoroughly obscene and an offence against the Holy Spirit.

Whereupon, urged by the Angel Gabriel, with whom he was in constant communication, he went for them with a sledge hammer to smash the nude marbles and daub paint all over the priceless pictures, lost for ever to posterity.

After this, Hortense, having suffered seven years of him, would suffer him no longer. Suddenly, in the middle of the night, accompanied by a retinue of servants, she rode off to seek adventure. Through Switzerland, Italy, Germany and Holland she travelled, cross-saddle, on horseback and wearing a man's habit and peruke. She starred in various scandalous intrigues, the lover of many, the mother of one, whose father was never her husband; but he who might have been the sire of her son she was not particular to know.

And so, her fortune dissipated by her own and Armand's imbecile extravagances, with her twenty servants, a dozen dogs, an aviary of birds and a little servant boy, she ended up in London.

It was a case of the cat among the pigeons with a vengeance, to cause flutters in the dovecote and consternation at Versailles when de Courtin, back again as Ambassador, replacing de Croissy, reported the fervent welcome she received from Charles. In this exuberant *cosmopolite,* the associate of the most brilliant intellects of France and her native Rome, Louis saw a political threat to Louise, his puppet secret agent. She, too, was in a panic, fearing to find her unique position in the service of two masters snatched from her by another who, despite her eccentricities, was vastly her superior in physical attraction and intelligence. She saw her empire falling and the newcomer given place of honour above herself and all other peeresses at the opening of Parliament. Her cup of bitterness was filled to overflow when Waller, the Court poet, who never missed a chance to extol the latest Favourite, put her into execrable verse:

When through the world fair Mazarine had run
Bright as her fellow traveller the sun,
Hither at length the Roman Eagle flies
At the last triumph of her conquering eyes.
... Legions of Cupids to the battle come
For Little Britain these and those for some

The allusion to 'Little Britain' was pointedly directed at Louise, the 'Little Bretagne', and after more of it in this same awful panegyrical vein, he finally winds up with:

Her matchless form made all the English glad
And foreign beauties less assurance had.

One foreign beauty, entirely deflated of assurance, took herself, on medical advice, to Bath; and naughty Nell appeared at Court in deepest mourning, 'as a mark of respect,' she told sympathetic enquirers, 'for the death of the French whore's hopes.'

While all this was going on in the vicinity of Whitehall, and Hortense had been temporarily installed in St. James's Palace, the Queen, islanded in her self-chosen solitude, heard of but took no part in the lavish entertainments provided for *la Mazarine*. But because Maria, Duchess of York, was first cousin to Hortense, Catherine felt in courtesy bound to receive her, and at once fell a victim to her charm.

With consummate tact if not with absolute veracity, Hortense made it clear that the warm reception accorded her by Charles was prompted only by respectful friendship; nothing more. Catherine chose to believe her, but would not have been greatly troubled had she not. Hortense had known Charles long before she was aware of his existence other than the name, discussed among her schoolmates at the convent, of a penniless Prince, son of the King of England who had had his head cut off.

Ever a good listener she enjoyed to hear Madame la Duchesse talk — and how she talked; incessantly. She spoke fluent English interspersed with French, as she told of her girlhood in the Palais Mazarin, touching lightly on her love affairs with — all sexes. For men she gave the impression that she had little use: 'Since they have only one use for us. I much prefer the society of women.' And with her bold magnificent eyes she stared at Catherine as if she could see through her to her bones.

'You are very thin,' she said, 'but *infiniment* more attractive than these large Englishwomen — 'she described in the air an imaginary protuberance of bust — 'who have breasts like cows' udders. Ah! I see you are a little shocked. Yes? When you come to know me better you will find that I do not — how you say — *mince* my words, but what is delicate in French is hideous in English. It is your heritage from the time you were barbarians and went naked, covered in blue paint — and their language is still spoken in Wales, I believe.'

'You must not say *my* heritage,' Catherine told her. 'I am not English although I am married to an Englishman.'

'As I might have been.' Hortense transferred her searching appraisal of Catherine to the fire, where logs blazed on the wide stone hearth. It was a day of ice and snow. Outside the bare tree branches traced a skeletal pattern against a sky of steel. 'Yes,' Hortense nodded at the fire that cast a flickering glow on her ash-blonde hair dressed in Medusa curls. Her beauty was of the sculptural Greek rather than Roman, and of Nordic colouring; her skin, from exposure to all weathers under hot skies, was tanned to a sun-warmed brown. In the firelight her chin, firmly rounded, and the curve of her finely chiselled upper lip showed faint golden hairs. 'Yes,' she repeated, 'I might have been where you sit now, sharing England's throne. Thank God,' she flung out a dramatic arm, 'that my uncle, the cardinal, the most odious of men ... how I and my sisters hated him. The only good he ever did me was to die and leave me a fortune — which is finished, gone! — and to forbid the marriage between Charles Stuart and myself. I could not have endured my life in this frightful sea-coal smoke and fog of London, and even at Windsor you have these damp death-cold mists ... brrr! Your winters are a frozen hell. As for your senseless gibbering women, I have seen not one except your charming little Frances and another, a daughter of Charles, I believe, is she not? — the young Lady Anne Fitzroy, married now to Lord Sussex — whom I find attractive. Of course those two — they are impossibly silly, *mais, ne m'importe que tu sois sage, sois belle et sois triste* — which applies more to you, *chérie*, than to these *idiotes*, for to me you *are* beautiful, and sad with the sadness of a Leonardo angel. We had such a one at the Palais Mazarin, which my imbecile husband — may he rot! — destroyed. Then I am horrified at your men, who fornicate so clumsily. They lack *finesse*, even Charles who is half French, he —' She pulled herself up abruptly and shot a glance at Catherine, who returned it with her small half-smile that exposed those two little upper teeth.

'How prettily you smile to or at yourself!' exclaimed Hortense. 'I think you are much to be admired for your tolerance of *les peccadilles* of Charles, for you are so essentially a woman with all of a woman's possessiveness. Now me — I am not possessive in the female sense. For example, I was never in love with Charles, nor he with me. He was in love with love and I was in love with — Hortense!' She threw back her head, laughing widely, to show her red palate down to her uvula. 'I am, you see, a *Narcisse*. You know the story of Narcisse, the lovely boy who saw his reflection in the water and became enamoured of himself, as I was, and as I am. Love? Pah! What is it? There are not sufficient words for love in any language, not even French. Me, I love my dogs, I love my horses, I love my food, I love my wine, I love riding, I love money, but when I had it I lost it — one always loses what one loves — and I love pretty boys, I adore pretty girls, and I hope I love God, but I have never, never, never loved a man.'

'Tell me about Charles,' ventured Catherine when Hortense paused for breath. 'What was he like when you first knew him?'

'Like? A gipsy. That is how he was when I first knew him, with his hair cut short and his face so brown. He had just come to France after his escape from England, and I remember his shabby clothes and the dirt in his nails — so grimed they were it must have taken him a month to clean them. He was shy, but perhaps that was because he could not speak well French and I not so well English then. Later when he learned how to behave as a French gentleman and not as an English scoundrel, he was *ravissant*, with his dark intense eyes and the way his mouth went up and his nose came down when he laughed. But he did not laugh often enough.'

Always, after these talks with Hortense, Catherine felt she had been buffeted by a high wind, nor was she singular in that respect. The descent of *la Mazarine* on Whitehall was cyclonic. She swept aside any who stood in her path to be scattered like leaves in a storm. Gossip whirled about her name and her startling idiosyncrasies; how that with the King she would ride to hounds dressed as a man in breeches and periwig; of her passion for cards and how she played ombre and basset for the highest possible stakes and invariably had the devil's own luck to win. If ever she lost, which was seldom, Charles, as usual, paid her debts.

De Courtin at the Embassy, and Louise, returned from Bath, viewed the King's interest in the Amazonian Hortense with considerable concern. Among various rumours to cause further vexed questions in French circles were the constant visits and marked attention paid by *la Mazarine* to the little Lady Sussex, daughter of Barbara Cleveland, supposedly by Charles. That this association might have a deleterious effect upon the youthful Countess in view of Hortense's singular activities, did not at all disturb de Courtin or Louise.

What did disturb them was not that Anne responded with infatuated ardour to this interesting attachment and had separated from her husband as result of it, but that her apartments in Whitehall, formerly those of her mother, were directly above those of the King. Thus Charles had easy access to his daughter's privacy, shared by Hortense; there they danced together, sang together, and indulged in childish games, all, to be sure, of the most innocent, and in which Charles, presumably to keep a paternal eye on Anne, would often participate.

Certain intelligence gleaned from servants' quarters — de Courtin had a purse well lined with *louis d'or* to reward the vigilance of a *femme de chambre* or a little page — gave it that long after Anne had been despatched to bed by her father, he would stay till all hours with Madame la Duchesse, talking — of what? Of those nostalgic days at the Palais-Royal or of matters more intimately urgent or — political? It was known, or guessed, that she, Arlington, and Danby were in league with the pro-Dutch element to declare war on France. They need have had no fear of that. Even while Hortense was exerting all her Circe charm for the bewitchment of Charles, he had signed a pact with Louis in which each King was pledged to aid the other in event of war.

Then, just when gossip for want of new excitement concerning the 'Roman Eagle' staled, she, the unpredictable lured to her eyrie another willing victim: this, the handsome young Prince of Monaco who had followed in her train across Europe, but had never yet succeeded in attracting her attention. He now had left his castle overlooking Monte Carlo to throw himself and his heart at her feet.

Charles, furious at being displaced by a younger, more personable and profitable prince — for Monaco was rich and he, by reason of his costly seraglio, was not — rebounded, for consolation, to Louise. All, joyfully for her, was as before; and in the intimacy of her bedchamber the affairs of nations were discussed between the King of England and the secret emissary of France, to her increased advantage. She had looked to lose the benefits conferred on her by Louis with the ascendance of Hortense, and now with the fulfilment of her trust restored, she reaped the ripe reward of it in a golden harvest from *le Roi Soleil.*

Lord Chancellor Danby watched with unease this Papistical influence threatening the monarchy: a Papist mistress as France's secret agent — no secret to the lynx-eyed Yorkshireman; a Papist heir presumptive to the House of Stuart, married to a Papist wife; and, although of little consequence, unwanted by the people, uncared for by her husband, a Papist Consort, still of child-bearing age, was a constant menace to the throne…

In her quiet palace by the river, storm clouds gathered darkly around the cloistered Queen.

'But this is unpardonable! I will not have it! I'll not give my consent!' James, his face haggard, his peruke awry, burst in upon the King in his laboratory. 'I will not,' James reiterated loudly, 'give my consent to it. You understand? I am most aggrieved and immeasurably shocked.'

'Amazing,' murmured Charles, engrossed in microscopic examination of a lump of meat that stank to heaven and on which an army of white maggots voraciously fed. 'Athanasius Kircher is a man of prodigious parts, and a Dutchman to boot. You must not disparage the Dutch, Jemmy, least of all as a son-in-law, for they are far in advance of us, not only in the arts — take Van Dyck, who actually is Flemish, and that remarkable young genius, Gibbons — but also as physicians, *vide* Kircher, the first investigator to employ the use of this,' he laid a finger on the microscope, 'as is demonstrated in his *Scrutinium physico-medicum Contagiosae Luis, quae Pestis elicitur dicitur,* and is also the first to express the illuminating doctrine that contagious disease is spread by small living animals, visible or invisible to the naked eye. This would, of course, apply to animalculae in a cut from a putrefying joint of beef, and to the presence of fleas in a certain type of rat which are a primary cause of the plague. You were saying?'

James was not saying, he was thinking: *if Charles were not my brother, I might, God forgive me, become ugly.*

'My patience,' he managed to articulate, 'is well nigh exhausted. You take too much upon myself — I mean yourself. That I, against the dictates of my conscience, have never attempted to convert my daughters to the Faith is a concession to the monarchy, but while I deplore your determination to maintain the Anglican Church in your kingdom, I realise your motive for so doing. The country is not yet ripe for its conversion — or yours. The risk to your throne would be too great, although for my part I would renounce my right to the succession sooner than renounce my Faith. But to marry my daughter to our nephew of Orange — to that, Charles, I will never consent. You and Danby between you have brought this about, and why? For what purpose God knows!'

Charles pushed back the fall of his heavy periwig, and straightened up.

'For the purpose of strengthening the House of Stuart in both countries, to bring peace to Europe and — Now what's the matter?'

'I am unwell,' muttered James, turning yellow. 'The stench of your nauseating — uh — uh — ugh!' Violently retching, he made a bolt for the door.

To Le Fèbre, the King's laboratory assistant, who was grinning behind his hand, Charles said, 'Our brother has as little stomach for science as he has for the Dutch.'

'If I may venture to correct Your Majesty,' Le Fèbre subdued his grin to say, 'Kircher, of whom you were speaking, is, to the best of my belief, not Dutch. He is German.'

'A deliberate *lapsus linguae.* I am well aware of Kircher's nationality, yet because of my brother's opposition to the marriage of Princess Mary to her Dutch cousin, William, I endeavour to paint, not the lily but the — Orange. As for the Duke's refusal to consent to it, God's fish! he *will* consent, or I'm — a Dutchman!'

And James, as ever, over-ruled by his brother, did consent; and in due course there came to England, William, Prince of Orange, the accepted suitor of his cousin, Princess Mary.

She, even more opposed to the match than was her father, implored Catherine's intercession with the King to break it off.

'Madam, I can't — I *can't* go on with it!' she sobbed. 'He is odious! He smells. I think he never washes, or shaves himself but once a week. His chin is full of bristles, and when he kisses my hand — thank God he doesn't kiss my face! — he is as prickly as our hedgehog. And he's so spindle-legged and round backed — he almost has a hump, and do you know, Madam, what they call him? Caliban! Oh, Madam, save me, save me!' she flung herself on her knees and clutched at Catherine's hand. 'You are the Queen, you surely could persuade the King how detestable this marriage is to me! I hate him! And to think I shall have to go to *bed* with him! I'd as soon go to bed with a gorilla!'

Ineffectually Catherine offered comfort by suggesting: 'You must not judge a man by his outward appearance, Mary. The King has the highest opinion of his intellect and —'

'Intellect! What intellect? I've seen no sign of it. He never speaks to me if he can help it. Just sits and hawks — he has a filthy cough — and picks his nose. His manners are disgusting.'

'After all, my dear,' Catherine reminded her, 'you will go to your new country accompanied by your husband. When I came here, I came alone. I had never even set eyes on my husband, whereas you —'

'Yes, Madam,' Mary hysterically interposed, 'whereas I was almost sick when I set eyes on *mine,* or on him who will be mine, unless I kill myself!'

But despite all Mary's protests, tears and threats of suicide, the wedding preparations went unjoyfully apace; and on 21 November, 1667, the unwilling Mary was led by her equally unwilling father to the altar, and handed over to the man destined to rob him of his crown.

This son of the deceased Princess Royal of England was, at the time of his marriage, in the direct line of succession after the daughters of the Duke of York, whose Duchess was about to give birth to a third child. If a boy, it would deprive William of the hope that his wife, now second in succession to the throne, would ever ascend to it; and this apprehension, in view of the imminent labour of the Duchess, did nothing to lighten the gloom of the sullen bridegroom as he knelt beside his weeping bride.

Yet none who watched the dismal ceremony could have guessed that the weakly stunted frame of this Dutch princeling housed a spirit of indomitable courage, whose whole life's aim and purpose was pledged to avenge himself on his enemy, the tyrant, Louis of France, who not only had encompassed the ruin of the Dutch Republic but had seized part of his own principality.

A confirmed misogynist, the posthumous son of his father, brought up by a termagant grandmother, Amalie of Solms, his childhood had been unhappy, his life loveless, his knowledge of women, if any, of the crudest. He had entered into this marriage with his cousin, twelve years his junior, solely as a furtherance to his political ambition, which, at the moment, depended solely on the sex of a child about to be born.

Such was he, William, Prince of Orange, future Sovereign of Great Britain and Ireland, the most detested ruler of the Stuart Dynasty, yet one whose brilliant statesmanship and consummate diplomacy was to place him among the highest before or after him.

'I, William, take thee, Mary ... for better for worse ...'

But how much for the better, or how much for the worse, none, not even he who spoke those words in his slow cool foreign accents, could have told.

ELEVEN

On a warm sunny morning in August, 1678, the King, as always unaccompanied, exercised his dogs on his daily walk in St. James's Park. The path he had taken was virtually deserted. Promenaders in the park were not as a rule up betimes nor out so early as the King; but, as he sauntered back from the lake where he had been feeding his waterfowl, a husky voice at his elbow swung him round.

'Sire, Your Majesty's pardon.' The owner of the voice was a shabby individual with a five days' growth of beard on his chin, and a cocked hat on his head with which he cringingly swept his knees. 'If I may crave a word —'

'What the devil!'

'Sire —' a furtive glance across his shoulder preceded the stage whisper — 'a word in Your Majesty's ear?'

Charles drove a look at him, disliked what he saw, and: 'If you're here to beg,' he was bidden, 'be off.' Then, as his spaniels came yapping at the stranger, 'Hark, hark, the dogs do bark, the beggars are coming to town. You'd best go join 'em.'

And he strode away with the fellow at a trot behind him.

'Sire, of your clemency —' he had all to do to keep up with that long-legged stride — 'yes, I *am* here to beg, but not for alms. I beg Your Majesty to heed me, for I come to warn you, Sire, that enemies, the Papists, do threaten regicide. Your Majesty's life is in danger.'

'If so,' was the cool response, 'it will not be the first time my life has been in danger — or in pawn, as it was for ten years.

Here, Lulu!' he stayed to whistle a dog that was scrabbling in a hedge. 'As for you, whoever you are —?'

'Kirby is the name, Sire. I see Your Majesty does not remember me. I was once employed by Mr. Le Fèbre in your laboratory.'

Charles looked at him more closely, with recognition dawning.

'Ah, yes, but a long time ago, surely, during the plague when we were short of assistants?' And Le Fèbre, having found him unsatisfactory, had dismissed him. He was vaguely reminded that the fellow had got himself involved in some shady speculation.

'Did you not later become financially — disadvantaged?'

'Your Majesty's memory is infallible. The prerogative,' again he bowed, 'of royalty. Yes, Sire, I did at one time fall upon pecuniary misfortune through none of my own fault. 'Twas from ill advice, but,' he hastened to add, 'it is not in the hope of monetary reward that I come to warn you, even at the risk of Your Majesty's displeasure at my presumption … Sire, I have certain information of that which threatens, not only Your Majesty's sacred life, but the whole structure of the Established Church and your constitutional government.'

'I'll tell you what to do with your certain information,' was all Charles had to say to that. 'You can put it up your — h'm — and keep it there.' And again he walked on, and was again detained.

'Sire, I implore you, do not continue your walk alone. Your life, I again repeat, is in danger. At this very moment —' he hushed his voice; his little beady eyes, deep set in a face like a slab of dough, shifted uneasily from those of the King, who, from under his beetling brows, examined him as if he were one of his microscopic specimens. 'At this very moment,' came the urgent repetition, 'there are those who lie in ambush to shoot you as you walk. Your Majesty's every move is watched. I implore to be allowed to accompany you.'

'Certainly not.' Charles thought it best to humour him. 'There's no sense in both of us being shot. And you'd better not dawdle here. Go back where you belong.'

Which he hazarded could well be Bedlam. He knew that in the recent removal of the asylum from Bishopsgate to Moorfields, several of the inmates had escaped. This Kirby probably was one of them.

But the fellow was not to be so easily shaken off. 'Sire, I implore you to heed me!'

'Oh, well,' Charles resignedly conceded, 'get on with it. Let's hear what you've to say.'

What Kirby had to say was so fantastic a farrago that more than ever did Charles doubt his sanity; but he heard him out, for, even were the man a lunatic, he might have gleaned from anti-Papist propaganda a modicum of fact.

As averred by Kirby on his solemn oath, and in that same conspiratorial stage whisper, there was a plot afloat to shoot the King with a silver bullet fired from a screwgun while he took his morning walk.

'A silver bullet!' quizzed Charles. 'Lead is good enough for commoners, but silver for a King! I should be honoured.'

'Pray, Sire, believe me. This is no idle talk. I swear to the truth of it. There is a plot devised by the Jesuits, not only for the extermination of your royal person but of the Protestant religion in your Kingdom.'

'I see. So I'm the first to be exterminated. But what if he who fires should miss me?'

'Then, Sire, the alternative is — poison!' was sepulchrally announced, 'which the Queen's physician, Dr. Wakeman, has undertaken to supply.'

'Hah! So does he? Here's gratitude! I only knighted him last week. And now he's going to poison me. How does he propose to administer the dose? In a cup of wine? I'll be wary of inviting him to dinner.'

'Sire, I beg you not to make a jest of this. The Jesuits are fomenting a rebellion in Ireland. France is supplying them with arms —'

'Trust Louis for that!' muttered Charles.

'— and substantial subsidies. Sire, I have proof positive of what I say.'

'Very well, produce it.'

'Not here, Sire. If I am seen or overheard — for I, too, am watched — my life, as is yours, would be forfeit.' With another secretive glance around he took a step nearer. 'If I may crave audience of Your Majesty in private I will bring with me a friend who can give you indubitable evidence of this most diabolical conspiracy.'

'I can scarcely wait to meet your friend,' declared Charles, bent on humouring him whom he judged to be mad, 'nor to hear the evidence of this diabolical conspiracy. So, you may attend me, if you will, at Whitehall tonight — you can ask for Mr. Chiffinch — and in the meantime I advise you to go home, if you have a home, and cool your head.'

Passing Nell Gwynne's house on his way back to the palace, he stopped to give the time of day to her who leaned over her garden wall, but not now to laugh and chaff with him. There was no laughter in her face when, in hurried undertones, she said, 'I saw you with that Kirby. Have a care! I know summat of him and naught to his good. He used to hang around me at the Playhouse — a smooth-tongued devil, he — with a gift of the gab that 'ud earn him a fortune on the boards, but he's got bigger fish to fry along o' them what's out to hook our dismal Jemmy and your Queen, poor innocent, who wastes her lovin' heart on you who's done her wrong, though you do right by some what don't deserve so much as a kick up the arse! Take heed, Charlie, from one who hears more of what's goin' on in and outside of Whitehall than you'd ever know of. There's traitors in your bed *and* in council chamber, and none so blind as you, me darlin', who can't see what's under your nose. Keep your eyes and ears open for Shaftesbury. I'd as soon trust a rattlesnake as him — the shifty sod. Will you be in to sup with me tonight?'

Not tonight, he told her. He had arranged an assignation with — 'this Kirby, whom I intend to hand over to his wardens to hold him where he ought to be — in the madhouse.'

'D'ye mean to say that you'll let him come at you again?' cried Nell, aghast. 'Then 'tis you for the madhouse, not him!'

'Sir, if you do not treat this matter in the light of what is here, I'll not answer for the consequences.'

It was Danby who spoke in the privacy of the King's closet, where Charles lounged in a chair beside a table littered with documents collected from Kirby and the 'friend', one Tongue, he had brought with him that evening.

'Foh!' scoffed Charles, 'you can't seriously believe in this mazy hotch-potch? The fellow's mad, I tell you.'

'There is method,' murmured Danby, 'in some madness. And this Dr. Tongue appears to have procured proof enough for its support.'

'Support of what? Blood-curdling melodrama prompted by the ravings of a Bedlamite? And who *is* this Tongue? Israel

Tongue — what a name! It smacks of a Jew or Nonconformist.'

'Maybe.' Danby thrust out a dubious underlip. 'But I understand he is a Doctor of Divinity, and is, or was, incumbent of St. Michael's in Wood Street. A poor living, it would seem, for he has lately relinquished it for literature.'

'Of a highly imaginative quality, no doubt. And what of his familiar, another "Doctor", Titus Oates? Their nomenclatures would look well on a play-bill — who is he to whom they allude as endowed, if not with divinity, with Divine Right?'

'Of him I know nothing — as yet,' Danby said, very glum. 'I will, however, make full enquiries, and report to Your Majesty my findings.'

Charles got up, yawning widely. 'I am off to Windsor in the early morning and have sat up half the night talking to no purpose of these absurdities. So whatever your findings, which I'll wager will be less than will sit on a codpiece, take them to the council and don't bother me. I've more to do than listen to tales told by an idiot.'

So that was how it all began; but neither Danby, the cautious, not he, who shrugged it off so lightly, could have foreseen how it would end.

The result of Danby's 'findings' brought him posthaste to Windsor to lay before the King more material produced by Tongue and Kirby, from which he had extracted certain facts of so ominous a nature that they could not, he insisted, be ignored.

'These are no maniacal ravings,' he assured the incredulous Charles, 'but a carefully organised Catholic conspiracy to effect a wholesale massacre of the Protestants. In short —' and he tabulated the main points of the plot, of which the primary intent was to assassinate the King and the Duke of York, and set fire, for the second time, to London. 'Your Majesty must be aware that the great fire of '66 was generally attributed to the Catholics. I am therefore come,' said the stolid Danby, 'to obtain Your Majesty's permission, as you did suggest, whether in earnest or not, that I bring this case before the council for immediate examination.'

'What! And raise a scare to make those who would never have thought of it think to murder me and my brother? Not on your life! We don't know, even among my most trusted, who...' From under his hooded lids he shot a narrow glance at the Yorkshireman standing squarely before him, his heavy jaw out-thrust. *Yes,* thought Charles, *you're trusty enough* and *tenacious. You don't breed bulldogs for nothing. Like master, like dog, and once you get your teeth into whatever you've tripped up, be it man or beast, you'll not let go.* And he said again, 'who — even among my most trusted of the council — may be gnawing at my vitals, in the dark.'

There was one, however, not now of the council, whom Charles had trusted, and by whom he knew that he had been deceived. Shaftesbury, nursing a sour grievance, had long watched and awaited opportunity to avenge himself for his dismissal of the Chancellorship. He had faced failure at every turn. He had made a hash of the Cabal; and, although he had brought in the Test Act to exclude all Catholics from holding high civil or military office, he had failed to secure a Protestant succession.

Bitterly did he brood over that rebuff when he had failed to persuade the King to divorce his Catholic Queen on the grounds of her infertility to take to himself a Protestant Consort, so to save the Stuart dynasty from the invidious corruption of the Papists. He would not easily forget how the King had turned on him, his fist upraised as if to strike, nor the dark look that flashed with the words: 'If my conscience would suffer me to divorce my wife, it would suffer me to murder her!'

He believed it was this suggestion of divorce that had got him in the Tower, and not that trumped-up charge against him for having denounced the present Parliament as an 'unlawful assembly'. But more than all of this was his obsessive hatred of the Papists personified in those two nearest to the throne; the one the King's heir, the other the King's wife, still young enough to breed... unless he could be rid of them both and prove Monmouth, the King's adored and eldest son, to be no bastard but — the *rightful* heir!

And now fate had flung in his path the instrument through which he might achieve his deadly purpose.

Titus Oates.

'Who is he? What is he, this Titus Oates?'

From Whitehall to Wapping that name and question was in every mouth to strike with fear the hearts of all who heard the awful tales floated round the Town about them and about — the Papists!

All through that exceptionally hot summer, omens of evil had been seen and prophesied by soothsayers of calamitous portent to King and country. Talk went, in whispers, of mysterious comings and goings of emissaries from the Pope to the Queen at Somerset House, and to the King's brother and successor, York, an avowed convert to Rome. The old Gunpowder Plot was still fresh in the minds of some whose grandfathers had lived through it, and, farther back, those blood baths of Mary Tudor's day, and the human torches flaring in the smoke of Smithfield. Were the bedevilments of a powerful Church come again to overthrow their liberties and drag to the stake or the gallows those who upheld the Faith of their elders and of their King?

In the council chamber — for Danby had insisted on an inquiry — members listened in amazement to him who stood before them, offering to their shocked credulity his monstrous fabrications.

How this Oates, with a head clamped between his shoulders as if he had no neck, and a chin so abnormally long that it looked half the size of his face and that face, under a yellow curled wig, of a low cunning and hideous pallor, could have obtained a hearing much less have been believed, is as astonishing as his horrific disclosures. But there it was, and there is he, arch-liar and perjurer of all time, to be acclaimed 'Saviour of the Nation'.

He, himself, a lapsed Catholic who, only the previous year, had been admitted to the order of Jesuits, far from arousing suspicion offered further proof of his veracity when, with hands upraised, he swore before Almighty God and His Angels that he had gone among the Jesuits solely to gather evidence of their infamous intent. He had been, for a while, employed in the Catholic household of the Duke of Norfolk, where he had overheard certain visiting priests muttering among themselves of a dastardly design to resuscitate the Church of Rome in these realms. It was this that first determined him to pursue his inquiries, to which end he enrolled as a novitiate in the Jesuit college at Valladolid in Spain. There he indulged in various relaxations, which he understood were permitted by the Roman priests. He did not enlarge on the nature of these 'relaxations', for which he had been summarily and, he declared, most unjustly dismissed.

Back in London he posed as a Doctor of Divinity, purporting to have taken his degree at the University of Salamanca. He had never been to Salamanca, nor was he a priest, and how he got away with it none will ever know, but get away with it he did for he was nothing if not plausible, and decorated his narrative with forty affidavits.

At the primary hearing he stated that the Jesuits had been appointed by the Pope to hold supreme power in the kingdom. The King, named by the Jesuits the 'Black Bastard', was the first to be annihilated, for 'if he did not become R.C. he could not remain C.R.'.

This, delivered in the ridiculous drawl he affected, was taken by the pop-eyed councillors as gospel, and by the King with guffaws. 'God's fish! The man's a wag! 'Tis as good as a play. Go on, let's have some more of it.'

More there was and, fabulously, more of it.

Four Irishmen had been bribed with the sum of ten thousand pounds to shoot the King, the money to be handed over to them by Père la Chaise, a Jesuit priest in Paris, as witnessed by Oates who by some unexplained chance had happened to be present at the time. When Charles, the only one of the council to see through the whole grotesque tissue of lies demanded where this transaction had taken place, Oates at once drawled out: 'In the hahouse of the Jaysuits next to the Pahalace of the Louvre.'

'Man!' roared Charles, 'there's no house of the Jesuits within miles of the Louvre.'

But none of the gullible council's crew were to be put off by that. He had his audience and he held them.

Further lively inventions from Oates gave it that Don Juan Paulos de Oliva, General of the Society of Jesuits, was the prime instigator of the Plot.

'What sort of man is this Don Juan?' was asked by the King. 'Describe him.'

'Sir, he is a tahall leean man,' came the answer, 'Black haired and daark visaged as Your Majesty.'

'Oh, so is he?'

Charles passed a hand across his mouth to hide a grin. He had known Don Juan in the past, and remembered him as squat, fat, fair-skinned and red-headed; but he let him go on, and he let himself out and went off to Newmarket to find more amusement watching his two-year-old, Blue Cap, put through his paces than in any performance of Oates'.

But on his return to London he found the city in a panic and his brother James in bed.

'I sent for you, Charles, because I — ach-tchew! — pardon me, I have an abobinable cold and my doctor says I bustn't get up. By stobach's queasy, too, with all this upset.'

Charles took a seat, and from his pocket a pomander which he applied to his nose, saying, 'I don't want to catch it. And what *is* all this upset? As I drove into Town I saw crowds of folk stampeding as if the plague had come again.'

'The plague it is,' said James stifling another sneeze. 'That monster Oates has idfected the council with his lies and now they ah-ah-tchew! — they're after Coleman, Maria's secretary.'

'Coleman? Why, what's he done?'

What hasn't he done, the fool! James began picking at his thumb. He's beed in correspondence with Père la Chaise in Paris — you remember Oates mentioned him at the preliminary hearing, or so you told me — and now he's got hold of a cock and bull story spread by Oates, that the English Catholics, with me at their head and Coleman as my lieutenant, are in league with France to bring about a conversion of England with the financial backing of Louis. Like all converts,

Coleman is over-zealous — I'b afraid I am, too — and he airs his views broadcast concerning the one and only Faith. That set Oates on his tail, and he and his lot searched Coleman's rooms and found a bundle of what they call "incribin-ating evidence" hidden in a box up the chibney, and although he destroyed most of the documents he forgot those he had shoved up the chibney and now all hell is let loose. Your precious council is convinced this gives substantial grounds to believe in this villainous Oates and the plots we Papists are supposed to have hatched. You will have to put a stop to it, Charles, or they'll put a stop to us — ah-ah — tch — Dabnation! Where's my handkerchief?'

'Soak your feet in hot mustard water. I wonder Chiffinch didn't tell me of this.'

'You didn't get back till last night, and anyhow, I don't suppose he has heard of it yet. I didn't until this bordig — it only happened yesterday, but the Catholics here in London are already getting away — at least all who can. I shall have to get Maria away. Coleman is — or was — her secretary.'

'I told you long ago to get rid of that meddlesome big-mouthed ass,' said Charles, unhelpfully.

'I know, I know,' fretted James. 'And I did get rid of him, but he wheedled his way back and then Maria took him over. She was sorry for him. I will — I *bust* get her away. I don't want her brought into it, poor child.'

'She won't be brought into it, I promise you that.' Charles got up and moved to the door. 'I'll try to drive some sense into my mutton-headed council. It will all be forgotten in a month, when we've given Oates rope enough to hang himself.'

'I hope you're right.' And as James raised a hand to wave him out, Charles noted with a pang that his wigless head revealed a bare patch and the hair, once blond, was grey.

'Pray God,' he heard James mutter, 'that none but Oates will hang.'

'Madam!' Frances, with a basket full of flowers and her face full of fear, met the Queen as she came from her chapel at Somerset House, 'I sent my page on an errand to the Exchange this afternoon, and he has told me something terrible he heard there.'

'Terrible?' smiled Catherine, who knew how Frances picked up and relished to exaggerate every drift of gossip. 'How lovely these are.' She stooped to a rose. 'I thought they were almost finished.'

'They are a second blooming, Madam. Yes, indeed, 'tis terrible. My page, he says they are all talking of it in the Exchange. Sir Edmund Berry-Something has been murdered!'

'Not Sir Edmundberry Godfrey?' cried Catherine. 'Not that good man? He only dined with us at Whitehall last week when the King entertained the magistrates to a banquet. Did you say — murdered? How? When?'

'It must have been just after the banquet, Madam. They say he disappeared. He went out early one morning and never came back. My boy tells me his body was found in a ditch in the country beyond Mary-le-bon marshes. He had been stabbed and the sword — his own sword — was left sticking in him — and oh, Madam, I feel quite sick. May I sit?'

She sat, and Catherine seated herself beside her on the stone parapet of the terrace.

'And, Madam,' blurted Frances in a tremble, 'they say 'tis the Papists who have killed him!'

'They would say that,' murmured Catherine, pale.

'Yes, and my page — he's a Catholic — he says they were at him with their fists, and hooted him, yelling "Papist", and "no

Popery!" and "Murderers!" And oh, Madam, they flung him down and kicked him and he came back with a black eye and all over bruises, and he says that Mr. Coleman, the Duchess's secretary at St. James's who was a friend of this Sir Godfrey, is one of those who killed him and now all Catholics are suspect!'

Catherine put an arm round the girl's shoulders. 'Suspicion is no proof. Poor child, how you shake. Come along in. I will give you a posset. You have had a shock.'

Not only Frances, but the council and all London had a shock. Like fire spread the news of Sir Edmundberry's murder; but Coleman, although suspect of having had a hand in it, was not thought to be the chief perpetrator of the crime. It was known that Oates had deposed evidence of a Catholic plot before Sir Edmundberry as a Justice of the Peace, and those 'hellish Jesuits' were the culprits. *Drops of wax, such as Catholics use for the candles at their unholy rites, were found on his clothes.* — this according to Bishop Burne, who claimed to have seen the body. The discovery of Coleman's letters, however, proved him implicated, not so much in the murder of Godfrey as in treason.

To Père la Chaise, the French King's confessor, Coleman had written:

We have a mighty work upon our hands, no less than the conversion of three Kingdoms, and by the subduing of a pestilent heresy which domineered over a great part of this northern world. There never was such hope of success since the days of Queen Mary ... But that which we rely upon most next to God Almighty's providence and the favour of my master, the Duke of York, is in the might of His Most Catholic Majesty...

Louis! From whom Coleman had accepted twenty thousand pounds to serve France in the Catholic cause.

What more proof than this to brand him a traitor to his King and country?

He was apprehended and thrown into prison to await his trial with other Catholic suspects. And Oates was the hero of the hour: 'Doctor' Oates their 'Saviour', who had so courageously unearthed the dark Terror that threatened the lives of all adherents to the Established Church.

The wildest rumours were afloat. The King would be killed, his brother York set upon the throne, and London burned to cinders. A French fleet had been sighted in the Channel, advancing to bombard the Kentish coast. The Papists were mustered in their thousands to lie in wait in cellars underground, armed with muskets, cannon and cutlasses supplied by the French, ready to rise and fall upon the Protestants in every city, town, and village in the land. It would be a massacre of innocents. The streets would run rivers of blood. Shaftesbury's wife, at her husband's command, carried a pistol in her muff. Other terrified ladies followed suit, scarcely daring to show themselves at windows. Householders quaked behind doors barred and locked against Catholic raiders. And still the King remained convinced that the whole thing was a monstrous hoax devised for his own mercenary ends by Oates, now installed in a suite of apartments in Whitehall, with a handsome salary for his maintenance and a bodyguard for his protection.

Immediately after the murder of the hapless Godfrey, a broadside appeared entitled *England's Grand Memorial,* dedicated to Shaftesbury, leader of the new Whig party and President of the famous, or infamous, Green Ribbon Club held at the King's Head Tavern in the City. Here the latest developments of the Plot were discussed with hordes of disreputable witnesses, sprung from the slums and stews of London, bribed to repeat the perjuries of Oates. Wearing his yellow wig, a clerical gown, a smug smile on his face and an almost visible halo round his head, he sat in the place of honour between Shaftesbury and Monmouth. They made a striking contrast; the beautiful youth, attempted usurper of his uncle's future throne, and the hideous monstrosity to whom half England's population said its prayers.

In the crowded rooms of the Green Ribbon, hazy with tobacco smoke, reeking of wine, the members a heterogeneous collection of lords and commons, pimps and poets, lawyers, jailbirds, gentlemen and thieves, rubbed shoulders together and toasted — 'Doctor Oates'. From the balcony that overlooked Temple Bar, where the mouldered heads of those doomed to die their martyred deaths were soon to rot on spikes, this choice assembly of patriots, pledged to save their King and themselves from the Terror, watched a howling mob parade with grisly pomp the body of Godfrey, steeped and putrefying in its blood, the first victim of 'Popish bedevilment'.

Nation and Parliament alike were panic-stricken. When, in October, the Commons met to sit upon and incubate the Plot, Members were on their feet demanding the removal of all Papist recusants, while in the Upper House one of the Lords expressed the sentiments of his Protestant peers in a roof-raising oration:

'I would not have so much as a Popish man or a Popish woman in our midst! I would not have so much as a Popish *dog* or a Popish bitch — no! Nor a Popish *cat* to mew about the person of our King!'

The Commons, greedy for more revelations from the redoubtable Oates, had Coleman brought up for trial before

Lord Chief Justice Scroggs, to be indicted with a batch of Jesuit priests on a charge of conspiring for the King's assassination. All were duly done to death on the gallows, with the usual barbarous brutality of disembowelment while still alive; and this on the sole adumbrated evidence of 'Doctor' Oates.

Having disposed of these, his earlier victims, twenty-six more including five Catholic peers, Lords Powis, Petre, Axundell of Wardour, Bellasis and the septuagenarian Stafford, were apprehended, condemned, and clapped into the Tower to await their trial for treason; they, whose only crime was their creed. And Oates, inflated with success, triumphantly pursued his fiendish works, regarded by his adulatory dupes as a 'Sublime Mission'.

He had secured a worthy accomplice whose career of Machiavellian cunning equalled, if it did not surpass, his own. This, one William Bedloe, a horse-thief recently released from Newgate, swore to have evidence that the murder of Godfrey was committed by the Catholics at Somerset House; that the body, having first been strangled, had been placed on the High Altar in the Queen's chapel, where it had lain for fortyeight hours before it was decided to cart it off to Primrose Hill, beyond Mary-le-bon marshes. It had been ascertained that the hapless victim was stabbed after death and left in a ditch that the deed might be attributed to highway robbery, notwithstanding that his money and jewels had not been stolen.

Somerset House, and in the private chapel of the Queen!

The hunt was on full cry, with Oates, the Master, leading his bloodhounds hot on the scent for — the kill.

PART FOUR

Nothing is there to come and nothing past,
But an eternal Now does always last.
   Abraham Cowley

TWELVE

Some few weeks later Charles, raging up and down his closet, gave James a report of the renewed hearing of the Godfrey murder with further evidence from Bedloe.

'He has now dragged in the names of two more Catholic priests, whom he swears have jointly confessed to have been involved in the crime, aided by three of Catherine's servants.'

'Catherine's ... Good God!' James slumped in his chair; his face was white.

'And also her goldsmith, Miles Prance, in charge of the chapel's ornaments. That those gullible fools can take the word of so palpable a liar is past all power of credence. He has been well schooled by that reptile Oates.' Charles swung suddenly round. 'And not even when I sent him with Monmouth to show him where the body had been hidden —'

'You sent Monmouth with him!' ejaculated James. 'Would you trust *him* as witness to these consummate lies?'

Charles eyed him coldly. 'Would I not trust my son?'

'If he *is* your son,' muttered James. He got up and went to him. 'Charles, you should know — or don't you *wish* to know? — how this young braggart, backed by Shaftesbury, swears you were legally married to his mother? Is your love for him so blind that you can't see how he and Shaftesbury are hand in glove with Oates and his venomous plot to be rid of *me* and proclaim Lucy's bastard — Prince of Wales? He even has the Feathers blazoned on his coach and has erased the bend sinister from his arms. Have you not heard that?'

Said Charles, from out of a dry mouth: 'If I *had* heard that, I'd see him hanged on Tyburn gallows before I would believe it.'

'You may have to believe it. So what did Monmouth find when you sent him ferreting with Bedloe?'

'Hah, yes!' The moment of tension passed; Charles resumed his restless stride. 'Bedloe got himself well trapped when he showed Monmouth the back stairs where the body was supposed to have been hidden before they lugged it up to Primrose Hill. Those back stairs, as he called them are no *stairs,* but a passage used by the footmen to bring Catherine's meals from the kitchens to her table. It would have been impossible for a dead cat, much less a dead man, to have lain there for two hours, let alone two days and nights, without being seen. But, as I was about to say when I questioned him — for no one else did — as to why so public a place should have been chosen for the concealment of a body, and if any other than Bedloe had seen it, he said none save himself had seen it; and even then, with the stink of his lies on his tongue, they accepted his evidence and none of the Queen's household called, or *allowed* to be called, to deny his perjuries. And why?' Wheeling round again, Charles trod the tail of a spaniel. 'Well, it's your own fault — you shouldn't get under my feet. There, then, there,' he stooped to lift the offended one into his arms, and went on from where he had left off. '*Why* were no witnesses called? Because that double-dyed villain accused them, the Queen's servants, of having aided and abetted the murderers and of having been bribed to keep silent. And now those God-damned councillors are singing hosannas to Bedloe and their Saviour, Oates!'

'But what,' asked James, helplessly, 'are we to *do?* We can't stand by and see innocent men sacrificed to false swearing.'

'The first thing to do,' Charles told him, 'is for you and your wife to leave the country, and —'

'And leave you here to bear the brunt of it?' broke in James. 'Never! Am I a rat — to run?'

'You are my heir. Will I stand by and see *you* sacrificed?' And forestalling an answer to that: 'It is an order,' said Charles, the King.

Yet despite his anxiety for James his first thought had been for Catherine. At last, with awful certainty, he had come to realise that Oates was drawing his bow not at one royal quarry, his brother and Papist successor, but at another, his wife!

He had now removed her to Whitehall to be under his protection, safeguarded within her own apartments adjoining his. While taking these precautions for her safety in view of this 'scare' as he called it, he had been careful not to alarm her nor to give her an inkling that she might be suspect of implication in the crime. From his account of Bedloe's lying evidence, although it greatly shocked her to think that murder should have been committed under her roof, and, as alleged, by some of her own staff, it never entered her mind that she would be considered in any way involved. Her one concern was for her servants.

'How can they believe that my men and my good Prance who makes such beautiful ornaments for the Altar could have done this dr-r-eadful thing?' Her English, now almost fluent, still retained a slight attractive accent. 'I should have think your council have more sense, and Lord Danby also. I never like him, Charles. He is so rough and — red! But how can they believe? For — don't you remember — you were with me on the day when poor Sir Edmund — when it happened? You were reviewing my footguards, and there were sentinels at every entrance. Not possible that anyone would dare make murder when the King was at my house. You do not believe it, Charles, do you, that my own people — ? No! you cannot believe it!'

'You *know* I don't believe it.' But he forbore to remind her that, so paralysed with terror were the council and everybody else at the inventions of Oates, they would believe anything of the Catholics, even murder. Instead, his eyes weighing on hers — wide and startled and softly brown in her small pale face, like the eyes of his white hind — he had said, with a catch in his voice, 'I want you to come back to me. We must never live apart any more. I want you with me now, not for a day or a week or a month but for — always.'

She drew in a breath. After all these years of loneliness withdrawn from him, except when her presence was demanded at State functions, that he should want her with him now for 'always'!

Henceforth she must do everything in her power to assist in the discovery of the murderers. It had been suggested that Somerset House should be searched for further evidence as to how or at what time of day the crime had been committed, and at once she gave her permission in a message to the House of Lords that the search be made, and received from them a vote of thanks and an expression of their confidence in her good will to facilitate their efforts...

She had yet to see the writing on the wall.

Her thirty-eighth birthday. From the window in her bedchamber that overlooked her privy garden at the palace, she watched the slow death fall of November's yellowed leaves. Each autumn, through these seven dreary years since Louise had snatched from her all that she cherished in life, she had seen the end of yet another year in this, her birthday month. And tonight there would be held here in Whitehall the usual celebrations with a grand ball for its finale. And again she would be led out to the dance with Charles, but not now with an empty heart. Her heart was filled with the joy of this reunion. Yet, while she gladdened, she grieved that men must die as a result of the lying accusations and false witness brought against them. For how long must the innocent suffer for the guilty? *Surely*, she thought, *God works in mysterious ways that through blood and martyrdom the Word and the Truth shall live...*

The short day was closing in with shadows and a clammy fog wreathed the garden in scarves of grey; and, as she turned sharply from the window, her little body stiffened. She felt that she was being watched but saw no living thing, heard no sound more than the crackling logs on the hearth that gave out a warm glow to darkening corners. Then footmen came to draw the curtains and light candles, and, from her anteroom whose door stood ajar, there rose a sudden chatter of women's voices, and that of Frances, shrill:

'But I tell you I *know!* That Horror has gone before the council today for an extraordinary meeting...'

'All meetings to do with him are extraordinary.' This another voice she recognised, that of Anne, the young Duchess of Buccleuch, wife of Monmouth, who had been given the Dukedom of Buccleuch in '73 on the death of his wife's father. 'My husband had to meet him when the King sent him to Somerset House to show him the place where — Oh, Your Majesty!'

Catherine stood in the doorway, and the two Duchesses, and one or two maids of honour who were there, curtsied to the ground. The Queen distributed smiles.

'I overheard what you were saying, and the least said of it the better. We have talk enough of horrors.' And to her Lady of the Robes, who at that moment entered, 'Ah, Lady Suffolk, I was about to send for you to discuss the gown I wear for the ball. I think my white and silver and the rubies, yes?'

So now it was all of gowns and jewels and furbelows, for she must look her best tonight.

That 'Horror' had timed his challenge to a nicety. On the eve of the Queen's birthday he had sworn before a stunned council to have personal knowledge of a plot in which Sir George Wakeman, the Queen's Catholic physician, had conspired with Her Majesty to poison the King. Of this same regicidal intent His Majesty has already been informed by one Kirby in the previous August.

Whether or no Oates was directly suborned by Shaftesbury and his faction in the council, the fantastic tale received credit enough for the horrified councillors to insist on an immediate inquiry. Charles, who believed that Oates and his monstrous lies would never stand up to cross-examination and that he would be exposed and condemned for perjury, agreed that an extraordinary meeting be called, which, accordingly, was held the next day, as prelude to the Birthday Ball.

And while Catherine dressed for the festivities, all unaware of the net closing round her, Oates, assured that he held the trump card, confidently played it.

Wearing the episcopal gown he adopted in anticipation of the bishopric promised by the infatuated council, he declared he had seen a letter written by Sir George Wakeman, in which it was stated that Her Majesty had been brought to consent to the assassination of the King.

Eyes to heaven, hand on heart, he also swore, 'As Gard was his witness', to have seen certain Jesuits at Somerset House who had come to confer with the Queen. By some providential chance he had been there at the time, waiting in an anteroom to be presented to Her Majesty.

The purpose of this presentation was neither asked for nor, by Oates, explained. Sufficient for the day that he was there, and that the Jesuit plotters had conveniently left open the door of the Queen's Closet that he might hear a female voice exclaim, 'I will no longer suffer these indignities to my bed and person!' — 'An allusion, my lards,' bowing to the benches, 'to Her Grace of Portsmouth.'

'And how,' Charles afterwards reported to his brother, 'I kept myself in my seat and my hands from his throat, I do not know, only that he has no throat to throttle with that neckless head of his!'

The voice went on to say, continued the imperturbable Oates, that she would assist in procuring the death of the King for the propagation of the Catholic Faith in this kingdom.

Perceiving the council to have gulped down every word of it, he was emboldened to enlarge.

When the priests came out of the Queen's Closet, he asked if he might now be admitted, and was graciously received by Her Majesty, the only woman present, and no other woman had left the room for there was but one exit, the door by which he had entered. Moreover the voice was unmistakably that of the Queen with her slight foreign accent.

Charles, who in boiling silence had listened to this fabulous tale, now for the first time spoke.

'Describe the Queen's Closet and the anteroom where you overheard this remarkable conversation.'

This was a poser; and Oates, who had never been inside the Queen's private apartments at Somerset House, was for the moment caught up; but he got over that by giving a description of the rooms to which the public were admitted. As every member of the council knew, the Queen's Privy Chamber was so far distant from the rooms described that even had she shouted at trumpet blast her intention to murder the King, her voice could not have carried through a series of apartments; and:

'The case,' said the King, 'is dismissed.'

But was it?

Although flabbergasted by these obvious discrepancies, which the majority of the council were inclined to accept without further inquiry or denial of the charge from other witnesses, they decided to bring the case before the House of Commons. Charles, disgusted as much with his idiotic council's credulity as with the loathsome Oates and his outrageous lies that involved his innocent Queen, left them to it, and went back to his quarters to dress for the ball.

When his valets had done with him, and very fine he looked in crimson velvet and glittering with orders, he sought his wife and found her in her bedchamber surrounded by her women. She bade them, 'Go', and as they fluttered out, 'Charles!' she turned to greet him, her face joyous, 'How you are grand.'

'And you — how lovely!'

She was in white and silver with pearls in her hair and rubies at her throat; and at sight of that blood-red streak encircling her neck a coldness came upon him, and going close to her he whispered, 'Turn about.' Wondering, she obeyed him that he might unclasp the necklace, and then he bent to lay his lips to her nape where the soft dark tendrils curled. 'This,' he said, 'needs no adornment,' and tossed aside the rubies.

She gazed up at him and saw that even when he smiled, his eyes were haunted, it seemed, and his cheeks hollowed; as often in a day or an hour, his face, were he harassed, would sink.

That this night of her birthday should go unmarred by the least shade of danger, which, he dared not think, might threaten her life, Charles determined the ball should lack nothing of carefree enjoyment. Taking their cue from him, the company went to it with abandon: and if among them were those few of the Faith who had not fled the Terror, they gave no sign while so gaily they danced what might be their dance of death.

After opening the ball with the King, Catherine dutifully partnered James. He had not yet left the country for Holland, where he intended to visit his daughter Mary, and so circumvent, as advised by Charles, any suspicion of 'ratting'.

Then Monmouth, as premier Duke, second only to the brother of the King, must be given precedence above all other members of the House of Lords. And even though she knew him for what he was, his father's idol and York's enemy, unstable, unscrupulous, marking impatient time to claim his false birth-right, she was not proof against his devastating charm.

As ever insincerely fulsome with his compliments, 'Your Majesty,' he told her, while they jigged to the coranto, 'outshines them all tonight with your air of a little *nonnette,* as my Grandmam, the Queen Dowager, used to say.' She let that pass, though inwardly she seethed. Was there no end to his insolence?... 'Not a day older than when I first saw you, was it ten years ago?' His eyes narrowed in an impudent raking glance, and he held her closer; the cool curls of his hair, for he wore no wig, brushed her cheek. 'Though for some you may not be a beauty, for me you have that something more than beauty which must fade with time, but not for you, my second mother, for you... are ageless.' The music twanged to its end. 'Shall we sit? Or will Your Majesty take refreshment?'

'I prefer to sit. And if you wish for refreshment, you may leave me.'

'To leave you, Madam, unattended? Am I not to be allowed the privilege of waiting on you?' He said it pleadingly, his mouth curved upward in a faun-like smile: so young he looked, young enough, almost to be her son. If only he were!

He led her to the high-backed gilded chair reserved for her next to that of the King, and with a 'By your leave, Madam,' sat himself beside her. He had no right to be seated there in the King's chair, and he knew it, but though her cold silence expressed her displeasure it had no effect on him to stay his dexterous talk, light as thistledown; yet each word held a barb.

'I see the Mazarin, *la belle Romaine,* has discarded her prince from Monaco and takes to herself a new paramour, or should one say — paramour*ette?*'

Hortense, in cloth of gold made with a cutaway coat in the style of a man's riding habit, her arm round the waist of a pretty young girl, led her out to the music of the Branle.

Monmouth raised a quizzing glass.

'Queen of the Lesbians,' he murmured.

'Queen of... what?'

He turned laughingly to tell her:

'I adore you, Madam! You are so deliciously naive. Hortense, or her prototype, Sappho, was a celebrated beauty more than two thousand years ago in the Greek island of Lesbos. Her passions were varied and violent. She kept a retinue of lovely boys — and girls, as does *la Mazarine,* that she might school them in the joys of — Aphrodite! This is a new capture, I take it.' Up went the glass again. *Ravissante!* And look who is here — our homing pigeon from Paris, the Cleveland. An ill-timed flight when other birds of her kind are on the wing, chased by the carrion Protestant crows ... Madam, you are pale.' He was all concern. Rising and bowing, he presented a jewelled pomander. 'Pray, honour me by keeping this trifle. I find it a necessity when I walk, which is seldom, but often enough to deplore the stench of my fellow men *and* women, in our London streets. And even here in the palace, many of our loveliest ladies are not particular to wash below — the belt.'

Would he never have done? Under all his badinage she detected a smear of vulgarity, inherited, or the result of his early upbringing. And still, despite discouragement, he rattled on. She was relieved when Shaftesbury, much as she distrusted him, detached himself from a group of men surrounding Louise.

Since Catherine's return to Whitehall, Louise had kept almost exclusively to her own apartments, was rarely seen at Court and received few visitors, other than Shaftesbury. Fearful though she may have been for her own fate as a Catholic, she knew that none but he could protect her from persecution. To save her skin, or her head, she must show herself his partisan in his proposed Exclusion Bill to throw York out of the succession. From a corner of her eye she watched Shaftesbury bow in exaggerated homage to the Queen.

'Madam, your most humble servant.'

She was compelled to extend him a greeting. She could not ignore this ex-Lord Chancellor, now leader of the Whig Opposition party; but neither could she repress a shudder at the touch of his lips to her hand.

A pigmy of a man, overdressed and undersized, she knew him to be responsible for the dismissal of all English Catholic priests, with exception of Father Huddleston whom Charles had insisted should remain in charge of the Oratory at Whitehall. But for how much longer, Catherine wondered with a sickness at her heart, would the Padre be safeguarded?

Well did she know that another potent enemy was here, who, even as he offered honey-mouthed congratulations — 'On Your Majesty's glorious birthday, and may God send you many more with which to bless you and us, your faithful servants,' his pack were baying their wolf-cry at the palace gates: *'Popery is slavery!"* and chanting the jingle bawled at his Green Ribbon Club:

'Sceptre and Crown
Must tumble down...'

The Great Hall was thinning, the music ending, the noise, the laughter, the jigs, had ceased, and the last guest had melted away when a foggy dawn lifted night's curtain.

In her lonely bed, Catherine, sleep-forsaken, could hear Charles in his adjoining room, restlessly moving. A spear of candlelight pierced through the half-open door, and in a mirror on the wall, she could see, every so often reflected, a glimpse of him in his night-shift, padding back and forth with long barefoot pantherish strides.

'Charles,' she called; and swiftly he came to her.

'Yes, love, what is it? Why are you not asleep?'

'And why,' she smiled up at him, 'are *you* not asleep?'

The lamp at her bedside table showed her lying there in the great four-poster he had used to share with her, but not now, never now; nor would he force himself upon her until cured of his infection, lest she be sullied...

So little and so lost she looked among her pillows that although he answered her smile he felt a tug at his throat as he said, 'I have the belly-ache from a surfeit of French wine and — Whigs.'

Her faint eyebrows lifted. 'Wigs?'

'Not those that are worn here,' he touched her hair, and seating himself on the bed, 'What,' he asked, 'had Shifty Shaftesbury to say to you?'

'He wished my happiness for my birthday, full of flattery and ... words. I do not like that man. He has the voice of a snake, if a snake could speak.'

'Yes, the snake that bites its own tail. He may bite more of his than he can swallow.' And smoothing back a curl that had fallen on her forehead, he thought: Should he warn her of the dire charge with which so soon she must be faced? No, he could not. It was *his* fight, and to the last drop of his blood he would fight it.

Give her, dear God, he prayed, *these few more days of peace.*

THIRTEEN

I, Titus Oates, do accuse Queen Catherine, Queen of England, of High Treason.

On 28 November, three days after the Birthday celebrations, that strident drawling voice trumpeted its deadly charge at the Bar of the House of Commons.

Those who had not heard the previous accusations sat appalled; others who had listened to the lying statements of their 'Saviour' and his mouthpiece, Bedloe, were more than ever convinced of the Queen's guilt.

High treason!

The axe was raised and now about to fall.

But they had reckoned without their host. In this dark hour all the protective chivalry and dormant love of Charles was reawakened in defence of his innocent wife. No longer must she be kept in ignorance of the fearful accusations brought against her that, should he for one moment relax his watch and ward, could bring her, a helpless victim, to the block.

Gently, even casually, to spare her, he told of: 'An infamous charge made by that maniac Oates who throws up another gobbet of lies, this time against Wakeman and — you.'

But the nature of those lies he did not, at once, divulge. He must lead up to it warily.

'Me! Against *me* — and my good Sir George, my doctor? What possible charge can he make against us? That he should dare!' Nothing in her face of fear, only the hot flush of indignation. 'What charge? Of what are we accused more than that we are of the Faith? Must I, the Queen, also be put to prison for my belief in the true Church?'

How to tell her of the damning perjuries spewed from the leprous mouth of Oates? How to prepare her for this calumnious threat to her life?

He caught her to him. His fierce grip was on her shoulders and the hurrying breath of his words on her lips as he said, with forced calm, 'He, this glib liar, this Oates, will have it that you and Wakeman,' he manufactured the semblance of a laugh, 'conjoin to kill me with a dose of poison in a — posset!'

'Poison!' She wrenched away from him, still unafraid or unaware of the awful implication that lay behind those words so lightly spoken. 'Me! to accuse me of — never!' An upsurge of fury overwhelmed her; incredulous, she stared at him. 'That he, this animal, should be allowed to speak such wickedness and before them — your council, is it?'

'Yes, and Danby, my Lord Treasurer, and the whole accursed House!'

'You — too! With them!'

In this convulsion of rage her English was chaotic as she poured forth her scathing opinion of him — 'for allowing these, your Parliament, to insult me — not me alone for I am less to be insult than you, the King! But for them to hear these dr-r-readful lies and you not to dismiss them but to sit there and — and *listen*! Oh, it is too much!' She crashed one little clenched fist into her open palm. 'You are more to blame than your Parliament — those fools, those heretics who hate me for my Church. Now, I finish with you. Yes! I bear with enough. I bear with your women. I bear with not having my money for which you marry me, I bear with everything, but I no bear with this — that I be accuse for to *kill* you!'

She was as one possessed. Not since their bridal days, when she had stormed at him because of the Castlemaine's invasion, had he been given a glimpse of those volcanic eruptions that fermented beneath her douce exterior. 'You must break with them — your Parliament. They are bad for you. I know it, me! I say nothing, but I know. You think because I sit so quiet that I have no eyes nor ears, but I see and I can hear, and I do know that you are too *easyy* Charles. You let them lead you, not you to lead them. How come it that this Oates, this madman, should go before your Parliament to make lies of me in so wicked a charge as to kill my husband and — my King! You must put that Oates — a wild beast — in a cage, pull out his lying tongue — put them *all* in a cage, yes, all of your government — how you say — dissolve! If you not do this and stop the persecution of my people, the Catholics, and my priests and me! Yes, it is *me* they will persecute with all others of my Faith, then I go back to my own country. My brother, he shall hear of this. I write to him. I tell him that now they fall upon — the Queen!'

And watching her as she thrashed about the room, her small body quivering, her cheeks aflame, he thought excitedly: By God! she's more of a man, and more of a King than I! Yes, he would dissolve Parliament, make a clean sweep of the old Cavaliers who had grown stale and as bigoted as Cromwell's Puritans ... A painful stab of reminder shot through him. Was that the only reason for a dissolution, or was it to save Danby from the impeachment that should be his, the King's! Danby had urged him against it, that secret treaty with Louis — another secret treaty — to withdraw his troops from Flanders, when Parliament and the whole country were clamouring for war with France in the spring of this year. And he had sold himself and British interests for French gold. None but Danby,

Montagu, God damn him, his Ambassador in Paris and Louise, had known of this until Shaftesbury and his Whigs had got hold of it a week ago when Montagu in collusion with the Whigs had sent Danby's letters, written at his command, to the Speaker of the Commons, and Danby must carry the burden of his country's betrayal on *his* shoulders — not the King! Only an immediate dissolution could save him, his trusty Danby.

'And who,' Catherine was saying, 'is at the roots of it?'

Roots of what? He had missed that. He pulled himself and his errant thoughts together. 'I tell you who is at the roots of this evil against the Catholics and against me and against James and against *you*! It is that Shaftesbury, that snake — *he* is the poison they would give to kill you!'

And at that he shouted inly, *O, but she's rare, this girl of mine,* for girl she still appeared to be, unchanged and virginal with those small breasts and a skin unlined as when he first had seen her. The sheer stunning wonder that the ferocity of circumstance, this abysm yawning at her feet, uncovered unimaginable depths in her not only of courage, but of defiance to challenge political corruption, drained him of his self-command and — self-esteem. What would she think of or have to say to him could she know of his shameful negotiations with France? He stood abashed before her who was no defenceless victim, cowering for shelter beneath his Crown, but Majesty outraged.

'Shaftesbury!' She spat the name at him. 'The nasty little man, he is the poison who creeps and crawls into your council chamber and into the chamber of your ... of the Frenchwoman whom I did love until she stole my ... my all from me.'

That broke him and he took her. She let herself be taken. He had the salt taste of her tears in his mouth from her trembling lips that, for one fleeting second, clung to his before she left his arms, chokingly to say:

'Not for me do I cry.' And with a childish gesture she drew the back of her hand across her eyes. What a creature of surprises, he marvelled, was this wife of his whom he had only just discovered. In one minute a termagant, queenship offended; the next, with an almost *gamine* unselfconsciousness, snivelling tears up its nose!

'Not for me,' she repeated, lifting her love-warmed face to his, 'but for you. It is at *you* they strike, through me. I am — how you call it — an escape goat. If they will crush me, like this —' she ground her heel into the carpet — 'as I would crush them if I could and as you will not — then let them *kill* me if it will satisfy them to throw out a Catholic Queen and save your throne and — you!'

The reality of her love that would accept the awful penalty exacted, however false the charge should she stand condemned, 'to save him' who had given her nothing, had squandered his life on worthless trash, hit at his heart.

'You tear me to pieces,' he muttered; and a wave of contempt for the loss of all he might have been overswept him.

With something like a groan he turned from her to bow his head on his arms against the oaken mantelshelf not to see the wistful urgency in her eyes, nor her tender smiling mouth as she said, 'I have no fear for myself, so — do you not fear for me.'

And in a voice, sob-shaken, 'I die a little death,' she heard him say, 'to find in you my — resurrection.'

The dying year saw the Popish Terror sweep through the country trailing the blood of the innocent amid roars of triumph in Westminster Hall, in the Law Courts, and from the crowds around the gallows on Tyburn Hill, where the tortured bodies of the martyrs swung, creaking, in their chains.

Immediately after those startling disclosures made by Oates in the Commons, he repeated his elaborate lies before the Upper House, backed by a petition from Parliament that 'the Queen, her Household and all Papists or suspected Papists be removed from His Majesty's Court at Whitehall'.

It was thrown out by the Lords with a bare majority on the grounds that they could not take action on the uncorroborated evidence of one who had proved himself an unreliable witness. The falsity of his statement locating the room where he swore to have heard the Queen declare she would agree to the assassination of the King, was the one slender thread on which her life depended.

Yet although the Commons, with the bulk of the people solidly behind them, were for committing Catherine to the Tower, not she but Oates was confined there at the King's command.

He had won the first round in the defence of his Queen, but for how long? The furious clamour raised against such monstrous injustice to the nation's 'hero', who sought only to save the King from regicide and the kingdom from disaster, compelled Charles to allow his release. In the frenzied excitation of the mob, and the unscrupulous zeal of the antiCatholic Whigs led by Shaftesbury, Charles saw that the imprisonment of Oates would only cause a further outcry to hasten the end of his blameless wife.

But while Catherine grieved for and suffered with those done to death for their Faith; while she feared for the fate of her doctor, her priests and her innocent servants, she still had no fear for herself though each day brought in more mysterious discoveries, more causeless trials, more false accusations.

One Samuel Atkin, an Admiralty clerk who worked for Pepys, had been arrested and imprisoned on the lying testimony of Bedloe as having seen him assist in the disposal of Godfrey's body. Nor did Pepys escape suspicion as involved in the Plot to secure the accession of his master, the Duke of York. So he, too, must join Sir George Wakeman and the five Catholic peers awaiting trial in the Tower.

The arrest of Pepys, as Catherine well knew, was another blood-stained pointer at herself and James to incite the insurrection of a populace terrorised by the revelations of their 'Saviour'. Any man, whether Protestant or Papist, who held a government position and whose work was closely connected with the Duke and devoted to him — though few enough were devoted to her — must be penalised. And although overwhelming forces were bent on her destruction, her courage never faltered. With Charles for her champion in this life and death contest she was upheld and fortified, unflinchingly to face her ordeal.

Her failure to be intimidated by the foul defamations bayed at her by Oates and his bloodhounds aroused the reluctant admiration of the Lords, and caused Shaftesbury in the Green Ribbon Club to flourish his flail with increased avenging fury. Despite that his plans to eliminate Catherine on a charge of treason had gone awry, he had a 'rod in pickle', he gloatingly informed Louise, 'with which to flay all Popish traitors of the King'.

He had serpentined his way into the graces of the Portsmouth who, since Catherine's return to Whitehall, was mortified that Charles no longer sought her company either in or out of her bed. True, he paid her an occasional visit, but rather from duty than desire, and he still respected her advice on matters of state but nothing more.

And Shaftesbury, watching her face settle in a frown at that deliberately tactless remark concerning 'Popish traitors', a face no longer babyish but rather resembling a double-chinned full moon, he cattily noted, and, with studied nonchalance, said, 'I am told by my sister, Lady Sunderland, whose husband hopes for a Privy Councillorship in the event of a dissolution —'

'Dissolution?' Her eyes widened. 'I had not heard that the King will dissolve Parliament.'

'You have not heard?' He professed surprise. 'You who have the King's confidence, you, the power behind the throne! If women were allowed to sit in Parliament what a politician you would make.'

'Milord has ever *le mot juste* for flattery. What then,' she asked, carefully indifferent, 'does your sister, Lady Sunderland say?'

'That the King is so impassioned of the Queen since this unfortunate affair of a charge — ' he spread his womanish hands; his mouth, full of gleaming white porcelain teeth, stretched to a smile, 'that the wife is now become — the mistress.

A flag of colour rushed to her face and, though her answering smile stayed, her eyes held twin sparks of anger.

'I am enchanted to hear of this reunion. *Helas!* That it cannot bring the King a son and heir.'

He leaned forward, and now he was not smiling any more. 'Madam, the King already has a son — and heir. Monmouth. Ah!' The angry flush deepened; her lips parted to her quickened breath. 'How? If that be so, prove it.'

'Your Grace,' he rose and bowed to her as if she were the Queen, 'I will and I *can* prove it — to the King, to the kingdom and — to you.'

After he left her she sat churning over in her mind those oblique words of his. Why had he come? Not to provoke her with Court chatter of the King's renewed 'impassioned interest' in his wife. Pah, that! She took a brandied cherry from a comfit box beside her and bit into it so savagely that the liquor spurted out over her chin. As if one cared. Charles was spent. He could no more serve a woman now that could a eunuch. No. Shaftesbury was after some deeper motive in approaching her...

Ah, yes! She saw it all. *She* was to be used as 'the power behind the throne'. He was counting on her influence with Charles to secure Monmouth for the succession, and if she refused? 'A rod to flay all Popish traitors' ... A threat. A bribe? Should Shaftesbury expose her as a paid servant of the King of France, the one King to whom she owed allegiance, she would be dragged to the block for a spy!

Sacré nom de nom! Why had she ever come to this accursed land peopled with madmen who burn images of His Holiness, the Pope, in the streets, nail cats to the Cross, cut out men's entrails and fling them to the dogs for 'eating their God', as they so blasphemously say, and do saint that murdering Oates, all in the name of their heretical religion. Her lips snarled back against her teeth. *I hate them,* hate *them, these English, more than they could ever hate me!* But if she did not hold out her hand to Shaftesbury — and Monmouth — she too, would be thrown to the dogs.

'Mama!' Her boy, her heart's idol, burst open the door and ran to her. 'Look what Lord Shaftesbury has given me.' He held out an orange modelled in gold. 'See, you do so —' He pressed down a finger to open it and reveal a tiny watch set round with diamonds.

'When did Lord Shaftesbury give you this?'

'Just now. I was coming in as he was going out. I had been playing ball with the pages, and he stopped me and gave it to me now for a Christmas present, he said, it being only two days to Christmas. Is it not kind of him?'

'Very kind.' An eyelid drooped over her wandering eye. She clutched him to her, gazing down into his laughing face. Tall and long-limbed as his father, no mistaking whose son was he with his gipsy-black hair, that large nose and square underlip. What proof could that pink-and-white little bastard of one who was anybody's bawd show against *this*?

She released a held breath. If the fight for Monmouth failed, then here was a ... certain son!

The first general election for eighteen years drove out the old Royalist party, now called the Tories, and brought in the Whigs with a council headed by Shaftesbury as President. His hopes for a Protestant succession went rocketing with James an exile in Brussels, and the Queen's brother, Dom Pedro, Regent for the deranged Alphonzo, demanding her instant return to Portugal.

This was welcomed by Shaftesbury as an easier riddance of the Queen than the scaffold that would bring the whole of Catholic Europe up in arms against Britain, and in all probability lose *him* his head should his enemies in the Lords turn the tide in the Queen's favour. But when Pedro despatched his emissary, the Marquez d'Arouches, to fetch her away and home to her own people who were in a turmoil of indignant protest at the monstrous condemnations levelled at their adored Princess, Catherine stubbornly refused to go. Her place, she declared, was by her husband's side. She was Queen of England and would remain so; nor could all the persuasions of Pedro nor the insistence of d'Arouches, weaken her determination to defy her persecutors.

Another setback for Shaftesbury, who had not reckoned on her indomitable courage, nor on the King's unshaken loyalty to his wife. *There is nothing concerns me more,* she wrote to Pedro, *than to tell you how completely the King releases me from all troubles by the care he takes to protect my innocence.*

It was patently clear that, although the country thirsted for the Queen's conviction, Shaftesbury must direct his attack along more positive lines.

His first move was to bring forward in Committee that a Bill be passed 'to disable James, Duke of York, from inheriting the Imperial Crown of this Realm.'

Four days later the Exclusion Bill had its first reading in the Commons, whereupon Charles prorogued Parliament, refused to sanction it and left for Windsor to enjoy with Catherine a brief respite from the storms and passions that looked to blast not their lives alone but the whole nation.

Shaftesbury, however, was not to be foiled in his determination to oust James from his heritage and Catherine from the kingdom. In the Green Ribbon Club, members were excited to hear of a mysterious black box that contained damning evidence to prove the Queen's marriage invalid.

When, in hushed conclave, this evidence with the necessary documents was produced, a great roar went up amidst the smoke and reeking wine fumes: 'Shaftesbury! King-maker! Another Warwick!'

On a boisterous March day of wind and rain, Charles, returned to the castle from hunting the stag in Windsor Forest, was met by a white-faced courier who had that to tell the King which brought him, mud-bespattered and rain-soaked, to his wife.

'I have to leave you — just for a day or two. I must go at once to London.'

'Why?' A hand sprang to her heart. 'Not my doctor — not Sir George? Is he…?'

'No, not yet. The trials are scheduled for July. There is something else afoot.' Then, seeing her deathly pale, 'There's no cause for alarm,' he assured her. 'Just another hornet's nest to be smoked out in the council chamber.'

But under his easy manner she detected a tension, and in his eyes a sombre fury.

'If you must go,' she said, 'then I go with you.' She came close to him, saying in a little beseeching voice, 'Please, Charles.' There was an angry cut on his cheek where a low-lying branch had caught it. 'This bleeds.' She touched it. 'You are hurt. Let me bathe it.'

'A mere scratch.' He put his arm around her shoulder, pressing her head against his breast.

'And you are wet.' she felt his coat, 'you will catch cold. You must change your clothes.'

'I'll change in the post-chaise. No time to be lost.'

'But what is it that takes you away in such hurry? I won't let you go alone. I must come with you — not for myself,' she whispered, 'it is for you, I fear. Please, Charles … tell me what has happened?'

'Not now. When I come back. Tomorrow or the next day.' He touched her forehead with his lips, and without another word or look, was gone.

At the gates of Whitehall, a huge crowd collected to read, in stupefied astonishment, a proclamation signed by the King.

For the evidence of any dispute which may happen in time to come concerning the Succession of the Crown, I do declare in the Presence of Almighty God that I never gave nor made any contract of marriage to a woman whatsoever but to my present wife, Queen Catherine, now living.
Charles Rex.

Again Shaftesbury, 'the King-Maker', was foiled. That a marriage between Charles and Lucy Walters, purported to have been solemnised by the Bishop of Durham, Dr. Cozens, long since dead and therefore unable to bear witness to it, of which Monmouth could be acknowledged the issue, had been publicly denied by the King, made Shaftesbury look, if not a rogue, certainly a fool even to his most staunch adherents.

'What I cannot understand,' said Catherine when Charles, back again at Windsor after a stormy scene with the council, told her the reason for his hasty visit to Town, 'is how Shaftesbury could be so *stupid* as to bring a certificate of marriage from a dead bishop who could never have been in Holland at the time you were there. I know he is a snake, but he shows not the cunning of the snake in this.'

'He is counting on public opinion which runs mad, thanks to his piddling schemes, at the likelihood of a Catholic succession; so he plays Monmouth for all he is worth, knowing he has made himself the people's idol and, God help me,' Charles turned his head away, 'as he has made himself ... mine'.

Yes, she thought, *a false idol,* for he could have been any man's son born of her who was everybody's woman.

Charles was saying, in a thick choked voice, 'James warned me months ago that Monmouth goes about bragging of his

Blood Royal and followed by a mob yelling, 'God save the Prince of Wales!'

Her heart ached for him, and the thought came to her that she was to blame for this misery brought upon them both. Had she borne him a child or had he allowed Parliament to divorce him, for as a Protestant it would have been no sin of his, nor of hers, who, in her Faith, could still have been his wife, then there would have been no fight for the succession. He would have been spared the tortures suffered by the Faithful, which were his tortures too. She knew he felt each death warrant bearing his signature to have been signed in his own blood. She would have given her life to spare him this. But nothing of her pain for him was in her face as she said lightly, 'Let us now forget our worries on this so lovely day. See, the sun is out, the clouds have gone and I go for my ride in the park. You come with me, yes?'

They remained at Windsor during the spring and early summer. Charles, a keen angler, spent most of those May days fishing with Catherine. He had taught her to cast a fly; she soon became adept and keen as he. And there in the peace of a Thames backwater, where no sight disturbed them more than the sapphire flash of a kingfisher's wing skimming the reeds, nor any sound other than the mating song of birds in the green-grey willows, it was as if the cataclysmic circumstances of this past year had flung across their lives an invisible cord to bind them together in a shared intimacy, born not of passion but of mind and spirit. He realised at last the enormity of her sacrifice; she, who at his bidding had renounced her pride and wifely rights, uncomplainingly to endure his blatant infidelities... The ineffable generosity of her love abased him, stripped him of all he had believed himself to be. All that he had sought in carnal satisfaction, in the greedy possessiveness and flattery of women, had resulted in an arid waste, not only of his potentialities but of the selfless love she yielded up to him and which he had so indifferently ignored.

It may have been in some soul-searing revelation such as this that the brilliant politician, whose laziness and self-indulgence had almost lost him his throne, was driven by a newly awakened respect for his wife to commandeer and amplify his latent political ability. He, who for so long had been led by knavish ministers, would now, with consummate skill, play them as he played the darting fish upon his line.

Meanwhile Oates, glutted with the adoration of a populace in the throes of a massed epilepsy, continued to batten on the blood of his victims. But even while he held a terror-stricken nation in the hollow of his hand, and each day brought more arrests, more impeachments, more cartloads of the doomed trundled up to Tyburn, the red-stained tide had reached its height and was now about to turn.

In July Wakeman, charged with conspiracy to poison the King, was brought for trial. Catherine, who had come from Windsor against the advice of Charles, waited hourly for news of it carried back and forth by messengers to Whitehall.

The King attended the trial incognito and, accompanied only by Chiffinch, sat at the back of the Court, the collar of his cloak drawn up and his hat pulled down over his eyes. He wore no full-bottomed black wig to betray him.

It was, in effect, Catherine's trial, for if Wakeman and the others were found guilty, a death sentence was certain, and then ... no power on earth could save her.

Chiffinch, beside him, saw how the King bit on his thumb to draw blood, and he, who had known him as a boy, remembered that trick of his when fretted. So did his brother, the Duke, but not to gnaw, as did the King, like a dog at a bone. Not in these twenty years had Chiffinch seen the King revert to his old habit.

He heard his master's snarling whisper. 'What hope have we with Scroggs to try him? He's a rabid anti-Papist and soused in drink from morning till night. God send him sober now!'

Better he were not, thought Chiffinch, with a sidelong glance at that muffled figure, his bleeding thumb between his teeth, and staring at the red-robed judge whose blotched drink-sodden face under the towering wig boded ill for a fair verdict whether drunk **or** sober. Yet, Chiffinch strove to cheer himself, were he in his cups, which by the look of him was likely, his wits might not be so brisk to gauge the evidence…

But it was Oates whose wits were not so brisk. Having sworn to have seen Sir George Wakeman give a prescription for poison to an apothecary, Wakeman was at him to ask, 'Then why, if you knew this, did you not mention it when I was examined before the council?'

To which Oates, in his loathsome drawl, his eyes heavenward, replied, 'Ai refuse to answer thaat question.'

Scroggs, glaring down at him, pounced. 'You *must* answer the question.'

Whereupon Oates, who had turned a sickly yellow, asked his lordship's leave to retire. 'Ai feel unwell.'

'You will stay, Dr. Oates, until the defence is heard.'

Charles released his bitten thumb. 'Not so soused,' he muttered aside. 'I take it back.'

On and on it went with Oates on the verge of collapse, while the spectators in the crowded Court, fearing to be done out of another *raree show an Tyburn Hill*, were shouting abuse at Scroggs to lift the roof.

'Silence!' roared the judge, 'or I'll have the whole lot of you pilloried!'

Charles nudged Chiffinch. 'I'm going. You stay. There'll be an acquittal — or I'll eat Oates' head. Come to me when all's done and report.'

To the King in his closet came a buoyant Chiffinch. No need to tell him the result. Charles took the words from his mouth.

'I was right!'

'Yes, Sire, and when Bedloe croaked out from the back of the Court that his evidence had been wrongfully summed up, the judge, he turned on him to say in high heat: "I know not on what authority this man should dare to speak!" And then, Sire, he, the judge, said, very strongly, that they must consider their verdict only in the light of the evidence heard, so they retired and after three hours brought in a verdict of-not guilty!'

Said Charles on a long-drawn breath: 'I must go to the Queen.'

The acquittal of Wakeman roused a storm of fury against Scroggs. He was libelled, abused, assaulted, impeached. The body of a hanged dog was flung through the window of his coach as he drove from the Court; and Shaftesbury complained to the council of a 'gross miscarriage of justice'.

The nation was divided into two halves: those who began to see themselves the victims of a gigantic fraud, and those who believed in their 'Saviour', Oates, as they believed in God. Even when Bedloe fell fatally ill and made a deathbed confession before Lord Chief Justice North, Scroggs' successor, that the Queen was entirely guiltless of any attempt on the life of the King and that the whole of his evidence had been false, even then the majority of public opinion refused to declare against Oates.

Shaftesbury, blind with rage at his failure to prove Catherine neither legal wife nor Queen, whipped his rod out of pickle to point it again at her. Conniving with Monmouth, his puppet, he brought the Duke's cook to depose before a secret committee that he had heard one of the Queen's priests whom he named Hankinson — possibly meant for Huddleston — and another, Father Antonio, a Portuguese priest, plotting 'to bring along four Irishmen to do the business for them'. The 'business' was translated as a further attempt, prompted by Catherine to kill the King.

At another extraordinary meeting of the council, and despite the acquittal of Wakeman that had also acquitted the Queen, it was decided she be brought to trial and her infamies exposed, with all punitive measures.

The news of this latest attack came to her at Windsor, where she and Charles were enjoying the peace of a lull after the storm.

'Will they never have done hunting me,' she cried, 'until they have my head?'

'Not yours, my little.' Charles took her face between his hands. 'I'll have theirs,' he told her grimly, 'every damned one of them — grinning on the spikes of Temple Bar!'

'I would not have one life, no, nor one head lost for mine.' She took his hand to her lips. 'I have only you to save me when I — how do you say when the fox runs away?'

"Tis they who'll run — to earth before I've done with them,' he said through his teeth; and was off post-haste to London to harangue the council, and in white-hot fury to forbid 'any such infamous charge against my Queen, which I,' he thundered at the quaking council, 'take as a charge against me, your King, and punishable to as — High Treason!'

He had turned the tables on them, stopped their tongues, though not the hunt that, with Shaftesbury and Oates as joint Masters, continued to overflow the prisons with their captures awaiting a barbarous end.

Yet although this haunting, ever-present danger clouded those quiet summer months at Windsor, Catherine was at peace. The security of her husband's love, if not that of a lover but rather of a father for a smitten child to be guarded lest it be snatched from him, was joy unbelievable to her abandoned lonely heart. She felt herself to be at fault to know happiness in the midst of the incalculable sufferings of her fellow creatures and the hate that so many of her husband's subjects had for her. Why, she would wonder, but not to ask Charles, whom she knew grieved so bitterly to see it, why did they hate her so, that they wished only to have her dead?

Even at the castle gates, in Windsor's Royal Borough, a yelling mob chanted a doggerel from the poison pen of Marvell, the lampoonist.

With one consent let all her death desire
Who durst her husband's and her King's conspire

She could hear the drift of it booed at her where she and Charles walked among their flower-beds on that hot August day. His face was carved in harsh deep lines, but hers was smiling.

'They do not hurt me, so let them not hurt you more than their noise that do disturb the fish so they won't rise. We have had no catch since this *canaille,* as Hortense calls them, have come to mock at me in Windsor.'

His fingers, hard and strong, crushed hers so fiercely she had all to do not to cry out with the pain of it; and, pulling her round to him, he gazed down into her upturned face with that still childish surprised look of hers, unchanged since his first sight of her; and with a half comical, half despairing wonder he thought: With all hell's demons howling for her head she can only tell me that their 'noise' disturbs the fish!

'Dear, don't be so sad. Why are you sad?' She tiptoed to lay a finger on the fallen corners of his mouth. 'These people out there — they do not hurt me with their rude songs any more than naughty little boys who learn to say rude words and write them up on walls.'

And at that he let out a great laugh to bring Lord Bruce, his favourite young gentleman, who had been hovering in the background with a racket in his hand, hurrying to say:

'Sir, you desired to play me at tennis at three o'clock. It is now half past the hour.'

'Surely so! I had forgot. I'll in to change and meet you at the courts in ten minutes.'

The game had already started when Catherine arrived at the courts with Hortense. She was one of the few women whose company she enjoyed. A never-failing source of entertainment, she shared with Catherine her abhorrence of Louise. Moreover she could be relied upon to garner any shred of information concerning *'cette chatte intriguante'*. Catherine, however, was careful to avoid any detrimental hint to Charles against her whom he still believed to be, as Hortense scornfully conveyed, *'sans peur et sans reproche'*.

'Charles,' she said, 'will soon see his pudding-faced Duchess is not without *peur* or *reproche*. I know what I know and what Chanticleer will know when another cock crows on his dunghill...'

It was stiflingly hot in the dedans. The fierce August sun poured through the narrow slats set high in the main wall, striking sparks of gold from the braided tunics of the pages as they ran for the balls. The heat brought a gentle dew to Catherine's forehead and a stench of perspiration from the heavily upholstered male spectators in the corridors.

Charles, on the hazard side, had won a short chase from Bruce, and was loudly applauded by Hortense.

'I play a good game of tennis,' she told Catherine, 'but not here, where the women only play *one* game,' and she glanced contemptuously around at those who were there fanning themselves and ogling the men. 'I played much tennis in Vienna after I left my husband and went riding *en garden* over the Alps.' She gave out another loud laugh. 'I was more in demand as a boy than as a girl from those of my *beaux amis* who had a preference for their own kind until they — and then were they furious when I — Oho, bravo, Charles! Well placed!'

A fine stroke into the winning gallery had brought the score to deuce.

Hortense leaned closer to Catherine's ear to hiss into it: '*Cette chatte* has always Shaftesbury in her pocket and Monmouth in her bed — no, wait! I say bedroom, where she plays the cat and mouse game with him but not the game of the cat with two backs, ha, ha! Those three, they make more dirt now between them, and with another whose name you must remember for you will hear it very soon. Fitzharris. Mark that name ... ah, milord,' as Bruce approached to take up a ball from the trench in front of the dedans. 'Your service is *épouvantable!*'

'But no match for the King,' he told her. 'I have lost the first set to him and three games of this.'

And Catherine, fanning herself, thought, *Fitzharris.* A newcomer to the Court from Ireland whom someone — was it Lady Sunderland? — had informally presented when walking through the galleries with Charles. What had Louise to do with him?

She was soon to know.

'Game to His Majesty,' droned the marker.

'Come on, Bruce,' chaffed the King, 'you are not in your play to give me this. You, who will band a ball at six paces mounting ... Service!'

Bruce won the next game and the score stood at three-one.

Catherine said, 'I find it too hot here. I think I will not wait for the end of the play.'

But Hortense stayed and Catherine left, attended by Lady Sunderland and Frances.

She was in the privy garden, sheltered from the sun under a wide-spreading cedar, when Charles, with Bruce, crossed the lawn and came to her.

'Who won?'

'The King, Madam. I am sadly off my play.'

'By one game only in the last set, and if you hadn't crashed your ball into the grille we would still be at it, neck to neck.' Charles mopped his face. His sweat-sodden shirt clung to him. He wore no wig, and Catherine saw, with a pang, that his hair was greyer than when she had last seen him wigless, and that his dark scalp showed through the whitening streaks. 'Bruce and I,' he said, 'are going down to the river to fish for an evening catch and cool ourselves.'

'But not without your coat,' she advised him. 'You will take cold while you are so hot. Lord Bruce, bring His Majesty a coat and do you put on your coat, too.'

But when Bruce sent a page for a coat, Charles refused to wear it. They stayed fishing till the moon was up and the day was done, and night brought with it a refreshing west wind. It also brought to Charles, over-heated, over-cooled, a fit of ague followed by a dangerously high fever.

For three days and nights his doctors despaired of his life, and Catherine was frantic when he told her who had never left his bedside save to peck at her food, 'I have sent... for James... the succession...' And fell suddenly, and to those who watched, alarmingly, asleep. But Catherine, in a tremble of hope, felt his forehead; it was wet. She chafed his hands, wet ... wringing wet.

'Thank God!' she cried, 'the fever passes.' And to Chiffinch, on his knees in prayer at the foot of the bed: 'Go, bring me hot towels. He must be dried — not lie in his sweat. I know these fevers from my own country. They come and they go quick. No — no doctors. I'll not have His Majesty any more bled. He needs all his strength.'

When James arrived he fully expected, from what he had heard, to find the halls of Windsor draped in black, himself again flung out of the kingdom, and Monmouth proclaimed King by a mobbing hilarious crowd. Instead he was greeted by a lively convalescent sitting up in bed and gnawing the leg of a partridge.

'A false alarm, Jemmy. My wife, God bless her, knows more of these seizures or tertian fevers or whatnot than all the whole College of Physicians. She berated me soundly for disobeying her orders and cooling off without a coat after tennis. Have you dined? Here, page, another brace of partridge, and pour yourself a cup of this good French wine, Jem. Louis sent me a pipe, about the only good thing he has sent me this year, damn him. Drink up, lad, drink up. I am not gone yet and when I am you'll sit where I sit now and where none other but you shall sit. Tell me, what do you fancy for Newmarket tomorrow? I'm off at crack of dawn to see Blue Cap win me the Plate. He's running at six to one. Will I put a hundred on for you? No? Come on, be a sport! I'll pay your losses if you lose. Say a pony each way — and here's to it!'

Another year gone; and Shaftesbury, crippled with gout, racked with hate and frustration at the defeat of his Exclusion Bill of the previous year by which York would have been deprived of the succession, struck another hammer-blow at Catherine.

Once again he urged his lickspittle part to press for a Bill of Divorce as the sole remaining chance to free the King of his Catholic wife to marry a Protestant consort, and beget him an heir to secure the throne for legitimate issue.

The atrocious suggestion, received by Charles with forcible protest and threats delivered individually to each of the Lords should they agree to any such disgraceful measure, caused the death of the Bill at its abortive inception.

And now it was to the knife between Shaftesbury and the King.

The second Exclusion Bill, resuscitated by the newly elected Whig Parliament, was carried unanimously into the Upper House. Charles, watching the debate hour by hour, heard Monmouth, most loved of his byblows, plead for the Bill, as 'necessary to put an end to these Popish Plots against my father's life.'

'The kiss of Judas,' groaned Charles; and those near him saw blood drawn from his bitten thumb.

At Whitehall the Queen waited all day and half the night, dreading to hear what well might bring about her end if not by death, of which she had no fear, but worse, much worse: severance from Charles. Nothing, neither the power of his word nor his fight for her could keep a Catholic Queen here in his kingdom, were James, his heir presumptive, disinherited and exiled. She, too, would be exiled, returned to her own country, as Pedro had demanded, or — brought to the block.

Another woman in her privy chamber, more luxurious than any in the palace, waited to know the result of that battle in the Lords, which would decide her fate as well as that of the Queen and York to the tune of — eight hundred thousand pounds!

That was the bribe offered by Shaftesbury were Charles persuaded to accept the disinheritance of his rightful heir and to name a successor of Shaftesbury's choice. If Monmouth, as favourite in the race for the succession, should find the odds against him, a new entrant for the sovereign stakes had been tipped by Shaftesbury and by Louise backed to win... Richmond, her son, and she the mother of a future King!

But her golden dreams looked to be fading, her influence with Charles lost as the charms that once had enslaved him; her wiles wasted as the words with which she begged him to consider: 'Should you acknowledge James your heir against all Protestant opposition, it will bring about another Civil War.'

And at the look he turned on her she quailed. 'Before God,' he had said, 'I swear I will never abandon my brother, nor will I ever abandon my wife!'

Waiting with her where she sat, tearing a flimsy handkerchief between her restless fingers, Louise was watched by one whom Shaftesbury had brought to her from Ireland.

Edward Fitzharris was the son of a loyal Cavalier, a gentleman of polished parts and manners, whose interest in her and her future could be bought ... at a price; and that price had been named for a pension and more intimate favour, perhaps. And, with his eyes on her face that had lost some of its plumpness, the lips pinched as if she had no mouth, he said, coaxingly soft, 'On whatever side the balance weighs, Your Grace holds the crown in your hands.'

'Once,' she muttered. 'Once. Not now.'

'More than ever now.' He rose and came to her, dropped on one knee, took her hand to his lips, closed her palm with a kiss in it, and asked, 'Do you know of Sir Edward Deering?'

'Sir — who? No, no.' And fearful of another who might snatch from her that on which her last hope hung, 'What,' she said, 'is he to do with me?'

He got up from his knees and moved to the window, saying with his back to her, 'Have you not heard the predictions of Sir Edward Deering, a notable astrologer whom the ignorant — and not so ignorant, for even Shaftesbury consults him — believe to be a wizard?'

'A wizard? Pah!' she scoffed. 'You, as a Catholic should know it is a sin to believe in or consult with wizards?'

'But not with one who reads the stars.' He turned to tell her coolly: 'Deering had prophesied that after the — probable — death of the Queen, the King will remarry and,' he came close to lean over the back of her chair while his hands strayed to her breasts, 'his wife will bear the King a legitimate son from a consort who renounces her Faith for — the Queenship.'

She jerked away from him, an angry flush on her cunning little face. 'That? Never! You sicken me with your *bavardage*. I feed on fact, not fiction. Go!' She pointed to the door. 'Bring me news of the Bill. I have sent messengers to the House all this terrible day, but they tell me only that still they sit and they sit *en discutant. Mon dieu!* These long-tongued English who talk and ever talk and say nothing. Go, then. Hurry!'

Outside her chamber, connected to the King's by a secret stair, now seldom used, he found her woman, Mrs. Wall. Pale, shifty-eyed, sandy-haired, she had her lady's confidence and some, not all, of his.

Flicking her cheek with a fingertip, 'The imprint of the keyhole,' he told her, 'plays you false. There's nothing to be learned from a closed door, and all doors look to be closed to us now, unless … Come here.'

He beckoned her to follow him to a window at the far end of the corridor, deserted save for a group of pages who scattered as the two approached.

Flinging wide the casement, he said over his shoulder, 'I heard something of this while in conference just now with her,' he jerked his head in the direction of the Duchess's apartment, 'and if you listen you will know that when one door is shut another... opens.'

Beyond the sleeping gardens, under the wintry sky pricked with a few faint stars, a mighty roar as of a herd of wild beasts rose up: 'A Monmouth! A Monmouth!' and 'Down with York!' followed by a chanting of the popular jingle bawled about the streets:

Your Popish Plot and Smithfield threat
We do not fear at all,
For lo, beneath our 'Saviour's' feet
You fall, you fall, you fall!'

Fitzharris closed the window.

To Catherine, when dawn was in the sky, came Charles, exhausted, but jubilant.

'The Bill is defeated. Thrown out by a bare thirty-three!'

With the rejection of the Bill, the rage of the Commons broke loose to fall upon another helpless victim. The last few months had seen the white-hot flame of the Plot burn slowly down; whereupon, to save its extinction, Shaftesbury and his Green Ribbon gang decided that, if further evidence against Catherine could be produced, belief in the Plot and her part in it would blaze up with renewed fury.

It was Lord Stafford, one of those five Catholic peers imprisoned in the Tower, whom they selected as their most vulnerable prey. Old, ailing, enfeebled, they thought him the more likely to be twisted with the promise of his life to declare against the Queen.

They were mistaken.

Weak in bodily health though he was, this septuagenarian's spirit was strong and not to be bought at the price of his Faith or his honour.

The trial by his peers, the most brutally unjust that has ever disgraced an English Court, was held in Westminster Hall before the Lord High Steward.

Scaffolding, soaring to the rafters, had been erected for the benefit of spectators, loyal to their Church and King, come to watch the great event of the year and, with howls and execrations, see punishment done to yet another Popish traitor to the Crown.

The galleries for the accommodation of the privileged, ladies of the Court, foreign Ambassadors, the King's gentlemen, and others who had cadged a seat with no right to be there, were crammed to capacity, presenting a lavish spectacle of crimson robes, coroneted heads, the colourful gowns of women and glitter of jewels as for a gala performance at the Playhouse.

Those of the prisoner's peers who were his judges sat with the witnesses and Counsels for the Prosecution in the well of the Court; the King, with a face of stone, sat solitary in his private box, and the Queen in hers, so pale, it was as if the blood in her veins had ceased to flow.

When at last the long procession had filed into the Hall, and the Lord High Steward, immense in scarlet, was enthroned upon the Woolsack, the Serjeant-at-Arms made proclamation for the Lord Lieutenant of the Tower to 'bring forth William, Viscount Stafford, your prisoner to the Bar.' And the hideous travesty began.

Frail, bent with age, debilitated from want of sleep and two years' imprisonment, his sparse white hair in wisps about his old cold face, motionless he stood within the Bar to hear the charge of high treason pronounced against him who had been denied a Counsel for his aid; nor had he been given one day in which to prepare his own defence, so swiftly, without warning, had they dragged him to his doom.

As in previous trials, discrepancies and contradictions passed unquestioned while witness after witness was called, and their fabricated evidence believed. As before, Oates, swearing by 'Almighty Gard to speak the Truuth and naathing baht the truuth', performed his part, his flabby face and elongated chin exuding a slime as of a shell-less snail's, while the juror Lords hung on every word drawled from his lying mouth.

With pachydermatous effrontery he and his perjured witnesses brought up the names of the Queen and Duke of York in connection with the letters of Coleman as cognizant of the Plot. And again, despite his acquittal, Sir George Wakeman was accused of having undertaken to administer the lethal dose of poison to the King.

Catherine sat through the first three days of the trial. It went on for a week and was for her a nightmare, unbelievably horrific, to see that defenceless old man fighting for the short span of life left to him; to hear his foul accusers maul his every attempt to justify himself and declare his innocence against the relentless prejudice of those by whom his fate must be decided. And as she listened to the accusations hurled at her as privy to the Plot, she knew that he, whom they tortured, suffered in her stead; and her heart screamed within her: It is I, the Queen, whom they dare not bring to trial, who have brought this misery upon the kingdom of my lord and King. It is me they would kill, and all of us who are of Mother Church and must bear the Cross along the Via Dolorosa, even as He whom they crucified for love of us ... as they crucify this old, old man.

She saw Louise, seated with her menfolk, dispensing sweetmeats and smiles among them, and the Irishman, Fitzharris, debonair and elegant in raspberry velvet, whispering something that amused her for she laughed and tapped his cheek with her fan. She saw Frances in the stalls reserved for the Queen's ladies, quietly sobbing into her handkerchief, and Hortense, her handsome face in a scowl, taking snuff, a latest gentlemen's addiction much in vogue with the sparks of Whitehall. She saw the carven face of Charles, his sombre stony eyes and cheeks hollowed. She saw the old man trembling, swaying, clinging with pitiful blue-veined hands to the edge of the Bar for support, and the executioner with his axe beside him She saw the vast Hall whirl slowly round her, and the crowded company, the red-robed peers, and that stern, implacable image presiding, fade ... and fade away. And she prayed, *Dear God, don't let me faint ... no sign to them of weakness while he, their captive, stands.*

She dug her nails so deep into her palms that the skin was pierced.

'The Court,' she heard, 'adjourns.'

There was no hope for him; he stood condemned 'on testimony,' as Evelyn tells us, 'that ought not to be taken on the life of a dog'.

Around the black-draped scaffold on Tower Hill swarmed a screeching mob come to see legalised murder done and that innocent white head, fallen under the axe, held aloft by the executioner for their delight.

But with this last of Oates' victims the Terror's tide had turned. Only the memory of those tormented years remained to leave a scar upon the soul of a blood-sickened nation.

FOURTEEN

What revelations in the world have been;
How are we changed since first we saw the Queen.
She like the sun does still the same appear,
Bright as she was at her arrival here.

May every New Year find her still the same,
In health and beauty as she hither came.

How were we changed indeed! This New Year's panegyric offered up to Catherine by the Court rhymester, Edmund Waller, reflected the protean temper of a people who, with one mouth, cried havoc to bring her down, and when fear and horrors faded as the thunder of a dying storm, so did they fawn at her feet to raise her up.

But she had suffered too much and too long with those whom she was persuaded to believe had been sacrificed for her, to be consoled by flattery. Although these recuperative years had brought contentment and sporadic shades of happiness, sorrow had left its ineradicable mark, seen in the faint coin-like tracery of lines around her eyes and in the few silver threads of her hair.

She was looking back along the past five years on a cold February day when, with Hortense, she returned from her ride in the Ring. She sat before the fire toasting her stockinged feet outstretched to the logs. She had sent away her women and ordered tea for herself and Hortense, who refused to drink what she called 'cat's piss' and asked for wine.

'You are thoughtful, *ma chérie,*' she said. 'Of what do you think with your face behind a cloud?'

'A cloud of memories.' Catherine's underlip quivered. 'I was thinking of that poor man, Fitzharris.'

'Poor? You pity him, pah!' Hortense spat as if in the dead man's face. 'I warned you long ago of him and of — Louise.*

'I know.' Catherine fell to silence, staring into the fire as though to see, in the fitful leap and dying down of the fierce tongues of flame, the agony of those long desperate years fallen now to ashes, even as that smoking log burned itself out on the hearth.

Fitzharris. The last to bring a charge against her of attempt to poison the King. But Charles had done with him as with all who dared accuse her. And they hanged him without mercy and with every barbarous excess, as accorded by the law, cut down alive, ripped up, his heart and entrails. 'Oh, no!' she shuddered and cried aloud. 'Not to any who have wished me dead would I have wished them so! Although,' she gave a mirthless laugh, 'they would have me named a Borgia.'

Hortense poured herself another crystal cup of wine, held it to the light and, screwing an eye at it, said, 'I was at the trial of Fitzharris. I have never told you that, have I?' Catherine shook her head. 'I was disgusted to hear your pigs of judges swallow his lies as God's truth and feed themselves on every word until he made his fatal mistake of calling Louise and her woman in evidence.' She drew a deep breath and said with calm hate, 'But she lied herself out of it, and her woman too.'

Catherine moistened her dry lips. 'Did he bring in her woman — as well?'

'Yes.' Hortense drained her cup. 'A rat-faced bitch as ever I saw, bribed to hold her tongue of what she knew and in panic spilled it. I think Charles has never forgiven Louise for her association with Fitzharris, using him to partner her with Shaftesbury and Monmouth, although she swore that she had only offered him charity from the kindness of her heart. *Mais!* this is all *vieux jeu. Tout passe, tout casse?* She leaned forward to lay a tapering finger on Catherine's knee. 'You are too forbearing. Were it myself, I would have seen her hanged as they hanged her dupe, Fitzharris.'

Catherine's eyes slid into the distance.

'Vengeance,' she said, 'is not mine.'

'Nor,' Hortense retorted, 'does it seem to be the Lord's. That serpent, Oates, he still goes free, although they got him in a debtor's prison. And then his fellows killed the mastiff guarding his cell — you didn't know that either, did you? — so he got away. Me, I never cease to wonder at the stupidity and complaisance of the English, who let a nation run raving mad because they beg to differ in their worship of God and who take for Holy Gospel the inventions of a lunatic dressed up as a bishop, and will cut off the heads of innocent men as they cut off the head of their King, while the guilty go unpunished. Charles disappoints me. He should never have signed those death warrants for the murder of the guiltless.'

'For my sake.' A painful flush flooded Catherine's face. 'He did it, against my will, against my prayers, for *my* sake. He said that had he pardoned one he must pardon all who were convicted of treason against him, even if the convictions were false, for then he could not have protected me. They would have said he was shielding me who was the guilty one. O, God!' She covered her eyes. 'It was I for whom they died. I wish,' she said in a muffled voice, 'I wish they had taken me and so saved them.'

'Let us not indulge in sentiment.' Hortense got up. 'I am a cynic and I do not deceive myself. I know what I am, too much the lover of *me* to lay down my life for my friends.'

Catherine smiled faintly.

'Dom Patricio, my good priest and tutor, he used to say that cynicism is the hairshirt of the hypocrite.*

'I seem to remember reading somewhere — was it your Milton, that arch-hypocrite with his piety and eyes to heaven while he beat his ill-used wife, who said hypocrisy is the only evil that walks invisible except to God alone? Ah, well,' she stretched her long arms above her head and, bending, touched her toes. 'This is a good exercise for keeping the figure. I will never allow me to become a cow. The Cleveland woman and Louise — they both are cows. They have let their bodies swell that they are like bladders of lard. I am not so young as I feel and you are not so young as you look. You have kept your youth *à merveille*. I go now to rest before tonight's festivities. There will be dancing and I must be fresh for it. So! *Au revoir*'

Long after Hortense had left her she sat, hands folded in her lap, reliving that tumultuous journey of the last five years through which she and Charles had travelled together, hand-fasted.

Receding farther and farther into the mists of memory, she saw him, who was the centre of her life, driven by storms on to perilous rocks that had almost wrecked him and his kingdom. She saw how Monmouth, ill-fated tool of Shaftesbury, had betrayed him … Only a miracle had saved Charles and his brother from assassination. If one of the grooms in charge of the stables at Newmarket had not dropped smouldering ash from his pipe in the straw to start a fire and demolish the house and stables, burned to the ground with a strong wind blowing … and oh, the poor horses! How Charles had wept for his horses. Some were rescued but not all. And because the house was a pile of rubble, Charles, and James who had been there with him for the races, went back to London two days earlier than they intended — but for that their coach would have been held up by a haycart blocking the road hard by a house at Hoddesdon in Hertfordshire, Rye House, while riders galloped on to London to proclaim Monmouth leader of the new Republic, and Charles and James would have been lying dead in the lane from a dozen bullet shots fired by their would-be murderers, hidden in the hedge...

She pressed the palms of her hands against her cheeks; a little moan escaped her ... More torrents of blood had flowed from the block on Tower Hill and into the shambles at Tyburn when the conspirators of the Rye House Plot were brought to justice.

Monmouth would have been the first dragged to the scaffold in his father's vengeful anguish at the discovery of that dastardly attempted crime in which his weakling son had been involved.

She remembered how Charles had come to her late at night after a long session with the council, looking less like a man than the ghost of one there in the dimly lit chamber, with only the flickering candle flames to light his face.

'This is God's vengeance for my way of life and the pain it has caused you,' he had said in a harsh strained voice, 'My son ... a patricide!' And he sagged forward on to the bed.

'No, no!' She started up and put her arms round him. 'Never that. We know he was urged by Shaftesbury to raise a rebellion against James — not you. Nor would he ever have plotted to — kill you. You can't, you must not believe it.'

'I do, and *will* believe it.'

His face so dark and stern, his eyes smouldering under their hooded lids...

'Charles, my dearest!'

She had taken his bowed head to her breast and felt his body shake with his soundless sobs. She was faint with love and pity for him. How to bring him comfort, whose heart was torn? She heard herself soothing him as a mother will tend a hurt child. For, under all his unquenchable spirit and his cynical assessment of human values he, who had proved himself the supreme master of statecraft to overcome that which in any other monarch would have brought about a revolution, she recognised the sensitive fugitive boy, bereft of his heritage, hunted and beggared, suspicious of every man, and his own son's hand against him.

'You must never believe it!' she cried again. 'And if you do not pardon him, God will not pardon you, for you know Our Lord tells us to forgive as we hope to be forgiven.'

She had won, had saved him an everlasting torment of remorse. Monmouth had confessed to a knowledge of a conspiracy to raise a rebellion, but not of attempted regicide.

Unconvinced by his whining protests and grovelling pleas for mercy, Charles said, 'It is the Queen, not I, who saves your life.'

Yes, she had saved him, yet she could not have foreseen that her intercession was only an indefinite reprieve. James, when his time came to pardon, would less readily forgive.

And Shaftesbury was gone. He had fled the country when the fury of the people fell upon the Whigs, and in particular that shady Green Ribbon Club of which he was the founder.

He sought refuge in Holland with William of Orange and died, not the traitor's death that he deserved but in his bed, of the gout in his belly.

She made a little movement with her hands before her eyes as if to brush away those dark veils of remembrance it were better to forget; and at the sound of men's voices below in the King's privy garden, overlooked by the windows of her closet adjoining his, she got up and went to the casement.

The sun, red as a holly-berry seen through a wintry haze tinged the westward clouds with pale rose as the short day sank to its end. A feathery fall of snow had mantled the distant roofs and draped skeletal tree branches with a shimmery transparency. Topaz points of light shone on slender spires, vanes and roof-tops; the vague outlines of this brave new city, risen from the ruins of the old.

The days were drawing out. Soon it would be spring again, and this cruel hard winter passed, the coldest of the century when the Thames was frozen solid and an ox roasted whole on a fire that could not melt the ice.

Down there in the garden two figures moved into her line of vision: Charles in his red-coated falconing suit — he had been hawking in Epping Forest; but he should not, she thought, go hatless, for his periwig was powdered with snowflakes and he wore no cloak. Always so careless of himself. She saw, too, that he limped as he walked from that unhealed ulcer on his leg he insisted on treating with a concoction of his own.

Beside him walked, or rather trotted, Mr. Pepys, taking three steps to one stride of the King's despite his limp. Stout, stocky, muffled to the ears, he was *not* careless of himself, this good Mr. Pepys, recently returned from sea, superintending the fleet as Secretary to the Admiralty. He had also suffered from the Terror, but had been released when the prisons disgorged their captives.

Charles was pointing eastward and, following the direction he indicated, she saw the scaffolding that surrounded a vast dome poised like a grey gigantic bubble in the sky topped by a glimmer of gold, and something — what was it? A basket with a man in it diminished to a fairy's size — of course! The surveyor who went up to instruct the workmen with the final building of this great St. Paul's, the pride of the city and Sir Christopher Wren's masterpiece.

Then Charles, turning, looked up and, seeing her at the window in the gathering dusk, waved his hand. Mr. Pepys bowed with a flourish of his hat, and she, smiling, lifted her hand in response, and heard, 'Madam, by Your Majesty's leave…'

Her women had come to dress her for the evening. There would be dancing and music and all the usual Saturday night's jollifications, for tomorrow would be Sunday.

The Lord's day, and gaming at the tables piled high with guineas, and Charles mingling with his guests, throwing a word to each, watched anxiously by Catherine, for surely his leg dragged more than when she had seen him in the garden yesterday? But when she asked if it were paining him, he told her no, the discharge had stopped. Yet she did not think he looked too well for all his gaiety. He was ringed round with men who listened delightedly to his wit and wisecracks, complimenting Mr. Dryden on his latest play, quizzing Mr. Wycherley whose comedies so much amused him; and there was that pompous Mr. Evelyn, his eyes everywhere, critically observant, and James, threading his way through the chattering throng to seat himself beside her and talk, at boring length, of yesterday's hunt in Windsor Forest that she could scarcely stifle her yawns. How his horse had taken a brook like a bird and James had taken a toss, but the body of the pack and all the rest of them had gone by the bridge and only himself and a couple of hounds, and so on and on, until…

'God bless me! Who is *this* Charles has picked up?'

'This' was a little French boy brought by the King to sing for Catherine.

Charles called for silence and Mr. Evelyn, glowering, pulled a long lip. Singing. On the Sabbath. And in French... As he runs to record it, 'In that glorious gallery while about twenty dissolute persons were at basset with a bank of at least two thousand guineas in gold before them and the King sitting and toying with his concubines, Portsmouth, Cleveland, and Mazarine...'

But his concubines could not now trouble his wife. Cleveland, back at Court after her long retirement collecting new amours in Paris, had, Catherine noted, not without some satisfaction, become quite disgustingly fat, had lost all her beauty and did all the toying, much to the obvious embarrassment of Charles. Louise, whose face carried not one but two chins, looked twice her age; and Hortense, in whom Mr. Evelyn may have been mistaken in naming her one of the 'concubines', had a pretty young girl in tow and was charging her supercilious nostrils with snuff.

Then as the noise and laughter died down at the King's command, a boy's voice rose sweet and clear:

Jeune j'etais trop sage
Et voulais trop savoir;
je n'ai plus en partage
Que badinage...

There were calls of 'Encore!' and Hortense, in a resonant contralto, sang another line of it:

Et touche en dernier age
Sans rien prevoir.

When Catherine, having left for bed early, lay reading her missal she heard Charles, who left late, talking and laughing with Bruce in his closet. He seemed in highest spirits when he came to bid her goodnight and stayed long after the clock had struck the first morning hour. He had all to tell her of the wonderful new house Wren was building for him at Winchester.

'It is too cold for you to take that long drive in this weather, but when the spring comes back to us you shall see it. I'll be happy in my house to be covered in lead.'

A page stood at the door with a candle to light him to his bedroom, when suddenly the flame went out and the long gallery was plunged in darkness. The dogs were restless and whining, Charles was calling, 'Let there be light!' And all the clocks chiming, so many chimes…

But while Charles slept Catherine did not. She tossed and turned, with fear in her heart. She had thought him overexcited and strange in his talk of.;. his 'house to be covered in lead'.

She slept at last, exhausted, and was awakened to find Lady Suffolk at her bedside.

'Madam, the King…'

As suddenly as that candle flame had been extinguished, and even while his barber shaved him, Bruce, who was with him, saw him stiffen and his head sink on his breast. His face was grey, his mouth foaming, and his eyes rolled up to show the whites.

His doctor, hastily summoned, lanced a vein while Bruce rushed for James, who came with one shoe on, the other off, in his hurry.

All that day, Catherine knelt at the end of his bed chafing his feet, refusing to take food or leave him who had asked for her

... 'My wife ... I want my wife...' so soon as those grey distorted lips could move to speak.

His doctors, an army of them, plied him with bleedings, blisterings, plasterings, purgings. He bore it all without complaint, denied the only remedy he wished for: peace, quiet, and his wife. But she too was denied him. She had fainted and been taken away by her doctor, bled, and lost of what little strength was left to her.

Three days passed and still no change reported to the huddled waiting crowd outside the palace gates until, on the third day, news went out that the King had rallied from his seizure, and the city broke into frantic rejoicing. Bells pealed from every steeple, and in the taverns men gave 'A health unto His Majesty', with grateful tears pouring down their cheeks.

But that short rally was delusive. The bishops, gathered round the bed, headed by the Archbishop of Canterbury, offered him Holy Communion. Tortured with pain as result of the violent treatment recommended by his doctors, including hot coals applied in pans to all parts of his agonised body, he evaded an answer to that, and again asked for his wife. She, who had passed from one fainting fit to another from constant bleeding, staggered up and went to him. One thought possessed her ... a priest. She must send for a priest. She saw again that scene, re-enacted, in a white-walled chapel at Moseley, when a hunted fugitive had knelt with Father Huddleston before the Altar in God's Presence with the vows of Faith unuttered, but spoken in his heart ... Father Huddleston! She must find James and tell —

In the darkened chamber, filled with clergy, doctors, ambassadors, peers, her husband lay, his eyes fixed and staring at the ceiling.

Those who crowded round the bed made way for her to pass. She fell on her knees to take his hand and whisper with her lips to his ear. His wigless, grey, almost bald head nodded. James, kneeling on the other side of the bed, looked up. She beckoned him, and he came to her. 'You know,' she managed to articulate, 'it is his wish ... to be received ... the Last Sacrament...'

He caught her as she fell.

Father Huddleston, whom Chiffinch fetched, was secretly conducted up a back stair, disguised in wig and cassock, for his life would be forfeit were his holy errand known.

James ordered the assembly out of the room, saying that so many people disturbed the King, with the exception of two Protestant peers whom he could trust, Lords Bath and Feverisham. And when all had filed out, Chiffinch brought Father Huddleston to the bedside.

Kneeling beside his dying brother, James said, 'Here is the man who saved your life. He is come now to save your soul, if you...?' His words sank with the sobs that tore him as he heard the answer, weak but firm.

'With all my heart, I *will*.'

Thus in humility and thankfulness in these, the last and greatest hours of his life, was the King received into the arms of Mother Church for whom so many of his subjects had been martyred, and in whose Divine Faith, until a century past, his predecessors on the English throne had lived and died.

When those who had been excluded from the bedchamber crowded back, they paused on the threshold in wonder to see Father Huddleston, his disguise discarded, holding the Cross above the pale face of the King that, cleared now of all pain, shone with a quiet ineffable content as though inwardly illumined.

From that moment, about ten o'clock at night, when he had received Extreme Unction, the King was fully conscious. He spoke lightly of his sufferings, could even make a jest of them: 'I'm an unconscionable long time dying!' As if he hid a chuckle in his shroud.

Catherine, who, between her bouts of fainting, was on her knees to him, begged his forgiveness, 'for anything I may have done to hurt ... or to ... displease you,' thinking back on those early days of their marriage. But, 'No!' the weak voice gained strength to tell her. 'No, it is I to ask forgiveness of you for ... your hurt love,' and tenderly, for her ear alone, *'minha pequena rosa.'*

Toward morning he asked that the curtain of his windows be drawn that he might see the sunrise; and to Chiffinch, weeping the slow painful tears of old age: 'Don't forget to wind my eight-day clock. 'Tis winding day ... tomorrow ... Jemmy. My dear...' His hand went out to James, who was uncontrollably sobbing. 'Forget ... all I may have done that you resented ... only for your good. I leave all to you that you may carry on with ... my blessing and God's guidance, and —' a touch here of the old whimsical humour — 'don't let my poor Nelly starve.'

A great hush had fallen on the palace, broken only by the whimpering of dogs at a closed door.

In her lonely room, the stricken Queen, roused from her stupor, heard the echo of a cry ring through the empty galleries down to the silent watchers at the gates.

'The King is dead. Long live ... the King!'

AFTERWORD

Although volumes have been written on the life of Charles the Second, his biographers give us but the barest glimpse of his marriage or his wife. Even those historians who write of the Titus Oates Plot scarcely mention the Queen around whom the whole Papist Terror revolved.

In presenting this marriage of one of our most popular Kings I have endeavoured to point that which seems to have been overlooked by his many biographers: the psychological effect upon him of his wife's patience, forbearance, and courage when confronted by those iniquitous persecutions that might well have brought her to the scaffold. Not until his full realization of her true worth, during these years of Terror, does the King emerge as the wise and brilliant politician acknowledged by modern biographers, in contrast to the Victorians' opprobrium of a self-indulgent profligate, spendthrift, and womaniser.

Little is known of Catherine's widowhood more than that she remained at Somerset House until the flight of James II with his Queen and infant son, when she returned to Portugal to escape further persecution under William and Mary.

The failing health of her brother, Pedro, then King, decided him to appoint Catherine as Regent for his young son by a second marriage.

She proved to be a wise and conscientious ruler, but her Regency was all too brief. Two years later she died at the age of sixty-seven, beloved and revered by the people of Portugal.

Among the numerous authorities I have consulted in the compilation of this biographical study of Charles II and his wife, in which no characters, no events, nor letters quoted are fictitious, I am particularly indebted to:

G. M. Trevelyan: *England under the Stuarts,* Agnes Strickland: *Queens of England,* Vol. 8; Arthur Bryant: *King Charles the Second; Life of Edward, Earl of Clarendon,* written by himself; *Twelve Bad Men, Original Studies by Various Scoundrels* edited by Thomas Seccombe; Janet Mackay: *Catherine of Braganza,* Lilias Campbell Davidson: *Catherine of Braganza;* Bishop G. Burnet: *History of His Own Times,* Arthur Irwin Dasent: *The Private Life of Charles II;* G. Steinman Steinman: *A Memoir of Barbara, Duchess of Cleveland; The Letters, Speeches, and Declarations of King Charles II* edited by Arthur Bryant; Julia Cartwright: *Madame, daughter of Charles I;* the Diaries of Samuel Pepys and John Evelyn; Hilaire Belloc: *James II* and the *Memoirs of Comte de Gramont,* translated by Peter Quennell.

Doris Leslie

A NOTE TO THE READER

If you have enjoyed this novel enough to leave a review on **Amazon** and **Goodreads**, then we would be truly grateful.
Sapere Books

Sapere Books is an exciting new publisher of brilliant fiction and popular history.

To find out more about our latest releases and our monthly bargain books visit our website: **saperebooks.com**

Manufactured by Amazon.ca
Acheson, AB